TEXAS PREY

BY
BARB HAN

Published in Great Britain 2015
by Mills & Boon, an imprint of Harlequin (UK) Limited,
Eton House, 18-24 Paradise Road, Richmond, Surrey, TW9 1SR

© 2015 Barb Han

ISBN: 978-0-263-25318-4

46-0915

Harlequin (UK) Limited's policy is to use papers that are natural, renewable and recyclable products and made from wood grown in sustainable forests. The logging and manufacturing processes conform to the legal environmental regulations of the country of origin.

Printed and bound in Spain
by CPI, Barcelona

Barb Han lives in North Texas with her very own hero-worthy husband, three beautiful children, a spunky golden retriever/standard poodle mix and too many books in her to-read pile. In her downtime, she plays video games and spends much of her time on or around a basketball court. She loves interacting with readers and is grateful for their support. You can reach her at www.barbhan.com.

To Allison Lyons for the opportunity to learn so much
with every book. To Jill Marsal for unfailing
wisdom and support.
To Brandon, Jacob and Tori for inspiration and kindness
(I love you!). To John for finding true love.

This story is as much about friendship
as it is about love.
To Emily Martinez, Lisa Watson, Caroline York, and
Raymon and Amanda Bacchus for yours!

Chapter One

Rebecca Hughes held her chin up and kept alert as she thrust her shopping cart through the thick, oppressive North Texas heat. She blinked against the relentless sun, a light so intense her eyes hurt.

The van parked next to her car in the grocery store lot pricked her neck hairs. Blacked-out windows blocked her view of the driver's side or anything else that might be lurking, waiting, ready. A warning bell wailed inside her head as she neared her sedan.

Today marked the fifteenth anniversary of that horrible day when both she and her younger brother were abducted, and it always put her on edge. The two had been isolated in separate sheds. When an opportunity had presented itself to run, Rebecca had escaped, thinking she could bring back help. Instead, she got lost in the woods and never saw her baby brother again.

Steering her cart toward the center of the aisle, she made sure no one could surprise her by jumping from between two cars. Tension squeezed her shoulder blades taut as memories assaulted her. Those thirty-six hours of torture before she escaped without her little brother, the horror and Shane's disappearance would haunt her for the rest of her life.

Shuddering at the memory, she tightened her grip on the handle and pushed forward. The early Friday-morning crowd was out. Most people were just beginning to run errands at the same time her workday ended. Her overnight shift at the radio station kept her sane after years of being afraid to be home alone in the dark.

She and Shane had been twelve and seven respectively when she'd sneaked out to play that stupid game with her friends. They'd been told to stay inside while the annual Renaissance Festival was in town, in full swing. Parents were busy, distracted. Strangers in costumes were everywhere. People came from nearly every state, descending on Mason Ridge in RVs and trailers and filling camp sites. And Shane was supposed to be asleep when she'd slipped out her bedroom window to meet up with her friends, not following her.

But none of that mattered. She should've realized sooner that the little stinker was trailing behind, his favorite blanket in tow. Shane had been her responsibility. And she'd let him down in the worst possible way.

The unfairness of his disappearance and her survival still hit with the force of a physical blow. His screams still haunted her. An imprint left by the horrible man who'd been dubbed the Mason Ridge Abductor was the reason she still watched every stranger warily.

When no one else had disappeared and all leads had been exhausted, law enforcement had written the case off as a transient passing through town. Logic said the man was long gone. Point being, he couldn't hurt her anymore. And yet, every time she got spooked he was the first person who popped into her thoughts. That monster had caused her to lose more than her sense of security. He'd shattered her world and taken away her ability to trust.

Her parents had divorced and become overbearing; friends looked at her strangely, as if she'd become an outcast; and she'd eventually pushed away the one person she'd truly loved—Brody Fields.

The van's brake lights created a bright red glow, snapping her focus to the present. Panic pressed heavy on her arms. Maybe she could circle around the next aisle and get back to the store before being seen.

There were a million wackos out there waiting to hurt unaware women, surprise being key to their attacks. Rebecca was fully present. She tightened her grip on the cart handle a third time, turned around and stalked toward her car. No one got to make her feel weak and afraid again.

Reaching inside her purse as she neared her vehicle, she gripped her Taser gun. Anyone trying to mess with her would get a big surprise and a few thousand volts of electricity. She wouldn't go down without a fight. Not again. She was no longer a shy twelve-year-old who could be overpowered in the dark.

With every forward step, the tension in Rebecca's body tightened. Her gaze was trained on the van.

She heard footsteps coming toward her from behind. Turning in time to catch a glimpse of a man rushing toward her, she spun around to face him. He was less than three feet away, moving closer. He wore a sweatshirt with the hood covering his hair and half of his face. Sunglasses hid his eyes. Before she could react, he slammed into her, knocking her off balance. She landed flat on the ground.

This time, she knew it was him—*had* to be him. She'd recognize that apple-tobacco smell anywhere. The scent had been burned into her senses fifteen years ago.

With the Taser already in hand, she struggled to untangle her purse strap from her arm. She shook free from his grasp, but not without upsetting the contents of her purse.

"You sick bastard. What did you do to my brother?" Aiming the blunt end of the Taser directly at his midsection, she fired.

The man fell to his knees, groaning, as she scrambled to her feet.

"What are you talking about, lady? You're crazy," he bit out through grunts and clenched teeth, convulsing on the ground.

Shaking off the fear gripping her, she snatched her handbag and ran to her car. She cursed, realizing some of the purse contents were on the ground. No way could she risk going back for them. Not with him there.

She hopped into the driver's seat, then closed and locked the door. Her fingers trembled, causing her to drop the keys. Scooping them off the floorboard, she tried to force a sense of calm over her.

Fumbling to get the key in the ignition, her logical mind battled with reality. That had to be *him*, right?

This wasn't like before when she'd mistaken one of the garbagemen for her abductor. Or the time she'd been certain he was posing as a cable guy. Anyone who'd come close and roughly matched her abductor's description had given her nightmares.

The sheriff had been convinced that no one from Mason Ridge was capable of doing such a horrific act. He'd said it had to be the work of a trucker or someone else passing through because of the festival. The FBI hadn't been so sure. They'd produced a list of potential suspects that had pitted neighbors and small-shop owners against one another. Personal vendettas had people coming forward.

As the investigation unfolded, there was no shortage of accused. And a town's innocence had been lost forever.

Determined investigators had traced freight cars and truckers that had passed through Mason Ridge the night both her and Shane had been abducted. In the days following, they'd scoured known teen hangouts, drained a lake and even set off dynamite in the rock quarry. But they'd come up empty.

They'd been reaching, just as she was now.

Guilt hit at the thought she could be overreacting. She'd never actually seen the face of the man who'd abducted them all those years ago. Had she just nailed a stranger with her Taser?

A quick glance in the side mirror said it didn't matter. This guy wasn't there to help with her groceries. The hooded man on the ground inched toward her, a menacing curve to his exposed lips, his body twitching.

She turned the ignition again with a silent prayer.

Bingo.

The engine cranked and she shifted into Reverse. Her tires struggled to gain traction as she floored the pedal. Fear, doubt and anger flooded her.

She checked the rearview again as she pulled onto the street. When she could be certain he wasn't following her, she'd pull over and call 911.

A few seconds later, she turned right onto the road and then made another at the red light, zipping into traffic at the busy intersection. A horn blared.

Adrenaline and fear caused her hands to shake and her stomach to squeeze. Tears stung the backs of her eyes. A couple more turns, mixing lefts and rights, and she pulled into a pharmacy parking lot. She reached for her purse, remembering that half the contents had spilled out in the parking lot. Had any of her personal information fallen out? On the concrete? Right next to him?

But it couldn't be *him*, could it?

Why would he come back after all these years?

The festival? The radio show? Every year she mentioned her brother near the anniversary of his disappearance and got threatening letters at the station. The sheriff's office followed up with the same result as previous years, no enthusiasm, no leads.

Rebecca couldn't write it off so easily, had never been able to. She scoured social media for any signs of Shane. Last month alone, she must've sent a dozen messages to people who matched Shane's description. Although she still hadn't given up, her results weren't any better than the sheriff's. But her resolve was.

Maybe it was her own guilt that kept her searching. Or, a deep-seated need to give their mother closure.

Rebecca rummaged through her bag, desperate to locate her cell, and found nothing. It must've fallen out of her purse. The sheriff's office was nearby. She'd have to drive to the station to file a complaint against her attacker. She cursed. No way could she get there in time for them to take her information and then catch him. He'd be long gone, most likely already was. She fisted her hand and thumped the steering wheel.

If her on-air mention of Shane hadn't rattled any chains, the media might have. Every year before the festival the local paper ran some kind of article referencing Shane's disappearance. This year being the fifteenth anniversary had brought out the wolves. A reporter had been waiting in the parking lot at work two weeks ago, trying to score an interview. He'd said he wanted a family member's perspective. She'd refused and then gone to the sheriff to ask for protection. Again, they did nothing to stop the intrusion, saying no laws had been violated.

Even Charles Alcorn, the town's wealthiest resident, had reached out to her. He'd helped with the search years ago and said he'd like to offer assistance again. What could he do that hadn't already been done?

This time, the sheriff's office couldn't ignore her. They would have to do something. The attack was concrete and too close for comfort. The man had shown up out of nowhere. She'd been so focused on getting away that she hadn't thought to see if he'd retreated to a car. A make and model, a license plate, would give the sheriff something to go on.

Her best chance at seeing him behind bars, overdue justice for her brother, had just slipped away. *If* that was him, a little voice inside her head reminded.

Did he have her cell phone? A cold chill ran down her back.

Wait a minute. Couldn't the sheriff track him using GPS?

Anger balled inside her as she drove the couple of blocks to the sheriff's office. What if they didn't believe her?

She hadn't physically been there in years, and yet she could still recall the look of pity on Sheriff Randall Brine's face the last time she'd visited. His gaze had fixed on her for a couple seconds, contemplating her. Then, he'd said, "Have you thought about getting away for a little while? Maybe take a long vacation?"

"I'm fine," she'd said, but they both knew she was lying.

"I know," he'd said too quickly. "I was just thinking how nice it'd be to walk through the surf. Eat fresh seafood for a change." Deep circles cradled his dark blue eyes and he looked wrung out. She'd written it off as guilt, thinking she was probably the last person he wanted to see. Was she a reminder of his biggest failure? Then again, it seemed no one wanted to see her around. "We've done everything we can. I wish I had better news. I'll let you know if we get any new information."

"But—"

His tired stare had pinned her before he picked up his folder and refocused on what he'd been reading before she'd interrupted him.

Rebecca had wanted to stomp her feet and make a scene to force him to listen to her. In her heart, she knew he was right. And she couldn't depend on the sheriff to investigate every time something went bump in the night or a complete stranger reminded her of him.

Somehow, life had to go on.

Heaven knew her parents, overwrought with grief, had stopped talking to each other and to their friends. Instead of real conversation, there'd been organized searches, candlelight vigils and endless nights spent scouring fields.

When search teams thinned and then disappeared altogether, there'd been nothing left but despair. They'd divorced a year following Shane's disappearance. Her dad had eventually remarried and had two more children, both boys. And her mother never forgave him for it. She'd limited visitation, saying she was afraid Rebecca would feel awkward.

After, both parents had focused too much attention on Rebecca, which had smothered her. There'd been two and a half years of endless counseling and medication until she'd finally stood up to them. No more, she'd said, wanting to be normal again, to feel ordinary. And even though she'd returned to a normal life after that, nothing was ever normal again.

Although the monster hadn't returned, he'd left panic, loneliness and the very real sense that nothing would ever be okay again.

Since then, she'd had a hard time letting anyone get close to her, especially men. The one person who'd pushed past her walls in high school, Brody, had scared her more than her past. He'd been there that night. He'd stepped forward and said she was meeting him to give him back a shirt he had to have for camp so she wouldn't have to betray her friends. Her mother had never forgiven him. He'd been the one person Rebecca could depend on, who hadn't treated her differently, and he deserved so much more than she could give. Even as a teenager she'd known Brody deserved more.

Separating herself from him in high school had been the right thing to do, she reminded herself. Because every time she'd closed her eyes at night, fear that the monster would return consumed her. Every dark room she'd stood in front of had made her heart pound painfully against her chest. Every strange sound had caused her pulse to race.

And time hadn't made it better.

She often wondered if things would have turned out differently if she'd broken the pact and told authorities the real reason they'd been out.

Probably not. She was just second-guessing herself again. None of the kids had been involved.

Once Shane had been discovered following her, they'd broken up the game and gone home. Nothing would've changed.

Rebecca refocused as she pulled into a parking spot at

the sheriff's office. By the time she walked up the steps to the glass doors, she'd regained some of her composure.

The deputy at the front desk acknowledged her with a nod. She didn't recognize him and figured that was good. He might not know her, either.

"How can I help you?"

"I need to speak to the sheriff."

"Sorry. He's not in. I'm Deputy Adams." The middle-aged man offered a handshake. "Can I help you?"

"I need to report an assault. I believe it could be connected to a case he worked a few years ago." She introduced herself as she shook his hand.

The way his forehead bunched after he pulled her up in the database made her figure he was assessing her mental state. Her name must've been flagged. He asked a few routine-sounding questions, punched the information into the keyboard and then folded his hands and smiled. A sympathetic look crossed his features. "I'll make sure the report is filed and on the sheriff's desk as soon as he arrives."

Deputy Adams might be well intentioned, but he wasn't exactly helpful. His response was similar as she reported her missing phone.

Not ready to accept defeat, she thanked him, squared her shoulders and headed into the hot summer sun.

Local law enforcement was no use, and she'd known that on some level. They'd let the man slip through their fingers all those years ago and hadn't found him since. What would be different now?

She thought about the fact that her little brother would be twenty-two years old now. That he'd be returning home from college this summer, probably fresh from an athletic scholarship. Even at seven, he'd been obsessed with sports. Maybe he still was. A part of her still refused to believe he was gone.

Rebecca let out a frustrated hiss. *I'm so sorry, Shane.*

What else could she do? She had to think. Wait a minute. What about her cell? If her attacker had picked it up, could she track him somehow? Her phone might be the key. She could go home and search the internet to find out how to locate it and possibly find him. And then do what? Confront him? Alone? Even in her desperate state she knew that would be a dangerous move.

Could she take Alcorn up on his offer to help?

And say what?

Would he believe her when the sheriff's office wouldn't?

She needed help. Someone she could trust.

Brody? He was back from the military.

Even though she hadn't seen him in years, he might help.

If she closed her eyes, she could remember his face perfectly. His honest, clear blue eyes and sandy-blond hair with dark streaks on a far-too-serious-for-his-age face punctuated a strong, squared jaw. By fifteen, he was already six foot one. She couldn't help but wonder how he'd look now that he was grown. The military had most likely filled out his muscles.

When she'd returned to school after a year of being homeschooled, kids she'd known all her life had diverted their gazes from her in the hallway when she walked past. Conversations turned to whispers. Teachers gave her extra time to complete assignments and spoke to her slowly, as if she couldn't hear all of a sudden. Even back then, the pain pierced through the numbness and hurt. She'd felt shunned. As the years passed, she realized no one knew what to say and she appreciated them for trying. She got used to being an outsider. Her tight-knit group of friends had split up. She'd figured they were afraid to be connected with her or just plain afraid of her.

Not Brody. He'd stopped by her house every day after the incident even though her mother refused to allow him inside, especially after he'd stepped forward. It had been easier to take the blame than to admit why they'd really been out that night—to play Mission Quest. They'd had good reasons to lie, too. First of all, they weren't supposed to be playing that online game, let alone sneaking out to meet up with strangers to capture their friends' bases. And then there was the sheriff. He'd been looking for any excuse to bust their best friend Ryan's older brother, Justin, the guy who'd let them into the game in the first place. If they didn't cover for him, the sheriff would go after Justin like an angry pit bull. It would be his third strike and a one-way trip to a real jail. No more acting-out-against-an-abusive-father juvenile stuff. He'd be shipped off for good if their dad didn't beat Justin to death first.

Justin had cleaned up his act. And he deserved a second chance. Besides, it was no surprise that he'd taken a wrong turn in the first place with a father as cruel as his. The real miracle had been that Ryan hadn't followed in his older brother's footsteps.

Even though it would have meant turning on their friends, Brody had visited Rebecca in the middle of the night to tell her that she didn't have to keep the pact. Ryan would understand.

But Justin didn't have anything to do with Shane's disappearance. And there was no reason to screw up another family.

Shaking off the memories, Rebecca slipped into the

driver's seat and started the engine. She put the car in Reverse and tapped the gas a little too hard.

An object flew forward underneath her feet. She hit the brake, bent forward and picked it up. Her cell. It must've fallen out when she was rushing into her car earlier.

A mix of relief and exasperation flooded her as the thought of tracking her assailant via her phone disintegrated.

It was too early to give up hope of finding him this time.

She couldn't do it alone. Brody had bought the old Wakefield Ranch. Rumor said he'd become a warrior overseas. Would he help? Could she reach out to him after all these years? How hard would it be to get his phone number and find out?

Rebecca pulled into another parking spot and thumbed through her contacts. Her finger hovered over Ryan's number. They hadn't spoken in years, but she figured it wouldn't hurt to reach out to him. She sent a text message to him, unsure this was his number anymore. It didn't matter. It was worth a try. He still owed her one for helping to protect his brother.

The text came thirty seconds later with Brody's information.

Seeing it, needing to reach out to him, made this horror so much more real. And her heart pitched when she thought about facing him again.

BRODY FIELDS LEANED against his truck. The call from Rebecca Hughes had dredged up old feelings best left buried. He'd almost ended the call without finding out what she'd wanted. Except he couldn't do that to her. It was

Rebecca. The sound of her voice had stirred up all kinds of memories. Most of them were good.

He'd known her since they were kids, but they'd been teenagers when he'd fallen for her. There was so much more than her physical beauty that had drawn him in. She'd been the only female Brody had ever trusted and allowed inside his armor after his mother had betrayed the family, stolen money from the town and then disappeared.

The mental connection he'd shared with Rebecca had been beyond any closeness he'd experienced. Looking back, maybe it was the loner in him that could relate to her isolation.

When she'd pushed him away and said she'd never loved him, it had hurt worse than any physical blow. Soon after, she'd left for college, and then eventually moved to Chicago. He'd been the most surprised to learn that she'd moved back to Mason Ridge.

For a split second, he'd hoped she'd called for old times' sake. Then, he remembered what day it was—the anniversary of Shane's disappearance—and he knew better.

The conversation had been short. She'd told him what had happened and requested to meet face-to-face at The Dirty Bean Coffee Shop. He'd agreed, ending their exchange. The place was on his way home. Driving to the meeting point had taken ten minutes.

The pale blue sedan parking next to his truck had to be hers.

Knowing she was about to step out of her car and he was about to see her again hit him hard. How many times had he secretly wished he'd run into her in the past few months? Where'd that come from?

Hearing that her abductor had returned hadn't done good things to Brody's blood pressure. He wouldn't refuse her plea for help. And a little piece of him hoped he'd figure out if her case and the memories were the reasons she'd rejected him all those years ago. He'd been a boy back then. Helpless. *A lot's changed.*

He'd grown up. Survived his mother's betrayal of his family and the town. Served his country. Gone on to become a leader of an elite-forces team. Spent time with a lot of interesting women. To be honest, not all of them were interesting, but they were smokin' hot.

He crossed his arms over his chest and tucked his hands under his armpits.

The first thing he noticed as Rebecca exited her vehicle was her jean-clad long legs and red boots. His body instantly reacted to seeing the woman she'd become. There were enough curves on her lean figure to make her look like a real woman. She still had the same chestnut-brown hair that fell well past her shoulders in waves. She'd be close enough for him to look into her light brown eyes soon. Were they still the color of honey?

Why did seeing Rebecca reduce him to being that heartsick seventeen-year-old brat again?

Brody ignored the squeeze in his chest. Fond memories aside, he didn't do that particular brand of emotion anymore.

That she moved cautiously, surveying the area, reminded him why she was there. It wasn't to talk about old feelings.

"It's good to see you." She took a tentative step closer to him.

Yep. Same beautiful eyes. Same diamond-shaped face. Brody hadn't expected her voice to sound this grown-up. Or so damn sexy. He didn't want to think about her in a sexual way. She'd been all sweetness and innocence to him at seventeen. And this wasn't a date. He glanced around the parking lot to make sure no one had followed her.

"Wish the circumstances were better. I'm glad you called." The conversation needed to stay on track. So, why did he feel another physical blow when he saw disappointment flash in her eyes? "Tell me why you think I can help."

"He's after me. Neither the sheriff nor the FBI caught him before. I'm scared. You're the only one I can talk to who knows what really happened that night." Her eyes flashed toward him nervously. "I've heard about the things you did overseas. I know you've done some security consulting on the side since you came back. I'd like to hire you to protect me while I sort all this out."

"I don't need your money. I'll help." He didn't have to think long about his answer. Brody had experience tracking down the enemy, and this case had always eaten at him. Guilt?

"I'd still like to pay you something. In fact, I'd rather do it that way. I'm not a charity case." She stared at him, all signs of vulnerability gone from her almond-shaped eyes.

He stared back. "Fine. We'll figure something out."

"Thank you."

He hadn't expected her to look so relieved. "You want to grab a cup of coffee while you fill me in?"

She nodded.

Brody followed Rebecca to the counter, where they placed their orders. She reached in her purse to pay for hers. He caught her arm. Big mistake. An electric volt shot through his hand, vibrated up his arm and warmed places that he didn't realize were still iced over.

There'd be no use denying he felt a sizzle of attraction being near Rebecca again. It was more than a mild spark. She'd grown into a beautiful woman. But if he didn't watch himself, she could put a knife through his chest with just a few words. And Brody had no intention of handing over that power again to anyone.

When their coffees were ready, she located a table in the corner. Brody followed, forcing his gaze away from her backside, ignoring how well the jeans fit her curves.

She took the opposite seat, her gaze diverting to someone behind him. Brody turned in time to see a fairly tall man sit a little too close for comfort. Then again, these coffee shops sure knew how to pack a hundred people into two-foot-square spaces. Brody had had to squeeze between the stacked tables to fit into the tight spot.

"Can you start right now?" Shoulders bunched, jaw set, she looked ready to jump if someone shouted an order over the hum of conversation. Tension practically radiated off her.

"Yes. I'll need to arrange care for my horses. I can make a call to cover that base. If I'm going to be able to help, you'll have to tell me everything." His voice was gruffer than he expected, borderline harsh. Between his need to be her comfort and inappropriate sexual thoughts, being near her wasn't exactly bringing out the best in him.

She glanced from side to side, told him what had happened that morning with more details this time, and then focused those honey browns on him. Tears welled in her eyes. "After all this time, he's after me, Brody. Why? It doesn't make any sense. Where's he been all these years?"

"That's a good question. One I intend to answer."

"And what about my brother? Is there any chance he could still be alive?" Her voice hitched on the last word.

"We'll find out." Brody gripped his cup so he wouldn't

reach out to comfort her. "You've already been to the sheriff or you wouldn't be calling me."

She lowered her gaze. "Yes."

"What did he say?" The way she kept one eye on the door had Brody thinking he needed to ask her to switch seats so he'd have a better view. As it was, he didn't like his back facing the door.

"That I should be careful and to call if I see or hear anything suspicious."

"Did you tell them that's why you were there in the first place?" Frustration ate at him. He needed to control it in order to focus on the mission. Why would the man who'd abducted her and her brother all those years ago come back? To finish the job with her? She'd never been the intended target. When she'd witnessed a man grab her brother and run, she'd chased him into the woods. He had to know she hadn't seen or remembered enough of him to help the law track him down or he'd already be in jail. "It's been fifteen years. Why now? Where's he been?"

"Wish I knew." Her gaze ping-ponged from the front door to the exit. Fear pulsed from her. "Then again, the papers always dredge up the past."

"That wouldn't suddenly bring him out. They run stories every year." Brody tapped his finger on the table. "I've thought about this a lot over the years."

"Did we do the right thing back then? I mean, we were just kids protecting our friend by keeping that secret. What if that cost Shane his... What if someone saw something?"

"They would've come forward on their own if they had. Unless you think Justin was somehow involved?"

"No. It wasn't him. This guy was too tall. Plus, I remember that smell. No one in Ryan's house smelled like apple tobacco, least of all Justin." The admission brought a frown to her lips.

"The sheriff wrote the case off as a transient passing through town before and found nothing. It's time to change things up. We need to look at this through a new lens. Our guy could be connected to Mason Ridge in some way. This is where it all started and this is where it ends." Brody had every intention of following through on that promise.

And if that meant breaking the pact and digging up the past, so be it.

Chapter Two

Rebecca's shoulders slumped forward. "It's no use. We've been over this a million times and we never get anywhere. I've scoured the internet for years trying to find Shane. The case is closed. It was most likely a random mugging this morning. Even the deputy thinks I'm crazy."

"Except that we both know you're not." Brody resisted the urge to take her hand in his, noticing how small hers was in comparison, how much more delicate her skin looked.

"The sheriff told me years ago the trail had gone cold. I just didn't want to accept the truth. They're probably right. Shane's…long gone." Her almond-shaped eyes held so much pain.

"I know why your parents didn't leave the area after they divorced. They never gave up hope of finding him, especially your mother," Brody said, leaning forward. Everyone in town had held out the same hope Shane would be found. Hope that had fizzled and died as the weeks ticked by. "And neither did you."

"Seemed like a good enough reason to stay in the beginning."

"There's no reason to give up now."

"Do you know how slim the chances of solving a cold

case are? I do." When she looked up, he saw more than hurt in her eyes. He saw fear. He already noted that she'd positioned herself in the corner with her back against the wall, insuring she could see all the possible entry points. And didn't that move take a page out of his own book?

"Except the case isn't cold anymore. He struck again. We know he's in the area."

"Do you have any idea how that new deputy looked at me when I reported the crime and he pulled me up in the system? No one believes me." Tears welled in her eyes, threatening to fall.

"I do." Brody meant those two words.

"He could be anywhere by now."

"And so could you. But you're not. You're here. And so is he." Brody needed the conversation to switch tracks. Give her a chance to settle down. It was understandable that her emotions were on a roller coaster. Her need to find her brother battled with the fear she never would. "What about after college? You disappeared. I heard that you swore you'd never set foot in Mason Ridge again. What happened?"

"I did. I moved to Chicago and got a job at a radio station. I came home three years ago because of my mom's health. She took a turn."

"I didn't know." Again he suppressed the urge to reach across the table and comfort Rebecca, dismissing it as an old habit that didn't want to die.

"I had no way to reach you while you were overseas. Doubt I could've found the right words, anyway."

Brody understood the sentiment. How many times had he thought about looking her up on social media over the years but hadn't? Dozens? Hundreds? "Is it her heart again?"

Rebecca nodded. The sadness in her eyes punctuated what had to be another difficult time for the Hughes family.

"What'd the doctor say?"

"That she isn't doing well. They're doing everything they can, but she's refusing to try a new medication that will help her. Says she's afraid of being allergic to it, which is just an excuse." She shrugged. "I always stop by and see her after I get groceries on Fridays. I couldn't go today, after what happened this morning. I called to let her know and prayed that she didn't pick up on anything in my voice. She shouldn't see me like this. It'll just make her worry even more."

"I'm truly sorry about your mom." And so many more things he wasn't quite ready to put into words. His own mother had freely walked away from his family after getting folks to hand over their hard-earned money under the guise of making an investment in Mason Ridge's future. She had no idea what it was like to stick around.

"Thank you." The earnestness in her expression ripped at his insides. "I can't help but feel that trying to reopen Shane's case is hopeless. The task force took all the facts into account fifteen years ago when they investigated his disappearance. All the leads from the case are freezing cold by now. My brother is still missing, probably dead. We're right where we started, except now this jerk's back as some twisted anniversary present to me." Tears streamed down her cheeks.

Brody reached across the table and thumbed them away, ignoring the sensations zinging through his hand from making contact with her skin and the warning bells sounding off inside his head.

She glanced at him and then cast her gaze intently on

the table, drawing circles with her index finger. "It's all my fault. If I hadn't told him to sit down and wait for me by the willow tree so I could finish the mission he'd still be alive today."

"Don't do that to yourself. None of this is your fault."

Her shoulders slumped forward. "What else can we do?"

Yeah, her stress indicator was the same. And Brody wanted to make it better.

"I'll figure out a way to get a copy of the file so I can review the list of suspects again. I have a friend in Records and she owes me a favor. Fresh eyes can be a big help and might give us more clues." Brody rubbed the stubble on his chin.

"With the festival going on this guy could blend in again, couldn't he?"

"Yeah. We have to look at everything differently this time. He might be someone local who hides behind the festival. Maybe he knew that was the first place law enforcement would look."

"You're right. He could be a normal person, a banker or store clerk." A spark lit behind her eyes, and under different circumstances it'd be sexy as hell.

"It's likely. He could be married and involved in a church or youth group. He might be a bus driver or substitute teacher. It's very well possible he could work with kids or in a job where he has access to families. We have to consider everyone. Those are great places to start."

"I just focused on what the sheriff had said before, him being transient. None of these options occurred to me." She shuddered.

Brody sipped his coffee. "It's not a bad thing that you don't think like a criminal."

"If we need help, Charles Alcorn offered," she said.

"A man in his position would be a good resource to have on our side." Brody leaned forward. "So this is how it's going to go. I follow you. Everywhere. You got a date, I'm right behind you." The thought of sitting outside her house while another man was inside doing God knows what with her sat in his stomach like bad steak. And yet, they were both grown adults. It shouldn't bother him. Wasn't as if he'd been chaste, either.

"I'm not dating."

Brody suppressed the flicker of happiness those words gave him. He had no right to care.

"And I don't want to stop you from doing…whatever," she added quickly.

Why did the way she said that knife him?

"Don't worry about my personal life. I'm here to do a job. That's all I care about right now." Why was that more of a reminder for him than for her?

Working with her was going to be more difficult than he'd originally thought. And not because errant sexual thoughts crossed his mind every time he got close enough to smell her shampoo. It was citrus and flowery. Being with her brought up their painful past, but they'd shared a lot of good memories, too. Like their first kiss. They'd skipped the Friday afternoon pep rally junior year and headed down to the lake in the old Mustang he'd bought and fixed up using money from his after-school job at his dad's garage.

As they sat on the hood of his car parked in front of Mason Ridge Lake, she'd leaned her head on his shoulder. And then decimated his defenses when she looked up at him with those honey browns. His heart had squeezed in the same way it did earlier today when he saw her again.

She still had that same citrus and flowery scent and it made his pulse race just as it had before. He remembered the warmth of her body against his side, her soft lips as they slightly parted.

Brody had leaned in slowly and her lips gently brushed against his; her tongue flickered across his mouth.

Afterward, they'd just sat there, silent, before he'd pulled her into a hug.

The kiss had lasted only a few seconds but was burned into his memory. How many times had he thought about those sweet lips when he was an ocean away with his face in the dirt? How many times since? *Too many.*

Brody glanced at his watch. "I'll connect with my friend and see what I can find out about that file."

"Okay." She leaned forward, rubbing her eyes, suppressing a yawn. "What else?"

"You used to look for Shane everywhere. My guess is that you haven't stopped. Am I right?"

"Yes. I scan social media on my days off."

"Any hits?"

She shrugged. "Not real ones. I've been hit on plenty, though."

"Men can be such jerks."

"Women are far worse. You'd be shocked at the messages I get from someone calling herself Adriana." Rebecca rolled her eyes.

"I have a few like those, too," he said in an attempt to lighten the tension.

"I'm sure you've been exposed to worse, having been in a war zone."

"I've seen my fair share of everything, here and abroad," he said. "You ever follow up on any of those real messages?"

"A handful. Why?" She paused and her eyes grew wide. "You don't think one of them could be stalking me?"

"Not sure. I was thinking it might be a good place to start."

She brought her hand up and squeezed the bottom of her neck on the left side, subconsciously trying to ease the tension in her shoulders. Her face muscles bunched. Signs her stress levels were climbing.

"Has anything else out of the ordinary happened to you recently? He had to know your schedule to know where you'd be this morning. I don't believe the grocery store was a random encounter."

"Now that you mention it, I've been hearing noises in the evenings before I leave for work. I thought it was the neighbor's cat at first. Now, I'm wondering if it could've been him."

"We'll check the perimeter of your house. The recent rain might have left us with evidence."

There'd been one of those open-up-the-sky-and-let-the-rain-pour-down-in-buckets storms North Texas was known for the other night. She scooted her chair back and slung her purse strap over her shoulder.

"There was also that unusually persistent reporter last week. I think his name is Peter Sheffield. I got off a few minutes early, so I was alone in the parking lot. He nearly gave me a heart attack waiting at my car after my shift at the radio station. Do you think he could be involved?"

"From here on out, I want you to suspect every sound, every person." Brody's gaze narrowed.

"So, what you're saying is…act like I always do."

He didn't like the sound of those words. "This guy might've been trying to scare you into an interview."

"That's crazy. People actually do that?"

Brody tapped his knuckles on the table. "I remember him now. He used to hang out with Justin, didn't he? Then he dropped out of Texas State U to join the military."

"That's right. He did. Are you saying you think he might be involved?"

"We need to look at everyone who was out that night playing the game. And especially Justin's friends."

Rebecca nearly choked on her sip of coffee. "I hadn't thought about it being someone so young. The apple tobacco. I just figured it had to be someone older."

"Maybe it is. But we're not taking anything for granted this time." He took the last swig of coffee, tilted the cup and glanced at the bottom, then fixed his gaze on her. "You ready to do this?"

She nodded, stood, walked past him and headed straight to the door.

"I'll follow you home in my truck." He threw away their empty cups, checking to make sure no one in the place seemed interested in either one of them. No one did.

Outside, the midday sun shone bright. Rebecca hesitated before spinning around to face him. He expected to be confronted with the same fear in her eyes, but she popped up on her tiptoes and brushed a kiss to his lips. "I'm not sure what I would do without you. Thank you, Brody."

The way his name rolled off her tongue brought back all kinds of memories he didn't need to be thinking about right now. "I haven't done anything yet."

"Yes, you have. An hour ago I was afraid of my own shadow."

"And now?"

"I'm relieved you're here. You look good, Brody."

The warmth her words spread through his chest almost

made him wonder if going to her place was a good idea. He was a grown man, now. And he had desires to match.

"You do, too. Better than good." Brody took her hand in his, ignoring how right it felt, and walked her to her vehicle.

Once she was safely inside, he hopped in his truck and followed Rebecca home. Her house, a two-bedroom bungalow, was fifteen minutes from the coffee shop. He parked behind her car as he surveyed the quiet residential street. Since the attack had happened hours ago, the monster could be anywhere. No red flags, yet.

"How long have you lived here?" he asked, once they'd both exited their vehicles, examining the front windows for any signs of forced entry.

"I rented it three years ago when I moved back." Her hand shook as she tried to unlock the door.

"I can do that for you." He looped his arm around her waist as she turned to face him. Touching Rebecca came a little too naturally, so he pulled back rather than allow himself to get sucked into the comfort.

"Guess I'm still a little shaken up." She smiled weakly as she handed over the key ring. Her fingers brushed against his flat palm, causing a sizzle to spread through his hand.

"You're doing great, honey." He closed his fist around the key, then stepped beside her before unlocking and opening the door. A high-pitched note held steady until she hit numbers on the keypad, four beeps followed by silence. The state-of-the-art security system was no surprise, given her past.

This place was all Rebecca. Soft, earthy feminine colors. Furniture he could see himself comfortable on—especially with her nearby. Her place was exactly as he'd imagined it would be, which had him thinking about the strong mental connection they'd shared. Still shared?

That was a long time ago. People change. He'd changed.

Walking around the living room, he ran his hand underneath lamp shades, tables and other flat surfaces.

The coffee-colored cabinets in the kitchen were his taste, too. He checked them and then swept his hand along the white marble countertops, stopping at the sink. There was a nice-sized window looking onto the backyard. The best thing about this part of North Texas was having trees. Her yard was a decent size, so someone could easily hide and watch her while she worked in the kitchen. Especially if she stood at the sink. His first thought was to install blinds.

Brody started making a mental to-do list as he moved through the house. He'd run to the nearest big-box store and pick up supplies later. He could make the changes himself.

She had a decent alarm.

"Do you live here by yourself?"

"Yeah." She bit back a yawn. Dark circles cradled her brown-as-honey eyes.

"You should try to rest. I'm not going anywhere. I'll wake you if I get any new information."

"I'm okay." She moved to the kitchen. "Besides, my nerves are too fried to sleep. I can't force down another cup of coffee. Want some herbal tea?"

"No, thanks." He still needed to check the master bedroom and he couldn't stall any longer. He shuffled his boots down the hall. The thought of being in the exact place she brought other men didn't sit well. There'd been no framed pictures of her with another guy so far. Brody didn't want to admit how happy that made him.

Hoping his luck would continue, he breached her bedroom. He'd open the nightstand drawer last, in case there were condoms. It wasn't his business what she did anymore, or with whom, but he couldn't help feeling territorial about his first love. The thought of her in bed with another man would rank right up there as one of his worst mental pictures. And he really didn't want to see any leftover men's clothing or shavers in the bathroom, either. Which was exactly the reason he'd put off checking her master bedroom.

As he walked the perimeter of the room, nothing stood out.

"Everything okay in here?" The sound of her voice coming from the doorway coupled with the visual of her bed didn't do good things to him.

"Doesn't look like you slept here last night."

"I work deep nights at the radio station."

"Right. Of course." Why did that ease his tense shoulders?

She stopped, almost as if she was hesitating to cross the threshold. Did she sense the heat filling the short distance between them? All he had to do was reach out and he could pull her close to him, protect her.

Brody mentally shook off the thought and moved on. "What time did you go to work last night?"

"I go in at ten o'clock. The show airs from midnight to six. We always wrap afterward."

"Any new employees in the last couple of months?"

"No. Not much ever really changes in this town." Her smile warmed his heart, threatening to put another crack in his carefully constructed armor. He took a couple of steps toward the door.

"The body needs sleep in order to perform. Why don't you close your eyes and rest while I check out the grounds?"

She looked up at him with big, fearful brown eyes. "You're not leaving, are you?"

"No. You're stuck with me. Like I said, I'm not going anywhere without you until we figure this whole thing out." He shouldn't notice how good he felt when her face muscles relaxed into a smile. "I need to make some calls, though, and you might as well get some shut-eye."

"What if he…" She didn't finish, but Brody knew exactly what she was going to say.

"I doubt he'll show up while I'm here. Think about it. This creep snatched little kids before and then surprised you this morning, which sounds like someone who's afraid of confrontation. I doubt he has the gall to try something with me around."

She nodded and her shoulders lowered.

"You have an extra key?"

"Sure." She disappeared down the hall, returning a moment later with a spare held out on the flat of her palm. She relayed her alarm code.

Taking it caused his finger to brush her creamy skin again. The frisson of heat produced by contact pulsed straight from his finger, to his arm and through his chest. In the back of his mind, he was still thinking about the feel of her lips against his at the coffee shop, the taste of coffee that lingered.

Physical contact was a bad idea. If he couldn't find and keep his objectivity in this case, the moral thing to do would be to help her find someone who could.

"You need me, just shout," he said, resigned. He needed to get in touch with the sheriff's office, too. See if Brine would offer information about the case.

"Okay." She paused. "Any chance you could stay inside until I get out of the shower?"

"I'll be in the living room," he said, hearing the huskiness in his own voice. The last thing he needed was the naked image of her in his thoughts.

He almost laughed out loud. They'd been together in high school. Not in the biblical sense, but they'd been a couple. Twelfth grade was a long time ago. Feelings changed. Their current attraction was most likely residual. She was beautiful. No doubt about that. And she was exactly the kind of woman he'd ask out if they'd met today and could forget about the past. But all the extra chemistry he felt had to be left over from before. That was the only reasonable explanation. Because Brody hadn't felt like this toward any woman since her. And he'd been in several relationships over the years. Yet, something had always stopped him from taking the next step. Marriage was a huge commitment, he'd reasoned. There'd been no need to rush into a big decision like that.

"I saw a laptop in the living room. Mind if I use it?" he asked.

"Not at all. Go right ahead," she said.

"What's the password?"

"Capital *N-V-M-B-R*. Then the number fifteen."

Brody turned without giving away his reaction. November fifteenth was his birthday.

REBECCA CHECKED THE CLOCK. She'd showered, hoping the warm water would relax her strung-too-tight muscles, before the tossing-and-turning routine began. She flipped onto her right side and placed a clean sock over her eyes to block out the light.

Rolling back to her left, she repositioned the sock.

No luck.

The sun was firmly set in the eastern sky. She'd closed her black-out curtains. This was normally the time she'd be asleep, but the way her mind was spinning no way could she rest. All she could think about was the possibility of Shane being alive. Even she knew the chances were slim. And yet, odds didn't matter in her heart, where she still held hope.

She'd need more than a piece of material to block out her thoughts. Time was the enemy. A killer was after her. Thoughts of being locked in that shed brought the terrifying sensation of her abduction back. And everything that had happened after…

When she'd returned, the town had been in chaos. Volunteers were assigned to a search team. Hundreds of people fanned out over the fields surrounding Mason Ridge Lake. Others opened car trunks and abandoned structures. People carried guns and set up neighborhood patrols. Even the wealthiest man, Mr. Alcorn, had thrown considerable resources into the effort.

Later, searchers joined hands as they walked in a line through the fields near Mason High School.

Two FBI agents had taken up residence in the Hughes's front room. A half dozen crop dusters and military planes had circled the sky, searching. The 4-H club had sent riders out on horseback.

Local law enforcement had encouraged people to keep their porch lights on at night and be ready to report any activity that might be suspicious. The Texas State Police had set up a half dozen roadblocks. Railroad cars, motel rooms and the bus station were searched—as was every house in the city.

Shane's comb had been shipped off to the FBI lab near

Washington for analysis. As had his favorite toys—trucks, LEGO and his handheld game system.

Rebecca had suddenly found herself under twenty-four-hour watch. Dr. Walsh, her pediatrician, had checked her for signs of sexual assault.

When a week of fruitless searching had passed, authorities had alerted residents to look out for scavengers, believing that Shane's body might have been tossed into a field or nearby farm. They'd been told to keep an eye out for large gatherings of buzzards and crows and were advised not to touch a body if one was found.

It wasn't long after that the FBI ran out of steam. Reporters had been a different story. They'd followed her parents for months, relentless.

Normally, Rebecca forced those thoughts out of her mind, unable to think about them. Having Brody in the next room brought way more comfort than it should. She told herself no one would care about her more than him, and that's why his presence gave her such a sense of well-being. Nothing about her current situation should cause her to let her guard down. The last time she'd gone against her better judgment, she'd ended up in a shed out in the woods. And her brother…

She couldn't even go there. Couldn't sleep, either. She tossed the covers and pushed off the mattress. She threw on a pair of shorts and a T-shirt, pulled her still-damp hair into a ponytail and met Brody in the living room.

He glanced up from the laptop, a look of determination creasing his forehead, and offered a quick smile. "Can't sleep?"

"No. This time of year is always…challenging. So, dealing with all this other stuff has my system out of whack." She threw her arms up, exasperated.

Brody studied her. His clear blue eyes seemed to see right through her. "I've said it before, but we will figure this out. I already reached out to Ryan and he's following up with the others, trying to see if we can figure out a good time for everyone to meet." He patted a spot on the sofa right next to him. He looked good. Damn good. He'd filled out his six-foot-two frame nicely. He was all muscle and strength and athletic grace. His blond hair was cut tight with curls at the collar. He wore a simple shirt and jeans.

Rebecca took a seat next to him, ignoring how her stomach free-fell the minute she got close. "Have you heard anything from your contact?"

"Yes. She emailed as much as she could. The suspect list is long." He had a pen and notepad out, scribbling notes as he flipped through a file on-screen. "I'd also like to take a look at your social-media account."

"Sure." She waited for him to click on the icon before giving him the password. "Nice pen."

He glanced at it and nodded. "A present from the old man."

"How is your father?"

"He's getting older, but he'd never admit it." Brody half smiled, still maintaining focus. "I've been thinking of moving him onto the ranch. Hate the thought of him being alone. But he's stubborn."

"Sounds like someone else I know." She laughed. "I doubt he'll give up his own place without a fight. He's a good man. I always liked him."

Brody nodded, but his expression turned serious again as he studied the screen.

"Find anything useful?"

"Hold on." He clicked through her chat messages,

studying the accompanying faces. He stopped at one, considered it for a long moment and then clicked on the image, which opened the guy's home page. "There's something about this one. Randy Harper."

"If Shane was still…alive, I'd imagine him to look just like this. I mean, he and I look related, don't we?" Her cell, on the coffee table, buzzed. She picked it up and checked the screen. It was her father. She hit Ignore and tucked it half under her leg.

Brody had seen who the caller was. She steadied herself for the inevitable questions about why she was refusing to take her father's calls. The cell vibrated under her leg, indicating he'd left a voice mail. She didn't want to get into it with Brody right now, didn't want to think about her father's new life while she still hunted down what had truly happened to his old one.

She glanced up, catching Brody's stare. He didn't immediately speak. Then he said, "The others resemble you, too, but there's something special about Randy."

"I had the same feeling."

"How long ago did you find him?" he asked.

"Six months or so."

"He doesn't live far."

"Nope. But he didn't respond to my message. I've been doubling my efforts with him and a few others lately."

"The city of Brighton is located two counties east of here. I used to know a girl who lived out there while we were in high school…." His voice trailed off at the end, as if he suddenly realized who he was talking to.

Sure, a twinge of jealousy nipped at her. More than that, if she was being totally honest. But she had no right to own the feeling. Shoving it aside, she smiled. It was weak, at best, but Brody took the peace offering, returning the gesture.

He scrolled down the page. "He hasn't posted anything in months. He either hasn't been online or he's abandoned his page altogether."

"We can rule him out as a phony, then. He can't be a crackpot trying to rattle me if he doesn't even realize I've tried to contact him. Plus, he's too old to be Shane. Look at the birthdate."

"You're probably right, but if it was him, then he might not really know when he was born. I've read about cases of abducted kids being told lies about when and where they were born to make it more difficult for them to dig around in the past."

"Wouldn't he need an actual birth certificate to enroll in school? My stepmother had to produce that, shot records, and a current electric bill for my half brothers," Rebecca said. She didn't want to feel the spark of hope that Shane might actually still be alive. She wanted her brother to be somewhere safe—had dreamed it, hoped it and prayed it. But she didn't want to create false expectations based on a social-media page.

"A birth certificate can be made. For a price. The rest would fall into place from there. Maybe we can find some of Randy's friends. Dig around a little in his background. Pay him a visit." Brody scribbled down a few names. "I don't want to invite them into your social network, so we'll have to reach out another way."

He scanned through photo after photo on the home pages of the people connected to Randy. A good fifteen minutes had passed when Brody made a satisfied grunt. "Look here. At this pic. And this one. Then, this one. See what's in the background?" He displayed the pictures in a larger window to view one at a time. Three friends had tagged Randy at a local restaurant called Mervin's Eats.

"When was the last picture posted?" Rebecca asked as another flicker of excitement fizzed through her.

"Three months ago." Brody glanced at the clock on the bottom right-hand corner of the screen. "Too early to go and check out the place now. Looks like we just figured out where we're eating tonight, though." He pulled up another screen, his fingers working the keyboard, and pulled up the address to Mervin's Eats in Bayville, Texas. He copied down the address in his notebook.

This was the first promising lead she'd had in fifteen years. It was hard to contain the enthusiasm swelling inside her. "For so many years, everyone's said he's gone. What if they were wrong?"

"I have plans to track down every possibility. That means we're going to run into dead ends." His honest blue eyes had darkened with concern.

"Believe me, I know better than anyone about disappointment." He was trying not to get her hopes up in case he had to dash them, and she appreciated him for it. "I've handled it before and I will again. It just feels nice to have a little hope for a change."

His nod and smile said he understood. "We need to keep working other trails, too. If we can figure out why or how our guy was connected to Mason Ridge before, maybe we can figure out what he's doing here now."

"I can't stand waiting around. I'd like to go out looking for him."

"Okay. Give me a chance to study these notes so I have a better idea where to start searching. See if I can find some connection either to this town or to your family."

She shivered as an icy chill ran down her back. That

thought was unnerving. Could someone close to them have orchestrated Shane's disappearance? She hadn't considered it before.

Brody's gaze trained on her. "Have you eaten anything today?"

"Not yet. Stomach's been churning all morning. My brain, too. I was thinking about the fact the places where he took my brother and me weren't secure. It couldn't have taken him more than a half hour to get us both there, so they were close by. He had to know the area, which, now that I think about it, would rule out a random person passing through town. I told the sheriff all this before, but there's another thing I can't stop thinking about. He didn't want me. He wanted my brother. I got in the way when I followed them and the guy was distressed about it."

"Makes me think it might've been his first time to kidnap someone," Brody said quietly.

"Not the work of someone used to slipping into a strange town to snatch a kid."

"What else did the sheriff say?" Brody asked, his interest piqued.

"That he probably improvised, saw a couple of abandoned buildings and hid us there. But why? Wouldn't he want to get out of town as quickly as possible?"

"And the response to that?"

"Nothing to me. I did hear someone from the FBI tell my parents later that the guy most likely hadn't preplanned the kidnapping."

If she could go back and trade places with her brother, she wouldn't hesitate. How many times had she wished she'd been the one to disappear, to die?

There was a slim chance that Shane was still alive, she reminded herself. The odds weren't good, Rebecca knew that, but she also knew better than to focus her energy on the negative.

That bastard had made a mistake once. She was living proof. All she needed was another misstep. With Brody's eyes on this case, maybe he would figure it out and bring the monster to justice. Rebecca would do whatever it took to help. "If only I remembered more…"

Brody's arm around her shoulder, his fingers lifting her chin, stemmed the emotion threatening to unravel her.

"I hate that you're going through this again. I'm sorry it happened to you in the first place. Believe me, I'll do everything I can to find that jerk."

A mix of emotion played inside her. Fear. Anxiety. Sadness.

Hope?

"Let's get something to eat and we'll hit Woodrain Park. He's probably smart enough to pick a new place, but we have to cover it, anyway." His words wrapped around her like a warm blanket. She leaned over until their foreheads touched.

"I won't let him hurt you again." He said other sweet words—words that made her want to yield to his strength.

And yet, getting too close to Brody wasn't a good idea. No one could quiet the monster's voice in the back of her head for long. He would return. He always returned. And she'd slip into her armor, blocking out the world.

"I'll fix something to eat." She rose and walked toward the kitchen, stopping in front of the sink.

Brody followed. The gun tucked into the waistband of his jeans was a stark reminder of the dangers they faced. He rummaged around the fridge, tossing up an apple. "Not much here to work with."

"I left my groceries scattered across the lot."

He nodded and then searched the pantry, pulling out almond butter, bread and cinnamon grahams. "These'll work."

She nodded.

He moved to the sink with the supplies, glanced up and froze. His gaze fixed on something out the window.

Cursing, he palmed his weapon and adjusted his position, stepping away from the window. "Get down. Now."

Rebecca dropped to her knees as panic roared through her, making her limbs feel heavy. "What is it? What's going on?"

"Someone's out there watching."

Brody crawled past her with the agility and speed of a lion zeroed in on his prey. "Lock the door behind me. Wait right here until I get back."

"No," she pleaded, trying to stop her body from shaking. She opened the drawer and gripped a knife.

"Take me with you. I don't want to be here alone."

Chapter Three

"Stay close." Brody didn't like the cold chill pricking the hair on his arms. He didn't like how easily a stranger could watch Rebecca while she was in the house. And he sure as hell didn't like the fact that the man who'd tormented her and changed her life forever was most likely back.

Brody crouched low as he cleared the back door.

The figure, tall and thick-built enough to be a man, darted into the trees.

"Go inside, lock the door and set the alarm."

She didn't respond, but he heard her backtrack as he broke into a full run. No way could she keep up, and he didn't want to risk them being separated in the trees, leaving her exposed and vulnerable.

The unforgiving dirt and shrub stabbed his feet as he bolted across the yard. Brody regretted kicking his boots off and getting too comfortable. The male form disappeared to the left as Brody hopped the chain-link fence and breached the tree line.

Forging through the mesquites, maples and oaks, Brody winced as he stepped on scattered broken limbs. He pushed the pain out of his mind, maintaining full focus on his target. He could hear crunching ahead of him, although he couldn't judge the distance or the gap between them. At this point, the noise could come from an animal he'd spooked. Based on the weight, it would have to be one big animal. Even so, it was still possible. There was no telling for sure until he got eyes on whatever it was.

A dark thought hit. Brody was being drawn deeper into the trees; the underbrush was thickening, and Rebecca was alone at the house. Brody couldn't take the chance he'd been lured away.

Besides, the rustle of leaves was growing more distant, indicating the guy was too far ahead to catch.

Circling back, the pain of bare feet pounding against hard soil made running a challenge.

He didn't know how long he'd been going, but it took a good fifteen minutes to jog back to the bungalow. His feet had been cut and he was leaving a trickle of blood across the lawn on Rebecca's quarter-acre lot.

She must've been glued to the kitchen window, because as soon as he stepped onto the back porch, the door swung open and she rushed into his arms.

"Hey, hey." He took a step back as the full force of her impact hit him.

"I'm sorry." She buried her face in his chest.

Brody should put a little space between them. He should take a step back and not be her comfort. He should keep a safe distance.

Should.

But couldn't.

Not with the way she felt in his arms. Not with the way her body molded to fit his. Not with her scent, citrus and flowery, filling his senses.

A tree branch crunched. Brody scanned the yard, didn't see anything.

Outside, they were exposed.

He guided them inside the house, then closed and locked the door behind them.

"It's okay," he soothed.

"I know," she said quickly, and he knew it was wishful thinking on her part.

He heard her muffled sniffles and suspected she wasn't stepping away from him because she didn't want him to see her cry.

Before he could debate the sanity of his actions, his arms encircled her waist, hauling her closer to him.

Flush against his chest, he could feel her rapid heartbeat. The whole scenario might be erotic if she wasn't shaking so damn hard.

"Should we call the sheriff?" Maybe they'd believe her this time with Brody there to corroborate her story. Rebecca took a step away from him, and then stared out the window.

"And say what? I saw a guy in the tree line? He didn't break any laws being out there," Brody said, a frustrated edge to his tone.

"He knows where I live. God only knows how long he's been out there spying on me." A chill raced down her spine at the thought of him watching her through her windows. She wasn't safe even in daylight now.

Brody took a step toward her and put his hand on her shoulder.

She turned to face him, ignoring the shivers his touch brought. Determination set his jaw, and the cloud forming behind his eyes said he wasn't sure she would like what he had to say.

"I don't know if I can protect you here. We most likely

scared him off and he may not return, but it's a risk I'm not willing to take with you."

Those words sent an entirely different shiver down her body, a cold, icy blast that said everything she knew was about to be taken away from her again.

"Meaning what?"

"I need to take you someplace safe."

This bungalow might not be much, but it was her home. The thought of allowing that twisted jerk to force her out of her house churned in her stomach. He'd taken away so much already—from her, from her family. Part of her wanted to dig in her heels and argue because anything else felt as if she was sacrificing her power all over again. Except the logical part of her brain overrode emotion.

Brody had military experience. She'd hired him to keep her safe. Not listening to his advice would be more than stupid—it could be deadly.

His gaze stayed trained on her as she mentally debated her options. Options? What a joke that was.

So, she wouldn't be stupid. Of course, she'd go where she could be safe.

"I'll do whatever you need me to." The words tasted sour. Putting herself in Brody's hands wasn't the issue.

Relief relaxed the taut muscles in his face. "Good. Then, pack a bag and let's get out of here."

"Can we search for him? Go after him for a change? Maybe even put him on the run?"

"If that's what you want." His blue eyes darkened, the storm rising.

"I know what you're thinking. Yes, looking for him could be dangerous. I understand that and I need you to know I'm scared. But I'm also determined. He doesn't get to take away my power again. Sitting around, waiting for him to strike makes me feel helpless."

"I'll have your back. He has to get through me to touch you. And, darlin', that isn't happening on my watch."

Rebecca had sensed as much when they'd dated in high school. She'd gotten so used to being alone, to the isolation that came with being "damaged" and different. She'd quickly figured out where the term *kid gloves* came from. The sentiment might've been wrapped in compassion, but that didn't change the message to a child.

Well, she was no longer a child. And that psychopath didn't get to make her afraid anymore. Sure, she'd had a moment before in the kitchen. There'd be more, too. And she refused to apologize for her moments of weakness.

Being afraid was a good thing. It would make her cautious. It would keep her from making a stupid mistake that he could capitalize on. It would drive her to find him and possibly her brother, if Shane was still alive. Besides, being fearless had put her in this situation. She'd had no business sneaking out that night. Mason Ridge might've been the Texas equivalent of Mayberry, but complacency meant being vulnerable.

"I just need a minute." She moved to the bedroom and opened a suitcase, thinking about the few items she couldn't live without. A sad note played in her heart. She had a few articles of clothing that had a special meaning, but that was about it. Shane's Spider-Man watch, his favorite possession on the earth, was inside her drawer. She retrieved it and pressed it to her chest.

She missed him.

Still missed him.

Everything good about childhood disappeared that hot night in late June. It was as though her mother and father had died along with the memory of Shane. Rebecca had no recollections of spring-break trips or campouts. Her parents had become obsessed with keeping her alive and in sight. Sleepovers stopped. There were no more séances or s'mores over a campfire, like there had been when Shane was alive.

It was as though all the color had been stripped out of life. No more blue skies or green grass. No more laughter. She'd been so distraught with grief at the time she didn't notice that while other kids gathered outside at the park for ball, she'd engaged in therapy with one of her many doctors.

She'd existed, had been treated like fine china, put on a display shelf and only handled with the utmost care. She'd spent most of her time in her room because being downstairs with her parents while they fought that first year had been even more depressing. Books had given her an escape and kept her somewhat sane, somewhat connected to the world playing out in front of her, all around her and, yet, so far out of reach.

When her parents had divorced, the rest of her fragile world shattered.

The truth was that Rebecca couldn't connect with anyone after losing Shane. Deep down, she didn't blame her father for wanting to start a new life. He'd tried to include her, make her feel part of his new world. But that would've been a slap in the face to her mother. And Rebecca already felt as though her mother had suffered enough.

She placed the watch gently inside her bag, then opened the next drawer and pulled out a few pairs of jeans, undergarments, and a variety of shirts, shoving them inside.

Rebecca stomped to her closet and jerked a few sundresses off their hangers. After rolling them up, she stuffed them inside the bag, fighting the emotions threatening to overwhelm her.

Toiletries from the bathroom were next on her mental checklist. She moved into the en suite and grabbed her makeup bag.

A wave of nausea rolled through her. His voice. The apple-tobacco smell. Her brain had blocked everything else out. She couldn't remember what he looked like other than a nebulous description.

Not even her psychiatrist had been able to hypnotize that out of her. She wished like hell she would've been able to give the sheriff and the FBI more to go on. She was the only one who'd had a glimpse of him, the one who'd lived, and she couldn't pick him out of a lineup if her life depended on it.

And, now, it would seem that it did.

Rebecca didn't realize she was shaking, until Brody's steady arms wrapped around her, stabilizing her. "I was just thinking that I could've stopped all this if I'd just remembered."

"It's not your fault." His warm breath rippled down the back of her neck.

"I know, but—"

"It's not your fault."

Hadn't she heard those four words strung together a thousand times via counselors, teachers, her parents? "It just feels like if I'd been able to describe him—"

"Honey, there were grown men trained to track predators like him who couldn't get the job done. Him getting away wasn't the fault of a twelve-year-old girl."

On some level, she knew Brody was right. And, yet, guilt fisted her heart, anyway. He was being kind, so she'd spare him her true feelings. She tucked them away and forced a smile, ducking out of his hold.

"Good point." She moved to the bed, closed the suitcase and zipped it. "I've been thinking a lot about the old group. Think Ryan got ahold of them? All of us were out there that night. Maybe someone saw something they didn't realize could be important."

"I've been thinking the same thing. Ryan's working on getting everyone together. Dawson's not far. Dylan moved a town over, so he won't be hard to track down. We'll have to ask around for James. I don't know what happened to him after I left for the military. What about the girls? You talk to any of them?"

"Other than exchanging Christmas cards with Lisa and Samantha? No. Janet still lives here but I can't remember the last time we spoke and I don't think she was out that night. Melanie moved to Houston and never comes back."

"At least you have a few addresses. That's more than I have to go on. Maybe the others will know once we get the ball rolling." He paused. "I don't remember seeing Melanie that night, either, or James for that matter but we should try to reach them, anyway."

Brody walked over and gripped the handle to her suitcase. "I can take you home with me, or we can go to a hotel. The choice is yours."

"We should be good at a hotel." A neutral place might keep her thoughts away from how much Brody had grown into a man she could respect. She led the way through the house, stopping in the living room to grab her laptop. "Not sure when I'll be back, so I better take this."

"I'm going to want to dig deeper into a few of the responses you received to your social-media messages."

"I almost forgot about the letters."

"You still have those?" Anger flashed in his blue eyes.

"Turned most over to the sheriff, but some new ones have turned up recently." She moved to the laundry room, where she'd been keeping the stack of mail.

More anger flashed in Brody's expression as she handed them over.

"There must be fifty letters here."

"This time of year always brings out the crazy in people." Arming the alarm, Rebecca had the feeling that once she walked outside she'd never be the same.

She locked the door behind them, hoping she could remember something else about that day…anything that might make the nightmare stop.

Chapter Four

Brody shouldn't want to show Rebecca his ranch, shouldn't want her to be proud of him. Hell, he'd already had her in his arms twice and he couldn't deny just how much it felt as if she belonged there, especially with the way her warm body molded to his. She'd asked to go to a hotel instead and his chest had deflated a little. The facts still remained the same. She'd rejected him and stomped on his heart before and she'd do it again. She wasn't cruel, just scared and confused. And it was all too easy for Brody to slip into his old role of being her shoulder to cry on, her friend. She'd confused those feelings for something else when they were young and she was doing it now. That was the only reason she'd go down that path again. How stupid was he not to figure it out before? Then again, Rebecca Hughes was his kryptonite. He reminded himself of the real reason she was there in the first place. She'd asked for his help.

All he was doing was helping Rebecca get her life back. He owed her that.

Or maybe he owed it to himself. If he got her squared away, he could put the past behind him and move on. He could stop thinking about those hauntingly beautiful eyes, the fear he saw behind them, the frustration he felt when he couldn't take it away.

"Got a different idea of where we can hang out the next few days instead of a hotel."

"Oh, yeah. Where are we headed?"

"How do you feel about camping?" He stole a glance at her as he pulled out of the drive, needing to see the look on her face. She might've been born in the country, but Rebecca Hughes didn't sleep outside.

Based on the look she shot him, his attempt at humor had only made things worse.

"Is that your idea of a joke?" She tapped his arm.

"Yes. It is." Something needed to break the tension. Get the conversation on a lighter track. It looked as if her muscles were strung so tight she might snap.

"Well, it's not funny." Her face screwed up. And she finally smiled, too.

"Sorry about the joke. But your reaction made me laugh. And I needed that."

"Okay, funny man. Where are we really going?" There was something special about the curve to her lips, the way her eyes flashed toward him looking so alive. The few times he'd broken through to her in high school were some of his happiest moments. And how sad did that make him sound? Then again, after his mother had ripped off the town and disappeared, life had become dark and complicated for him and his father.

"How do you feel about a serious change in plans? Hanging out in a cabin in Texoma for a few days until we sort all this out instead of a hotel? No roughing it. The place will have all the modern luxuries."

She was shaking her head from the second she heard "Texoma."

"It's too far. By the time we drive out there and back,

we'll lose four hours. No way." Her body had started shaking again, all hint of playfulness gone from her expression. He wondered if she even realized she was doing it.

"You sure you don't want to get away? I mean *really* get away?"

"I can't. I don't want to be that far from my mother. I need to call work, too. In fact, I should do that right now." She made a quick call and then dropped her phone in her purse. "I could always stay with my mother."

"That's not a good idea. Unless you want to tell her what's going on."

"No. You're right. It's bad enough that I skipped our visit this morning. That won't work. I'd rather keep her out of this as much as possible."

"I figured that's what you'd say."

"She needs me here. Can we get another place? Something closer?"

Brody stopped at the four-way stop sign at the end of her block. "My ranch is the perfect place."

"You bought the old Wakefield place, didn't you?"

"It's less than twenty minutes from here and it'll make it easier for me to check on the horses. If you really don't want to go there, my dad's house is another option."

"It would be nice to see him again. I'd like to stay at your place, though, if we can't stay at a hotel."

"It might be best if we don't leave a credit-card trail." He turned the steering wheel right. Pride he had no right to feel tugged at his heart. He needed to remember to keep a safe distance from the emotion. Nothing good could happen from touching a fire twice. "Let's swing by and get you settled before heading out to search for this guy."

"That's a better plan."

"Can I ask a question, though?"

"Okay." Her tone was tentative.

"Why didn't you take your father's call earlier? You two still at odds?"

"I'm not sure 'at odds' is the best way to describe our relationship. We don't really have one."

"Why is that, if you don't mind me asking?"

"It's complicated."

"I know." He kept his gaze on the road ahead. "I realize why you kept your distance before…how screwed up your mom was. I'm sure you felt conflicted. Love him and it betrays her. I get it. But, why now? Your mom's sick. You're doing all this alone and you don't have to."

"She's not his problem anymore."

"He said that?"

"No. Not in so many words. But he walked out. Divorced us."

"Her. He divorced *her*. There's a big difference."

"Same thing."

"Is it?" He shrugged. "I see Dylan with Maribel and just because he's not together with her mom doesn't mean he loves that little girl any less."

"Dylan has a daughter?" She couldn't contain her shock.

"Long story, but yeah. He's a great dad, too."

"He's the last person I'd expect to have a family. Especially after what happened to him with his own parents. Didn't we vote him most likely to become a career criminal?"

"What can I say? The guy cleaned up his act. He'd do anything for Maribel. He's a changed man."

Brody's phone vibrated again, another text. "Can you check that for me?"

Rebecca picked it up from the seat and checked the screen, staring for a long moment.

"It's from Ryan. He spoke to Lisa and she said one of her cousins was in Woodrain Park when a strange-looking guy ran past. He fit the basic description of our guy." Her voice cracked on the last few words.

Brody gripped the steering wheel so tight his knuckles went white. He ground his back teeth. "Looks like we have a place to start our search."

"Something's been bothering me about this whole scenario." Brody finally broke the silence. "You asked the question before and it's the same one that's been on my mind. Why now? What's so significant about today?"

"I keep racking my brain, too. I always go back to the fact that it's the fifteenth anniversary."

"Yeah, but what's so important about this one? Why not the fifth, or the tenth?"

Good question. "Could it be the extra newspaper coverage we're getting this year?"

"It's possible. They run stories every year, right?"

"Uh-huh."

"Makes me think there was some kind of trigger that we haven't figured out yet."

"That makes sense. But what? I haven't done anything differently. I've been here working, taking care of my mother. My routine hasn't changed." Her life sounded depressing when she spoke about it out loud. It was true, though. Her entire world had been about existing and nothing more for more years than she could remember. Maybe didn't want to, either.

"You moved back a few years ago, so that's not it." He tapped the steering wheel with his thumb. "Any new friends?"

"I don't have time." She glanced down at her feet

when she said it. Was that true? Or had she simply not made time?

"What about those letters? Anything stand out?"

"No. I get the same stuff every year," she said on a sigh.

"Any new employees at work?"

"We have a summer intern who started last month."

"Male or female?" His tone deepened a fraction, but she noticed it. He was onto something.

"Male. What are you getting at?"

"Who is it?" Brody's gaze stayed fixed on the road ahead.

"Alex Sweeny. Why?"

"How tall is he?"

"Six feet, I guess." Surely Brody wasn't saying what she thought. That Alex was somehow involved. She was already shaking her head. "He's way too young to be the guy we're looking for. Plus, he's related to the sheriff."

"You're right. We have to explore every possibility, though. And one of those prospects is that this guy could be involved somehow or wanting you to relive the past." His jaw clenched and released. His tension level matched hers.

"You mean like a copycat?" Rebecca didn't want to consider the possibility. If this was some twisted person trying to remind her of that horrible summer, then her chances of figuring out what had happened to her brother were nil.

And if not?

Then she had to face the horrible truth that any whack job could send her spiraling back to that dark place by imitating the crime. "What about the apple tobacco? The officers and FBI were careful about not letting that leak into the press exactly for this reason. How would he know about that?"

Rebecca kept on alert for two things. One was the scent of apple tobacco. The other was Shane's birthmark. He had a birthmark that looked like Oklahoma on top of his right foot.

Brody's face set with concentration for a long period. "With Sweeny being related to the sheriff he could get inside information of your case."

"I hadn't even thought of that. He would know about the threatening letters. The reporter. It was all common knowledge around the radio station."

"Why?"

"My boss wanted everyone on the lookout. He figured the best way to protect me and keep his other employees safe was to keep everyone informed." But could Sweeny, a young kid, pull off an attack at the grocery store without her realizing who he was? "I still think the kid is innocent."

"And he might be. But until we figure this thing out, we follow through on every possible lead." Brody turned into Woodrain Park's lot.

Rebecca hadn't been back to that place, to those woods…ever. Icy chills raced up her arms. She crossed them to stave off goose bumps.

As if a door had been opened, emotions flooded, crashing into her.

The shed.

The desperation.

She stopped for a moment to stem the tears pouring down her cheeks. "I can't remember much of what happened in the shed. I must've blocked it out or something."

Brody had pulled over and parked. His hand covered

hers, which did little to stop the shaking. "He can't hurt you anymore."

"What if I can't do it? Can't go back in there?" She motioned toward the wooded path.

"Then we'll look somewhere else. The chance he'd return is slim."

His words, his touch, breathed life into her. And a bit of courage. Besides, she couldn't avoid those woods forever. Maybe going, facing that horrible place, might help her remember something else. "You're right. He's most likely long gone by now. And even if he's not I have to do this. It might help. I keep thinking about how my brother's disappearance is my fault." A sob racked her. "I wish he would've stayed home that night instead of sneaking out to follow me. Wish I hadn't gone out that night and then none of this would've happened."

"I remember how close you two were. How you stood up for him when that bully threatened to beat Shane up after school."

"And you showed up at the rock quarry to make sure the bully never pulled that on younger kids again," she said.

Brody shrugged.

"Sorry about the black eye he gave you."

"That healed. I'm not so sure my pride ever recovered," he said with a smile that could melt Glacier Bay.

She leaned into him, into his comfort. She rarely ever spoke about the past, let alone laughed at some of the memories. Being with Brody was slowly bringing her back to life. He seemed to understand her need to keep everyone at a safe distance. He did the same. Maybe it was that she knew he'd been a loner most of his life and she could relate—she'd felt the same every day since that summer night when her life inexplicably changed. The only happy thought she'd held on to through college was Brody. He'd been her safe landing.

Regret filled her as he sat there quietly reassuring her, and for a split second she wished she could go back and make things right. Would she have pushed him away if she'd known no other man's touch would make her feel the way his did?

"You don't have to do this." Brody's voice, warm and understanding, pulled her back to the present. "We can go. Let the others look here. Ryan's on his way as we speak and he's bringing Dylan."

"I want to." How did she explain that while she realized facing these woods, that shed again, would be the most difficult thing in her life, it was also the only way to begin healing? All these years, she'd been going through the motions of her day, numb. Being with Brody, remembering that it was possible to feel things again, made her want to keep going. Do more than just exist.

"I don't want to go, believe me. Everything inside me is telling me to run the other way. But I'm afraid I'll feel even worse if I don't. What if I could have saved him and didn't because I was scared to go back? I can't live with that."

"I understand." And the hitch in his voice said he meant those words. He got out of the truck and then opened the passenger door. "It's not still there, you know. The shed."

"What happened?"

He rolled his shoulders in a shrug. "Me."

"You came out here?"

"It was after you left for college. I'd signed up for the service. Didn't want to ship out with unfinished business here."

She understood he wouldn't see another answer to his emotions. Brody had been quick to anger before and ready to fight the world. Except when it came to her and his family. He'd been tender and kind, which had made pushing him away all that much more painful.

The military looked to have done good things for him. He seemed to have grown into his own skin, was more at peace with himself and the world. Except when it came to her. There, he seemed as confused as she felt.

"I couldn't stand this place for what it had done to you. The fact that it was still standing six years later made me furious. I had to make sure another soul would never be taken to that place again. So, I tore it apart with my own hands to make sure."

"Thank you." She could totally see Brody doing something like that to protect her, to protect others. Maybe even out of frustration that the guy got away with it. His angry streak never would have been aimed at her or any other innocent person. But a bad guy, someone who was downright mean to others, should watch out.

She'd noticed it before, but there was a sense of purpose to Brody's stride now. Less anger, more determination. He was quiet calm, but, just like the surface of the ocean, danger lurked below. She had no doubt that if Brody met the man who'd hurt her today, he'd unleash hell. Just like he'd done all those years ago when faced with a bully. This time, Brody would win.

He took her hand as he guided her toward the pathway in the woods.

His cell buzzed. He checked the screen. "It's Dylan."

"Let's hope for good news."

Brody tipped his chin. "Tell me you found something we can work with."

He said "uh-huh" a few times into the phone, but Rebecca could tell from his tone there was nothing new to go on.

"We're at the park. We just got here." He went quiet. "Then you're not far from us." Another pause. "Yeah. That's exactly where we're headed. I know, man. I hear you."

She knew immediately that they were surprised she'd want to go back there. She couldn't say she was shocked at their reactions. No one in her right mind would do it. Maybe if she followed the killer's trail, she'd find something. It was a long shot but she had to try for Shane. She'd been a kid before, helpless, but she wasn't anymore.

She'd thought about this a million times. If she'd screamed for help instead of following and confronting the kidnapper, would things have turned out differently? Or what if she'd left some sort of trail so that others could find them?

A knot formed in her chest, tightening like a coil with each forward step.

It wasn't hard to tune out the rest of Brody's conversation. Rebecca was half-afraid of what Dylan thought about her after the way she'd left things with Brody, and she was afraid she'd overhear him warning Brody to stay away from her or something.

The only thing keeping her feet moving at this point was Brody's hand on her lower back, guiding each forward step, reassuring her.

"Dylan and Ryan are near Mason Ridge Lake. Said they'd head this way."

She needed to focus her attention on something besides the horror inside her escalating the farther they walked. "How are they?"

"Dylan and Ryan? They're good. I already told you about Dylan's little girl."

"You said he was bringing her up alone. What happened?" She needed to distract herself. Her pulse was rising and she needed to think about something else besides what lay ahead.

"He met someone on leave and fell pretty hard. Guess he was missing home and she reminded him of it. The relationship didn't last long, which is a long story, but he got Maribel out of it."

"What about the mother?"

"She was really sick when she finally told Dylan he had a child. He got to see her one last time before…"

"That's so sad. He didn't know?"

"No. She didn't tell him. Said she was afraid of what his reaction would be."

"He always said parenting was the cruelest thing people could do to children. She must've known."

"He didn't keep his feelings a secret. You should see him now. Maribel came to live with him when she was two. He had a rough year adjusting, but you wouldn't know it to see them together now."

It was hard to think of Dylan being tender with a toddler. If Brody had been tough back in the day, then Dylan had been an outlaw. Throw them both together and they'd be deadly.

Seeing Brody now, thinking about children, made Rebecca wish she'd handled things differently. The deep-seated sense of trust they'd shared was gone. She could see unease in his eyes. He was still as protective as he'd always been—some things would never change.

There were new scars on his body that weren't there before. He might've filled out in good ways, all muscle and strength, but he'd been hurt, too. Her heart squeezed thinking about the pain he must've endured. Rebecca knew full well external scars hurt far less than internal ones.

She'd lied to him and pushed him away. The only other time she'd been untruthful was for their friends.

Small towns were known for being bad places to hide secrets. Yet, they'd had to protect their friends. A cold chill raced up her spine, gripping her heart. A mistake?

The uneasy feeling intensified. Her feet felt heavier, legs weaker. A ball tightened in her chest.

Brody stopped. "You sure you want to keep going? You've been too quiet, which used to mean you were overthinking something. Now, I have no idea if it still means that. But I can tell that whatever's going on is spiking your blood pressure."

A branch snapped.

She turned around and gasped. "Oh. God. No!"

Brody instinctively reacted, dropping down low and pulling her down with him, a second too late to miss the large metal object from cracking his skull.

Chapter Five

Brody fought against the darkness trying to invade his body. The blunt-force blow to his head scrambled his brains. He instinctively felt around for a knot. Didn't take long to find one the size of an egg.

There was blood on his hand when he brought it back down. Lots of blood. He felt around in his pocket for his cell. It must've fallen out when the blow knocked him off balance.

Dizzy, vision blurred, he scrambled to stop a tall man from dragging Rebecca into the thicket. She fought like a wildcat, kicking and screaming, but she was outmatched in height, weight and strength.

Brody grabbed dirt, stumps, anything that would help him gain purchase as he crawled on his belly toward the attacker. He reached out in time to catch the guy's ankle and latched on to his pants.

The last thing he remembered was being dragged several feet before the darkness clawing at him won.

Now, he forced his eyes open, unsure how long he'd been out.

Dylan was there, consoling Rebecca, who looked shaken to the core.

She caught Brody's gaze and locked on, immediately moving toward him. "Thank God, you're awake."

Brody tried to speak, but his mouth didn't immediately move. He took a few slow breaths and reset.

"What happened?" he managed to get out. Brody didn't even want to think about what would've happened to Rebecca if the others hadn't shown.

"He was here." One look at Rebecca's dilated pupils, her wide, fearful eyes, and Brody figured she'd retreated to that space deep inside her that no one could reach. He'd seen it a few times in high school and nothing good ever came of it. The most notable time was when she'd broken up with him.

"Did you guys get him?"

She shook her head. Damn if her disappointment and fear wasn't a sucker punch to his gut. Not to mention the way her hands shook when Dylan gave her a bottle of water.

"When did you guys get here?" Brody was still fuzzy. He remembered having a conversation with Ryan a little while ago.

"We were nearby. Called the sheriff as soon as we got here. They're searching the woods for him as we speak. We'd be out there, too, but—"

"Thank you for sticking around." His gaze immediately shifted to Rebecca.

"No problem, bro. She fought like a banshee. It's the only reason she's still here and not God knows where."

Dylan helped Brody sit up and handed him a bottle of water. "Did you get a good look at the guy?"

"He's tall and thin, but quick. She got the best view. He nailed me before I had a chance to react. He knows these woods." Brody glanced around, trying to get his bearings.

"Think you can help her work with a sketch artist?" Dylan asked.

"Yeah. I can try. Like I said, he practically cracked my skull in two when he surprised me, so mostly he looked like a tall, skinny blur." Brody made a move to get up but sat right back down when his head felt like someone had split it open with an ax. "Any idea what he used on me?"

"We're lucky it wasn't a gun."

Brody glanced at Rebecca, who stood there stiff, looking like she might jump out of her skin if someone said boo to her.

"Get her out of here."

She whirled around on him. Determination set her jaw. "No. I'm not leaving. Not without you."

"Ryan can take you to the ranch and stay with you there." He checked his head and came back with more blood on his hand. "I'm not getting up anytime soon."

She stood there, brown eyes piercing through him. "I'm not going anywhere."

"How long was I out?" Brody's gaze shifted from Rebecca to Dylan.

Dylan cleared his throat before he spoke. "Not long. I'd say we arrived within a few seconds of you blacking out."

Rebecca might be there, standing close, but a wall had gone up around her. Her muscles were stiff, her jaw tight, and her arms were crossed over her chest. Everything about her body language had changed. "I'm not leaving with you still here."

"She should be fine. We're all here," Ryan said as he walked over. "EMTs are close."

About that time Brody heard sticks crunching in the brush behind him, growing louder. "You guys can't stay here. This is the closest anyone's been to him. I'm fine and he can't be far. Go, get him. I'll pick up the search when I'm cleared."

Ryan's expression said he'd carry Brody to the hospital himself if he had to. Dylan was just as unmoving.

"Let the paramedics get here and take a look at you first. Then, we can go together," Ryan said.

Brody blew out a breath, closed his eyes and leaned back. They were saying that they didn't want him doing anything stupid, like not getting proper medical attention. "Fine. But I'm going out there." He motioned toward the thicket. Nausea gripped him as blood trickled down his nose. He didn't want to admit how close he was to passing out again. It was in that moment his drill sergeant's words chose to wind through his thoughts. The first rule of being a good soldier was to take care of injuries.

The next time Brody woke, he was in the back of an ambulance.

He blacked out again, then woke to the news he was in the hospital being treated for lacerations and a possible concussion. "How long was I out this time?"

"A half hour?" The muscles in Rebecca's face tensed and he could see her pulse thumping at her neck. She was stressed. As shaken as she was, and emotionally closed off, she'd refused to leave Brody's side. He didn't want to acknowledge what that did to his heart.

"What's going on? Is everyone okay?" he asked.

She thanked the nurse and then waited for the older woman to leave the room and close the door behind her. "No. You're seriously hurt. And it's my fault."

He put his hand up before she could get too worked up. "Hold on a minute. This has nothing to do with you."

"Yes. It does. I brought you into this mess and now look." When she turned to him a tear spilled down her cheek. Something quick and explosive hit his chest when she made eye contact.

"Sweetheart, none of this is on you. If anything, I should've been more careful in the woods. I should've realized he would know that area like the back of his hand. Plus, we got a look at him this time. The sheriff has a better description to work with. And that's a good thing, right?"

She nodded as a few more tears escaped. She quickly wiped them away.

"Look at me. I'm here because I made a mistake. I underestimated the situation. I won't do that twice. And, I'm going to be okay. Believe it or not, I have a pretty hard head."

At least that last comment got a smile out of her.

The haunted look in her eyes had returned, though. Brody had no idea how to break through that. He'd tried and failed before. Didn't figure much had changed since then. Even so, it was good to see her again. Better than he wanted to admit.

And that was most likely because he'd missed home, too. Being far off in a desert, away from everything familiar, had a way of playing tricks on a man's mind and making him weak. Brody reasoned that was why he still had residual feelings for Rebecca. She was "known," and it had nothing to do with the curve of her hips into those long legs. Or her laugh, which sounded like music to his ears. He had missed her quick mind, her will to live even under extreme circumstances. She'd felt like home to him years ago. Those feelings resurfaced and that's why his heart hurt being close to her.

"Where are Dylan and Ryan?"

"They stayed with the sheriff to help search the

thicket." She folded her arms. "Think I should call Alcorn? He might be able to get more resources out there."

"I want this guy caught, too, but that might not sit well with Ryan," Brody said.

"Right. I almost forgot how much they don't like each other." She rubbed her arms. "Besides, the guy is probably long gone by now."

"Dylan said something about a sketch artist."

"One is being sent over now." She glanced at her watch. "In fact, he should be here any minute."

REBECCA DIDN'T WANT to admit how great it felt to see Brody sitting up, awake, sipping water. Or how much she wished she could get closer to him, touch him again. But she wouldn't, for her sake as much as his. And especially because his compassion was evident in his words and actions, but that was all he felt for her. He'd been clear.

A knock on the door made her heart leap. Resentment hit fast and hard that an unexpected noise had that effect on her again, just like before, just like she'd sworn would never happen again.

Well, the bastard wasn't going to get away with it this time.

"Come in," she said, popping to her feet, needing to walk off her nerves.

An older gentleman with a sketch pad tucked under his arm walked in, accompanied by a deputy.

Brody was already up, sitting on the edge of the bed, which agitated the machines he was hooked up to. They beeped loudly.

The older nurse rushed in.

"Mr. Fields, you need rest."

"Do whatever you need to me while I'm here, but as

soon as this meeting is over, I'm walking out that door."
He looked at Rebecca when he said, "Did you see my cell?
I lost it back there."

She produced it and he took it from her, heat pulsing
from where their fingers met.

"I wouldn't advise that. The doctor wants you to stay
overnight for observation," the nurse warned.

"With all due respect, we're in the middle of an investigation and I don't have that kind of time."

She glared at him as she fiddled with dials, her gaze
bouncing from him to the machine to Rebecca.

The deputy introduced both himself and the artist
while Rebecca pulled extra chairs next to the bed. Brody
made a move to help, but she motioned for him to stay put.

When the artist put the finishing touches on his sketch
and showed it to her, dread wrapped around her shoulders. The finished product was still too vague. "That's
not going to help. He's great at keeping his face hidden."

"It's a start," Deputy Holder said, and she could tell he
was reaching. At least he wasn't looking at her as if she
had six foreheads, half curious, half afraid, and expecting her face to explode. "We'll circulate this. See if we
can't stir the pot a little."

At least the sheriff's office took her seriously now.
She thanked the men and closed the door behind them.

The nurse turned toward Brody. "Any chance I can get
you to change your mind and stick around a little while?"

"No." He shot an apologetic look. "I know you're doing
your job, but I have to do mine."

The nurse gave an understanding nod before saying
she'd be back and then leaving.

"I didn't get a good look at him." Rebecca sat on the
edge of the bed, facing him without looking at him.

"This will help. The sheriff's office will start getting more leads than they can handle."

"It feels...hopeless." She threw her hands up in the air.

"One thing I learned on missions was to stay focused on a positive outcome no matter how bad things look. A thousand things can go wrong when you're out there, but thinking about them doesn't do any good. Positive thinking has more power to create change than I ever realized. If others knew how strong their minds were, people's lives would be very different."

"What did you focus on? What was home for you?"

He shifted his position, breaking eye contact. "I had a lot of things to come back to. Buying the ranch for one. My dad for another. Texas, my home."

A little piece of her heart wished he'd said her. But why would he? Not after the way she'd hurt him.

"Those are great things to keep you grounded." Rebecca had very little to keep her centered. She had her mother, whom she loved. What else did she have besides work and a couple of friends? Sadly, not much. Even her bungalow was a rental.

Her father was remarried with two boys, her half brothers, whom she'd never really been able to connect with no matter how much they'd tried. They weren't bad kids, but they weren't Shane, either. She could see the selfishness in those feelings now, but her teenage self had been less aware. And maybe it was her dad's new life that she never felt she fit into after he left.

Had Rebecca really made an effort?

Or had she expected him to go the extra distance to make her feel comfortable. He hadn't, so they'd drifted apart for a few years until she stopped visiting altogether.

There'd been so many people poking around in her

head, and all she'd wanted to do was be left alone and seem as normal as possible. Except she wasn't. She was damaged goods.

Had it been too easy to keep everyone at a safe distance? And now? What had changed?

Rebecca had taken over as her mother's caregiver, helping coordinate doctor appointments and medicines, and that had taken her mind off her own problems. A little part of her had been relieved not to be the focus for a change.

If she were being honest, she'd admit that being near Brody awakened pieces of her she'd ignored for so long.

"Did you bring the laptop?" Brody asked, breaking through her heavy thoughts.

"Yeah. I drove your truck."

"You thought to bring it to the hospital?" He glanced up, and what looked like pride was on his face.

Her heart fluttered. "I knew you wouldn't want to wait for someone to pick us up, so I drove. They wouldn't let me ride in the ambulance, anyway. I'll run down and get the laptop."

"That'll give us something to do while we wait for my release papers." He smiled.

She would never get used to the flush of warmth rolling through her at seeing him look so pleased with her. Maybe it was the way she'd left things all those years ago, the hurt in his eyes she remembered to this day, but she wanted Brody to be happy because of something she did.

It took all of ten minutes for her to retrieve the laptop and return. She set it on the bed, where Brody immediately opened the file.

"We recognize a face, get a name and maybe we get lucky with an address." Brody pulled up the list of suspects.

"There are so many familiar names. Do you remember who that is?" She pointed to the top name.

"Wasn't he our bus driver in middle school?"

"Yes." Her shoulders sank forward. "It makes me so sad to look at these names and think they might be such horrible people."

"We've known them most of our lives."

"If it's someone local, then they've hidden it for this long. There's no way they'd let this kind of secret out now."

"Don't be discouraged. No one's had this much information to go on before. We have a general description."

"It's still pretty vague," she pointed out.

"Once we narrow the list by height, we'll rule out a substantial amount of suspects. We know it can't be our bus driver. Mr. Alba was our height in middle school." His joke was meant to lighten her somber mood.

It helped. "True. Do you know how many men there are in Texas over six feet tall?"

"Yeah. We grow everything bigger in Texas." Brody laughed, and her tension eased. "Still, knowing this guy is six foot two will be a huge help."

"What if they were right all along? What if he was just passing through town all those years ago?"

"That's possible. Then we look outside of Texas."

"And what if this isn't him? What if it's some whack job imitating him?" She knew she was letting her fears get the best of her, but there were so many questions.

"Could be. But then we have to consider both sides of the coin."

"Okay, say we get a name. He'll surely go into hiding now. Not only did he slip out of my sight fifteen years ago, but he's done so twice today. No way will he stick around after this. How will we ever find him now?" Bile

rose from her stomach, burning her throat. She wrung
her hands and paced.

"I thought about all those things, too. We might keep
looking and not find anything to go on. We might dig until
we've dug to China and come up empty-handed. But it
won't be for nothing. You'll know something. You'll know
that you've given this your best shot. And that will help
you put this to rest when the time comes." He held steady
to her gaze. "First things first. We search these files while
we give my pain a chance to ease and make sure I'm not
going to pass out when I walk. Then, we head out and investigate. We don't stop until we find answers."

"And what if none of it helps?"

"It will."

She didn't respond, couldn't respond. She only wished
she had his faith as she walked another ten steps to the
window and back.

"Hey, come here."

She stopped, but her heart kept racing.

Brody patted the bed. "Let's look through this together.
Maybe something else will stick out that the investigators
missed before. You were closest to the scene and sometimes visuals help stimulate memories."

"Okay. You're right. Maybe we'll find something, and
if we don't I'll figure out a way to live with it."

Rebecca's cell buzzed. She took the call, thanked the
caller and then fixed her gaze on Brody.

"It's the nurse at the care facility. My mom needs me.
I have to go."

Chapter Six

"Then let's go." Brody stood. His knee gave and he almost fell. He caught himself by grabbing hold of the chair.

"This is not a good idea. You should stay here until you're better. I'll go check on my mother and pick you up in a little while." She palmed the keys and slid her purse strap over her shoulder, giving the universal sign of a woman ready to go.

"Absolutely not, Rebecca. I will not leave you alone. You can drive, but I'm going with you." He'd regained his balance and looked steady on his feet. Steady and stubborn.

"The doctor hasn't released you yet, remember?"

"I'm not waiting around for someone to tell me to stay in bed for the next three days and rest. Besides, I'm better at assessing my injuries than anyone else. I know what my body can and can't handle."

She didn't want to think about why he knew how much punishment his body could take. Did it have to do with the three-inch scar running down his left arm?

He closed the laptop. "Besides, I can study the folder and make a few calls on the way to see your mother. That's the most efficient use of our time, anyway."

She stood there staring him down for a long moment.

He was in a weakened state and she wanted, no, needed him to get better.

And yet he had that determined set to his broad shoulders and prominent chin. His sturdy jawline anchored his steady gaze, which was fixed on the door.

When Brody Fields made up his mind about something, he followed through. Period. He could be as obstinate as a bull terrier and, injuries or not, just as lethal. No way was he listening to her.

The nurse shuffled into the room.

"Bring whatever paperwork you need to keep the lawyers off your back, but do it fast. You have about a minute before I walk out that door." He inclined his head toward the only exit in the room.

The nurse yelled out for someone and Rebecca assumed it was the floor supervisor.

"Forty-five seconds."

The woman blew out a frustrated breath. She stared him down before calling out the name again.

"Thirty."

A disgusted grunt came. "Fine. If you're determined to hurt yourself, I have no legal grounds to stop you. I'll get your paperwork. Stay right here."

"No, thanks. Time's up." Brody leaned forward. Everything about his body language said he was about to walk out that door.

"Will you stop by the nurse's station to sign a release form?"

Brody clenched the muscles in his jaw, nodded.

"Follow me."

SIGNING OUT TOOK all of ten minutes. Brody didn't want to give the nurse a heart attack, so he cooperated while she printed form after form and asked for his signature a dozen or more times.

Billing had decided to pay him a visit before he left, too. He'd given his credit card and signed for that, as well.

Once inside his truck, he checked in with Ryan. His friend had no news to report, which was expected since there hadn't been any texts or phone calls.

Dawson, another childhood friend, was tending to Brody's horses, so he gave him a ring, too. Last week Brody had gotten an injured stallion who might be ending his racing career. Lone Star Park kept him in horses that needed rehab. He also took in neglected animals. A dozen mares had been rescued days before dying from starvation because of an irresponsible breeder last month and they were doing nicely. He'd witnessed firsthand what humans could do to each other in war and at home. Seeing what they could do to animals hit him in a whole new place of frustration. Brody needed to check on his horses at some point this evening. There should be plenty of time to visit Mrs. Hughes and follow up on the restaurant lead they'd uncovered earlier.

"If it's not too late when we finish with your mother, I'd like to go to Mervin's tonight. See what we can find there, which might be nothing," he quickly warned.

"Okay. I don't think we should go alone, though."

Good point. He wasn't up to par in his weakened physical state. He was one more surprise attack away from being chained to a hospital bed with an IV that had something besides coffee in it. "I'll see which of the guys can go with us."

"I heard you invite them to Mother's," she said.

"Figured we could talk while you visit. I'm not going

inside her room, considering I'm pretty much the last person she'll want to see. I was never her favorite person."

"That was a long time ago."

"Some things don't change."

She broke into a smile. "True. But she'll tolerate pretty much anything if it means I'll spend more time there."

Brody shouldn't say what he was about to say, but he couldn't help himself. "You have the same shy smile you did in high school."

And the same eyes, serious and intelligent.

"Do I? Here I thought I'd grown up so much. Guess not."

"Not so fast. There's nothing wrong with looking like you're still in high school. Some women might even consider that a compliment." He laughed. "I'd like to see more of that thing curving your face, though."

"Oh, Brody. It's been so long since I..." The smile faded too quickly. So did the sparkle in her eye.

"Go ahead. Finish your sentence," he urged.

"It'll make me seem even sadder than I already am, especially to you."

"It won't. Come on. Tell me. Please."

She compressed her lips.

"I said 'please.'"

"Okay, fine. Have it your way. It's been so long since I had anything to really smile about."

He shook his head. "That's a damn shame. A woman as intelligent and kind as you, as beautiful as you, should have everything she wants. Love. Laughter. Children."

Rebecca shrugged.

"Don't tell me you never think about having a family someday." He couldn't hide his shock.

"Have it your way. I won't tell you, then." No hint of a smile on her face now.

"Seriously?" Didn't every little girl dream of having a fairy-tale wedding, a big house and kids? Brody didn't have siblings, so he couldn't speak from personal experience on what little girls dreamed of, but they'd been portrayed that way his whole life. "You never think about it?"

"Not really. Not since I was a little girl and unafraid of the big bad wolf. Now that I know wicked things happen to children and what that does to a parent, I can't think about going down that road as the mother. I've seen what it did to mine."

"I get that." He could see anguish fill her. If she didn't fight, it would swallow her whole.

"It's not so bad, you know." She tapped her finger on the steering wheel. "I'm used to being alone."

Those five words haunted him more than he wanted to admit. Was it because he was the same? Had she hit a personal note?

He mentally shook it off. This was not the best time for a conversation about having children, not when emotions from the past were being dredged up. Besides, the incident in the woods had sent Rebecca into an emotional tailspin. He'd seen that lost look on her face once. Right before she'd broken his heart. No matter how close they were, now or then, she'd never be able to meet him all the way. Whoa. Why was he thinking about the two of them in a present-day relationship?

It didn't matter. He still didn't have answers to her case. He was considering all the options and yet the simplest explanation, the one the Feds kept coming back to, was that the guy wasn't connected to Mason Ridge. If he had been, then Brody's job of finding the jerk would've

been easier. The faster he could bring this monster to justice, the better. If only he could help bring peace to her
family. The man responsible for Shane's disappearance
needed to pay.

Brody had every intention of burying the bastard.

Time had come to get back to the basics in this case.
He opened the laptop and then the file, studying it again
as she drove toward Apple Orchard Care Facility, where
her mother lived. The suspect list seemed never-ending.
If he searched long enough, there had to be a connection
somewhere. He'd been looking for an association to the
town or the family. Maybe he needed to look harder for a
link within their group of friends. Maybe Justin's friends.

"It's okay, you know," Rebecca finally said. "I'm not
going to fall apart like my mother."

No. Rebecca was a survivor. Even after all these years,
she kept her chin up, kept searching. "I know."

She stopped at a red light. "Why did you call the guys?
I mean I know what you said, but there's more to it, isn't
there?"

"I'm interested to see if anyone remembers anything."

"It was a long time ago, Brody. I doubt anyone besides
me even thinks about it anymore."

The light changed and she pressed the gas.

There's where she was wrong. How could Brody forget? How could anyone forget who was there that night
or in that town? He already knew Ryan had thought about
it, as did Dylan and Dawson. That night was etched into
everyone's memories.

Brody had called a secret meeting after Shane had
disappeared. Rebecca couldn't be there, of course. But
everyone else had shown. Parents had strictly forbidden
kids to leave the house, so Samantha, Lisa and Mela-

nie had arranged to be together, watched by Samantha's older brother. Every available adult was out on a search team, scouring fields and abandoned buildings. No one wanted to leave their children unattended after the incident. Brody's father had allowed him to join the search, so he hadn't needed an excuse to be out. Brody and the guys had sneaked inside Samantha's first-floor bedroom window, risking everything to meet.

None of their friends had admitted to seeing anything. Afraid of being busted, everyone had scattered. But had they been lying? Surely they'd seen something. Maybe if they talked it through again, as adults, a detail would pop.

Brody figured the real reason Rebecca couldn't let this go was because she'd yelled at Shane when the game broke up, humiliating him, so he ran to get away from her. The weight she carried was so much more than letting him down because she'd always watched over her little brother. At first, she'd told him to sit by a tree and wait. He didn't listen. She'd embarrassed him in front of her friends, telling him he had no business following her. Teary eyed, he'd broken into a full run, little athlete that he'd been. Even then, he'd been fast as a whip. And she'd completely underestimated him. By the time she'd apologized to everyone for her little brother ruining their mission, he was gone.

The bullet that was Shane had already disappeared out of view. Rebecca had told Brody that she wasn't worried about losing sight of her brother. He'd head home. Where else would he go?

A noise had spooked the rest of the group. The game had been a bad idea that night. There were too many people out after dark because of the festival. Afraid of getting busted, they'd scattered in different directions.

Brody had offered to help find Shane. Rebecca had said she'd be fine. A few minutes later, alone, she'd heard a muffled cry.

The rest was history.

And Brody felt responsibility, too. What if he'd insisted on helping her search? Would he have made a difference? Surely, the kidnapper wouldn't have been able to subdue three kids. Even at twelve, Brody had been substantial. He might have been the tipping point they'd needed. How many times had he asked himself that question?

It still didn't matter. Brody hadn't gone. Shane had been kidnapped. History couldn't be revised.

At twelve, Rebecca had been a tower of strength.

Even now, she dug her heels in and went full force chasing a lead rather than roll over. She threw herself into the investigation even if it meant shutting out everything else around her. But then, she'd been good at that before, too.

With her mother gravely ill, Brody wondered who Rebecca would have left after her mom was gone. Her father? They weren't close anymore. Was that part of why she'd clung to the idea that Shane could be alive? Fear of being alone?

Where did that leave Rebecca?

Brody wanted to be there for her, to see her through this now in a way he couldn't before. He hated the thought that she felt alone again, fighting for the life of someone in her family. She didn't need advice or someone to tell her what was best for her. He'd be there if she needed him, if she let him.

Watching her pain nearly killed him, but he knew the only way to put the past behind her was for him to be strong and, better yet, bring justice.

"Did you call your father back?"

"I've been with you every minute."

"I thought maybe you'd returned his call at the hospital when I was out."

"No. Not yet. I will, though." Her voice was unsteady, as if she was still trying to decide.

"When?"

"Soon."

"Why not now?"

"Can I ask you a question?" Rebecca's voice was far less frail and afraid than it had been earlier. He sensed that she was gaining her strength. She might've been shell-shocked, but she wasn't broken. Not even the Mason Ridge Abductor could take that away from her.

Too many places inside him needed Rebecca to be okay.

"Yeah. Sure."

"What happened with your mother? I mean, I've heard the rumors about her convincing the town to invest in a lakefront resort and then disappearing with the money. That true?"

"Yes."

"Does it still bother you?"

"No." Brody had hoped this one time that she couldn't read his mind. They'd shared a mental connection in high school that had him wondering if dating her had been a good idea. He wasn't sure he wanted someone to understand the pain he was in. He was a kid, and he'd been feeling sorry for himself.

"Are you in contact with her?"

"No."

"Why not?"

"Other than the fact that she hasn't tried to get in

contact with me once since she left? I don't have anything to say to her."

"That all? You can be honest with me, Brody. I won't tell anyone. Not like I have a bunch of people to tell, anyway…" Her words trailed off at the end and he could tell she tried to come off as unaffected by the truth in those words. "It's more than that, isn't it? You value family."

Did he? He'd spent his teen years bitter about his mother's actions, his father's lack thereof. "I value loyalty more."

"That, too. But you never talk about her. I mean, you must feel something. Like with my dad, I was angry with him for starting another family. Especially since this one felt so…unfinished."

"Have you forgiven him? Moved on?"

"I guess not. But I am trying."

"Really? How so? By not answering his calls?" He glanced at her in time to see regret darken her features. Damn. He didn't expect her reaction to hit him so hard.

"I deserve that." Chin up, she seemed ready for another punch.

"That wasn't fair of me—"

"Yes, it was. I'm the one who brought up the subject. I shouldn't dish it out if I can't take it, right?"

"I still didn't mean it."

"Don't worry. I get it. You're doing the same thing I do. Push those feelings down so deep that no one can touch them. They're buried. They can't hurt you. But, lately, I've been wondering if that's the right thing to do."

"Meaning you want to call your father." Was she right? Brody had done his level best to forget the feelings existed.

"For one. I mean, part of me wants to talk to him. The rest thinks it's too late to start our relationship now."

"He wouldn't try to get in touch if he didn't want to spend time with you. My situation's different. My mom took off and that was it. I never heard from her again. No birthday cards. No surprise high school graduation visit. She hasn't tried to get in touch once. And it's bad enough she stole from the town, but look what she did to my father. He never stopped waiting for her to come back, never got over her. She had to know how much he loved her, I loved her. And not one word in more years than I can count. Not exactly a person worth tracking down." Anger had those last words biting out. He never talked about his mother, not to anyone. He'd convinced himself that he no longer cared about her or the way she'd treated his father. Was that true? The venom he felt surging through him said otherwise. Was it good to dredge up the past?

"You're right. You're completely right. Our situations are totally different. But our way of dealing with them is pretty much the same." She hesitated. "I'm glad you talked about it. You never used to."

"Like I said, wasn't much to say before."

"And now?"

"Talking to you is different. We have history." It was more than that, but no way would he allow himself to dwell on that emotion. He didn't need to know how deep his feelings ran for Rebecca. The bottom line was that she'd shut him out just as his mother had. And Brody was nothing like his father. Brody wouldn't sit around licking his wounds, waiting for a woman who could so easily walk away from him to return.

He shoved those thoughts aside as Rebecca pulled into

a parking spot and cut the engine. "I'll stick around out here and keep digging in these files while you go inside."

She lightly touched his hand, and even that little bit of contact sent sparks flying. Another reminder it was a bad idea to get too close to her this time around. Sparks ignited flames. Unchecked, flames developed into full-blown fires. A raging fire destroyed everything in its path. Just like his mother had. And his father had simply stood in its way and gotten burned.

But Rebecca's situation with her father couldn't be more different. "It's okay to love your father, you know."

"I do now. But by the time I realized it, his calls had slowed and it just seemed easier to leave things alone. Sleeping dog and all that. Now I'm thinking maybe I just took the coward's way out."

"You? Not a chance." Brody shook his head. He brushed against her right cheek with the backs of the fingers on his left hand. "You're one of the strongest people I've ever known."

She smiled, warming him, warning him that getting too close to fire would engulf him just like it had his father. Brody wasn't objective when it came to Rebecca. And that was dangerous.

"I'm sorry about your family, Brody." Her look was all compassion and sympathy, creating an intimacy between them he didn't want to acknowledge, and it stirred something in his chest he had no desire to think about.

"I guess there's no chance I can convince you to come inside with me."

The others hadn't arrived yet. Brody texted them to say that he had. A second later, he got a message that the guys would be running late. Dylan had to swing by and check on Maribel who wasn't feeling well. "I doubt your mother wants to see me."

"You might be surprised." She unbuckled her seat belt and reached for the handle. "Why not see for yourself."

"Hold on a sec." Hopping out of the truck, his knee giving in the process, he steadied himself and rounded the front end, determined to open the door for her. Part of him wanted to be there for Rebecca, to hold her hand through it all, but the other part—the logical one—said going inside with her was a bad idea since he didn't want to upset her mother with his presence. Then again, the thought of Rebecca going anywhere alone didn't sit well, either.

Rebecca held out her hand.

Brody took it, ignoring how well hers fit.

"I know you're supposed to meet the guys out here, but will you go in for a minute?" she asked.

If she hadn't asked, he sure as hell wouldn't have volunteered. She had. Against his better judgment, he nodded.

She smiled and that annoying part of his heart stirred again. Sure didn't take much to get that going. *Way to be strong, Fields.*

But he was expert at swallowing his true feelings. Rebecca was no exception. Pretending he hadn't just told himself a big fat lie, he held out his arm for her.

The next touch, her hand to his forearm, was so light it barely registered. The electricity it sent up his arm was another story altogether. Frissons swirled up his arm, lighting a path straight to his chest. And he suppressed the thought that no other woman had that effect on him, chalking it up to unrequited love. Because if her feelings had run a fraction of his, then she wouldn't have been able to walk away all those years ago, would she? Unlike his father, Brody had no intention of being the fool twice. Between her and his mother, he was beginning to feel destined to associate with women who had no problem walking away from him. Wouldn't Freud have a field day with that one?

The facility was small and well kept. Purple and pink flowers lined the path to the front door of the two-story brick building. A large pot of flowers flanked each side of the oak door and white rocking chairs lined the over-size porch.

"You're sure this is a good idea? Me going inside?" Rebecca's mother had made her feelings toward Brody clear years ago, saying he wasn't good enough for her daughter. The fact that his mother later stole from the town hadn't improved his standing with Mrs. Hughes, even though he'd had nothing to do with it. Still, he didn't imagine her feelings had changed.

"I want you there."

"With her condition, I don't want to make things worse."

"It won't. She's changed a lot. For so many years she was afraid something else would happen to me. She didn't want me to leave the house for fear I wouldn't walk back in the door. Her feelings toward you back then had little to do with you and so much to do with everything else she was dealing with." Rebecca paused, stopping a few steps in front of the door. "Besides, she asks about you."

Well, didn't that last comment stop him in his tracks? "Me?"

The shy smile returned. "Yep. I know she wasn't nice to you back then, but if you could forgive her. I know it would mean the world to her."

"Already done. I don't have kids of my own, but I can only imagine what that's like after seeing Dylan with

Maribel. Hell, I'd give my life for that little girl and she's not even mine. I understand where your mom is coming from."

Rebecca didn't immediately start walking again. Instead, she turned to Brody. The equivalent of a thunderstorm brewed behind her eyes. "I think she held on for so many years to the hope my brother would come back alive. Now, she's suffering. Her body wants to go, but she can't. I think it's because she never found closure. A little piece of her half expects him to come walking through the door at any moment."

"Because they never found out what happened to him?"

She nodded. "Mom's just this shell of a person, hanging on. And I know it sounds awful, but I just wish she could find peace. I wish she could let go. She's so tired. Her mind is going. Sometimes she talks about him like he's still here. Yet, she hangs on."

The reason Rebecca wanted Brody with her made a little more sense now. Based on the anguish on her face, she was barely holding on, too. If she needed him to be strong for her, to get through this, he could do that. For her. For him. As a tribute to their past.

Without thinking much about it, he hauled her against his chest. She buried her face as he dipped his head and whispered in her ear. "It's okay. I'm here. Nothing else bad is going to happen."

She gave in to the moment, softening her body against his. And Brody couldn't help but notice for the second time how well they fit. This close, he could feel her heartbeat increasing and the smell of her shampoo, that same mix of citrus and flowers, engulfed his senses.

There was nothing more or less that he could do then except cup her cheeks in his hands and guide her lips to his. Kissing her felt like home. Light at first, deepened when she opened her mouth for him and slid her tongue inside. Her fingers tunneled into his hair as the urgency of the kiss amplified.

Brody's logical mind said she was seeking temporary shelter in a storm. As soon as this blew over, they'd be right back where they started.

With great effort, he pulled back first. "We'd better head down the hall. Since the guys are running late, I might just tell them to meet us at the restaurant in a little while."

Too quickly, her composure returned, her body stiffened. "You're right. I'm sorry."

"Don't apologize. I probably enjoyed that more than you did."

"I doubt it. And that's not where we need to be right now."

Didn't that confuse him till the cows came home? It had to be a strain to hold so much weight on her shoulders. "You know we're going to figure this out, right? You don't have to do this alone. I'm here. The guys are helping. Law enforcement's involved. He's not going to get away with this."

"I have to find him before he gets to me again, Brody."

A foreboding feeling tugged at him. "I know."

Chapter Seven

Rebecca clasped her hand around Brody's as they turned toward her mother's wing. Warmth spread through her from the contact and she didn't fight it. Instead, she relaxed into it, letting it drift through her, calming her, grateful to have Brody's support even if that's where the connection between them had to end—at friendship.

As they rounded the corner to her mother's hallway, she saw a couple hovering. A man she immediately recognized as the reporter who'd hassled her at her car stood behind them, looking down. Was that jerk trying to hide?

Rebecca squeezed Brody's hand.

He glanced at her, must've seen the shock on her face and tucked her behind him.

The couple looked at Rebecca in unison, their faces pale and desperate. Their gazes were intent as the woman rushed toward Rebecca.

"Ms. Hughes?" The panicked look on the woman's face said everything Rebecca needed to know as to why the lady was there. The expression was unmistakable, hope mixed with anxiety and fear. Gaunt eyes. Sallow skin.

"You want to get out of here?" Brody asked her quietly, his large frame blocking her view.

"Yes." She turned back toward the hallway they'd come from.

"Please, don't go." The woman's voice was full of terror. "It's our son. He's been missing since last year and we were hoping you could help. We're from Sunnyvale."

Hearing those words nearly ripped Rebecca's heart out again. Whatever had happened, Rebecca feared she wouldn't be able to help. She'd tried with her brother's case and look how well that had turned out. "I'm so sorry. I wish there was something I could do."

The woman's brows knit in confusion. "Peter Sheffield called and told us what happened." Brody took several steps forward, making progress toward her mother's door, using his body as a shield. He squeezed Rebecca's hand and she realized he was bringing her closer to her mother's room. She understood his message. Once she got close enough, she could duck inside and lock the door. Later, she'd have a conversation with security about how the reporter brought a couple into what was supposed to be a secure facility.

"It'll just take a minute of your time," the man Rebecca assumed was the father said. He had that same look—dark circles under his eyes, desperation written across his features.

Rebecca glanced at the reporter. Sheffield was tall and sinewy. He had the beady eyes of a rat. Why was he here? What kind of game was he playing?

"I'm sorry that Mr. Sheffield said I could help in some way. I'm afraid he's wrong." Rebecca had made a fatal mistake in making eye contact with the desperate mother. No way could Rebecca slip away now. Those eyes would torment her for the rest of her life if she didn't face the woman.

"He was seven. Just like your brother," the mother quickly added.

Brody's body stiffened as he folded his arms across his chest.

She touched his arm, moved around him, and whispered, "It's okay."

His brow went up when she passed him. He didn't make a move to stop her.

Meeting with a mother who was facing her worst nightmare head-on sent a jolt, like a shotgun blast, through Rebecca's chest. If there was anything she could say or do to ease this woman's pain, Rebecca would. "What do you think I can do to help?"

Sheffield pulled a small device from his pocket, no doubt ready to record everything he heard.

Rebecca shot a look toward Brody. He immediately bumped into Sheffield, mumbling an apology, knocking the recording device out of his hand. "Oops. Didn't mean to do that. Let me help you pick it up."

"No. I got it," Sheffield said, irritated.

Brody scooped up the device and took the battery out. He handed the small piece of metal over to Sheffield with a look that dared him to complain.

The woman's gaze flashed from Rebecca to Brody. "I'm so sorry to bother you. It's just we heard about your situation and we thought you might be able to help us."

"I'd like to, but I'm not sure what I can do. I have my hands full caring for my mother right now and my brother's case is fifteen years old." She was careful not to reveal too much, or talk about what she was really working on.

"You're the only one who knows what we're going through." The mother who was in her mid-to-late thirties wrung her hands together. Her light brown eyes were red rimmed and dull, the sense of helplessness and despair written all over the dark circles underneath. She was small framed and looked as if she hadn't eaten in days. With her long brown hair and big eyes, she would be considered attractive under normal circumstances.

Her husband looked to be just under six feet with a runner's build, light hair with blue eyes. He had that same haunted look on his face, the one so familiar to Rebecca. He stood off to the side, looking hopeless and helpless. Everything about his body language said he needed to bring his child home.

Rebecca tried to speak, to find some words of encouragement for the desperate couple, but none came.

"Why don't you tell us your son's name?" Brody interjected.

"Jason." The woman took a step forward and her knees buckled. Before she hit the floor, Brody was on one side of her, her husband on the other. She looked up at him and a tender look passed between them. The gesture tugged at Rebecca's heart.

The love and concern on the couple's faces, their tenderness toward each other, outlined just how much love they shared. Had Rebecca's parents ever felt that way toward each other?

They'd grown up in a small town, had been high school sweethearts and married after he graduated college, as everyone had expected. They had history, had tried to be there for each other. But Rebecca wondered if they'd ever had *real* love like this. Her father had it now. She'd seen it with his second wife. A piece of her had been sad and it made her feel even more out of place at his house, like Christmas wrapping paper left over from the year before. Useful, but not exactly what he wanted anymore.

"Take her into my mom's room. I'll get a nurse," Rebecca said to Brody, grateful her voice had returned. There had to be something she could do to help this sweet couple.

Sheffield tried to follow, but Rebecca held her hand out. "Absolutely not. Not you."

The two men carried the woman, stopping to gently lower her into the chair near Rebecca's mother, who had propped herself up when they entered the room, her gaze traveling over the faces.

Rebecca touched her mother's arm. "I'll explain in a minute and then we'll talk about why you called."

The woman apologized several times before Rebecca could reassure her that it was all right. Her mother looked no worse than usual and Rebecca wondered if the call was a stunt for attention.

Mother responded with a blank look.

If Mother hadn't had the nurse call, then it had to have been Sheffield.

Brody disappeared to escort the reporter out of the building.

"Sometimes, I just walk into a room and it's like all the air gets sucked out and the world tilts. I get dizzy. I'm so sorry," the woman repeated.

Rebecca sat across from the woman on the edge of her mother's bed, listening.

A nurse hurried in and examined the woman. "Everything looks fine. A doctor will be in to check on you in a minute."

"No," the woman said, waving away the nurse, "I'll

be okay. I just need a second to catch my breath and a glass of water."

Brody walked in, a confused look on his face.

"I'm sorry. Where are my manners? I'm Kevin Glenn, and this is my wife, Chelsea." He shook Brody's extended hand and then Rebecca's. "Our son disappeared last year. We spoke to law enforcement, FBI, and they haven't been able to find him."

"We know exactly how you feel," Rebecca's mother said, her chin out and determination in her gaze. "And we know exactly what you're going through. Come. Sit." She patted the bed near her, looking stronger than she had in months. "This is a lot to have thrown at you at once. Believe me, I understand."

Rebecca scooted down so that Kevin could sit next to her mother.

"Mrs. Hughes, I'm so sorry for your loss," he said, choking back a tear.

"Thank you," her mother replied. "What happened to us tore our family apart. I made a lot of mistakes. There comes a time when you have to focus on what you have left." Mother glanced from Brody to Rebecca. "And hope it's not too late."

Rebecca smiled at her mother.

Kevin's shoulders rocked as he swiped away tears. "I apologize for barging in like this. It's just when we heard about what happened to you this morning, we wondered if the kidnappings could be related. Sheffield had reached out to us to write an anniversary story on our son's disappearance. We haven't been speaking to the media, but then he said he thought our story might be related to yours somehow and that got our attention. Then he told us you had some kind of an accident in the woods. We've been waiting here ever since."

"We did and we reported it to the sheriff's office," Rebecca said, while holding her mother's gaze.

"You were with Sheriff Brine in the woods?" Mother gasped and brought her hand up to cover her heart.

"It was one of his deputies, but yes."

"What were you doing...*there*?"

"It's a long story, Mother. I don't want you to worry about me. I'm completely fine." Rebecca tried to smooth it over, but her mother's wild eyes said words weren't helping.

"You shouldn't have been there, Rebecca. You should let the sheriff's office do its job."

"They haven't done it so far."

"There's nothing else you can do. You have to let it go." Fear and panic raised her voice several octaves. All her mother's protective instincts seemed to flare at once. A spark lit her eyes as she sat up as straight as she could manage.

Rebecca moved to the side of her mother's bed, not wanting to rile her. Too much agitation wouldn't be good for her heart. "No. I can't. And not just because I want to find out what happened to Shane. The man is back and he's trying to hurt me. I can't allow it. And if I can find out what happened before...then I owe it to you and me to do so now."

"Don't do it for me. You don't owe me anything, dear. It's not safe for you out there. I'll talk to the doctor about making space for you here." This was the most life Rebecca had seen from her mother in years. A piece of Rebecca wanted a reaction from her mother just to know that she was still alive in there. Usually, she stayed in bed day after day, watching TV and sleeping. Her daily exercise routine consisted of six trips to the bathroom.

"I understand why you'd panic. I didn't mention it to upset you." Rebecca held her mother's hand. The iciness was gone now. Hot, angry blood ran through her veins.

"Rebecca, be reasonable. You can't go out there while he's around. What if he comes after you again? I can't do anything from this bed. I can't protect you from here."

Her mother's blood pressure was increasing to unhealthy levels. "I hear what you're saying, but I have protection."

Her mother's gaze shifted from Rebecca to Brody and back. "No one can save you against a monster like that."

"The best thing you can do to help me is calm down." Her mother's eyes were wild now and her breaths came out in short bursts. Her gaze darted around the room, landing on the Glenns and then Brody. "Not even you will be able to stop him. No one could before."

Brody took a knee beside her bed, lowering himself to eye level. "Nothing will happen to your daughter as long as there's air in my lungs."

Tense, Rebecca readied herself for the fight that was sure to come.

"The best thing you can do for your daughter is trust her, trust me." He took hold of her mother's hand and held on to it.

Instead of responding with anger, she blew out a breath. Her shoulders slumped forward and, for the first time, she looked almost relieved. "I know you're right. My girl is smart. She's a lot tougher than I ever was."

"No one blames you for your reaction. Hell, I'd be the same way," Brody continued, his voice a calm port in the sea of tension that had been surrounding them. "And no one should have to go through what you did."

Her mother eased back onto her pillow, keeping a tight grip on Brody's hand. "I was worried about her. That's the reason I called. I'm glad she has you, Brody."

"We have a chance to find him. To know about…" Brody didn't immediately finish his sentence. "That's why Rebecca and I went to the woods. And, yes, we were attacked, but she fought that creep off until help arrived."

"You were close to him?" Her mother's eyes were now wide blue orbs.

"Yes, Mother," Rebecca said. "I had to be. He won't be out there much longer. The sheriff can't ignore me anymore. He'll get him this time. And if he doesn't, we will."

The excitement looked to be taking a toll on her mother. Her gaunt features paled as she suppressed a cough. She had the disposition of a deployed airbag.

"You should rest. Keep up your strength." Rebecca might not be able to bring her brother back, but she could help find the man who had taken Shane from them. She didn't have the heart to think *Shane's killer*. The small sprig of hope that had refused to die inside her had prevented her from doing so. Hope that the young man she'd located on social media would turn out to be Shane. Hope that she hadn't wasted more than half of her life searching for a brother she would never find.

Had she funneled all her energy into finding him in order to avoid acknowledging his death?

Kevin made a move to stand. Her mother caught his arm with her free hand. "Stay."

"We don't want to intrude. Your daughter's right. You should rest," he said. "We were foolish to show up like this. Sheffield said you could help. I'm really sorry. Your family has been through enough already."

"Will you keep me company for a while?" Her mother's voice, frail and tired, trailed off at the end of her question.

Kevin nodded as she closed her eyes.

"You don't have to," Rebecca whispered just out of her mother's earshot.

"We don't mind. It's just the two of us now. If it's okay with you, we'd like to stay here. I know it's going to sound weird, but it's nice, for a change, to be with people who understand. Who don't look at us like we're about to freak out or break."

"Believe me, I do get that." Rebecca reached out and patted Chelsea's hand.

Mother smiled softly. "It's nice to have company."

Brody's cell buzzed. He excused himself and disappeared into the hall.

When he returned, the look on his face said the others had arrived.

"We'll check in on you guys later," Rebecca said.

As she walked toward the door, Chelsea touched her arm. "Good luck with your search. Will you let us know if you find anything?"

"Absolutely." Rebecca was grateful they were with her mother. The slight rattle to her breathing made her fear her mother didn't have much time.

"WHEN YOU CAME back into Mother's room earlier, you looked confused. What happened?" Rebecca asked.

She didn't miss a trick. Or did she just read Brody that well? Probably both. He'd work toward being less transparent next time.

"I went out to see to if our friend found the front door all right. He was too easy to escort out."

"So he got frustrated and left."

"I'm not so sure. Think about it. First, he brings that couple to you. Why?"

"Because he's been dying to get an interview with me."

"Exactly. And he had you right there. But then he left? Have you ever seen a reporter give up on a story so easily?"

"Good point. He went to all the trouble to make sure the Glenns came to see me. He wouldn't leave like that, would he?"

"And that's another thing that bugs me. How did he know where you'd be?"

"I need to ask my mother if he spoke to her before. I'm thinking he tricked the nurse and prompted her call."

"That's true. And he also told the Glenns about the attack in the woods. How did he know about that?"

Rebecca shrugged. "Who knows how reporters figure things out? Sources, I guess."

"And that could be anybody."

"He might have a contact at the sheriff's office. When we called it in they could've let him know."

"I just wonder what else he thinks he knows. He wouldn't have left here if he didn't think there was a hotter story or lead somewhere else." Brody didn't like the way the reporter had tried to bully Rebecca. He made a mental note to keep an eye on the guy.

The fact that Sheffield seemed to be watching their movements didn't sit well. Then again, maybe he was trying to make a name for himself. Solving the case the sheriff couldn't would be a huge boost to the guy's career.

THE RIDE TO MERVIN'S EATS was quiet. Dawson's black sport utility was parked in the lot.

"The place is busy. I wonder if any of Randy's friends will be here." Rebecca's expression was easy to read. Her wide gaze was more desperate than hopeful.

"There's a slim chance we'll get a hit on the first try, right? Let's get a feel for the place. See if we think it's a good idea to ask around. Someone might know something."

"They wouldn't likely tell strangers, would they?"

"We'll make something up." Brody scratched the scruff on his chin. It was long past dinnertime and had been a full day. He could use a hot shower and a warm bed. Thoughts of the kiss he'd shared with Rebecca edged into his mind. He pushed them away. "Ready?"

Rebecca took in a deep breath and grabbed the door handle. "Let's go."

Ryan hopped out of Dawson's SUV first, followed by Dylan and Dawson.

After hugs and greetings were exchanged, the five of them moved inside.

The place was a decent size and had a nice hometown feel to it. Lots of autographed snapshots of a man who Brody assumed was the owner with professional athletes and musicians lined the walls.

A surprising number of people filled the place given dinnertime had come and gone a good three hours ago. There was still plenty of seating for more. Brody stopped at a sign that read Please Wait to Be Seated.

Music played in the background, but it wasn't loud enough to drown out the buzz of lively conversation. The place was about half-full.

A hostess wearing form-hugging jeans and a Mervin's

Eats T-shirt greeted them. She checked them out and smiled. "Just five tonight or are you expecting more?"

Rebecca looked to Brody for a response.

"We're all here," he said.

"Do you want menus? The kitchen's open another half hour," she said, twirling her hair and leaning toward Brody.

He looked to the guys, who seemed about ready to bust out laughing. They shook their heads.

"Just two."

"Well, then, follow me." She pulled the requisite number of menus, flashed a smile and spun toward the grouping of tables to her left. She paused long enough to ask, "Booth or table?"

"We're not picky," Brody responded.

Another smile came and this time her cheeks flushed.

Rebecca elbowed him as he let her pass him to take the lead. Her eyebrows pinched together as though she were scolding him.

Now it was Brody's turn to try to hold back a laugh. If she'd noticed, then the hostess was most definitely flirting.

And, if he was being honest, his reaction would've been much worse if the tables had been turned. Even so, he put up his hands in the universal sign of surrender and whispered, "I didn't do anything."

The others jabbed him in the shoulder and arm as they walked past.

Ryan was last. "How's Rebecca?"

"Strong. I don't have to tell you what she's been through."

Ryan nodded as they approached the round corner booth. Each one filed in to the right.

Brody slid left, so he could sit next to Rebecca. He

liked having her positioned in between him and one of the guys. Anyone wanting to get to her would have to go through one of them first. Brody also liked the idea of having backup. The light dose of pain medication from the hospital was wearing off and a freakin' jackhammer pounded the spot between his eyes.

A waitress stopped by to take drink orders. Brody ordered chicken-fried steak with iced tea and smiled when Rebecca did the same. The others ordered an appetizer of chicken wings and a round of beers. Normally, Brody would join them, but tonight he wanted a clear head. Whoever was after Rebecca could strike at any time. Brody figured the guy wouldn't be stupid enough to try anything with the others around, especially since they were all big guys and this creep only struck like a coward. He didn't fight head-on. He hid in the trees, in the brush, the element of surprise his only advantage. His preferred target had been a child.

The thought of the Sunnyvale boy going missing last year near the anniversary of Shane's disappearance weighed heavily on Brody's mind.

When the waitress had thanked them and disappeared, he clasped his hands and intentionally kept his voice low. "It means a lot to both of us that you guys are here. We're hoping to connect with the whole group, but the girls have spread out so that's a bit trickier on short notice. Samantha's in Dallas."

"And Lisa moved a couple of counties over," Ryan added. "Anyone know where Melanie is?"

Dawson nodded. "I ran into her sister the other day. She moved to Houston, and never comes back to visit. I think she stays in touch with Samantha and Lisa, though. I can check with one of them."

Brody thanked Dawson for helping out with the horses earlier.

"Do you guys still hang out?" Rebecca asked.

Most shook their heads.

"That's such a shame. We were all so close when we were little. Remember how long we used to play outside?" Rebecca asked.

"Remember Red Rover?" Dylan chimed in.

Heads nodded and smiles returned.

"Sad that we didn't stay that way. It's my fault," Rebecca said.

"Everyone's to blame, not just you," Dawson quickly interjected. "We were kids. No one knew what to say or do. We were all scared. Looking back, I feel like we let you down."

"You didn't," Rebecca said. "I was out of school for a year and my parents didn't let me see anyone. I missed you guys, but everything was so crazy for such a long time. I think I forgot how to have friends."

The waitress arrived with drink orders and the appetizers, momentarily stopping conversation.

"All our parents flipped out after that. Everyone changed. *Everything* changed. And none of it was your fault, Rebecca. We wish we would've gone searching with you that night. If we had, things would've been different." Dylan lifted his mug. "The reason stinks, but we're together now. So, glasses up."

How many times had Brody had the exact same thought? Too many, he thought, as he lifted his glass.

Ryan leaned forward, his serious expression returned.

"Justin is grateful for everyone covering for him that night. I don't know if I ever thanked you guys for that."

"Sheriff Brine really had it in for your brother after he got caught breaking into school," Brody said.

"My brother was stupid back then," Ryan said. "He learned his lessons the hard way. Besides, the sheriff couldn't hurt Justin any worse than what he got at home."

Brody remembered that Justin had stayed out of school beyond his week's suspension when he'd been caught. The beating he'd received from his father had left permanent marks on the backs of his legs. "We all knew covering for him was the right thing to do."

"I appreciate it," Ryan said.

"Speaking of the sheriff's office, my friend gave me a copy of the Mason Ridge Abductor's file. According to the FBI profiler, he would most likely have had a job that required him to travel around the state."

"Like a festival worker?" Dawson asked.

Brody nodded. "They ruled out local bus drivers, shop owners, and everyone else with a stable job."

"I remember how adamant the sheriff was about this being a transient worker. Didn't they check out everyone connected to the festival?" Dylan asked.

"They did," Rebecca said. "But there are so many people who come through town this week for the activities. The RV park by the Mason Ridge Lake is completely booked. Has been for months. And it's like that every year. There are workers but then also tons of people who come just for the festival. It's impossible to keep track of everyone."

"So, they're saying it was most likely someone here for the festival and not necessarily someone who works there," Dylan clarified.

"Right," Brody said. "But here's the thing. The Mason Ridge Abductor was smart enough not to get caught, which took some doing. But then lower-IQ offenders are the ones who tended to spend time in jail. This guy has avoided capture for fifteen years. He didn't have to be especially brilliant, just smart enough to cover his tracks. He could be one of us."

"Are you saying you don't think law enforcement had it right before?" Dylan asked.

"The more I think about the facts in this case, the more I believe someone right here could've been involved." Seeing Rebecca's brown eyes look weary and pained caused Brody to clench his hands. He hated everything about this case, except the part about seeing Rebecca again. Even so, watching her expression, knowing how much she was hurting, felt like a clamp around his heart. "There's a reporter who is hot on the case. You guys remember Peter Sheffield?"

"He's a jerk," Ryan said. "But harmless. I heard he's trying to make a name for himself at the paper."

Brody had figured as much. He hoped the guy didn't get in their way.

Rebecca turned to him, a wishful look in her eyes. "Should we tell them about Randy?"

The others exchanged looks.

"Rebecca has been searching social-media sites and she came across someone who looks a lot like Shane. There are pictures online of him hanging out with friends here," Brody said. He fished his phone from his pocket and pulled up the social media site. He located the pictures and passed his phone around the table.

"He has the same chin as Rebecca," Dawson observed.

"That why we're meeting here?" Ryan asked, studying the photo.

Brody nodded.

"Good idea," Ryan said, his gaze shifting to the hostess. "Friendly place."

Brody knew that his friend was referring to her flirting. In fact, she'd kept her eye on the table and a smile on her face ever since. Rebecca seemed to notice, too.

Chapter Eight

Rebecca didn't realize she'd been holding her breath until Ryan returned. He'd offered to fish for information from the hostess, giving Brody an out so he wouldn't have to be the one to do it. "What did she say?"

He slid inside the booth. "She recognized him but didn't know him personally. Said he hasn't been in for months, though."

"Did she have a guess as to why?" Rebecca asked.

"I'm afraid not."

"What about his friends? Do they still come in?" she quickly added.

"Negative, but she wasn't surprised. Said groups of young people come and go, many of whom head off to college. A lot of them find jobs in bigger cities after school since professional jobs are scarce around here. Others go into the military."

Her chest felt like a balloon with a hole in it, slowly leaking air—and hopes of finding Shane along with it.

Brody perked up with the news. "The first place we'll check is the military. It'll be easy to find him if he enlisted."

Dylan nodded. "I have a contact, too."

A burst of optimism spread across the men's faces.

Rebecca, on the other hand, felt she was back at square one.

The food arrived, stalling conversation once more. After hearing the disappointing news, she was grateful to be able to fix her attention on eating.

It was probably too good to be true that Shane had grown up a couple towns away, safe, in a good home. If he couldn't be with her and her mother, she'd at least wished he'd be well cared for and happy. He was so young when he'd been taken she wondered if he would remember her at all. She'd read in an article a few years ago that people retained very few memories before age ten. Shane had been seven, well below the age of retention. Her own memories of him had faded over the years. If she hadn't had photographs of him everywhere, would she remember him at all? Being the oldest, she had to believe she would.

A strange thought struck. What if she found him and he rejected her? What if he didn't want to go back? What if he was perfectly satisfied with his life?

Could he be completely happy without ever knowing about his past? Was it selfish to want to force that on him if by some miracle she found him alive?

One thing was certain. Rebecca had to know what had happened to her baby brother. She prayed he was thriving. And if he was, when she saw him, knew he was fine, then she'd decide if she had any right to intrude on his life.

Dealing with her mother complicated the situation. On the one hand, her mother had a right to know about her son. On the other, Shane or Randy or whatever his name was deserved to live in peace, if that was the case.

Rebecca took a bite of chicken-fried steak and chewed.

Brody leaned toward her, his arm touching hers. He seemed to realize she'd gone inside her thoughts, gotten lost there. In barely a whisper, so only she could hear, he said, "This is good. We're making progress."

In difficult times she'd learned that it was best to focus on the here and now. Besides, he was right. They knew more than they had in years. And even if Randy wasn't Shane, at least they could rule him out. Progress. They were making progress. Progress would be her new mantra. She'd already learned the hard way that dwelling on the negative only brought her down further.

And with the guys back together, she was beginning to believe that anything was possible.

When the plates had been hauled away, she thanked them for coming.

"Is there anything else you recall from that night? Anything we need to be on the lookout for?" Dylan asked.

"The thing I remember the most is strange," she said. "It's a smell. Apple tobacco."

"That was never in the papers," Ryan said quickly.

Something flashed in his expression that sent a chill scurrying up her spine. Recognition? She carefully studied him. "The FBI wanted to keep it out of the news. They were already bombarded with leads and they said the more information we gave the bigger chance we had of copycats and false leads. Why?"

"It would've helped people to know what they were searching for," Ryan said, regaining his casual composure with what looked like significant effort on his part.

"Or tipped off the abductor on what we were looking for," she said.

"I thought law enforcement was focused on transients."

"The sheriff's office was. Brine refused to believe someone in town could've done this. The FBI wanted to cast a wider net," Rebecca supplied, still eyeing Ryan.

"What else did they keep out of the news that might've

helped?" he asked, and she realized he was most likely just as frustrated as they were.

"That was it." Time had faded so much of her memory. The FBI had also told her that she'd been in shock, and forgetting details was her brain's natural way of protecting her. Not even a hypnotist could pull any more information out of her then. Fifteen years had surely eaten away at anything that might have been left.

With a full stomach, exhaustion set in. Her bones were so tired they ached. She leaned back against the seat, not wanting to interrupt the conversation that had turned to what each of them had been doing lately.

Brody concealed a yawn and that kicked off one for her, too.

"We should probably head back. It's an hour's drive to Mason Ridge and Rebecca hasn't slept in a day and a half," he said.

"Don't break this up because of me. It's nice to see everyone again." She couldn't remember the last time she'd sat around with friends she trusted and had a drink. College had been a blur of classes, her job as a waitress and all-night study sessions just to keep up.

Heads nodded in agreement.

"Then I think we should barbecue at the ranch next Friday night. I'll have plenty of cold beer and beds to crash on so no one has to drive," Brody said.

"I'd like to reach out to Samantha, Lisa and the others," Rebecca added. "It'll be like old times." She stopped short of saying *like when she'd been happy.*

"Until then, promise you'll get some rest. The both of you," Ryan said. "And take care of that gash on your head."

Dylan added his agreement. "We'll keep digging and

let you know if anything comes up. Forward a copy of those social-media links. Maybe I'll make a few new friends between now and then."

"Will do," Brody said.

The bill came and Dawson covered it with his hand. "I got this. You two get out of here. We'll stick around a little while and chat up the locals. See if we can dig around a little more while we're here."

Brody argued over paying the bill, lost and then thanked his friends as Rebecca hugged each one.

She wanted to talk to Ryan about his reaction earlier but tabled it. *For now.*

NIGHT HAD DESCENDED around Rebecca and Brody by the time they reached the ranch. The truck's headlights cut through the darkness, lighting a path down the drive before moving across the large ranch house as Brody pulled into his parking spot.

Rebecca tried to shake off the fog that came with drifting in and out of sleep on the way there and then waking too fast. Twelve hours underneath a warm comforter would do her good.

She blinked her eyes open and glanced at the clock. It was eleven-thirty on a Friday night. Normally, she'd be doing laundry. How lonely did that sound?

As if her past hadn't been scarring enough, the few times she'd tried to date in college hadn't worked out. One of her most distinct memories was of her first boyfriend. He'd had too much to drink one night and thought slipping her a roofie would be fun so he could "experiment." Thankfully, he'd passed out before he could do anything sick to her, but the feeling of being vulnerable had shocked her back into protective mode.

Opening up, trusting again, had been next to impossible after that. She'd met a few men in Chicago. She'd watched her drinks like a crazed person whenever she was on a date. Taking her glass of wine or cup of coffee to the bathroom with her had solicited more than a few odd looks. She didn't care. They could judge her all they wanted, but she planned to be fully alert and in control. She involuntarily shivered at the memories and the all-true thought that Brody was the only man she'd ever felt safe around. No way would he try anything funny if her back was turned. Heck, she'd kissed him twice already and he hadn't tried to push for more even though she sensed that he wanted it as much as she did.

Since moving back to Mason Ridge three years ago, the dating well had dried up.

"Hey, beautiful. You're awake." Brody's voice wrapped around her, the rich timbre sliding through her, warming her. Being near him made her want things she knew better than to consider. Things like a real man to wake up next to, to feel secure with.

He turned off the engine, cut the lights, and put his arm around her after they exited his truck.

The porch light came on unexpectedly as they approached, lighting up the front of the expansive one-story brick ranch.

Rebecca froze. "Does someone else live here with you?"

"No. It's one of those motion-sensor lights." He moved his arm from around her neck and she immediately missed the weight of it, the warmth, the feel of Brody's touch.

"You okay?"

"Yeah," she lied. How did she begin to defend just how little it took to completely rattle her nerves?

He made a move toward the front door but stopped short. Instead, he turned, captured her face in his hands and pressed his lips against hers, hard, kissing her.

She opened her mouth enough for his tongue to slip inside, where she welcomed him. The taste of sweet tea still lingered on his tongue. She tunneled her hands into his thick hair and kissed him back, matching every stroke of his tongue. And she didn't want to stop there.

He managed to pull back first. Again. "There. I've been wanting to do that again ever since we left your mother's."

She didn't immediately speak. Couldn't. Not while she could still taste him. Besides, she'd probably just say something to ruin the moment, anyway.

He mumbled an apology before sliding the key into the lock.

"Don't be sorry. I'm not."

He turned, smiled and offered his hand. She took it, electricity and awareness zinging through her. Brody was the excitement of an electrical storm blowing right through her. It was strange how safe she felt with him even though he turned everything inside her upside down.

In the porch light, she could see his face clearly. A face she'd thought about so often over the years. Remembering his features had calmed her when she woke from nightmares.

"I missed you, Brody," she said softly.

He responded by hauling her against his chest. So close, her body flush with his, she could feel his racing heartbeat against her breasts. Awareness trilled through her. She reached up on her tiptoes and wrapped her arms around his neck.

He blew out a warm breath as his hands looped around her waist. "The problem isn't how much I want you,

Rebecca. You know that, right? I'm sure sex would blow both of our minds."

This close—her breasts against his muscled chest—her nipples beaded.

"I haven't done casual sex since returning from my first tour, and I have no plans to start now. Especially not with you."

Those last words stung. She pulled back, embarrassed that she'd given in so freely to her feelings. Rather than analyzing that to death, maybe Rebecca should be relieved she felt that way at all. If Brody could unlock those feelings, then surely someone else could. "I think you misunderstood. I wasn't suggesting—"

"You might not have been, but it's been on my mind ever since I saw you this morning. And I think it's been on yours, too."

Or maybe Brody was and would always be the one she felt secure enough with to let go. And look how that had turned out, two broken hearts.

She didn't want to look into his eyes while she felt so vulnerable. He lifted her chin and that's exactly what she did—looked into those blues. Why was it the only time she felt home was when she looked at him?

Hope of another man igniting those same feelings inside her fizzled. Brody was her weakness, her hot-fudge sundae when she was supposed to be on a diet, and maybe it was time to admit he would never be more to her than a temporary treat.

"Doesn't mean we have to act on it," she said.

"Nope. Sure doesn't." He didn't immediately move.

They stood there holding each other in the moonlight, staring for long moments as though cast in stone and neither could move if they'd wanted to. She wanted to lean further into the feeling, into him, and stay there as long as she could in his arms.

"We should probably go inside," she said, losing herself in his crystalized blue gaze.

Everything about Brody reminded her of being a woman, which was something she'd neglected for so very long.

She rose up on her tiptoes and pressed a kiss to his cheek. "You've done a lot for me, Brody. More than you'll ever realize. I didn't know what to do with that when we were kids, so I pretended breaking up with you was to save you. And part of it was. The other part, the part I still don't want to admit, has to do with me. I'm trying to get over what happened, and I get close. Then, he just reaches up and takes me back down. Whether it's in a nightmare or like now, he's always going to be there, holding me back, unless I do something to change it."

His body tensed as though every muscle was fighting against the words forming in his thoughts.

"I understand," he said. "I'm sorry for what happened to you. But when this case is over, we'll go back to the way our lives were before. Yours involves taking care of your mother and working at the radio station. Mine's here on this ranch. The horses. And we need to keep that in mind before we do something that'll burn us both. No use going down that path again, wasting time."

So many objections charged through her mind, but she couldn't go there. He was right. This case would be over soon, one way or the other. That jerk would end up where he belonged, in the ground or in jail. She refused to believe he'd get to her. And they would each go back to their respective lives. Rebecca would care for her mother in her final days, and Brody would go back to his business.

And all that was going to happen whether she wanted it to or not.

She couldn't control the future. But they had now, this moment, and she didn't want it to end. She shifted her weight to the other foot, stared him directly in the eyes, and said, "I hear what you're saying and I won't argue. But I do object to one thing you said. Time spent with you is never wasted."

"I didn't mean—"

"I know exactly what you meant and I understand where you're coming from. I'm grateful for your help, so I won't push for anything else." Even though she wanted him more than she wanted to breathe. She also recognized what a huge mistake they'd be making if things went any further. As long as her mother was alive, Rebecca was tied to Mason Ridge. From the looks of her mother's condition and refusal to take medication that could save her, that wouldn't be long. Rebecca had every intention of leaving and not looking back when her mother's long battle came to an end. Whereas Brody's life was right there, doing something he loved. Everything he was building for his future was inside that county. And she admired him for knowing where his place was, where he fit. Chicago had been wonderful, mostly because it was far away from Mason Ridge. She had yet to figure out where she belonged.

Rebecca turned toward the door, easing out of Brody's grip. "I love that you bought this place. It suits you. The work that you're doing is amazing. You seem happy here."

"It's been good for me." He led her into the house and turned on the light. "No one's here and my housekeeper doesn't show up until Tuesday so we won't be bothering anyone by being here. Make all the noise you want."

The open-space living room was massive. An oversize log fireplace anchored the room on one side, and the image of a fire, glasses of wine and a bunch of throw pillows on the floor in front crossed her mind. She shook it off, instead focusing on the wood beams across the ceiling. The place was comfortable and masculine. It had that warm lodge feel to it with comfortable furniture she could sink into. Everything about the space was a true reflection of Brody. She clasped her hands together, trying to conceal her overflowing pride. Brody had done good. Better than good. "It's perfect."

His smile shouldn't make her heart flutter, and yet that's exactly what it did.

"The place has two wings, one is made up for guests and the other's mine. You can stay in the guest bedroom unless I can convince us both one night in my room would be worth it." He grinned his sexy little smile where barely the corners of his lips upturned.

She hoped he didn't notice the flush of excitement those words brought. Because right here, right now, if he seriously invited her into his bed she'd say yes.

"I'll grab a towel so you can shower." He motioned toward the long hallway to the right.

A shower sounded like heaven about now. She suppressed another yawn. "I doubt I'll be able to sleep."

"There isn't much more we can do until morning, anyway. We'll be fresh and ready to go after a good night's rest," he said.

"I don't know."

"I'll grab your suitcase, so your clothes will be waiting." He stopped long enough to give her hand a reassuring squeeze. "We'll figure this out, Rebecca."

Brody had always been able to see right through her. "I know you're right, it's just…"

"You want so badly to give your mother good news."

She nodded. "I want to give her something to fight for."

"You already have. She has you." He paused. "Besides, anything happens tonight and I promise to wake you. But you're sleepwalking at this point and you need a few hours of shut-eye before you make yourself sick."

He had a good point. And when she really thought about it, exhaustion weighed heavily on her limbs. Thoughts of a shower and sleeping in a bed were almost too good to be true. She stood and followed him down the hall. He stopped in front of a linen closet, pulled out a fresh towel and pointed toward the first door on the right.

"You'll have all the privacy you need in there."

Probably more than she wanted about then. "You going to bed, too?"

He'd already started toward the front door when he stopped and turned, sexy smile securely in place. "After a long, cold shower."

BRODY HAD BEEN awake for three hours. He'd tended to the horses, eaten breakfast and polished off a cup of coffee. He'd wanted to go inside Rebecca's room to check on her a half dozen times just to make sure she was okay but didn't. He knew better than to trust himself with her while she was vulnerable. She needed some reassurance about life, and that's most likely why she'd made it clear last night she wouldn't mind a little fooling around.

He, on the other hand, couldn't risk it. His heart couldn't take another hit.

Brody made another cup of coffee, using one of the individual cups from the single-serving machine that his housekeeper had practically forced him to buy. He settled in at the kitchen table, studying the file again. Surely something was there he could work with.

His phone vibrated. He checked the screen, found a text from Ryan wanting to know if he could stop by.

Brody responded with a yes and said the front door would be unlocked.

Ten minutes later, Ryan showed. Tension radiated from him in waves.

"That was quick." Brody glanced at the time. It was almost noon and still no sign of Rebecca.

"I was in the area," Ryan said, heading toward the kitchen. "Mind if I grab a cup of coffee and join you?"

Considering Brody lived twenty minutes from the nearest store, Ryan couldn't have been close. Brody didn't need to see the worry lines on his friend's forehead to know something was up. "You know where everything is. Make yourself at home."

"What is this? Almond mocha?" Ryan wrinkled his nose as he picked through the little pods.

"My housekeeper forced me to buy the variety pack. Said it was good to try new things. As it turns out, I'm not so much of a flavored-coffee guy. I like mine straight up and strong." Brody finished the last of his, noticing the dark circles under his buddy's eyes.

Ryan made his own cup, joined Brody at the table and took a sip.

This close, his features looked haunted. An ominous feeling settled over Brody.

"We need to talk about something Rebecca said last night. Is she up yet?" Ryan asked.

"No. She's still asleep. At least I think she is. I haven't seen her yet this morning." Brody glanced toward the guest hallway. He didn't like the way Ryan's face muscles tightened when he'd asked about Rebecca. This was disturbing.

Ryan stared into his cup for a long moment. Then, he looked up at Brody. "Are you okay?"

"You want to talk about how I'm doing?" Brody asked, surprised.

"That's not what I came here to talk about but bear with me for a sec."

Brody checked his watch. "Good. Because I have a lot to do today and I don't like where this conversation is headed."

"Fair enough," Ryan obliged. "How are you doing with all this?"

"Fine. Why? Do I seem like something's wrong?" Brody finger-combed his hair.

"Thought I picked up on something last night and you look tired this morning." Ryan shrugged.

"So I tossed and turned a little last night. I've gone days without sleep on missions. This is nothing." Brody swirled the rest of the contents in his cup. "And the reason I didn't sleep last night is because the Mason Ridge Abductor is back."

"I'm not talking about that kind of okay and you know it," Ryan said plainly.

Brody didn't immediately defend himself.

Ryan took a sip of coffee. "I'm not trying to get you riled up or dredge up the past."

"Then don't."

"It's already here. What kind of friend would I be if I didn't speak up when I thought I should?"

"I know what you're about to say and I appreciate your concern." Brody could almost hear the next words spilling out of Ryan's mouth and he hoped to preempt them.

"Because I don't think you do, I'm not going to shut up yet." Ryan gripped his mug. "Things were bad before."

"I lived it. You think I've forgotten?"

"That's not what I meant. I'm not trying to put you on the defensive. I'm offering to help. We can find a safe place for Rebecca to stay without her staying here."

"You think I can't separate my emotions long enough to take care of business?"

"I saw the way you two looked at each other last night." Ryan rubbed the day-old scruff on his chin. "Everyone noticed."

Brody had already admitted to tossing and turning all night. He'd told himself it was because of this case and not because she slept under his roof. "She was special to me a long time ago."

"And an elephant doesn't forget. Tell me something that I don't know."

"I don't feel the same way toward her anymore. Whatever we had between us died when she walked out. You know what I'm about."

"Loyalty," Ryan said without hesitation.

"Exactly. If someone can't stick with you during the tough times, then you gotta keep walking, because life is going to dish more than you can handle sometimes. Last thing I need is to be with someone I can't trust to be there when it all goes south. You know that about me." Brody's tone was a little more emphatic than he'd planned for it to be.

Ryan nodded. "Even so, there's a connection between the two of you. And that kind of link doesn't listen to reason."

Didn't Brody already know that. Last night had been a prime example of hormones trying to take control, but he'd been strong. Of course, another few seconds of her body flush with his, her heart beating against his, and he knew the story might've turned out differently. And that would've led to all kinds of awkward today. He didn't want to think about what might've happened if he hadn't practiced restraint. He didn't want to talk about this. He wanted to focus on the case. And he knew Ryan had shown up to discuss more than just *this*. Brody figured he needed to throw his friend a bone. "I'd be lying if I denied having feelings for her. Believe me when I say that I know what's good for me in the long run. And the woman sleeping in the other room is not it."

He pointed toward the hallway where she slept and his gaze followed.

She was standing there, chin up, defiance in her stare. The exact look she gave when the pain was more than she could process.

Damn. Damn. Damn.

A few other choice words flashed through his mind. Brody hadn't meant for her to hear what he was saying. Truth was that he didn't know exactly how he felt about her. Yes, he had feelings. Yes, they were strong. Yes, he wanted to take her to bed more than he wanted air. But he had to consider the possibility that this need could be nothing more than residual hurt from a wounded teenager. He'd been destroyed when she'd broken it off with him.

At eighteen, he couldn't think of a future without her. His plans to go into the military, to come back and buy the ranch, all of this, had been to create a life for her. He could see the fault in that plan now. Both parties needed to be on board. He had never shared his ideas with her. And he was still asking himself why he'd returned to Mason Ridge when those plans had been blown to high heaven. He told himself that it was to be close to his father, but

Brody could've gone anywhere after the military. When the time came and his father couldn't take care of himself, Brody doubted it would matter where they'd settled.

Rebecca had wanted to be out of Mason Ridge as soon as she came of age. She'd said that she'd broken up with him to save him from himself. Had it really been to free herself so she could get out of this town and not look back just like his mother?

Plus, it wasn't like she'd come back for him. She hadn't reached out once since she'd gone. The only reason she was here now was to be near her ailing mother in her final months. Mrs. Hughes looked to be barely hanging on. As soon as death took her, Rebecca would disappear again. Just like his mother. And there Brody was, just like his father, waiting for a woman who could walk away so easily.

There was no denying that Brody and Rebecca shared feelings. There'd be no point fighting the fact that those feelings, whatever else they were, were strong. But it was probably just unfinished business between them. And even if it wasn't, no good could come from acting on it. Period.

Rebecca hadn't even stuck around for graduation. The last day of school, she'd gone home, packed her bags and caught a flight north to go to school.

Brody knew because he'd stopped by, lovesick, about to ship out but unable to go without seeing her one more time, without being sure that's what she wanted.

She was long gone. No goodbyes.

It had hardened Brody in a good way. Made him suck it up and endure basic training. Falling into his bunk every night exhausted had been a welcome relief to the living hell of realizing the one person who was everything good in your life didn't blink an eye about boarding a plane without a backward glance.

In some ways, he owed his elite status to her. It was because of Rebecca he'd worked his tail off, preferring to punish himself day after day in training so he could fall into bed numb every night. She was the reason he'd maintained focus when others couldn't wait for leave to see their loved ones. Because of Rebecca, he'd kept everyone but his father at a safe distance ever since.

No distractions.

And all those feelings dissolved as she stood there for a long moment, in the hallway, not speaking. Brody's oversize T-shirt long enough to hit midthigh. Then she said, "That one of those pod coffeemakers?"

Ryan's gaze bounced between Brody and Rebecca, stopping long enough to relay an unspoken apology to both. "I better head home. There's something else I'd like to discuss with you, Brody. I'll give you a call later."

"No, please don't leave because of me," Rebecca said, crossing over to the kitchen. "I'll join you both for a cup of coffee."

Ryan nodded.

She made a cup and took a seat at the table, pulling the shirt over her knees as she hugged them into her chest. "What's the plan for today?"

Ryan stared into his cup again for a long moment.

Tension was like a wall between them.

"You said something last night that I can't get out of my mind." His jaw clenched as he looked up at Rebecca.

The knowing look she gave Ryan when she nodded had Brody almost thinking she'd been expecting this conversation. What had he missed that she'd picked up on?

"You mentioned apple tobacco. I didn't know about

that before." Ryan paused, his gaze returned to the cup. "Before I say anything else, I just want to say that I'm sure my brother wasn't involved. I know him."

"What exactly are you saying, Ryan?" Brody asked.

Rebecca didn't budge and she looked small, sitting there. Brody fisted his hands to stop them from reaching for her.

"My brother came home smelling like that sometimes. I'd know that scent anywhere, Rebecca. The one you're talking about is distinct."

"I know it wasn't your brother, Ryan," Rebecca said reassuringly. "It couldn't be him. Your brother's tall and stocky like you. You guys have a football build whereas this guy is tall and slim. Plus, I think he's older than Justin."

Ryan didn't look relieved. "He'd smoke it with my uncle when they'd get drunk together back in Justin's troubled days. So, I lay awake last night asking myself if Justin didn't have anything to do with this, and I know in my heart he didn't, then who could it be? What are the chances a transient smokes apple tobacco. It's not exactly a common thing. If we stop looking at random people who could've been in town for the festival and set our sights on people right here, then that changes everything. And right now the evidence points to my uncle."

"What's his build?" Brody asked.

"He's tall and thin."

Chapter Nine

Rebecca touched Ryan's hand to comfort him. "Doesn't mean it was him."

"I hope not. But I gotta look at the facts and be honest with myself, with you," Ryan said, his anguish written all over his face. "He's been in trouble with the law, but I can't believe he would do something like this."

"We can see if he was a suspect." Brody studied the police file.

"Do you know where he lives? We can go talk to him," Rebecca offered.

"I haven't seen him in a while. Last I knew he was living in Garland."

"That's half an hour away from Mason Ridge at the most," Brody said. He stopped suddenly.

Rebecca didn't like his expression. But then, she was still reeling from Brody's words while she'd stood in the hallway. They stung, even though she knew he was just speaking the truth. Stuffing those feelings down deep, she took another sip of coffee.

"Turns out, your uncle Gregory was a suspect," Brody said, flashing an apologetic look toward Ryan. "He worked as a delivery driver for a Texas nursery chain around the time of the abductions."

"Which would put him on the highways," Rebecca said.

"The sheriff would've been able to match up his delivery schedule," Brody said quietly. He kept skimming the file.

"My uncle did stupid things when he drank, but he wasn't violent."

"There isn't much more in the file that I can see. Think we can speak to him?" Brody asked.

"No other kids have gone missing in the area since Shane. If his uncle was somehow involved, wouldn't there be others?" Rebecca asked.

"The Glenn boy last year in Sunnyvale," Brody reminded her.

"True." She nodded.

"I thought about that, too. My uncle moved to Garland two years after the disappearance," Ryan said. "Last time I saw him a few years ago his hands shook if he didn't have a drink by ten o'clock in the morning. He's done other stupid stuff, illegal. Been in jail a couple of times. My heart doesn't want to believe he's capable of such a heinous act and yet I can't ignore the facts. What if he did this?"

"I hear what you're saying. It's probably not even him, but it's smart to check into every possibility. I appreciate you coming forward. This must be really hard for you," Rebecca said. A man who couldn't go a day without drinking most likely wouldn't have the strength to subdue both her and Shane, could he? There was another way to solve this. She remembered that her attacker had spoken the other morning in the parking lot. If it had been Ryan's uncle, she would be able to recognize his voice. "I might have a way to resolve this. Does your uncle have a phone?"

"I believe so. Why?"

Brody was already nodding. He'd caught on to what she wanted to do.

"Call him and put it on speaker."

"Justin might have the number." Ryan pulled out his cell. After a quick call to his brother, he punched in the digits. The line rang three times before rolling into voice mail. Ryan's thumb moved over to end the call.

"Don't hang up. Hold on a second before you do that," Rebecca said, stopping him.

This is Greg. You know what to do at the beep.

Brody's gaze was intent on her, studying her.

"Doesn't sound like him," Rebecca said on a sigh of relief. She wanted to find Shane's abductor more than anything but not at the cost of one of her friends. "At least I don't think."

"We can't ignore the possibility that he might know something or be connected in some way," Brody said, looking to Ryan. "Does your uncle have any enemies?"

"My first thought would be Alcorn. He hates all of my family members. You think someone else might try to set him up?" Ryan asked, his voice hopeful. He deflated a second later. "Why would someone do that after all these years? And why to him? It's not like he's rich or powerful. There's nothing to blackmail him for. Even Alcorn has given up."

"The word about apple tobacco might have gotten out. This is a small town, and after running into Peter Sheffield last night I started thinking how hard it can be to keep secrets. All it would take is one leak. Someone had to have seen something."

"I'd like to chat with your uncle," Brody said.

"I'll arrange something and get back to you." Ryan's face muscles were tight.

Brody checked his phone. "I just got a text from Samantha. She's trying to pull together the other girls to swing by tomorrow afternoon. She's already in town to see her father, anyway."

Samantha had moved to Dallas after college for a job in the textile industry.

The reunion with the guys had gone well, so Rebecca was hopeful this would, too. Was it possible to pick up friendships after everything that had happened? Rebecca hoped so. It was a nice feeling to be with people she had so much history with. They were the few people who didn't look at her awkwardly anymore, as if seeing her reminded them horrible things could happen at any moment. "I can't wait to see her and the others. It's been such a long time. In the meantime, we'll keep following leads, right?"

"The festival rolls up the tents tomorrow. I'd initially hoped to wait and see if things calmed down after they leave. But then I checked online this morning and the Glenns' son, Jason, who disappeared in Sunnyvale last year, did so while the festival was packing up," Brody said.

Ryan perked up. "That's a strange coincidence."

"I'm not so sure that timing is accidental," Brody agreed. "Who's in charge of the festival?"

"Charles Alcorn heads it up every year," Ryan supplied.

"Isn't the festival too low-brow for him to be involved?" Brody asked.

"You'd think so," Ryan said. "But they use his land and he makes a fortune every year."

"I wonder if we can get a list of vendors from him? Names?" Brody asked.

"Doesn't hurt to ask," Rebecca said with a quick look toward Brody.

"He has offices downtown in the building next to the mayor's office, doesn't he?" Brody asked with a slight nod.

"He does. Nice building. I saw in a magazine that he renovated the whole inside before moving in a couple of years ago. Only the finest quality furniture. The best finishings. He donated the other half of the building to the city."

"How convenient for him to be right next door to the mayor."

"Easier to line Mayor Garza's pockets when he only has to walk four steps," Rebecca said. It was common knowledge he had a do-what-it-takes-to-get-the-job-done philosophy. It was half the reason she was tempted to take him up on his offer of help.

"In the meantime, we'll keep poking around until we figure this out." Ryan pushed his chair back from the table. "I have a few things to take care of. Keep me posted on what you find out. I'll let you know as soon as I arrange a meeting with my uncle. Stay close to your phone."

"Will do," Brody said, turning to Rebecca as soon as the door was closed.

"You noticed that, too, didn't you?" she asked.

"Yep. Ryan sure got out of here quick when we started talking about Alcorn." Brody stood, walked to the sink and rinsed out his coffee cup. "There's no love lost between their families. Ryan's dad wouldn't give Alcorn something he wanted years and years ago when he was still alive."

"That wouldn't have gone over well. Guess I wasn't

around much to notice." She'd been so wrapped up in her own family's issues she hadn't once stopped to consider her friends' problems. "I remember bad blood from when we were kids now that I think about it."

Brody crossed to the back door. "Some old wounds don't heal."

BRODY EXERCISED THE HORSES, taking care not to overtax his newest arrival, Storm Rival. The owner didn't have any use for the chestnut Thoroughbred when he developed shin splints after his last race at Lone Star Park. Brody just called him Red. Red had been a promising two-year-old until this happened. Now his future was uncertain. He had a true splint, the worst-case scenario for a race-horse, as evidenced by the bulge just below his left knee and on the inner side of his leg. The problem was all too common in young horses entering heavy training. Bad cases had ended plenty of promising careers.

His owner had been kind and this guy was going to get a second chance in life, a different life. The hefty donation would help keep things running, too.

Being in the barn, away from Rebecca, was a good thing. Her lips were too full, too pink, too damn tempting.

Work was the best distraction.

After he'd arranged care for the evening, he cut across the yard and back to the house.

Rebecca was still at the table, studying the screen on Brody's laptop.

On Brody's phone was a text from Ryan. "Ryan may have found something interesting and he wants us to come check it out. He isn't far from here. Are you good with that?"

Rebecca nodded.

"We can be out of here in fifteen minutes. I just need to get dressed," she said, disappearing down the hall.

Brody forced his gaze away from her backside. Self-discipline was the biggest difference between a man and a boy. While he waited, he took pictures of the suspect list so he'd have it with him in case they came across a name.

She returned ten minutes later, fresh-faced, hair pulled back in a ponytail. Her jeans, low on her hips, fit her curves to perfection. The material of her light blue blouse was just thin enough to allow a peek at her matching lacy bra. "Ready?"

For more than she knew. "Yep."

"I checked the news while you were taking care of the horses." Rebecca moved to the driver's side.

"I'm okay to drive."

She gave him the look that he knew better than to argue with, so he didn't. He held his hands up in surrender. "Okay. Fine."

Taking control behind the wheel, she held out his keys. "Didn't figure you'd get far without these, anyway. And your head is still healing."

"I've taken worse blows than that and survived." To his ego, for one.

"Can you give me directions? His position should be on your phone, right?"

Brody pulled up Ryan's location using the GPS tracker on his phone. He raised the volume and set the phone between them on the seat.

She cranked the ignition and backed out of the parking spot. "This has all been so crazy I don't think I stopped to thank you for what you did for my mother yesterday afternoon."

"Not a problem," he said casually, and meant it.

"I'm serious. She can be difficult to deal with and I think she was shocked to see you."

"Nah. She was fine. Plus, there was a lot going on. Under the circumstances, I thought she was rather nice."

"And if I admit to being wrong about something, will you promise not to rub it in?" she asked.

"Depends on what it is."

She stopped at the end of the drive long enough to jab his arm. "Be serious."

"I am. Scout's honor."

"Like you were a Boy Scout." She rolled her eyes and made a right turn toward town. "Fine, then I won't tell you."

"Oh, come on. You know I was just kidding." He used to love making her laugh in high school. Her smiles were rare, laughter even more so, and he figured that made them all the more special.

"So you think I'm going to tell you now that you've done a little begging?" She didn't hold back her laugh.

"Any chance it's working?"

"Okay, fine. What's it going to cost me?" He paused long enough to listen to the next instruction from the GPS.

She turned right, as instructed, then nodded. Her serious expression returned.

"You plan to tell me, or did you bring it up just to torture me?" he asked, trying to bring the lighter Rebecca back to life. She was inside there. He knew it and he wanted more of her.

"Fine. I lied to you before to trick you into seeing my mother. You were right. She didn't like you." She cracked a shy smile.

"I believe I won her over."

"Agreed. I wasn't sure what to expect, but you broke through to her." She paused. "I feel so bad for the Glenns."

"They've been through the ringer. It's obvious on their faces."

Again, she nodded.

"You rarely ever talk about Shane. Is that subject off-limits?"

Rebecca neither spoke nor nodded.

"You don't have to now. I just thought maybe it might help or some—"

"Don't feel bad about asking, Brody."

"I don't," he reassured, but she was dead-on. He felt bad for bringing up Shane.

"I should talk about him more. About what happened. Maybe it'll help us figure things out. You say we're down to a couple dozen names aside from Ryan's uncle, right?" She paused long enough to receive and follow GPS directions.

She didn't need to tell him about her pain. He felt it, based on the heaviness in her words, the determination in her features.

Brody leaned forward in his seat and stretched his arms.

"All I can really remember about my brother came from stories from my mom and pictures she showed. Other than that night, of course. I can't seem to forget that. All I keep thinking is who would do something like this to an innocent boy? I mean, the guy has to be a monster, right?" Rebecca's body shuddered just talking about it. "Or, maybe he's crazy."

"You won't get an argument out of me that the man's crazy or needs to be locked up with the key tossed away for good. Hell, give me five minutes alone with him and the bastard won't hurt another child for the rest of his life."

The GPS interrupted, stating that the destination was two blocks up on the right. The distraction gave Brody a minute to regroup as Rebecca drove to the spot and then pulled into a parking space.

"Odd. I expected to see Ryan's SUV here," he said.

"I did, too," Rebecca agreed.

"Something doesn't feel right about this." Brody surveyed the area. He phoned Ryan, but he didn't pick up. "I think you should let me drop you off in town so I can investigate."

"And leave you alone with those bumps and bruises? Not a chance."

"I'm better today. I'll grab Dylan or Dawson. It's the weekend. One of them should be around. On second thought, I'll call Dawson. Dylan will be with his little girl today." He prepared himself for a fight.

"Take me to Angel's. That way, when you come to pick me up, we'll be able to get a decent piece of pie," Rebecca said.

Grateful she didn't put up an argument, he palmed his cell and fired off a text to Samantha. He had no plans to leave Rebecca alone. "Mind if I arrange a little company for you? I don't want you to sit there by yourself going crazy worrying until I get back."

"What makes you think I'll do that?"

"Because I've met you before, remember? It's me, Brody."

"Okay, funny man." She paused, looking resigned. "But you're probably right. Samantha did say she'd be in town this weekend. Maybe we'll get lucky and she'll be available. It would be nice to see her."

Lucky. There was that word again. "Done. She just texted back to say she'd meet us there in fifteen. Okay if she brings her father?"

"All right by me."

The extra fifteen minutes it took to drop Rebecca off at Angel's had Brody's gut tied in knots. He sure as hell hoped Ryan wasn't lying in the woods somewhere, helpless. The image didn't do good things to Brody's blood pressure. He phoned his friend again. Same result.

Bringing Rebecca into those same woods where they'd been attacked felt all kinds of wrong. No way could he take a chance with her safety. And he had the very real feeling they could've been lured into a trap.

REBECCA HAD DOWNED another full cup of coffee and was feeling much more awake and alert by the time Samantha arrived with her father. Mr. Turner had aged quite a bit since Rebecca had last seen him. His entire head was covered in white and his frame was thinning. The hardware store he owned in town most likely still kept him in shape.

Throwing her arms up, Rebecca waved at the pair. She was greeted with a huge smile from Samantha, but Mr. Turner hesitated. He said something to his daughter, but they were too far away for Rebecca to make it out.

When Samantha pointed at Rebecca and nodded, Mr. Turner looked downright uncomfortable. Not an unusual reaction from people in town, but it reminded Rebecca just what an outcast she was in her own hometown. And as much as she'd love to keep her mother around for many more years, healthy, Rebecca was eager to move back to a bigger town. Chicago had been kind to her. And best of all, no one knew about her past there. She didn't get those same wide-eyed stares and behind-the-back whispers when people passed by her in the streets as she did in Mason Ridge. Don't get her wrong, she loved her hometown more than anything, just not some of the baggage that came with it.

Samantha led her reluctant father to the table and plopped down. He did not. "It's so good to see you, Rebecca. You remember my father."

"Of course. Mr. Turner, it's so nice to see you again." With her mother in long-term care and Rebecca herself living in a rental, she hadn't had much need to stop by the hardware store. She stood and stuck out her hand.

He obliged, shaking just long enough to be polite.

Rebecca noticed his palm was warm, sweaty. Since when did her presence start making people so nervous? She was used to seeing sadness in everyone's eyes. Some were upset even and she figured they didn't want to be reminded of that summer. But nervous? She'd moved into a whole new category. *Great.*

Maybe she had always made people feel that way and she'd been too trapped inside her own head to notice.

"I'm sorry I can't join you two," he started.

"Daddy saw some friends at the counter. He asked if we'd mind if he ate lunch with them."

"Not at all," Rebecca said, figuring he didn't look too sorry. In fact, he looked like he might jump out of his skin if she said, "Boo!"

He scurried off to join a couple of older men seated at the bar stools at the breakfast counter.

When he was out of earshot Samantha leaned in, embarrassment flushing her cheeks, and said, "Honestly, I don't know what's wrong with him lately. Getting old, I guess."

Rebecca figured she had a good handle on his sudden

need to eat lunch with someone else, anyone else. The man looked like he'd seen a ghost, which was par for the course for her and another reason she didn't mind working the graveyard shift. She figured most parents didn't want to be reminded what could've happened to their child instead of Shane. "It's fine. This will give us a chance to really talk. We'd bore him to death with our conversation, anyway."

Samantha flashed a grateful look and then summoned the waiter. "I swear he's starting to get senile. And the man doesn't sit still anymore."

"He's fine. Don't worry about it."

The waiter interrupted their conversation. Samantha ordered a club sandwich and sweet tea.

"I should have a salad, but I can't resist the burgers here," Rebecca confessed. "Looks like I'll be hitting the gym later."

"It's so good to see you. How long has it been?"

Rebecca didn't want to try to reach back too far. "I know I haven't seen you since we headed to different colleges."

"Our ten-year reunion is like next year." Samantha's look of horror brought a smile to Rebecca's face.

"Already? Man, time flies."

"I somehow got hooked with planning duties. I'm on the attendance committee, which basically means I'm responsible for finding everyone and making sure they show up."

Rebecca gave a full-body shiver. "Count me out."

"You have to come. If only to support me," Samantha said on a laugh.

"Do you stay in touch with Lisa or Melanie?"

"Mostly just Melanie. She moved to Houston after

college so we don't get to see each other as much as we'd like. Lisa's not too far, though. I've run into her a few times at the grocery with Pops. I meant to call her today."

"I'd love to see both of them again. I work deep nights, so even though I live nearby I never see anyone." She decided not to share just how on purpose that was. But seeing Samantha was nice. Rebecca hadn't realized just how much she'd missed having this kind of friendship. Ties that ran deep.

"Melanie never comes back." Samantha rolled her eyes. "Says her work keeps her too busy and she doesn't get a lot of vacation time. When she does, she likes to see someplace new."

That last bit of information came out a little too quickly. Samantha practically stumbled over the words in her rush to explain.

Rebecca had no intention of making anyone else uncomfortable, not on purpose. Most people didn't want anything to do with her anymore and she understood on some level. They couldn't help, so they'd wanted to forget. She was just a big old fat reminder of the worst summer in the history of Mason Ridge, of every parent's worst nightmare. Plus, everyone had known and loved Shane. She couldn't blame them for not wanting to be reminded of the horrible incident that took him away from them. If it hadn't happened to her family, she might be able to look the other way, too.

"Okay, you got me. I'll come to the reunion," Rebecca said, mostly to redirect the conversation.

"Seriously? You will?" Again, her friend looked grateful for the change of subject.

"If I'm in town." She wanted to add, *and still alive*.

Chapter Ten

Brody picked Dawson up at their meeting point on his way to find Ryan, regretting the extra five minutes it took.

"Have you heard from Ryan at all today?" Brody asked, checking his phone again after pulling into the spot he and Rebecca had occupied nearly half an hour ago. He'd brought his friend up-to-date on the short ride over.

"Nope. Not a word. But then that's not unusual," Dawson said, shoving the last bite of a burrito into his mouth.

Having along a guy as big as Dawson, with almost twice Brody's strength, was a good thing, Brody figured.

"Let's see if we can figure out what's going on." Brody didn't like how Ryan had looked earlier. The edge to his tone hadn't sat well with Brody. After the revelation about Ryan's uncle, he looked even more determined to figure out what was going on. Brody sent another text to Ryan and then waited.

There was no response. Again.

"Here's the most logical place to park, but Ryan's vehicle is nowhere." Brody checked the navigation system's map. If he could believe what was on the screen then Ryan was fifty feet or so off the road.

He and Dawson got out of his truck and headed toward the dot on the screen. As they moved, he thought about the missing Sunnyvale boy, the timing. There had to be a connection. What were they missing? But then, getting inside the head of a man who'd abducted a child wouldn't be easy. What about the age of the Glenn kid? He was seven just as Shane had been. Were there other cases in Texas of seven-year-olds going missing? Did the abductor live in Texas? Brody had to think so.

This far, they didn't have squat to go on except a vague description. The hoodie and sunglasses blocked his face and Rebecca had not been able to get a good view of the guy during either encounter, which was frustrating. No more so than the blow to Brody's head. Having his skull traumatized didn't make for the best recall. Brody made a mental note to run a search for crimes connected to seven-year-old boys in Texas.

The phone vibrated. Brody checked the screen. He had another email from the feed store. Still no word from Ryan.

Cell coverage would become spotty the closer he moved into Woodrain Park. On the other hand, the fact he hadn't heard from Rebecca was good news. Even so, a bad feeling crept up his spine. Call it instinct, intuition or a sixth sense, Brody didn't care. Whatever it was had kept him alive in more than one dicey situation in the military.

For Ryan's sake, Brody hoped like hell Greg hadn't been involved. Brody vaguely remembered the guy hanging around Ryan's house in the summers. Even then Brody knew the guy was no good. Did that mean he was a kidnapper? A murderer?

Rebecca had dismissed it, but Brody couldn't stop thinking about the apple tobacco. What was the chance that was a coincidence?

"I know this area," Dawson said. "These woods connect to Mason Ridge Lake on the south side."

"Which means the RV park where most of the festival workers stay is just on the other side of the lake," Brody agreed, now that he was getting his bearings. The workers pretty much stuck to themselves when they came through town, unlike the winter carnival crew, who would show up in restaurants, chat up locals and walk the town square. The only times he remembered seeing festival people were early in the mornings at the grocery when he'd had occasion to go. And, sometimes, late nights at the Laundromat, although they hung most of their clothes to dry near the lake. If one of their machines needed a part, they'd show up at the hardware store, but that was a rare sighting. The nearest auto shop was in Sunnyvale. If one of their vehicles had trouble, they'd have to go there or be towed. Brody hadn't thought much about their habits before.

Being a Renaissance Festival, people walked around in sixteenth-century costumes. There were horse games played and turkey legs for sale. The workers kept to themselves. He figured the lack of workers in town had more to do with them sleeping in mornings and the fact there wasn't much to do in Mason Ridge.

Dawson followed closely behind as Brody led the way through the thicket.

The lake was coming into view by the time they reached the spot where Ryan should be. "This is it."

"He has to be around here somewhere." The day was in full swing and Brody could see festival workers from across the lake. They looked to be gathered in a circle. Were they having a meeting? "What's going on over there?"

"Hard to tell from here." He moved out of the tree

line and to the water's edge. "It looks like they're sitting around having lunch."

Brody moved next to him. Kids ran around, kicking and chasing a ball. A woman was hanging clothes on the line she'd set up from a lamppost to her RV. Nothing suspicious appeared to be going on. It all looked like pretty normal stuff to Brody.

A text came through. Brody checked his phone. It was from Ryan. "He wants to meet at the picnic tables." Branches broke to their left.

Brody whirled around. The trees were thick enough to block his view. He locked gazes with Dawson and then motioned for him to break to the left. Brody broke to the right, his steps so light they made no sound. Dawson's hunting instincts must've kicked in, because he didn't make a noise, either.

The sound Brody heard might have been an animal and that was the most logical answer. No one, and especially not the Mason Ridge Abductor, would be dumb enough to attack them in broad daylight. Then again, he'd just tried that with Rebecca.

Let him pick on someone his own size, Brody thought, stepping ever so softly through the underbrush.

He and Dawson would come at whomever or whatever was making the noise from opposite sides. It was the best way to surprise him.

Another noise sounded, indicating more movement. Brody tracked farther to the left, hoping Dawson was correcting his position as well and that he wasn't being lured into a trap. This scenario had stink bait written all over it.

What if it was Ryan?

Brody reminded himself that cell coverage was spotty in the woods. Or…

A bad thought hit Brody. Ryan would answer his phone if he *could*.

Whatever was making that sound was on the move. And that had to be a good thing, because if it was Ryan that meant he was capable of walking.

Brody picked up a rock the size of his fist and hurled it toward a tree ten feet away to see if he could stir up more movement. An animal would react instantly to the sound and scatter.

He stilled.

Sounds of children's laughter floated across the lake. No bolt from an animal.

Meaning the noise was being made by a person.

A muttered curse followed a grunt and a thud. Then a call for help shot through the trees. Dawson.

Brody broke into a run toward the sound, branches slapping him in the face and underbrush stabbing needles in his shoes.

A large man was hovering over Dawson, who was on his side on the ground. Brody dove straight into the guy, knocking him off balance.

Dawson immediately rolled away and then jumped to his feet. He moved so quickly the guy didn't have time to react. Brody had already pinned the guy with his thighs. "You like sneaking up on people in the woods?"

"I was just thinking the same thing about you," the guy ground out. "What are you doing over here, sneaking around, watching my friends?"

Hope that this could be The Mason Ridge Abductor died instantly based on this guy's size and general stature. He was big and powerful. Not thin, like Rebecca had said.

"We're looking for our friend."

"Get off me and I'll help."

Brody nodded to Dawson, who eased off the festival worker. He was a big guy with a ponytail. He was a bit older, his white hair streaked with gray.

"If your friends are over there, then what are you doing sneaking around on this side of the lake?" Brody asked.

The man dusted the dirt off his jeans and then took the hand up Brody offered. "My name's Lester Simmons."

"We heard a woman was attacked at the grocery nearby and we didn't want to take any chances. We travel with our wives and children to a different city every week. We've seen and heard just about everything. No one wanted to risk it so we set up watch," Lester said. His deep-set brown eyes and permanent smile lines softened what could have been an intimidating figure. One phone call and he could have a dozen men bolting around that lake. The tables would be turned. Brody and Dawson would be completely outnumbered.

Brody gave a nod of understanding and provided a description of Ryan. "According to GPS on his phone, he should be in this area."

"Hold on." Lester pulled his cell from his back pocket.

"Whoa. Not so fast."

"I already have guys on their way. I'm not dumb enough to investigate a sound alone. Figure I'll give them a heads-up so they can look for your friend." Lester went to work on his phone.

"Thank you," Brody said. "Sorry about before."

"It's cool. Tensions are high around camp, too." Lester pocketed his phone. "Where'd you leave off?"

"The last message I received from him said he'd be near the picnic tables," Brody said, remembering the area.

"There's a set right over here. We come over sometimes

for dinner because the barbecue grills are less crowded on this side." Lester led them to the tree line."

Sure enough there was a set of picnic tables nestled near a cove. No sign of Ryan.

None of this made sense.

Brody fired off another text to his friend and moved to the location Ryan said he'd be.

No response. No luck.

More men arrived, coming from every direction, and offered the same response when asked if they'd seen anyone else.

The area had been thoroughly searched and there was still no word from or sign of Ryan. It wasn't like him to pull a prank or do something like this. Brody didn't like it one bit.

"Think we should check his place?" Dawson asked. "Maybe he gave up waiting and headed home."

"That's a good idea. There's no sign of him here and we've been searching for more than an hour." Brody had an idea. He called Ryan's phone and then listened. The buzzing sound came a few seconds later. Brody moved to it, located the device.

"Looks like he was here. I'll take this back to him." Brody swiped his finger across the screen. Sure enough, the texts were there. He scanned the log for any others that might give a clue as to where Ryan could be. There was nothing. Brody turned to Lester. "Your help is much appreciated. I apologize again for the misunderstanding earlier."

Lester's friends looked over at him in confusion.

"Not a problem. Like I said, everyone's on alert around here." Lester smiled and took the hand being offered in a hearty shake.

On the way back to the truck, Brody filled Dawson in on the phone's contents. Dawson double-checked the logs and didn't find anything that stood out, either.

At least they'd made a contact within the festival ranks. Having an ally there might come in handy later. There were so many of them around town for the festival, which wrapped up tomorrow. The more eyes and ears, the better. And it was also helpful to know his family and friends were as concerned as the rest of the town.

Turns out, the festival crowd wasn't so different from the people of Mason Ridge.

Finding Ryan had just become top priority.

The drive to his house took another twenty minutes. Brody parked across the street and then texted Rebecca to find out if she was doing okay.

Rebecca replied that she and Samantha were catching up and he could take his time getting back to the restaurant.

As Brody opened the door to get out, his phone rang. The name of the caller was Rebecca.

Odd.

He quickly answered.

"Brody, I thought you'd want to know that Ryan just walked in."

"He's okay?"

"Not a scratch on him," she replied matter-of-factly.

"Hold on to him for me, okay?" Brody stopped Dawson and ended the call. "False alarm. He just showed up at Angel's in town."

"That's strange."

"Isn't it? At least we know he's not lying in a ditch somewhere." Relief settled over Brody and he realized how clenched his shoulder muscles had been. "Want me to drop you off at your house?"

Dawson nodded as he got back in the truck. "It's been a crazy few days, hasn't it?"

It was more statement than question.

"Sure has." Brody gripped the steering wheel tighter, readying himself for more warnings about his relationship with Rebecca.

"You have everything covered out at the ranch?"

"Thanks for the other day. My neighbor helped out last night and my part-time help pulled an extra shift this morning. So far, so good."

"Call me if you need more help."

"Will do."

Brody shot Dawson a look.

"What?" Dawson asked.

"Nothing. I just thought you were going to warn me about spending time with Rebecca," Brody said, easing his grip on the wheel.

"Sounds like something Ryan would do."

"He already did."

"Then you don't need to hear it from me."

"No. I don't."

"Besides, I got a different opinion about that, anyway." Dawson chuckled. "And you know what they say about opinions and how much they stink."

"I sure do," Brody agreed. "I'd like to hear what you have to say, anyway."

"The two of you together is a good thing in my book. It's natural."

"Us being together has never been the tricky part. It's when she leaves that does me in."

Dawson nodded. "I get that."

"The last time wasn't exactly a trip to the state fair."

"I remember. You were a mess."

"Thanks," Brody said sarcastically.

"Anytime," Dawson shot back, clearly trying to work off the tension they'd both felt. "How do you know she'll do it again? I mean, give her some credit. She's a grown woman now, not some young kid scared of her own shadow."

"True," Brody agreed. "In my experience, when people tell you who they are, it's smart to believe them."

"And actions speak louder than words."

"Most clichés are rooted in truth. That's why they're repeated over and over again."

"Except that she's not the same person she was before. Not in my opinion. And I don't remember her making any promises she'd stick around before."

"Tell that to a kid. Here's another problem you might not have considered." Brody pulled up in front of their meeting place. He lived a few towns over. "Don't both parties have to want to be in a relationship for it to work?"

The door was open and Dawson was half-out when he turned. "Had your eyes checked lately? Because I'm starting to think you're going blind."

Was his vision impaired when it came to Rebecca? He felt the heat between them—there was no questioning their attraction. Could there be more?

It took more than good chemistry to make a relationship work.

Dawson held on to the door. "You remember to call me if you need a hand around the ranch. You hear?"

"I plan to take you up on that offer. And thank you."

"Good. Consider the other stuff I said, too."

"You bet." Brody obliged his friend and appreciated

his point of view. Ultimately, relationships came down to loyalty.

And he was grateful for Dawson's.

REBECCA DIDN'T REALIZE that she'd been in the booth for almost three hours by the time Brody walked through the door of Angel's. She waved him over, thinking how fast time had zipped by.

By the second hour, Mr. Turner had excused himself, telling Samantha he could walk home from the restaurant.

Of course, she'd tried to talk him out of going. He'd told her that he wanted to stop by some of the shops in the square, anyway.

Reluctantly, Samantha had let him go. She'd mumbled another apology, which was unnecessary, and had said that he never got over the abductions. He'd said that he wished he could help in some way but had felt as helpless then as he did now. Some people got over the past better than others. Since Rebecca and Samantha had been friends all those years ago, the whole ordeal most likely hit a little too close to home for Mr. Turner. With the loss of his wife the previous year, it might've been too much for him.

Rebecca understood and had assured her friend there was no harm done.

Those thoughts washed away as Brody opened the door and made a straight line to Rebecca. His head was down, but his gaze was intense and a little part of her wondered if he'd missed her, too.

Ryan, who had been seated next to her, stood as Brody approached the table. The two shook hands and then he leaned over to hug Samantha.

When Ryan sat down again, he moved across the table, leaving the spot next to Rebecca free.

"My phone's missing," he repeated, this time saying it to Brody.

"When did you notice it was gone?"

"Not until she asked me about the text message I sent." He motioned toward Rebecca. "Thing is, I didn't send it."

"You couldn't have," Brody said.

Chapter Eleven

Brody held out Ryan's phone. "There were all kinds of festival people in the area where someone told us to meet. They were trading watch."

"One of them must've lifted my phone at the gas station earlier when I stopped to get gas. I keep it in my pocket and hardly think about it until I need it. I've never been one of those people glued to the screen." Ryan took the offering. He should look relieved that his uncle might be innocent. Instead, he looked even more worried. "You think one of them tried to isolate you? Get you in the woods?"

"Makes me think someone's watching. Whoever's behind this is most likely still trying to get to Rebecca. But now I may have a contact inside the Renaissance camp." Of course, the guy could have been covering for one of his own. "I met a guy named Lester. He seemed like a good person albeit protective of his people. We might be able to get more information from him."

"We still need to circle back and talk to Uncle Greg," Ryan said.

Brody's coffee arrived.

"I stopped by Alcorn's office and caught a break when his admin was there working. I wasn't sure she would be given this is Saturday. I used Rebecca's name. She turned over a list of vendor names. We can check them against the suspect list to see how many hits we get. We'll focus on those first." Sitting so close to Rebecca had Brody's pulse racing again.

"I think we should speak to my uncle first," Ryan said.

"We can always drive to Garland and check his last-known address," Brody offered.

Rebecca touched his arm. He ignored the heat exploding through him. Everything inside him wanted to haul her in his arms. He picked up his coffee instead of reaching for her. This seemed a good time to remind himself of the fact that most high school sweethearts who went on to marry didn't make it to their third anniversary, or so he'd been told. He already knew how much it hurt when a relationship didn't work. His friends had offered all kinds of unsolicited advice and encouragement when she'd walked out before.

Dismissing the notion of him and Rebecca still together before it could gain traction and make him miss something he shouldn't want he said, "Ryan, you could drive."

"Or we could go back and rest first. I doubt you slept much last night," she offered.

If the Renaissance people were leaving tomorrow, then he'd rather go now. She was right, though—his head pounded and his eyelids were starting to feel like hundred-pound bales of hay sat on them as the adrenaline wore off from his earlier scuffle. "It's probably better not to wait until morning to follow through on this."

Ryan agreed, looking as if he might explode if he didn't get answers soon. His nervous tick of chewing on a toothpick had already surfaced.

"I hope you guys find him. This is scary," Samantha

finally said. She reached across the table and squeezed Rebecca's hand.

"He won't surprise us this time," she said. "You be careful, too. Take extra precaution if you're out some- where alone, day or night."

"I will. Speaking of which, I'd better get back to Dad. He's had a lot on his mind lately with the store. I guess the pressure of owning a business is getting to him more as he ages." She shrugged. "I'm so happy we got to see each other."

"Tell Melanie hello for me."

Brody picked up on a flash in Samantha's eyes. When he really thought about it, Melanie hadn't been back to Mason Ridge since college. "Tell her we'd love to see her sometime."

"Any chance she'll be coming back for the reunion next year?" Rebecca asked.

Samantha flinched, only for a brief moment. If Brody hadn't been watching her, he would've missed it.

"I doubt it," Samantha said. "Melanie doesn't like to come back. She doesn't have great memories from high school and her parents are almost always on the road now. They go see her in Houston."

Brody figured a small town like Mason Ridge wasn't for everybody.

Everyone stood and said their goodbyes. Brody re- quested the check and covered their lunch and drinks.

"You haven't eaten anything yet," Rebecca said stub- bornly when he tried to usher her out the door.

To appease her, he ordered a club sandwich to go. He tried not to think about how nice it was that someone was looking out for him for a change. Experience had taught him being dependent on others could backfire and the burn left a permanent mark.

Brody had always taken care of himself, especially after his mother had pulled her disappearing act. His father had buried himself in work, so Brody learned his way around the kitchen in order to eat. There wasn't much ceremony to it at first, mostly opening cans of soup and making sandwiches. He'd gotten better over time and once he was old enough to man the grill, his dinners got a lot more interesting.

Conversation flowed easily while they waited for his order. Later, he wanted to double check the social media messages and he still hadn't worked through all the threatening letters to see if anything was there. They had a list of suspects, sure, but he needed something to narrow it down. It was too much to hope for a name but that's exactly what he needed. Then, he could fit the rest of the pieces together.

"I'll drive," Ryan said. "We can leave your truck here."

Brody nodded, thanked the waitress and settled the bill. His left hand instinctively reached for the lower part of Rebecca's back as they walked toward the door.

Pulling it back, he held the door open and followed the others to Ryan's SUV.

"My uncle usually leaves his door unlocked when he's home," Ryan offered, trying the handle. It turned, so he opened the door. "He's most likely out back, drinking, if he still lives here."

Brody followed, linking his fingers with Rebecca's. To hell with what Ryan thought. Why did Brody feel guilty about holding her hand? Wasn't like he was making a move on her. And yet, having that link kept his heart from racing. It still pounded for a different reason. The vendors hadn't matched any of the names from the suspect list Brody had checked on the drive to Garland. That trail had gone cold.

He didn't have a list of all vendor employees, so festival workers couldn't be ruled out altogether.

Rebecca took two steps inside and froze. Brody immediately knew why. It was the smell of apple tobacco.

He squeezed her hand, urging her forward. Her hesitation disappeared as she powered ahead.

Inside was dark and sparsely furnished. Blinds were closed, only allowing a smidge of light to push through. An old couch with a couple of mismatched chairs pretty much covered the decor in the living room. There was an old TV with a protruding back sitting on an industrial wooden wire spool. The kitchen was on par with the rest of the place. Greg's house was what most people would call a dedicated bachelor pad. It would work for someone in college, but for a man Greg's age most people would consider the place sad.

"This has to be my uncle's place," Ryan said. "I remember this furniture."

Brody looked for any sign there could've been a child there. Of course, Shane had been gone for fifteen years, so whatever Brody saw wouldn't belong to him. If Greg abducted kids, there should be some evidence.

Nothing stood out.

The door to the back porch creaked as Ryan pushed it open.

"It's me, Uncle Greg." Ryan quickly added, "I brought company."

Uncle Greg was a tall and slight man, and it wasn't lost on Brody that he fit the description of the Mason Ridge

Abductor. His easy smile faded when his gaze stopped on Rebecca.

"What brings you and your friends all the way out here?" he asked, shifting his weight from one foot to the other, looking uneasy. He held tightly to a beer can as he took a swig. "You folks want something to drink?"

"Nothing for us, thanks," Brody said, noticing the tension around Ryan's eyes as he came up beside him. Play this wrong and his uncle might not talk at all.

Rebecca had eased behind Brody a little more, clearly uncomfortable being around Ryan's relative. Her discomfort wasn't full-on panic and Brody took that as a good sign to keep going. If her fingers stiffened any more, he'd excuse them both. There was no reason to put her through anything she didn't want to be part of and he'd wait with her in the SUV. Since she was doing okay, and he really wanted to stick around to see Uncle Greg's reactions to Ryan's questions, Brody stayed.

Ryan continued, "I need to ask you a few questions."

"Take a seat while I refresh my drink," Greg motioned to a mixed grouping of mismatched plastic chairs.

To be polite, Brody did.

"You remember my friends, Brody and Rebecca?" Ryan asked.

"Nice family, the Hughes." Greg popped open a fresh beer from the cooler, took a gulp and sat down next to Ryan.

Brody noted it was the farthest seat from Rebecca. He also noticed that Greg didn't mention anything about his own family. And that was probably for the best.

Rebecca had a death grip on Brody's fingers. He glanced at her to get a read on whether or not he needed to take her to the SUV. Her gaze was intent on Greg. The creased lines on her forehead indicated she was carefully studying him.

The pulse at the base of her throat beat rapidly but that was her only tell. Otherwise, she looked surprisingly calm. Then again, she had the most to gain from this interview.

No reason to leave yet.

"Tell me everything you remember about the night her brother was taken," Ryan pressed.

"I've already told the law everything I knew." Greg's expression dropped to frustration and despair. "Did they believe me? No. They hassled me for months after that boy went missing. I couldn't walk to the corner without being hauled in for loitering."

His expression was genuine. He had the worn look of an innocent man who'd suffered horrendous abuse at the hands of law enforcement. Brody could see Sheriff Brine pulling something like this.

Greg turned directly to Rebecca. He said, "I'm sorry for your loss, ma'am, but I want you to know that I had nothing to do with what happened. I've told the sheriff the same thing. But he didn't listen." He took another gulp of beer and Brody noticed Greg's hands shook. "I don't want to talk about it no more, either. Isn't it enough I moved out of town to get away from all the harassment?"

Brody hadn't thought about the fact that Greg might've been targeted all those years ago. Everyone knew Sheriff Brine disliked the Hunts. Guess he'd taken full advantage of what happened to demonstrate his power.

Ryan comforted his uncle, who was clearly shaken up just remembering.

"I'm the one who's sorry," Rebecca said, rising from her seat. She walked over and hugged Greg. "The sheriff shouldn't have taken advantage of what happened to my family to hurt you."

Greg blinked up at her, clearly stunned by her kindness. "I've done a lot of wrong things in my life but I would never hurt no child. I cried like everybody when that boy went missing."

She patted his shoulder. "I know."

He crossed his legs, the look of surprise still on his aging features. "If you ask me, the sheriff knew more than he let on back then."

Angry words from a man who'd been scorned. Brody couldn't blame the guy for lashing out. It was no secret that Brine didn't like any of the Hunts.

Rebecca thanked him for his time and turned to Ryan and Brody. "We should head back and leave this poor man alone. He's been through enough already."

Brody rose to his feet ahead of Ryan.

They said their goodbyes and moved toward the house.

Brody stopped and picked up the pipe on the plate being used as an ashtray. He turned. "Can I ask you something?"

"Shoot," Greg said, still visibly shaken at the memories of what Sheriff Brine had put him through.

"Why apple tobacco?"

"That's easy. Picked up the habit from an old drinking buddy who used to come to town with the festival." The man didn't flinch.

Greg took another drink and Brody tried his best not to look too interested in the answer to his next question. "Do you remember that guy's name?"

"Sure do. Thomas…oh, what's his name. Something. It's right there on the tip of my tongue." He banged his knuckles on his forehead. "I remember now. Last name was Kramer."

"Thank you. You've been a big help today. We appreciate you being honest with us."

"I do what I can."

"You don't happen to know where Thomas is now, do you?"

"Nah. I don't get to the festival anymore. I try to stay clear of that town with Brine breathing down my neck every time I walk on the sidewalk."

One look at Rebecca said she'd caught on.

They had a name.

"Any chance you can still describe him?" Brody asked.

"Sure," Greg said. "He was my about my height and build. Had brown eyes."

Find Thomas Kramer and they had a shot at finding out what had happened to Shane.

Brody thanked Greg for his time.

By the time the trio reached the SUV, Rebecca looked about to burst. She held it in long enough to open the door and slip inside.

"We have a name," she said.

"We sure do. And he matches the description, too."

"Thomas Kramer. Wasn't he one of the suspects?" Rebecca asked.

Ryan started the SUV, put the ignition into Drive and pulled away from his uncle's house. His worst fears put to rest, he looked relieved for the first time since this ordeal had begun.

"It's familiar." Brody checked his phone. "Sure is."

They owed the encampment a visit. He checked his watch. The festival wouldn't start for hours. It would be more difficult to find Lester with those costumes on.

Brody wished he'd asked what job Thomas Kramer had at the festival.

With this being the last night, Brody had very little time to work with. He wasn't sure it was safe for him to go on his own to the RV park where festival workers kept a close watch.

Based on the protection details they had going, it wouldn't surprise Brody if they carried guns for night duty.

Did they know they'd had a kidnapper among them? Were their efforts to keep out locals like they'd said, or were they protecting their own from a threat within? Lester had said that they'd started patrolling based on the grocery store attack.

In hindsight, their efforts seemed larger than the crime. A local woman was mugged at the grocery store and suddenly they're setting up patrols, attacking anything that moves in the woods?

Seemed like on over-the-top reaction to what the sheriff's office had said was a random occurrence.

Chapter Twelve

This was the closest Rebecca had been to a breakthrough in the case in years—she could feel it. Energy hummed through her at the thought they could be getting close to solving a fifteen-year-old puzzle and possibly finding her brother.

Thoughts buzzed around in her head. If Kramer had been a suspect, why would they have let him go? Wouldn't the sheriff have interviewed him? What about the FBI?

Of course, there were more leads than people to handle them back then. Even at twelve, Rebecca had known that much.

Ryan had been quiet for the entire half-hour trip so far. "My uncle is a drunk. It's possible he's remembering the name wrong."

"I thought about that," Brody said, flashing a knowing look toward Rebecca. "Never hurts to take it seriously, though."

Rebecca knew both men were trying to soften the blow if this turned out to be a nonlead, and she loved them for it.

BY THE TIME Ryan had dropped them at the restaurant where Brody's truck was still parked, Rebecca's thoughts ping-ponged from Thomas Kramer to Brody.

They had a name, Thomas Kramer, and the very real possibility he would lead her to the truth.

For the rest of the ride to Brody's place, she vacillated between excitement and fear. Questions assaulted her. What if they'd found him? What if they hadn't?

What if they wrapped this case and she and Brody walked away from each other for good?

The truth was that she liked being close, having him depend on her. Making sure he ate and didn't overexert himself were things that made her ridiculously happy.

There was something so right about taking care of Brody.

He'd barely set his keys on the table in the foyer when she said, "I'll grab the letters to see if one of them is signed by Kramer."

"While you do that, I'll see if I can find any news about him or an address," Brody said, moving to the laptop in the kitchen.

When he came back into the open-concept room, he brought the laptop with him and moved to the sofa. "It's more comfortable over here if you'd like to join me."

She did, tucking her foot under her bottom as she sat down. They had a name. And she had a feeling this all would be over soon. "We're getting close."

"We don't know if Thomas Kramer is our guy yet. If not, this isn't the end."

Tears rolled down her cheeks despite her best efforts to hold them back. She hadn't expected to get so emotional with him, dammit.

"You told me something the other day and it made a hell of a lot of sense," he said.

Wiping a few tears away, she said, "What was that?"

"Holding in emotion is dangerous. Not talking about

the things that bother us, bottling them up, doesn't lead to anything good. And I think you're putting on a brave front right now."

His words hit home and the floodgates opened. Tears streamed and she couldn't hold them back if she'd tried.

"Get over here," he said.

Rebecca was in his arms before she could recount all the reasons this would be a bad idea, her face buried in his strong chest.

"You're scared and there's nothing wrong with that," he said, his voice a deep, steady timbre. His quiet strength was like the river that cut through granite.

This was the closest she'd been to figuring out the past.

Rebecca pulled herself together. "I'll be okay."

She picked up the stack of letters and set them on her lap.

Brody kissed her forehead before opening the file on his laptop.

It didn't take long for him to say, "Look here."

Her heart skipped a beat as she read the screen. "Are those notes from his interview?"

"Looks like it," Brody said. "Did you notice this?"

"He had a child who died at age seven," she said, horrified. "Wouldn't that make him a prime suspect?"

"I would think so," Brody said quickly, his eyes skimming the file. "Here. It says that his alibi checked out and that's why he was cleared of suspicion."

"It says he was caring for a sick aunt that weekend," Rebecca said. "She could've lied for him."

"I'd put money on it."

"Any chance we can find his address?" she asked.

Brody minimized the window on his screen and then

pulled up a search engine. He tapped the keys on the keyboard. "Nothing. Although, his address might not be listed."

"Or he could live with someone else. Another relative," she said.

"True." Brody rocked his head.

"Any chance his aunt's name and address is in that report?" Rebecca's pulse raced in her chest.

Brody pulled up the file and scrolled through the entire page. "It's not here. When we go to the festival tonight, I'll ask Lester about Kramer."

"I feel like we should be doing something more right now," she said, feeling antsy. Answers were close. She could feel it.

"We are," he said. "And we will. I know patience is difficult right now, believe me, but the truth will come out soon enough."

"I want to talk to this Kramer guy."

"We will," he reassured. "Right now, there's not much more we can do until we talk to Lester tonight."

"You're probably right." Her heart trilled against her rib cage and she needed to slow down her breathing, find a way to calm herself.

Looking around Brody's place, at the comfortable decor, she could see herself living in something like this with him. In fact, this was exactly the kind of place she'd live in if she had a ranch. She loved the open space of the landscape, and the Texas sky was nowhere brighter in the day or more majestic at night than in Mason Ridge. Chicago had been wonderful, too, for different reasons. And mostly, it had been different.

Walking down the street there she could be anyone. She was no longer "that girl." No one whispered.

And yet, Mason Ridge would always be home in her heart.

Was it because Brody was there?

"I didn't leave you all those years ago, Brody, so much as run away from here, from everything I felt. I needed to sort out my emotions, but I hurt you in the process. I'm so sorry."

Brody lifted her chin until her face was raised and she looked into his clear blue eyes. She'd expected to find pity in them, but instead she saw something hungry, something primal. Need?

"What time should we leave?" she asked.

"We have a little while. The festival workers will be setting up for opening soon so I doubt we'd get in without a warrant, which we don't have."

"We have a little time to kill?" Rebecca ran her finger along Brody's strong jawline. Neither looked away.

Chapter Thirteen

Brody felt Rebecca's heartbeat pounding against his chest. The rapid rhythm matched his own. With her in his arms, he felt an emotion that was foreign to him—intimacy. And an overwhelming need to pick her up, take her to his bed and show her just how much a woman she'd become overtook him.

He'd experienced need but nothing matching the intensity of this feeling.

Somewhere in the back of his mind, he realized being this close was a bad idea. Staring into her honey-brown eyes, the smell of her shampoo drowning his sense, and all reasoning flew out the window.

Just when he thought he might be able to stop this from going any further, she shifted position enough to pull her shirt over her head and drop it on the floor.

"You can tell me no if you think this is a bad idea, Brody." The way his name rolled off her tongue made him want to hear her say it again and again as his tongue moved down her neck.

She stood and shimmied out of her jeans. Underneath, she wore matching lace panties.

Blood pulsed toward his already uncomfortably stiff length.

He tugged her toward him until she was standing in front of him, his hands to either side of her hips. Leaning forward, he rested his forehead on her stomach. "You have no idea how badly I want to do this."

He looked up at her as she stood there with defiance in her stare.

"But?"

"No buts. I want to make love to you, Rebecca. Now it's your turn to take an out, because I've already made up my mind. If you have any doubts about what we're about to do, you're going to have to be the one to stop this. In about two seconds, I won't be able to so I need to know that you want this. Me."

"It's always been you, Brody. I've always wanted you."

That was all the encouragement he needed. Standing, rising to his full height, he dipped his head down and claimed her mouth. Their lips molded together as he slid his tongue inside her mouth, the need to taste her overtaking every rational thought.

Her hands traveled across his chest, moving upward until they tunneled in his hair, pulling and tugging as her tongue swirled inside his mouth. She tasted so sweet.

His shirt joined hers on the floor.

By the time he reached for the zipper of his jeans, her hands were already there, so he let her do the honors. A second later, his pants were tossed on top of hers.

There in his living room wearing nothing but a bra and panties was the most beautiful woman he'd ever seen. She needed to hear it. "Rebecca, you're gorgeous, sexy."

Thoughts of the innocent kisses they'd stolen in high school were a world away. High school was a world away. And Brody couldn't say he was especially sorry they weren't those same two people they'd been.

He'd grown up, become a man.

His Rebecca, still sweet, had an incredibly sexy side. He'd noticed the way men looked at her. He didn't like it.

"I missed you, sweetheart."

"I'm right here, Brody," she said.

Standing now, he felt an all-too-familiar tug at his heart. Rebecca was the only one who affected him in that way, who reached beyond the mask of strength he wore. With her, he felt a strangely comfortable sense of vulnerability.

This time, he kissed her.

Their mouths moving together, the heat between them rose as his hands moved along her stomach, her breast. He palmed one and her nipple beaded against his palm.

It was her silky bra that hit the floor next. She was all curves and soft skin, and his groin tightened when he really saw her.

Brody took her by the hand and led her to his room.

By the time she was on the bed, all of their clothes littered the floor. *Rebecca on his bed.* He liked the sound of those words more than he should.

"Do you have protection? There hasn't been a need for me to be on the pill," she said.

"That can wait."

On his knees, he ran his finger along the tender flesh of the insides of her thighs. Her body quivered along the stroke of his hands.

"Brody, I want you *now.*"

"I have no plans to rush this." It had been a long time since Brody had been interested enough in a woman to take her to bed. He'd stopped doing casual sex.

Looking at Rebecca, at the perfection that was her, everything in his body begged for quick release, but self-discipline was his middle name and he had every intention of enjoying this to the fullest.

"Brody, are you planning to torture me by making me wait?" She sat up, took his arm and tried to urge him toward her. Her face was flush with need, and he felt her body humming with anticipation. "Because I can't."

He smiled at her, moving just out of her reach. She was everything he wanted in a woman—beautiful, intelligent, sexy. And not one female had lived up to the standard she'd set so many years ago.

"As a matter of fact, I had something different in mind." He leaned forward and kissed her to disarm her.

Tucking his hands underneath her sweet round bottom, he tilted her until her head rested on his pillow again.

"No fair…" She pouted until she seemed to realize what he was doing.

She was already wet for him when he inserted three fingers inside her and so he was the one who groaned.

He worked her mound with his thumb as he dipped his fingers again and again, loving the way her body moved and the sensual moans she made.

Pulsing faster, deeper, harder, her muscles clenched and released around his fingers.

"Brody," she whispered breathlessly.

He would never get tired of hearing her say his name.

REBECCA SHOULD BE embarrassed at how quickly she'd climaxed. She wasn't. Everything with Brody seemed right and the sexual tension between them had been building since they'd met up at the coffee shop the other morning. If she were being totally honest, it had been building long before that. In high school, they were too young to really know what it was or do anything about it.

Even though he'd tipped her over the edge once already, she wanted more. She needed to feel his weight on top of her, pressing her into the mattress. Him moving inside her.

She pushed up on her elbows, watching as his shaky hands managed the condom. "You need help with that?"

"I think I got it." He rolled it over his tip.

She reached over and guided it down his large shaft.

His guttural groan at her touch nearly drove her crazy. She wanted him to feel everything he'd just given her and so much more.

Pulling him over her, opening her legs to welcome him, he released a sexy grunt as he drove inside her. She opened her legs more, adjusting to his length.

Her hands mapped the lines of his back, memorizing everything that was Brody, and he thrust deeper, reaching her core. She matched his intensity, craving, needing more and more as they rocketed toward the edge.

He pulled out a little, his tip still inside, and tensed.

"What is it, Brody? What's wrong?"

"Nothing. It feels a little too right and I'm already there. I want this to last."

"Don't stop now. We can always do it again."

His smile faded as he reached the depth of his first thrust. She bucked her hips, needing to fly over the edge with him.

Harder. Faster. Deeper.

More.

Their bodies, twined, exploded with pleasure. A thousand bombs detonated at once, sending volts of electricity and pleasure rocketing through her. She could feel him pulsing inside her as her muscles clenched around his length.

When he'd drained her of the last spasm, he pulled

out and folded on his side next to her. The weight of his arm over her, his touch, quieted any protest trying to tell her that this might have been a bad idea. His heart raced, matching her tempo, as he leaned over and pressed a kiss to her temple. And then another to her forehead as he pulled her in closer. His body was soft skin over powerful muscle, silk over steel.

She wanted to say the three words roaring through her mind but stopped herself, refusing to think about the fact that he had built a life in Mason Ridge and she was a temporary resident.

Being with Brody was dangerous but far from wrong, even if it wouldn't last.

BRODY WOKE WITH a start. He'd only dozed off for half an hour and yet it had felt like so much longer. No doubt the result of a satisfied sleep that came with the best sex of his life. Rebecca lay still in his arms, the scent of her citrus and flowery shampoo filling the air around him. He could get used to breathing her in, lying next to her all night. Part of him wished they could stay right there.

The window of opportunity to track down Lester and, therefore, find Thomas Kramer, was closing.

In a few hours, it would be dark outside and the fireworks show would begin over the lake, signaling the end of the weeklong festivities.

The workers would scatter as the break-down crew went to work. By morning, there'd be nothing left of the festival but memories. He slowly peeled her arm off him, careful not to disturb her.

There was enough time for him to make a cup of coffee and he wanted to let her sleep as long as possible.

It took all the self-discipline he possessed to disengage

himself from her soft, warm body. Drawing on what was left of his willpower, he slipped out of the covers, located his boxers and put them on.

One last look at her while she lay there, her shimmering chestnut hair splayed across the pillow, and everything in his crazy world seemed right.

How long would it last?

Rebecca had been clear. She would leave town and not look back the minute she could.

He turned and walked out of the room.

The coffee was ready in a couple of minutes. His housekeeper had given good advice about stocking the shelves. And he was all right living by himself, wasn't he?

Didn't Brody prefer to do things his way, like keeping his shoes inside the door and not cleaning up the mud right away when it rained? He knew how to take care of himself, how to cook. Weren't those things important to him? He didn't have to explain where he was on a Friday night or defend having an extra beer while he watched the game.

After serving in the military, he'd wanted nothing more than to come home and be part of the community again. He figured he needed to get his bearings first before he tried to build onto his life.

Someday he planned to find the right woman and make their relationship permanent. Kids didn't seem like the worst idea at some point. He didn't care if he had boys or girls so long as they were healthy. Of course, if he had a daughter, he'd want her to look just like Rebecca.

Brody sighed sharply, ignoring the pain in his chest, and booted up his laptop, sipping his fresh brew.

Assessing how far he'd come should make him feel a sense of gratification. The house was comfortable and nice. He had land. His work rehabilitating horses was important and made a difference. He had enough money to be happy but not so much it was all he cared about.

So, why did he suddenly feel there was a gaping hole in his life?

A still-sleepy Rebecca shuffled into the room. "I can't believe I conked out."

"Come sit down. I'll make you a cup of coffee." He'd had time to reach out to a friend in the military about Randy the other morning and had been hoping to hear back. There was no response, which wasn't surprising. It had only been a day. *Give it time, Fields.*

He'd enlisted Dylan's help, as well. Brody would ask for an update when he saw his friend later. Patience racked right up there with second chances. Brody didn't care for either.

"Do we have time?" she asked, stretching. She looked sexy as hell standing in his living room.

"It'll only take a sec." He moved to the kitchen, popped a pod into the coffeemaker and returned a minute later with a fresh cup. "Here you go."

She thanked him with a kiss and a smile. "How's your head?"

"Better." He motioned for her to join him at the table.

"This coffee is fantastic." She was sitting on the edge of the seat, looking nervous.

Did she regret sleeping with him? He almost laughed out loud. That would be a new one. Wasn't he always the one keeping one foot out the door in every relationship since her? High school crushes hardly counted. Maybe he'd held everyone at a safe distance since his mother had ditched him. Brody hadn't had a horrible childhood. He and his father had been close, two bachelors under the same roof. His father had worked long hours to dig them out of the hole created by his mother.

Brody shoved those thoughts aside as he rose. "I'm going to hop in the shower before we leave. Care to join me?"

The smirk on Rebecca's lips was sexy as hell as she took his hand. "I'd love to, Mr. Fields."

After making love again, Brody dressed, thinking twice wasn't nearly enough. Could this, whatever *this* was, morph into something more permanent? He couldn't go there yet. What he could manage was enjoying what they had for today.

And he didn't have a whole lot of time to consider much of anything else considering time ticked away on finding Thomas Kramer. Brody's internet search had turned up unlucky. Then again, he hadn't expected to find Kramer easily. This guy had avoided capture for fifteen years. He traveled with a festival that was on the road forty-five weeks out of the year and could live anywhere.

Dawson texted that he was already at the festival with Ryan looking for Lester, and that Dylan was coming with Maribel. Said that Dylan had some news for Rebecca that he wanted to deliver in person. Brody hoped he knew what that meant. He wanted to keep a smile on her beautiful face.

"Think we have time to swing by and see my mother on our way? I spoke to her nurse earlier and Mother's having a good day. She had a great visit with Chelsea and Kevin this morning and they promised to stay in touch. They left their information with Mother. I guess having company did wonders for her," Rebecca said, entering the room. She'd dressed in a light blue tank top, jeans and sandals.

"It's on the way to the festival grounds, so that's not a problem." He withheld the information about Dylan's news. No sense getting excited about it before they knew what it was. Dawson had been tight-lipped so far.

"I'm ready if you are."

He nodded as her ringtone sounded in her purse. She retrieved her phone and checked the screen. "It's my dad. Do you mind if I take this?"

"Not at all." Brody smiled. From all he'd known, Mr. Hughes was a good guy. He deserved to know his daughter.

"Hi, Dad," she said into the phone, moving to sit on the couch in the next room. "I'm good. Thank you for calling." A beat of silence passed. "I'd love to come see you and the boys." Another hesitation. "Next Sunday? Barbecue?" She glanced toward Brody.

"Good idea," he whispered, just loud enough for her to hear.

"Would you mind if I brought someone?" Her eyes flashed toward Brody again. "Good. See you at six. Sure, I'll bring a swimsuit."

There was a moment of silence followed by, "I know I haven't said this in far too long. I love you, Dad."

She closed the phone and turned to Brody. "What are you doing next weekend?"

"Taking you to a barbecue." If she needed him there to ease her way back into her father's life, Brody didn't mind helping out. It was the right thing to do and he felt good about encouraging the reunion. Not everyone had a relationship with a parent worth holding on to. If someone did, they needed to grab hold with both hands and hang on for the ride. Those first steps toward the starting gate were often the hardest to take. "For what it's worth, I'm proud of you."

"You probably don't want to hear this from me, Brody." She glanced down to the floor and then back up at him. "I think you're a great man."

His heart skipped a beat because he thought she was going to say something else, the three words he wasn't ready to hear. Because when this was over, he had every intention of walking away.

REBECCA WAS HAPPY she didn't have to coax Brody to go inside with her to see her mother. Panic had engulfed Rebecca when they'd gone to her room only to find it empty. Turned out, her mother was in the recreation room playing a game of chess with another patient, looking pleased she'd made a friend.

They'd cut their visit short, promising to return the following day. Her mother had made Brody vow he'd return soon, too. Then she'd thanked him for looking after her daughter so well.

Since the festival was a short drive, Rebecca didn't argue when Brody made a move to drive again.

Neither said much on the ride over. Tensions rose the closer they got. Brody parked near Main Street and then texted the others to let them know he and Rebecca were there. It didn't take long to find Ryan and Dawson.

"We found our friend, Lester, from earlier," Dawson said. "He said Thomas Kramer was part of the breakdown crew. Or at least he had been until last year when they'd found him peeking through windows of the workers' RVs."

Rebecca couldn't help but think Kramer would have to be strong to do that job.

A text came from Dylan saying he was delayed with Maribel and would join them as soon as he could.

"Another reason their guard has been so high?" Brody asked.

"Exactly. Lester was up-front with us, but we both got the impression he was uncomfortable talking about one of his own," Ryan added.

"If they fired him last year, why come back? Why follow them here?" Brody asked, taking Rebecca's hand.

She wondered if the sudden urge to keep her close by came with knowing Kramer could be right next to them and they wouldn't know it. "Good question," Ryan said.

Dawson nodded. "I told Dylan I'd stick around the midway area. I'll keep watch. You guys should check the perimeter and see if he's hanging around, watching for another target."

Brody agreed.

Rebecca looked around, remembering the timing of Chelsea and Kevin's son's disappearance. "I wonder if they suspected him of the Sunnyvale kidnapping and that's why they beefed up their own security. It had happened on the last day of the festival last year."

Brody nodded. "There have been reports of him showing up in other places, but our guy says he hasn't seen Kramer," Dawson said.

"I ran a search of abductions of seven-year-old boys in the area and there haven't been many in the past fifteen years," Brody said.

"Maybe those are the only ones here." Rebecca didn't want to think about the truth in front of her. If Kramer had been the one to take Shane and he was still hurting boys, then it stood to reason that Shane was dead.

Chapter Fourteen

"I keep wondering why he'd come back. He had to know he'd be figured out eventually," Rebecca said as she, Ryan and Brody walked the perimeter of the festival while Dawson waited on the midway.

Brody didn't like the answers he came up with. "It's been a long time in between abductions here. Plus, he's bold because he's done a great job of hiding his activities so far. He knows this area, the woods. He's been able to slip under the radar all these years. But his time is up. We know who he is. He's going down and it's only a matter of time before we find him."

She paused, releasing a heavy breath. "Do you think it's possible that Shane's still…"

"I do. And you have to believe it, too." He didn't want to tell her what he thought Dylan's news would be just in case he was wrong. Brody and Ryan exchanged knowing glances.

Brody checked the surroundings. They were stopped near a farm road toward the back of the festival grounds. There were no residential developments for a good two miles on either side of them. He only had one bar on his phone.

Ryan pointed to a fresh trail that had been cut through

the brush. "Someone's been here. Could be teenagers looking for a party spot, or…" His gaze bounced from Rebecca to Brody.

Teens were known for searching out good places to build a bonfire and drink near the county line. And this had all the right markings for it.

"Except this trail has been trimmed and they don't normally use anything sharp," Brody pointed out, examining the marks.

"This might be another wild-goose chase, but it's worth looking into," Ryan said.

"Let's check it out. We can notify the sheriff if it's worth his time. I'm sure his office has been inundated with leads since the sketch hit the air."

Ryan nodded. "True."

Rebecca, on the other hand, remained perfectly still. Her face had gone pale. Brody didn't like having her along, but he didn't figure she'd let him go without her. He linked their fingers and took a step forward.

She followed until they moved into the tree line. She stopped, refusing to budge, except to grip his hand like death.

"Hold on a second, Ryan." Concerned, Brody turned his full attention to her. "What is it, Rebecca?"

She stood frozen for a long moment. "Do you smell that?"

"What?"

Ryan moved to Brody's side.

"I know that smell." Fear widened her eyes; the color drained from her face, and her fingers were icy cold.

"What is it, Rebecca?"

"Apple tobacco." Her moment of hesitation dissolved like salt in boiling water. Her gaze narrowed and her lips thinned as determination replaced fear. She stalked toward the woods.

Brody and Ryan kept close beside her, flanking her, as the sun kissed the treetops. She needed space and Brody intended to give it to her. Enough to work out her anger, but not so much as to leave her exposed.

Rage burned through Brody with each forward step. Even though the light was beginning to fade, he saw a small building positioned in the trees ahead coming into focus.

Rebecca had to have seen it, too. She didn't stop charging ahead. In fact, she increased her pace. Not a good idea. He couldn't let her be the first one to see what was inside that place.

Everything inside Brody wanted to stop her, to protect her from what he feared would come next. They could be walking up on a body, even Jason's from last year.

That there was no stench in the air was the only positive sign this might not go south.

He squeezed Rebecca's hand for support and exchanged a look with Ryan. She seemed to understand the need to move slowly and quietly, just in case Thomas Kramer was inside. Or watching from somewhere in the woods, setting another trap.

Brody would've liked time to gather intel before storming into the building, set a perimeter.

Instead, he signaled for the others to stop and listen.

There was no noise coming from the broken-down old shed.

A chill raced up Brody's back as he surveyed the area. The trees were thick enough to conceal the building, which was large enough to house a few people and supplies. "Hold position while I try to get a visual."

Rebecca and Ryan nodded.

This was exactly the kind of location Thomas Kramer would use. An abandoned shed in the woods that had been long forgotten. Unfortunately, there were far too many places like this in and around Collier County.

The suburban sprawl spreading from Dallas had not reached this place. And that was a large part of the reason Brody had returned. The other incentive had been to stay close to his father.

A little voice said he came back to be close to Rebecca, but he shut that down.

That same irritating voice said he came back because he still had feelings for her.

Was there any possibility that was true?

No.

Did he feel something when Rebecca was around? Yes. Love?

Brody shoved the word down deep as he moved stealthily through the woods. *Loyalty* was better.

The shed door had a place for an outside lock, which meant the original owner most likely had kept small farming equipment inside at some point. Brody inched closer without so much as snapping a twig. He didn't want to give away his location should Kramer be inside. Surprise was the best advantage and Brody had a lump on the back of his head to prove it.

There was no lock. Either the place was clean or they were about to walk into a trap.

Brody's need to protect Rebecca overrode his rational mind, because his first thought was to breach the building alone. No way did he want her within five feet of that shed. He circled back to her and Ryan.

"You sure you want to do this?" he asked.

She nodded. "Did you find anything?"

"There's no lock on the door. We shouldn't have any trouble getting inside." He hesitated. "I do want to remind you this could be a setup. Or you might end up seeing something you can't erase from your mind. I'd prefer to go first."

"I thought about that," she said ominously.

"And you still want to go in with me?" He looked her straight in the eyes. Any fear, any hesitation, and he'd go on his own. "Ryan can stay here with you."

Her head was already shaking, and Brody noticed that her body was, too.

"I can't live my life afraid anymore," she said.

As much as he wanted to stop her, to talk some reasoning into her for staying back, he couldn't. He understood her need to face her fears. Hell, he'd done the same thing. When his Humvee had been hit by an RPG, he'd volunteered for the next mission just so he'd have a chance to climb back in one and drive down that same street. He knew if he didn't, he might as well go home. In his eyes, being useless to the men who depended on him would be far worse than dying.

Brody linked his fingers with Rebecca's and led her toward what could be her worst nightmare. If she was ready to face her past, could they think about starting things up again? The thought caught him off guard. Did he want another chance with Rebecca?

Up to now, he'd convinced himself that he'd accepted this assignment for unselfish reasons, for her. Had he done it for himself all along?

Not ready to process that information, he tucked it away and moved to the door. He'd give her one last chance to reconsider. "Ready?"

BRODY AND RYAN moved like a well-rehearsed team, Ryan against Brody's back, insuring no one could surprise them from any angle. The two barely needed words between them to know what to do, their connection was so strong.

It wasn't so long ago that she and Brody had shared the same unspoken communication link. Had the years changed him or was he holding back with her because she'd hurt him? She'd felt the sparks between them, they'd made love, and she wondered if that could grow into anything more.

And yet, she knew that wasn't possible.

Good relationships were based on trust and communication. Without trust, good communication was impossible.

And above all, Brody valued loyalty.

She stood in front of the shed, her body trembling, and she wondered if it had anything to do with Brody as much as her fear. Yes, she was scared of seeing what was on the other side of that door. But the determined part of her kicked in and all she could see were Chelsea and Kevin's faces, their pain. The same expression had haunted her mother for so long.

Rebecca knew firsthand how devastating not knowing could be. Shane's disappearance, the years spent searching for him, had branded her. The situation had become worse when her father decided it was time to give up and move on. He'd said he didn't want to live in the past any longer. The same hadn't been true for her mother. She'd sworn she wouldn't rest until she found her son alive or brought his body home. On some level, she must've seen her husband's willingness to put the past behind them as a betrayal to their son, to her. Whatever love had existed between them had fractured. Her mother's relentless dedication to putting up new signs year after year had worn her father down even after their split. He'd said her activity was a slap in the face. He'd cry and say he was sorry that he couldn't bring their son back.

Rebecca didn't blame her father. She figured he was surviving the best he could under the circumstances.

Kevin and Chelsea's love for each other seemed to run deeper. Instead of standing on opposite sides of the room, they stood together. He'd been ready to catch her when she'd fallen. No matter the outcome of their case, Rebecca believed that couple would survive.

They were strong.

It was a safety net she'd never known as a child. Up to now Rebecca had believed relationships couldn't stand the test of time, not when something really bad happened, because of what had materialized with her own parents. And that made it harder to trust in her relationships.

Maybe there was hope for real love, a true connection.

Brody slowly opened the door. What was left of daylight filled the empty space.

That there was no stench had been a comfort. She knew they weren't going to find bodies.

Was anyone inside? It was too quiet. Another piece of her heart broke off that this would be another dead end.

Brody and Ryan stood in front of her, blocking her view. No doubt they felt the need to shield her from whatever horror might be inside the building.

"What's in there?" Rebecca asked as she tried to brace herself for whatever waited on the other side of that door.

"I'll keep watch out here in case he decides to come back to check on this spot," Ryan said, turning to place his back against the wall.

"Someone's been here." Brody took a deep breath and stepped aside.

There was just enough daylight left to see clearly. Bugs flew around her. She slapped her left bicep and then her leg. Mosquitos seemed to be everywhere, poised to take advantage of a quick meal. Dusk was a feeding frenzy.

Flies buzzed around her ears. Rebecca scarcely noticed. Her gaze was intent on the space she'd just stepped into. There was rope on the floor and empty juice boxes in the corner. Her legs almost gave when she took a step closer as horrible memories assaulted her.

"Yes, he has," she said through chattering teeth.

Brody palmed his cell and checked his screen. "According to my map, Mason Ridge Lake isn't far from here. He most likely wouldn't walk there and back, so there might be a source closer. Hold on, let me zoom in. Okay, we have a farmhouse about forty yards from here. Maybe they saw something."

"He was freaked out by me being there. Kept mumbling that I wasn't supposed to be around." Shivers rocked her body just thinking about it. She'd worked to erase those memories for so long.

Before she could ask, Brody was beside her. His arm around her waist steadied her.

"Ryan, call it in. There might be DNA evidence that can positively identify him," Brody called out. He turned to her and said, "Step lightly out of here. The sheriff won't be happy we've trampled all over their evidence."

"They've never been able to find his DNA before," she said. "He's clever."

"These aren't fresh. But, he might not have had time to wipe the place clean." Brody pointed to the empty juice cartons. "And they should be able to identify the child based on those."

Good point. Identifying a child and possibly Kramer would go a long way toward making sure this never happened again.

Brody helped her outside and held on to her while they waited for the sheriff to arrive. "That bothers me."

"What?" Rebecca asked.

"That they weren't able to find DNA evidence before."

"He's too smart," Rebecca said.

"Which doesn't exactly jibe with the theory of a transient. Kramer's tricky. I wonder what else he's has done."

"None of it has to make sense to us. We're normal people and this guy is a calculating monster," Rebecca said. "But the other issue I have is whether or not the sheriff will believe us. He could brush us off and say this could be from anyone."

"Unless the DNA on the juice boxes matches a missing kid in the database," Brody said.

Rebecca nodded, thinking about Jason and his parents, the agony of waiting.

Ryan's gaze moved from Brody's arm to his face. "You sure that you two waiting around here is a good idea?"

"We should head back to the festival. He could be there right now," Brody said.

"Absolutely not. I don't want to leave. Not until we have answers," Rebecca argued.

"Ryan makes a good point. There's nothing we can do to help. In five minutes, the place will be crawling with law enforcement, and we need to give them space to do their jobs."

As much as she wanted to protest, that made sense. Ryan's head was rocking back and forth in agreement, too. Plus, the sheriff didn't exactly believe her most of the time, anyway. Maybe it would be best if she was out of sight. "Okay, but let's walk the woods. Maybe there's another place nearby he stashed someone."

Brody shook his head. "He's gone. He wouldn't stick around."

"But we're so close. He was here. What if he—"

Brody's arm tightened around her waist. He leaned down and said, "I can only imagine what you must be going through. I'm so sorry."

He whispered other reassuring words—words that steadied her racing pulse.

"It's just that we're so close. I can feel it. He was here at some point, which means he comes back."

"He doesn't know we're onto him. And he won't have time to disappear before we find him this time. We're closing in. Plus, others are looking for him. He can't hide with the festival workers anymore. If he's around, we'll find him."

True. She knew that. But everything inside her wanted to keep looking for him in the woods.

She could hear footsteps and radio noise getting louder. "They're coming."

"I didn't think it would take long since they're close by, watching over the festival," Brody said.

Ryan gave Brody a bear hug first and then hugged her. "I'll stick around and give them a statement. You two get back to the festival."

"You sure?" Brody asked.

Seeing the exchange between close friends struck her in a place very deep. She thought about what Brody had said a million times about some families being made from the heart instead of shared tissue. He was right about that.

And a lot of other things, too. Most of all, he was right that no matter how much her heart ached to be close to him again, it was impossible to go back. Even though her pulse still raced with every brush of his arm against her.

And her heart beat heavy in her chest.

Because she also knew she would never feel like this toward another man for as long as she lived.

BY THE TIME she and Brody had finished walking the perimeter of the festival grounds with no luck Ryan had texted to say he was on the midway with the others.

Dylan walked up to the group with his daughter in tow as they arrived.

After hugs and greetings, Rebecca focused on the little girl to take her mind off Jason, Shane and the horrors that lay in the woods. Maribel had Dylan's bold green eyes. She also possessed his dark hair with curls.

Maribel beamed up at Rebecca and her heart literally melted.

Bending down to eye level, Rebecca said, "I've known your daddy since I was this tall." She held her hand up around four feet off the ground.

"Really?" Eyes wide, rosy round cheeks, Maribel was a cherub incarnate. Her *r* came out as a *w* and it was about the cutest thing Rebecca had ever heard.

"It's true. You look a lot like him."

Maribel took a step toward Rebecca and threw her pudgy little arms around Rebecca's neck.

Rebecca hugged the little angel back. She heard Dylan say something about Maribel normally being shy with new people.

Dylan inclined his chin toward the cotton-candy stand. Ryan took the little girl's hand and led her out of earshot.

Wiping away a loose tear, Rebecca said, "She's beautiful, Dylan. You did good."

"I'm lucky," Dylan agreed, but the look in his eyes said he was ready to change the subject. "You want to sit down over there?" He motioned toward a bench.

"No. I'm fine. What is it?" The seriousness in his expression tightened a coil inside her stomach.

A look passed between Dylan and Brody, causing an ominous chill to skitter across her nerves.

"Tell me," she said.

"It looks like I found him."

"Shane?" Surely her ears were playing tricks on her. Dylan couldn't possibly mean her brother.

"We believe it's him." Dylan nodded.

Brody was by her side, his warmth and his touch the only things keeping her upright.

"I have a contact in the military who found the name Brody gave us, Randy Harper. I had an idea which branch he might be in because Dawson took me back to that restaurant outside of town, Mervin's Eats. I brought Maribel, figuring we could gain the hostess's trust easier if my daughter came along. It worked. The hostess started talking about a friend of hers who'd dated him up until the time he left for the service. She couldn't remember his name or which branch, so I asked her to call her friend, and she did."

Air whooshed from Rebecca's lungs as she tried to let his words sink in. Could they have found Shane? Was it even possible after all these years? Tears were already streaming down her cheeks and she didn't bother to wipe them away. They were glorious tears of release. Tears that had been held inside far too long. Tears that needed to be set free. "Where is he?"

"All we know right now is that he's alive. He's in the army out on a mission. I'm told he's a great soldier."

"How can you be sure it's him?"

"We won't know for sure until he takes a DNA test but she said he had a birthmark that looked like Oklahoma on top of his right foot."

"That has to be him. What are the chances someone else would have that?"

"He doesn't remember much of his younger years. She said it bothered him because he'd been told his whole life that his parents had been killed in an accident, that he'd been sent to live with his Uncle Kramer on the road, and that he was an only child but he could swear he had an older sister."

Rebecca dropped to her knees, put her face in her hands and cried.

Everyone gave her space, even Brody. He seemed to know she needed a minute.

The release was sweet as she finally let go. *Shane, my baby brother, you're alive. You remember me. I've missed you so much.*

When she could stem the flow of emotion, she wiped her face and stood. "What else?"

"That's all I know for now. We're waiting for DNA confirmation, but that could take a little while since he's deployed. My contact says we can make contact when he returns to base."

"Do we know when that will be?"

"Sorry. That information is classified. My contact had no idea. My guess is a couple of days to a week at the most."

Rebecca threw her arms around Dylan's neck. "I don't know how to thank you. All of you."

"Us finally helping you has been a long time coming," Dylan said, hugging her back.

Maribel ran up with a big pink cloud-like puff on a stick. "Da-da!"

Rebecca took a step back and laughed as the little girl plowed into her father's legs with her cotton candy. He picked her up, not paying any mind to the pink splotches left on his jeans. Brody was right. Seeing Dylan with his daughter, the tenderness in his eyes, made her believe people could change for the better. She'd always loved her friend, but he was the last person she'd expected to see with a baby on his arm. "Seeing you with your daughter makes me think about life a little differently."

Dylan smiled one of those wide and genuine smiles. "Guess I never knew real love before."

Rebecca had. "You hold on tight to it."

"Yes, ma'am."

The little girl wiggled out of his arms and squealed as she ran through her dad's legs.

Brody and the others formed a protective circle around Maribel. He pulled Rebecca closer as his gaze surveyed the area. He had to know what she was thinking...*he's still out there.*

Chapter Fifteen

"We need to find Lester. Maybe we can pin him down for information about Kramer's whereabouts," Brody said, his frustration outlined in his sharp sigh. "He might know where his aunt lives and I have a feeling Lester didn't tell us everything."

"All I keep wondering is if his aunt lied to authorities before."

Brody's lips thinned. "I want to know why she would do that."

"It's a good deception. Places him away from the scene, gives him an alibi, and he gets free rein. Heck, he could've given her something to knock her out without her even knowing. I wouldn't put anything past a man like that."

Brody stopped suddenly. "That's him. That's Lester right there."

"The guy with the white streak in his hair?"

"Yes. Come on." Brody clasped her hand tighter, as though he knew she needed the extra support. Every step closer to finding Kramer tightened the coil in her stomach. How could the man who'd taken away her brother and ripped her family apart so easily slip through the system?

She wasn't crazy and she was so close to being able to prove it. The man who'd haunted her for fifteen years was real and he was right there in Mason Ridge. "Kramer was ruled out as a suspect too easily back then. We have to find that bastard and bring him to justice." Dare she hope they would find Jason? That Shane seemed to be alive and well was an encouraging sign. Rebecca said a prayer that the little boy was out there, somewhere close by, safe. She tried not to think about the fact that he'd missed a birthday with his family, or how many her brother had. A thought struck her. "I must've gotten too close when I found Shane—Randy online. That's why Kramer came back for me."

"Makes me think he won't leave until he finishes the job," Brody said. "We can't risk it, though. If he figures out we're this close, he could disappear."

Brody touched Lester's shoulder. The guy spun around a little too quickly, his eyes wild.

"Sorry, it's just me," Brody said.

Relief washed over Lester's features, but he tried to play it off. "No problem. We're all a little jumpy with this being the last night. So far, so good, though."

"This is my friend Rebecca," Brody said, introducing her.

After they'd shaken hands, he continued. "Thomas Kramer abducted her and her brother fifteen years ago. She got away, but they never found Shane."

Was Brody intentionally putting names and faces to the story? Lester's expression softened.

"I wish I could help you out, man. No one knows where he is."

"So you're saying that you haven't seen him at all?" Brody pressed.

Lester's gaze moved from Rebecca back to Brody. "Not me personally. One of the guys believes he did."

"Here?"

"Yeah. Earlier, though. I've been watching out ever since," Lester continued. "We put extra eyes on the campsite, too."

"That's smart. Just in case."

"Sorry to hear about your family," Lester said to Rebecca.

"My mom took things really hard. She never recovered." It was true. Rebecca also wanted to play the sympathy card in case this guy was holding back information.

"Kramer's aunt lied for him. Do you have any idea where she lives?" Brody kept pushing.

"I have a kid of my own, a little girl. I can't imagine." Lester paused. "His aunt Sally doesn't live far from here. She's in Brighton. It's why we're extra careful here and in Sunnyvale."

"You must've heard what happened last year," Brody said, glancing at Rebecca.

She made the connection, too. Randy Harper was from Brighton.

Lester nodded.

"Did you know Kramer very well?" Rebecca asked.

"We thought we did. Apparently not."

"According to the police report, he had a son who died," Brody said.

"We didn't know until years later about that. Way after the fact. It all started to make sense then."

"When exactly did you figure this out?" Brody asked.

Lester shrugged. "Not sure exactly. Heard it through the grapevine and couldn't be too sure of the source."

"And you didn't think to go to the police with it?" Rebecca fired back.

"No," he said with a look of apology. "We thought it

was all hearsay. Plus, if we don't run a tight ship then we don't get invited to places. None of us wanted to be associated with a person who abducts children. We couldn't afford to have that hanging over our festival. None of us would have a job."

"Even so, why didn't anyone come forward?" Rebecca asked. "That kind of information is pretty damning, don't you think?"

"We didn't know for sure it was him. Besides, we believed that he was caring for his aunt."

"Didn't you suspect anything when he suddenly showed up with a kid on the road?" Rebecca asked, mustering the kindest voice she could under the circumstances. The coil was tightening and it was becoming unbearable.

"That's the thing, he didn't. Not for a few years, anyway, and we didn't put it together back then. All of a sudden he would talk about his kid going to school, or playing some kind of sport. We figured we just didn't know him well enough to get personal before," Lester said.

"If he didn't take the kid on the road, then where'd he keep him?" Brody asked the question that was on Rebecca's mind.

"Must've been with his aunt Sally," Lester said. "I actually know her address. It's where we used to send his checks."

He pulled up her name on his contacts list from his phone.

Brody entered the information into his cell, and then thanked Lester as he and Rebecca made a run for the truck.

"Now that we have her address, we need to pay her a visit," he said.

"Do you think it's best to investigate without involving the sheriff?" Rebecca asked.

"Even if I trusted his judgment—and I'm not saying I do—the sheriff has to work within the law. We don't. And I have every intention of using whatever means necessary to make her talk. If that's where Kramer took Shane, then it stands to reason he'd take Jason there, too."

"You think we'll find Kramer there?"

"It's possible. If not, we might find a clue as to where he's hiding. All we need is a receipt or motel bill."

She didn't want to think about how relieved she was that the bogeyman who'd haunted her for a decade and a half had a face and a name. No longer was he a larger-than-life figure in a young girl's imagination. He was flesh and blood. Evil, but a man, nonetheless. And men could be taken down.

She glanced up and was startled to realize Brody was watching her as they ran. No doubt, her concern played out on her features.

"I know what you're thinking and we'll get him." Brody's words were spoken with a silent promise as they made it to the truck.

"We find him, we might find out what exactly happened to Shane. I have to think Kramer didn't do anything to hurt my brother, not now that I know he's grown and in the military. Plus, he seems to be taking these boys in an attempt to replace the son he lost."

She paused, trying to let that sink in.

"It makes sense. We don't have the details yet but it wouldn't surprise me to learn that he cared for Shane in the way he wished he could've for his own son."

"I hope DNA confirms that it is Shane for more than selfish reasons. I'd like to give that to my mom. She's been holding on so long. I want her to know what happened to her son, that he's alive." Tears welled in Rebecca's eyes. One broke free and spilled down her cheek. "I need so badly to tell her we found him, but I want to wait until we're one hundred percent sure. Otherwise, we'd break her heart again and she can't take that."

"Shane's alive. Believe it. And we'll get confirmation soon enough."

Brody climbed into the driver's seat and programmed his GPS with the address of Kramer's aunt.

"There isn't a day that goes by that I don't wish he'd kept me and set Shane free." More tears fell as she buckled her seat belt. She needed to tell Brody everything she remembered, to let it go. "We were so scared, but somehow I figured out that my bindings were loose. Shane was upset, crying, so Kramer was in a hurry when he put me back into my shed and he didn't tie me securely. It took me a minute to realize what had happened. He'd taken Shane to another building to calm him. It was dark outside and I remember my legs giving out as soon as I left the shed. I went looking for Shane. I thought if I could get to him, then maybe we could both get away. I was in shock. I couldn't believe I was free." She paused to stop the sobs. "When I couldn't find him, I thought if I could get away and go get help that we'd get back in time."

A few more tears flooded her eyes. She didn't realize she'd been squeezing her hands together until her fingers hurt.

"It's okay. You don't have to talk about this now," Brody soothed, guiding the truck onto the main road.

"I need to do this, Brody. I've been holding it in far too long. It feels good to finally let it out, to really breathe."

"Take it slow. Stop if you need to." He kept his steady gaze on the road in front of them.

"I got lost in the woods. I remember wandering around, afraid to make noise, stop or sleep. By the time they found me, I was dehydrated and delirious. The sheds had been cleared. Everything had been moved. Shane was gone. The monster who took my brother had disappeared." Sobs racked her, so she didn't fight them.

Saying the words made everything real. Being with Brody was different. He made it safe to open up those old wounds. He made her want to let go of the pain and finally talk about it.

She needed to hold on to the feeling while it lasted because as soon as this case was over, he'd be out of her life again. When she could return Shane to her mother, Rebecca would move away from this town and start a new life for herself.

Talking about the past was the first step toward letting it go.

Brody reached out to her with his free hand, patting hers but saying nothing. His touch was more reassuring than any words ever could be. His hand quickly returned to the wheel.

"And you already know we never found out exactly what happened to my brother until now. He was declared dead ten years ago but it felt so hollow. There was no body. No memorial service. Even after the declaration, my mom refused to accept it. She kept vigil. She talked about him like he'd walk through that door any minute and surprise us all. She made a birthday cake for him every year and brought out old photos."

More sobs came.

Brody just sat there, silently reassuring her.

"For years after she'd see him places—on the playground, driving away in the backseat of cars at the gas station, on a school bus. With every anniversary of his disappearance, those news articles would run, and she'd relive what had happened all over again. And yet, she never gave up hope of finding him. Now, he's alive and she deserves to know what happened to her son."

SITTING THERE, listening to Rebecca as she told her story, without being able to take away her pain or make the jerk who'd hurt her pay for his sin, was a knife stab to Brody's chest. Justice was coming, though. Even if this lead didn't pan out, Brody would find a way.

Hearing the words, the raw pain, seeing how Rebecca kept the weight of the world on her shoulders frustrated him to no end. He'd told her before but it was worth repeating. "None of this was ever your fault."

"I know."

"You were just a kid. We were just kids. You did the best you could to survive. That's all any of us can do."

She mumbled something else in agreement and he had to grip the wheel from wanting to reach out and touch her again. He was on a slippery slope with Rebecca, sliding downhill fast. There were no branches to grab on to, nothing to save him. His heart was falling down that sinkhole called love and nothing inside him could gain purchase to stop it on the way down.

They'd driven straight for an hour and a half when the GPS indicated they were getting close to their destination.

Brody slowed the vehicle when he entered the cul-de-sac. He parked two houses down as he watched a tall, thin man exit the ranch-style house.

Kramer?

Rebecca reached for Brody's hand and then squeezed.

The man took the driver's seat of a green sedan.

He was too far away to be able to tell for certain that it was Kramer.

Until the sedan slowed as it neared them and the driver saw Rebecca.

His expression said everything they needed to know. And then he accelerated, his tires squealing as they struggled to gain traction.

"It's him," Rebecca said, her voice no longer shaky with fear. "I saw his face."

Pride filled Brody as he banked a U-turn in the cul-de-sac and sped to Kramer's bumper.

Dark eyes stared at them from the rearview mirror.

"He makes it onto the highway and there's a good chance we'll lose him," Brody said. "Make sure your seat belt is secure."

"Catch him, Brody."

Kramer turned onto a farm road.

Brody maintained a safe distance without allowing Kramer too much leeway.

A few turns and they were following him onto a gravel road.

"He knows this area," Brody said. And Kramer was using it to his advantage as he maintained break-neck speed.

Brody's truck was heavier. He floored the gas pedal, trying to keep up.

Kramer must've panicked because his car veered left and then right. He cut through a corn field and then circled around toward the street they'd been on before.

Any number of innocent people could get hurt if Kramer was allowed to get back on a main road.

Brody gunned the engine, pulling beside Kramer, trying to force him off the road.

In response, Kramer drove his speed up past the
hundred-mile-an-hour mark.

The two-lane road was empty, save for Brody and
Kramer. That could change any second. Brody had to
decide if he should keep pushing the limit, or drop back
and follow. But then what? Allow this man to get away?
To reach the highway?

Brody gunned the engine, keeping pace with the sedan,
and then nudged the wheel right.

Kramer twisted his, jerking the vehicle away from
Brody a second before their side panels collided. Then,
Kramer overcorrected and his vehicle flew out of con-
trol. He sideswiped a tree and was sent into a death spin.

Another tree brought a sudden stop to the deadly roll-
over. The sound was deafening. The blaze ignited in-
stantaneously.

By then, Brody's truck was at a complete stop.

"Stay here," he said to Rebecca, who was already barreling toward the inferno.

She kept going.

All he could do at that point was try to catch up with
her.

The blast that came next caused them both to freeze.

Brody reached for Rebecca's hand. She spun around
and buried her face in his chest as they both fell to the
ground.

"It's over," she said, tears streaking her cheeks. "It's
finally over."

They stayed long enough to give statements to law enforcement and learn that an officer had been sent to the
aunt's house. No one was said to be home.

Once in the truck, Rebecca put her hand on Brody's arm as he cranked the engine.

"Can we go there?" she asked. "I need to see for my-self that Jason isn't there."

Brody nodded.

Twenty minutes later, he pulled into the familiar cul-de-sac.

Rebecca made it to the door first and knocked. Lights were out and everything was completely quiet. It didn't appear that anyone was home, just as the officer had re-ported.

"We can ask the neighbors who lives here. Maybe one of them will know something," Brody offered.

"That's a good idea actually. Surely, someone has seen something," she said, spinning around and heading toward the opposite house.

A middle-aged woman answered on the second round of knocking. Rebecca introduced herself and Brody. He hung back a little so as not to intimidate the woman.

"We're sorry to bother you, but we're trying to reach our friend Thomas Kramer. Is this still his address?" Rebecca pointed to the house in question.

The woman gave an odd look. "Do you mean Thomas Harper?"

Harper? Brody made the connection to Randy's last name.

Rebecca must have, too, based on the way her shoul-ders stiffened.

"Right, sorry. Having one of those days," Rebecca hedged, recovering her earlier demeanor.

"I'm Patricia and yes, that's his house," she confirmed. "Doesn't look like anyone's home. He travels most of the time for work. His little boy comes to visit sometimes."

"And his aunt?" Rebecca asked.

"Never saw a woman around." She shrugged. She had a solemn look on her face, completely unaware that her neighbor was a monster.

"How long have you lived here?" Brody asked.

"We moved in a couple of years ago," Patricia responded.

Brody wondered if the aunt was still alive. He gripped his phone in one hand and gently squeezed Rebecca's with the other as he thanked Patricia and told her to have a good night.

On closer appraisal of the house, a few of the side windows were boarded. The front room had a window AC unit. The door would be easy to breach. "His aunt might live somewhere else," he said. "She could be nearby. I'm guessing she keeps Jason when Kramer is on the road."

"I can't leave until I know for sure," Rebecca said.

"I know." Brody took that moment to kick the door. It flew open.

Stepping inside, he called for Jason.

There was no response.

It was dark and Brody had no idea what waited inside.

He clicked on a light. The room looked like something out of an episode of *Hoarders*. Stacks of papers and magazines were everywhere. Old pizza boxes and fast-food bags were piled on the coffee table.

Brody caught movement out of the corner of his eye, so he tracked it to the kitchen. "Jason. We're here to help. Your mommy and daddy are looking for you."

A whimper sounded from inside the pantry.

Opening the door slowly, Brody repeated the boy's name.

As light filled the little room, he saw the boy huddled

in the corner. His clothes were dirty and he was frightened. "It's okay, Jason. Take my hand."

The little boy started crying harder.

Rebecca dropped down to her knees. "Hey, Jason. My name is Rebecca and I'm here to take you home. I know a very bad man took you away from your family. He did the same thing to my little brother. It's going to be okay. I know you're scared. But you didn't do anything wrong."

In one swift movement the boy sprang into her open arms, buried his face and cried.

She soothed him, stroking his hair, and when she smiled up at Brody there was a deep sense of peace in her features.

"I'll call his parents first and then the police," he said.

She nodded, moving carefully as if trying not to disturb the boy clinging to her. "Have his parents meet us here. I want to stay until they arrive."

"Absolutely." Brody wouldn't have it any other way.

The Glenns made record time.

As soon as the little boy heard his mother's voice, he broke into a full run toward her. Brody watched Rebecca, witnessed the emotions playing out on her face as each parent thanked her and gave her a hug.

Brody stood back a little, taking it all in. The thought struck him that he'd believed Rebecca to be disloyal. What an idiot he'd been. She was the most loyal sister and advocate that anyone could hope to have in their corner.

As soon as the family walked away, Brody hauled her close to him.

"It all makes sense now," she said, looking into his eyes. "The timing of why Kramer attacked the other morning. He was getting desperate because he must've known I'd found Shane."

"You threatened to expose his lies and uncover the truth. He couldn't have that happen. His life would've been over."

She nodded.

"Are you ready to get out of here?" he asked.

"Yes. Get me away from this."

Brody didn't let go of her hand as they walked away from the house.

She glanced toward the house one more time. "He can't hurt anyone else, Brody. It's over."

THE RIDE BACK to town seemed to zoom by even though neither said much. Brody didn't mind. Silence was comforting as she sat in the middle seat, snuggled next to him, and there was something very right in the world.

Rebecca. *His Rebecca.*

There was a fork in the road ahead. Go left and he'd be taking Rebecca back to her bungalow. Make a right and he'd be heading to his ranch.

The road was split, but his heart knew exactly what it wanted, *if* she wanted him.

He stopped the truck in the middle of the farm road, put on his emergency flashers and opened his door. "Will you step outside with me?"

Surprise was written all over her face, but she did as he said. "Is it safe?"

"Should be at this hour." It was just past midnight. A new day had dawned. Could they make a fresh start?

He met her at the front of the truck, the headlights lighting a path, his heart pounding against his chest. "Rebecca, we can't change the past."

She dropped her gaze to the ground. "I know. And you don't have to say anything, because I already know how you feel."

"Do you?" He lifted her chin until her eyes met his, those intense honey browns vulnerable. "Because I don't think you do. As much as I loved you, I needed to grow up. I had too many wounds from the past, from my mother."

"I'm so sorry about the past, Brody, but I can't change it."

"I wouldn't want you to. We let go of what we had in high school and maybe that was a good thing. Life is crazy and it's uncertain. I'm only sure of about one thing. I love you."

Her eyes sparkled as soon as she heard the words. "I love you, Brody Fields. Always have and I always will. It's only ever been you. But you need more than my words."

He placed his hands around her neck and guided her lips to his, to home. "You're all I need, Rebecca. You're enough."

She kissed him slowly, sweetly; that shy smile had returned.

"I just have one question," he said.

"Which is?"

Right there in the middle of the road, he bent down on one knee, preparing to ask the woman he loved to marry him.

He didn't touch ground before she'd dropped into his arms and said the one word he needed to hear before he had a chance to ask.

"Yes," she said. "I'll be your wife."

Scooping her up, taking her to the passenger side, he

asked the other question on his mind. "You belong at the ranch with me. Are you ready to come home?"

Tears streamed down her beautiful face as she said, "You're home to me, Brody. I'm already there."

Epilogue

"Whatever will I do with one of those things?" Her mother's face screwed up as she motioned toward the laptop Rebecca was setting up on the side table next to her bed. Beside it, she placed Shane's Spider-Man watch.

"Believe me when I say that you're going to want to keep this close," Rebecca said, motioning toward the laptop.

"Tell her I don't know how to use it," Mother said to Brody. Her gaze stopped on the keepsake.

He smiled and his clear blue eyes sparkled. "Trust her. She knows what she's doing."

The past few weeks had been good to her mother after hearing news of Thomas Kramer's death and his aunt's arrest. Her mother had started leaving her room to play chess every afternoon and stopped resisting physical therapy. Every day she was getting stronger and the doctor was hopeful, especially following the initial results of how well her body was adjusting to the new medication.

Rebecca hadn't told her about all the events that had transpired. She'd been waiting for the right moment to talk about Shane. And this was it.

"I'd rather help make wedding plans than dicker around with one of those," Mother protested. Again.

"Just a second." Rebecca pulled up the program she'd installed to allow an overseas face-to-face chat. "There's someone who wants to talk to you."

"What's wrong with the phone? I know mine still has a cord, but people do use it from time to time."

"Nothing. But this call can't be made using one of those." Rebecca checked the screen, her heart thumping in her throat. "Are you there?"

Static and blur were all she had.

Then, the screen cleared up and she saw his face. It was Shane, her baby brother. She'd found him—tests had confirmed it—and she was about to share him with her mother.

Rebecca shifted the laptop so her mother could see. "Mother, it's Shane. He's alive. Your son is alive. And he has something he wants to say to you."

"I heard what happened. How you never gave up on me. I love you, Mom." He looked good, strong.

Her mother clasped her hands together and tears streamed down her face as disbelief transformed into joy. "How could I? You're my baby boy. I love you."

"There's so much I want to know, but I only have a few minutes to talk," Shane said. He had that proud Hughes chin and determined gaze.

"It's okay, son. We have the rest of our lives to get to know each other again." And from the looks of her, her mother planned to stick around to enjoy every moment.

* * * * *

"Do you think he could have been the one—" her throat moved as she swallowed convulsively, probably choking on nerves or fear **"—that put me in the trunk?"**

Dalton reached for her, sliding his arm around her shoulders to offer her comfort. She trembled against him, and he tightened his embrace. "Of course not," he said. "I wouldn't have brought you along if I thought he could be the one who had hurt you."

She had thought that all this time and had been willing to confront her attacker? He'd known she was strong, but her fearlessness overwhelmed him.

Instead of cowering, she opened her door and stepped out to confront her fear or her elusive memories. Dalton jumped out the driver's-side door and hurried around to her side of the car. They hadn't been followed. But if the killer had figured out that they might come back here…

He didn't want her far from his side in the dimly lit parking garage. He didn't want to lose her.

AGENT TO
THE RESCUE

BY
LISA CHILDS

Published in Great Britain 2015
by Mills & Boon, an imprint of Harlequin (UK) Limited,
Eton House, 18-24 Paradise Road, Richmond, Surrey, TW9 1SR

© 2015 Lisa Childs

ISBN: 978-0-263-25318-4

46-0915

Harlequin (UK) Limited's policy is to use papers that are natural, renewable and recyclable products and made from wood grown in sustainable forests. The logging and manufacturing processes conform to the legal environmental regulations of the country of origin.

Printed and bound in Spain
by CPI, Barcelona

Lisa Childs writes paranormal and contemporary romance for Mills & Boon. She lives on thirty acres in Michigan with her two daughters, a talkative Siamese and a long-haired Chihuahua who thinks she's a rottweiler. Lisa loves hearing from readers, who can contact her through her website, www.lisachilds.com, or snail-mail address, PO Box 139, Marne, MI 49435, USA.

With great pride and appreciation for my daughters, Ashley & Chloe Theeuwes—for being such strong, smart young women!

Chapter One

The noose tightening around his neck, Dalton Reyes struggled to swallow even his own saliva. His mouth was dry, though, because fear and nerves overwhelmed him. He tugged at the too-tight bow tie and thanked God he wasn't the one getting married right now.

He couldn't imagine promising to love one woman for the rest of his life and then to spend the rest of his life trying to make that one woman happy. Even though he didn't want that for himself, Dalton stood at Ash Stryker's side as the FBI special agent vowed just that to Claire Molenski.

Ash turned and looked at him, his blue eyes narrowed in a warning glare. Realizing he'd missed his cue, Dalton hurriedly reached into his pocket for the ring. Why the hell had he wanted to be the best man? Wearing the monkey suit was bad enough, but having to keep track of the damn ring, too...

It was too much. He would rather have mobsters shooting at him than this pressure of the whole church watching him. At least the church was small. But it was hot and stuffy, too. Sweat beaded on his lip, but then his fingers encountered the band. And he pulled out the delicate gold ring. It was tiny—just like the bride.

The first time he had met Claire Molenski, he'd thought the little blonde was hot. But she looked like something else in that white gown—like an angel. Dalton had always preferred bad girls, the ones who wore too much makeup and too-little leather skirts.

As soon as the ceremony was over, he rushed outside and gulped some air.

"You'd think you were the groom," a man teased him from the shadows of a huge oak. "With as much as you were sweating up there…"

"That'll never happen," Dalton replied with the confidence of a man who had never been in love and never intended to take that fall. "I won't ever be anyone's groom."

Finally the man stepped from the shadows. He'd beaten Dalton outside, so he must have been there before the ceremony had even ended. Apparently, though, he had been inside the church long enough to see Dalton sweating at the altar. Since he'd left early, he didn't seem to like weddings any more than Dalton did.

Then Dalton recognized him and realized why. "You're Jared Bell…"

The man was a legendary FBI profiler. Recruited out of college into the Bureau, he already had a long and illustrious career for his young age. But he was almost more legendary for the serial killer he hadn't caught than for all those that he had. The sick bastard who'd eluded him had had a thing for killing brides.…

It probably hadn't been easy for him to see Claire in that white dress and not imagine all those other brides who hadn't lived long enough to wed their grooms. All those victims…

Jared Bell extended his hand to Dalton. "And you're Agent Reyes."

He should have been flattered that the profiler knew him. But then Dalton Reyes wasn't so much legendary as notorious—for growing up in a gang but then leaving the streets to become a cop and then an FBI special agent assigned to the organized crime division.

"Nice to meet you," he said. With a glance back at the church, he asked, "I take it you know Ash…"

The grinning groom stood on the stairs of the stuffy little chapel with his smiling bride clasped tightly against his side. Ash Stryker couldn't take his hands off the petite blonde, but Dalton didn't blame him.

Bell nodded. "Yes, I know Ash. Not as well as you do, apparently, since you were his best man."

Reyes grinned at the surprise in the other man's voice. "You thought it would be Blaine Campbell?"

Bell nodded again. "Stryker and Campbell were marines together."

The two marines had known each other longer than Dalton had known either of them. So he was pretty sure that Blaine Campbell had been Ash's first choice, but somehow *he* had wound up with the honor. Ash and Claire had told him it was because they probably wouldn't have made it to the altar without him. A lot of people had recently been trying really hard to kill them. He had helped out, but he'd only been doing his job.

A job he loved. He still couldn't believe that Ash was cutting back—no longer going undercover. Dalton shook his head and sighed. He had wanted to stand up as best man for Ash, but he didn't agree with him.

His cell rang, saving him from making a reply to Jared Bell. He fished his phone from the pocket of his black tuxedo jacket.

"Good thing it didn't ring in the church," Bell remarked drily.

Dalton nodded in agreement. He probably would have been fired on the spot from his position as best man. He glanced at the screen of the cell phone. Why would the local police-post Dispatch be calling him?

"I have to take this," he said "But I hope we get a chance to talk some more at the reception."

Bell sighed. He probably thought Dalton wanted to talk about what everybody always wanted to talk about—that case that had never been solved.

Dalton clicked on his phone. "Agent Reyes here."

"This is Michigan state trooper Littlefield," a male voice identified himself. "I heard you might be in my area for a wedding."

Littlefield had helped Campbell, Ash and Reyes apprehend some bank robbery suspects at a cottage in a wooded area nearby this chapel. It was how Ash had heard about the wedding venue. And Littlefield must have heard about the wedding because he'd been invited.

"I'm in your neck of the woods," Dalton admitted. "Why aren't you at the wedding?"

"I'm working," Littlefield said. "I couldn't get off duty. I had Dispatch patch me through to your cell. Are you working?"

Harder than he'd thought he would have to as best man. "Not at the moment…"

"What I mean is," the trooper clarified, "are you still working that car theft ring?"

It seemed as if he was always working a car theft ring. He would no sooner shut down one operation before another would spring up. Sometimes he went undercover himself; sometimes he used informants, but he hadn't failed yet to solve a case. This case was giving him trouble, though—probably because the operation was a lot more widespread than he'd originally anticipated.

"Yeah, I'm still working it." He had recently put out a

bulletin to state police departments and sheriffs' offices
to keep an eye out for any suspicious vehicles.

"I just passed a strange Mercedes heading down a
dirt road," Littlefield shared, his voice full of suspicion.
"It looked vintage."

A vintage Mercedes on a dirt road? It was unlikely
that the car owner would have risked the paint or the
suspension of the luxury vehicle.

"Where are you?" Reyes asked. "And how do I get
there?"

"Aren't you at a wedding?"

Ash would understand. Maybe.

Dalton had been chasing these car thieves for a while.
But he hadn't caught them—probably because their chop
shop was off some dirt road in some obscure wooded
area.

Like here...

He tugged his bow tie loose as he headed for his
SUV. With its power-charged engine, he should be able
to catch up to that Mercedes in no time.

THE BRONZE-COLORED MERCEDES fishtailed along the
gravel road, kicking up a cloud of dust, as Dalton pursued it. He had caught up to it in less time than he'd anticipated. Now his anticipation grew. If he could follow
it back to the chop shop...

But the driver must have spotted Littlefield's patrol
car following at a discreet distance. And the Mercedes
had sped up to lose the trooper. The Bureau SUV was
more powerful, though, and had easily passed the patrol
car. Dalton had caught sight of the Mercedes, but had
the driver caught sight of him yet?

Could he see the black SUV through the cloud of dust
flying up behind his spinning tires?

Even if he hadn't seen him, the driver wasn't likely to go back to the chop shop now. He was more likely to try to dump the car since a trooper had seen it. Littlefield hadn't gotten close enough to read the plate, though.

Dalton was getting close enough, but too much dirt obscured the numbers and letters. Actually, he couldn't even tell if there was a plate on the car at all. Then the Mercedes accelerated again. The driver must have seen him.

Dalton pressed on his gas pedal, revving the engine. But his tires slid on the loose gravel. The road wasn't driven that often, so it wasn't well maintained. There were deep ruts, and the shoulders of the road had washed out into water-filled gullies on either side. If he lost control, he might wind up in one of those gullies. So he eased off the gas slightly and regained control.

A city kid born and raised, Dalton wasn't used to driving on dirt roads. The driver of the Mercedes had no such problem. Maybe he had grown up around this area, because the car disappeared around a sharp curve in the road.

Dalton cursed. He had been so close. He couldn't lose him now. He sped up and fishtailed around the curve, nearly losing control. The SUV took the corner on two wheels. Worried that he was going to roll the vehicle, he cursed some more. Then the tires dropped back down and the SUV skidded across the road—toward one of those gullies.

He braked hard and gritted his teeth to hold in more curses as the SUV continued its skid. He grasped the wheel hard and steered away from the ditch. Finally he regained control only to fight for it again, around the next curve. He skidded and nearly collided with the rear bumper of the Mercedes; it was the only part of the luxury vehicle that wasn't in the ditch.

Maybe its driver hadn't been as familiar with the roads as Dalton had thought—since he'd gone off in the gully himself. The tires of the SUV squealed as he braked hard again. He shoved the gearshift into Park and hopped out of the driver's side. His weapon drawn from beneath his tuxedo jacket, he slowly approached the vintage Mercedes.

Its engine was still running, smoke trailing up from beneath its crumpled hood. The water in the gully sizzled from the heat of it. The Mercedes wasn't going anywhere now. But the driver was gone—probably out the open passenger's window.

Dalton lifted his gun toward the woods on that side of the road. The driver had disappeared into them. But he could be close, just hiding behind a tree. Or he could be following a trail through those woods to that chop shop Dalton was determined to find. Since he was a city kid, he would probably get lost. But he started down toward the ditch, anyway, to follow the driver into those woods.

Then the smooth soles of his once-shiny black dress shoes slipped on the loose gravel and the muddy bank. He started sliding toward the water—which he wouldn't have minded falling into if the damn tux wasn't an expensive rental. To steady himself, he grabbed at the Mercedes and braced his hand on the trunk. But then his hand slid the way his shoes had. He glanced down and figured out why when he saw the blood on his palm. It was also smeared beneath the dust across the trunk lid.

Dread tightened his stomach into a tight knot. Growing up where he had and working in the division he worked, he had already found more than his share of bodies in car trunks. But he suspected he was about to find another.

He had nothing on him to pry open the lid or to break the lock. So he took the easy way and kicked in the driver's window, which started an alarm blaring. Then he reached inside for the trunk-lid release button. Fortunately the car wasn't so vintage that it hadn't come equipped with some more up-to-date features. The button clicked, and the trunk lid flew up, waving like a flag in the woods.

It wasn't a surrender flag, though, because the driver had fled into the woods and apparently for a damn good reason, too. Even if the car wasn't stolen, he would have had some trouble explaining the body in the trunk.

Sun shone through the trees of the thick woods and glinted off that trunk lid. It was such a beautiful day for a wedding. Dalton should have stayed at the stuffy little church and celebrated with his deservedly happy friends. Instead, he had nearly wiped out on some back roads and probably stumbled upon a murder victim.

He drew in a deep breath of fresh air to brace himself for what he would find in the trunk. Then he walked around to the rear of the Mercedes.

White lace, stained with blood, spilled over the bumper. He forced himself to look inside the trunk. The woman's face was so pale but for the blood smeared on it. And her long hair, tangled around her head, was nearly as red as her blood.

He recognized the dress, since he had just seen a gown eerily similar to it. But that bride had been alive and happy. This bride was dead. He reached into the trunk to confirm it, his fingers sliding over her throat where her pulse would have been—had she had one any longer.

Something moved beneath his fingertips—in a faint

and weak rhythm. He looked down again just as her eye-lids fluttered open. Her eyes were a pale, almost silvery, gray, and they were wide with confusion and then fear.

She screamed and struck out, hitting and kicking at him, as she fought him for her life.

THE SCREAM STOPPED him cold, abruptly halting his head-long escape through the forest. He had heard that scream before—seconds before he'd thought he had killed the woman. Hell, he'd been certain he'd killed her.

How could she be alive?

It wasn't possible...

More important, it wasn't acceptable.

He had let the state trooper distract him. With his heart pounding in his chest with fear and nerves, he hadn't known how to react to that police car behind him. At first he'd driven normally, hoping that the trooper wouldn't notice the missing plate—hoping that he would give up following him for some more interesting radio call.

But the trooper must have called in someone else—some other agency—because then he'd noticed the black SUV. And his every instinct had screamed at him to drive as fast as he could—to outrun that vehicle.

Instead, he had let it run him off the road—into that damn ditch. He'd barely escaped the vehicle before the guy had run up to it.

In a tux...

What kind of government agent wore a tuxedo?

The kind that had happened into the wrong situation at the wrong time.

He had to go back. He couldn't leave the woman alive. And if he had to, he would kill the man along with her. And this time, he would make damn certain that she was really dead.

Chapter Two

"It's okay…" The man uttered the claim in a deep voice. "You're safe." But he held a gun in one hand while he grasped her wrists with the other.

His hands were so big that he easily clasped both her wrists in one, restraining her. So she kicked. Or at least she tried. But heavy fabric tangled around her legs, holding her down…inside the trunk of a car.

Fear overwhelmed her as she realized that she had been locked inside that trunk—until this man had opened the lid. She needed to get out; she needed to run. But her head throbbed. A blaring alarm intensified the pain, and her vision blurred as unconsciousness threatened to overwhelm her again. She could barely focus on the man.

He was so big and muscular that he towered over her. Thick dark hair framed a tanned face. And dark eyes stared down at her. He looked as shocked as she felt.

She struggled again, tugging on her wrists to free them from his grasp. But his hand held her. She fought to move her legs, but they were trapped under the weight of whatever she was wearing.

She glanced down, and all the white nearly blinded her. White lace. White silk. Except for the red spots, which dropped onto the fabric like rain. She was bleeding. Not only had she been locked inside the trunk of a car, she had been wounded.

How badly?

Panic pressed on her, constricting her lungs. But she gathered her strength, opened her mouth and screamed again. Her voice was weak, too, though, and only a soft cry emerged from her throat this time.

"You have no reason to be afraid anymore," the man told her. "You're safe now. You're safe."

Her vision cleared enough that she could see him more clearly. He wore a black jacket with a dark red rose pinned to one of the shiny silk lapels. His shirt was whiter than the dress she was wearing. A black bow tie hung loose around the collar of that shirt.

He was wearing a tuxedo and she was dressed in what had to be a wedding gown. What sick scenario did he have planned for her? Or had it already taken place?

She couldn't remember what had happened and how she had ended up in the trunk of a car. Since she couldn't change what had already happened, she concentrated instead on the present—on what was happening now and where she was. She peered around him—to the forest surrounding the vehicle that was upended in a ditch. He had brought her to the middle of nowhere.

And she could think of only one reason for that. To dispose of her body...

Because no one would ever find her out here. She had no idea where she was. There were so many trees overhead that she could barely see the sky through the canopy of thick branches. She had no idea which direction was which—even if she was strong enough to escape him. She already knew he was strong from his grip on her wrists; he was so tall and broad shouldered, too.

"Please," she murmured. "Please, don't hurt me…"

She shouldn't have wasted her breath. Uttering those words had cost her so much of what little was left of her strength, and she had no hope of appealing to his sense of humanity. She doubted he had one. He must have been the person who had put her in the trunk, who had hurt her.

He was standing over her, restraining her…and he had the gun. He had to be the one who'd…

But she couldn't remember. She couldn't remember what had happened. The pounding in her head increased as she struggled to summon memories.

But her mind was blank. Completely blank.

She didn't even know who she was….

THE MAN WAS totally focused on the woman—so much so that he would be easily overpowered. And the blaring car alarm would drown out the sound of his approach. Ready to attack, he moved forward, but then sunlight seeped through the thick branches of the trees overhanging the road and glinted off the metal of the weapon the man held.

Just as he'd suspected, this guy wasn't just some Good Samaritan who had happened along to rescue the woman. Despite the tuxedo he was wearing, he had to be some type of lawman. An armed lawman.

Frustration ate at him—joining the bitterness he had always felt for law enforcement. The gun would complicate things. But it wouldn't stop him.

He would enjoy killing the man, too—now that he knew he was in law enforcement. But he would have to act quickly, before any reinforcements arrived.

He had to act now. He had to make sure that the woman really died and the lawman died along with her.

THE PANIC ON the young woman's face struck Dalton like a blow. Those already enormous silvery-gray eyes had widened more with fear while her face had grown even paler.

Aware that he was scaring her, that he was intimidating her, he stepped back. But he was afraid that if he completely released her, she might injure herself as she tried to get away from him. So he continued to hold her wrists.

"Don't move," he cautioned her. As wounded as she was, she shouldn't risk causing more damage to her battered body.

But she ignored his advice and struggled even harder, thrashing about inside the trunk. Maybe she couldn't hear him over the blare of that damn car alarm. But like her, it was growing weaker—probably either as the battery ran down or was damaged from the water flooding the engine, which had already died.

Now he just had to make sure that the bride didn't.

"You're hurt," he told her—in case she hadn't noticed the blood that had stained her dress and made her long hair wet and sticky.

She had lost so much blood that some had even pooled in the trunk beneath her. She needed medical attention as soon as possible. Or he wasn't sure that she would survive.

"You need to hold still," he advised her, "until I get help for you."

But to get help, he would have to put away his gun and take out his cell. He glanced around to see if the driver of the Mercedes had returned. The towering trees cast shadows throughout the woods and onto the gravel road—making the time of day appear closer to night than midafternoon.

The driver could have circled back around—could even now be sneaking up behind them. Dalton peered around—over his shoulder and into the woods, checking for any movement. Sunlight glinted within the trees.

Off a gun?

Or maybe it was a beer can that some teenagers or a hunter had tossed into the woods.

Dalton had spent his life on the streets; he knew what dangers he would face there. He had no idea what lurked out here—where it was so remote. He couldn't see anyone, yet the skin tingled between his shoulder blades. He felt as though he was being watched. Maybe being out of his element was what made him so uneasy—made him reluctant to put away his weapon.

But Dalton had no choice. He had to get help for the battered bride. She had already lost so much blood— maybe too much to survive.

"You're going to be okay." Because he had told so many over the years, lies came easily to him now. But maybe he wasn't lying; he wasn't a doctor. He had no way of knowing how gravely she was injured, so maybe she would be okay. "But you need to calm down. You need to trust me."

Because of all those lies he'd told and all those old friends from the gang that he had betrayed and arrested, few people trusted him anymore. Certainly no one who knew him.

But he was a stranger to her. Maybe that was why she stopped struggling. Or maybe she was just too weak from all that blood loss.

So he released her wrists, then holstered his weapon

and pulled out his cell. But the phone screen blinked out a warning: no signal.

He cursed. He couldn't leave her here while he drove around until his phone had a signal again. She might not survive until he returned. Either her injury might claim her life or the man who'd put her in the trunk might return for her.

Dare Dalton try to move her? To carry her to his SUV and drive her to a hospital? Hell, he didn't even know where a hospital was in this area.

Maybe she wasn't as weak as he'd thought, though, because she drew in an unsteady breath and then tried again to climb out of the trunk. He put a hand on her shoulder to hold her still, though he probably hadn't had to bother. The weight of the blood-soaked dress was already holding down her body.

"You have to take it easy," he warned her. "You have a head injury." At least that looked to be where her blood was coming from. Had she been shot?

In his experience, most of the people he had found in trunks had been shot, execution-style, in the base of the skull. But all of those people had died. If she had a bullet in her head, and he moved her...

She would probably die, too. But if he didn't move her, she still might die. There was too much blood.

She lifted one of her hands and touched her head. Her beautiful face contorted with pain and she jerked her hand back. Staring down at her fingers, which were stained with her own blood, she gasped.

"Do you know what happened?" he asked. Maybe she could tell him if she'd been shot.

But from the dazed and glassy look in her pale gray eyes, she appeared to be in shock. Or maybe it was the injury that had her so groggy and weak.

"Noooo…" she murmured.

Wouldn't she remember being shot? He remembered every time that he had been shot.

"Maybe you were struck over the head," he suggested.

She could have a concussion—some blunt-force trauma that was making her bleed so much. Dalton had seen that kind of injury a lot, too, over the years.

Or she could have been shot from behind, so that she hadn't realized what was happening to her—until it was too late. Until the bullet had been fired into her head.

Gravel scattered across the road, small stones skittering past him and into the water in the gully. Then metal clicked as a gun cocked. And Dalton realized that the same thing had just happened to him. Someone had sneaked up behind him to take him by surprise.

The damn driver must have circled back around—returning to reclaim his victim. To make sure that she was dead and couldn't identify him.

Her eyes widened with shock and fear. Either she could see the man over his shoulder, or she must have heard the gun cocking, too.

Dalton shifted his body slightly, so that he stood between her and the danger. If the man wanted to kill her, he would have to kill Dalton first.

He reached for his holster again—for his gun. But he wouldn't be able to draw it fast enough to save himself from getting shot. But maybe he could get off a shot himself and save her.

Chapter Three

The man had drawn his gun again. But she wasn't afraid *of* him this time. She was afraid *for* him. A shadow had fallen across the road behind him. And that soft click of metal must have been another gun, already cocking…

The bullet would hit the man first—before it hit her. He had positioned himself so that it would. He had positioned himself to protect her.

Maybe he wasn't who or what she'd thought he was. Maybe he wasn't the person who had hurt her. Maybe he wasn't a monster. But how had he found her?

"Who are you?" she whispered. But she wasn't asking for just his name.

"FBI," he identified himself—not to her but to whoever had come up behind him. "Put down your weapon…"

A man uttered a ragged sigh of relief. "Agent Reyes, I couldn't tell if that was you or not…from behind… and in a tux…but of course you were at the wedding…" The man's sigh became a gasp as he peered around the FBI agent and saw her in the trunk. "Is that the bride?"

"No," the agent replied. "Not the bride from the wedding I was at anyway. I don't know who she is. I found her in the car we were pursuing."

Unlike the agent who wore a tuxedo, this man was wearing a vaguely familiar-looking uniform. It was tan and drab like the dust coating the car, but he had a badge pinned to his chest. He was also a law enforcement officer.

She breathed a slight sigh of relief. Maybe she had been rescued—if only she remembered from what…

"Where's the driver?" the state trooper asked. He was shorter and heavier than the agent—with no hair discernible beneath the cap of his hat.

The FBI agent gestured toward the woods. "He ran off before I could even get a look at him. And then I found her in the trunk. She needs medical help."

She heard the urgency in his voice and knew her situation was as critical as she feared it was.

"Does your phone or radio work?" the agent asked the officer. "I can't get a signal."

The other man grabbed at the collar of his shirt and pressed a button on the device attached to it. "We need an ambulance."

They didn't need the ambulance. *She* did. She had been badly injured. All the blood was hers. No wonder she felt so weak—too weak to even pull herself out of the trunk. Too weak to fight anymore.

"Help's coming," the man called Agent Reyes assured her.

He had already helped her—when he had stopped whoever had been driving the car and opened the trunk for her. She wanted to thank him, but she struggled for the words—for the strength to even move her lips.

"Shh," he said, as if he sensed her struggle. "You're going to get medical attention soon. The ambulance is on its way."

But she was afraid that it would be too late.

"Hang in there," he urged her.

She shook her head and dizziness overwhelmed her,

making her stomach pitch and pain reverberate in her head like a chime clanging against the insides of a bell.

"You're strong," he said. Instead of clasping her wrists, he took her hand and squeezed it reassuringly. "You must be strong, or you wouldn't still be alive. You're a fighter. You can hang in there."

She had suspected he was lying to her earlier—when he'd told her she would be okay and especially when he had urged her to trust him. Now she was certain that he was lying. She had never felt weaker than she did right now. At least she didn't think she had…

Memories still eluded her.

"What's your name?" he asked.

She blinked, trying to focus on his face again. He really was quite handsome—with that tanned skin, those dark eyes so heavily lashed and his thick, black hair. It was a little long—longer than she would have thought a government agent would be able to wear his hair.

"What's your name?" he asked again. Moments ago he'd shushed her when she'd tried to talk. Now he was getting insistent, as if he needed her name in case she didn't survive until the ambulance arrived.

She gathered the last of her strength and admitted in a raspy whisper, "I don't know…"

Her memories weren't just eluding her. They were completely gone, as if they had seeped out with her blood—leaving her mind entirely blank.

"I don't know…" she murmured again…just as oblivion returned to claim her.

"WHERE'S THAT DAMN AMBULANCE?" Dalton demanded to know. Maybe the trooper had called only minutes ago for help, but it felt like hours—with the young woman lying unconscious in the trunk of the car.

Dalton had pressed her veil onto the wound on the back of her head, trying to stem the bleeding. But the fabric was flimsy.

Trooper Littlefield pointed down the gravel road where he must have abandoned his squad car, since he'd come up behind Reyes on foot. "I can hear them coming now."

The faint whine of sirens reached his ears, too. And in the distance a cloud of dust rose up into the trees.

"Help's coming," he told the woman, hoping that she could hear him even though she was unconscious. "Stay with me. Help's coming."

Then he turned back toward Littlefield. The trooper was older than him—shorter and heavier. And he was sweating so badly that it streaked from his bald head down his neck to stain the collar of his tan shirt. He probably hadn't chosen to walk the rest of the way down the gravel road. Had he crashed? Or had the car just overheated from the chase?

"Can they get around your car?" he asked.

He nodded. "I parked it off to the side—" he gestured toward the FBI SUV "—like you did."

Dalton hadn't exactly parked there; he had just been fortunate enough to have ended up there instead of in the ditch like the Mercedes had.

"Why did you abandon your car?" Dalton asked.

The trooper pointed toward the Mercedes. "I heard the cars stop. I wasn't sure what the situation was…" He glanced at the woman in the trunk. "I didn't think it would be this, though."

Despite all those bodies Dalton had found in car trunks over the years, this wasn't the situation he had expected, either. It was just too ironic and coincidental since he'd just been at a wedding himself that he would find a bride locked inside a trunk. Then he remembered that conversation he'd had outside the church—the one with profiler Special Agent Jared Bell.

Could this bride have been the next intended victim of Bell's serial killer?

As far as he knew, the guy hadn't killed another woman for a couple of years. He wouldn't claim this victim, either—if Dalton could do anything about it.

Finally the sirens grew louder and lights flashed as the ambulance approached. "Help's here," he told her. "You're going to be okay."

Her lashes fluttered, and she peered at him through her barely opened lids. "Don't lie to me."

"Help really is here." And as he said it, paramedics rushed up to the car. He released the blood-soaked veil to one of them and then he tried to release her hand— that he hadn't even realized he still held—and step back out of their way.

But she clasped his hand tightly in hers. She was stronger than she thought—stronger even than he had thought. "Don't leave me," she implored him.

Recently another agent had nearly lost a witness at the hospital when bank robbery suspects had tried to abduct her right out of the ER. Dalton wasn't about to take that risk. This woman had already been through too much.

"I need to ride along," he told the paramedics. Then he told her, "I won't leave you."

Her eyes closed again. Somehow she trusted him— when she had no reason to trust him or anyone else after what had happened to her. What exactly had happened to her?

"Was she shot?" he asked the paramedic who eased the veil away from her head wound.

The young man shrugged. "I don't know. They'll get

a CT scan in the ER. So we need to get her to the hospital ASAP." He and another man snapped a collar around her neck and then lifted her onto a board that they carried up to the gurney they'd left on the road.

Dalton had to run along beside the stretcher they rolled along the gravel road to the ambulance. He hurried inside the rig just as they closed the doors and sped away. From their urgency, it was clear that her condition was every bit as critical as Dalton had feared it was.

"How far from the hospital are we?" he asked.

"Twenty minutes out," the driver replied.

He would bet every one of those minutes counted in her situation. The paramedic in the back had administered an IV and an oxygen mask. It was more than he had been able to offer her. But it wasn't enough. Not if there was a bullet in her head.

"What is her name?" the paramedic asked.

"She doesn't know," Dalton replied. "Could she have amnesia?"

"It's possible if she has a concussion," the paramedic replied. "But what is her name?"

"She couldn't tell me," he pointed out, "so I don't know."

"You're not her groom?"

A strange shiver rushed over him. "Of course not. I'm an FBI agent. I found her in the trunk of that car."

The paramedic glanced down at Dalton's tux and nodded, as if humoring him.

"I just came from a wedding," he explained his attire. "It wasn't mine."

It would never be his.

"I don't know who she is," he repeated. But maybe something had been left in the trunk of the car that would have revealed her identity. A purse. A wallet. A receipt. Or the registration for the car that might have been hers.

He should have stayed behind at the scene. He could have done more for her there than by playing nurse-maid in the back of the ambulance. And why would the man who'd put her in that trunk risk showing up at the hospital?

If the guy was smart, he was still running.

"What the hell…" the driver murmured from the front seat.

Dalton glanced up and peered out the windshield—at the police car barreling down the road toward them with lights flashing and sirens blaring.

"Does he want me to pull over?" the driver asked as he reached for the radio on the dash. "Why doesn't he tell me what he wants?"

Another shiver rushed over Dalton, this one so deep that it chilled his blood. They hadn't passed the trooper's abandoned vehicle. He had a bad feeling that it was that vehicle heading straight toward them now.

But it was not Trooper Littlefield driving it. It wasn't the bald man behind the vehicle. This person had a hat pulled low over his face. But that wasn't the reason he was driving straight toward them. He wanted to run them off the road; he wanted to reclaim the victim who had nearly escaped him.

The ambulance driver jerked the wheel and veered toward one of those deep ditches. At the last moment, he jerked the wheel back and kept the rig on the road, riding along the steep shoulder. "What the hell's that trooper doing?"

"It's not the trooper." It had to be the man who'd run from the Mercedes. He must have circled back around and found the trooper's abandoned vehicle. "And don't pull over…"

"But he's going to kill us!" the other paramedic exclaimed. "He's heading straight toward us!"

But the man couldn't have expected that an FBI agent was riding along in the rig. So Dalton had the element of surprise. He pulled his gun from his holster, leaned forward over the passenger's seat and pointed the barrel out the open passenger's window.

Maybe the man saw the gun, because he sped up as if trying to run them off the road before Dalton could fire a shot. Dust billowed up behind the trooper's car, forming a cloud thicker than fog. Dalton could barely see through it, but he fired his weapon. Again and again.

He couldn't tell if he struck the car, though—let alone the driver. And the vehicle kept coming toward them. Faster and faster.

The ambulance driver cursed.

"Keep going straight," Dalton advised him. The road was too narrow; the ditches too deep and the gravel too loose. "Don't swerve."

But his warning came too late.

The ambulance driver didn't have the nerves for the dangerous game of chicken. Cursing, he jerked the wheel, and the rig teetered on two wheels.

The paramedic in the back shouted in fear.

The driver couldn't regain control of the van and it flipped—over and over—hurtling Dalton over the seat and toward the windshield. If he went through it—if he lost consciousness—he risked losing the bride…

But then the accident would probably be enough to finish her off. She was already critically wounded. He held his breath and tried to brace himself.

But it was too late.

THE AMBULANCE LAY crumpled on its side in the ditch, but its lights flashed and sirens blared yet. With a gloved hand, he turned off the lights and sirens inside the state police cruiser. But he could hear an echo of the ambulance's sirens in the distance.

More emergency vehicles were on their way to the scene. Maybe the trooper had called for more help. Maybe the agent had managed to get a call out before the ambulance had crashed. The agent was inside that crashed vehicle. He'd seen him climb into the ambulance with the woman—determined to protect her.

The agent had even shot at him; the windshield of the police cruiser bore holes too close to where his head had been. He shuddered at how close those shots had come to hitting him. Even with both vehicles moving, the agent had nearly struck him. He was a damn good shot. A dangerous man.

Maybe that was why he hesitated before approaching that crumpled ambulance. He didn't know what he would find inside: dead bodies or a still-armed government agent.

The ambulance sirens grew weaker, while those sirens in the distance grew louder as those vehicles approached. He could hesitate no longer. He had to hurry. Before the other emergency personnel arrived, he had to make certain that both the woman and the lawman were dead.

HER HEART AND her head pounded with fear and pain. Strapped to the gurney, she had actually taken little impact from the crash. Since the gurney was anchored to the floor, she hadn't been thrown around like the others.

The blond-haired paramedic who'd been in the back with her had bounced around like a rag doll and then crumpled against the side of the ambulance where it had come to rest in the deep ditch next to the road.

She couldn't tell if the man was just unconscious.

Or…

A cry burned her throat, but she held it in—refusing to panic. Yet.

Strapped down and hanging on her side, she could only twist her neck to peer around the vehicle—to see what had happened to the others. To the FBI agent.

The driver was pinned beneath the steering wheel, so he remained in his seat. Like the other paramedic, he wasn't moving. How badly was he hurt?

They had come to help her. But now they needed help. Because of her?

Guilt struck her with all the force that the ambulance had struck the ditch. Could this be her fault?

Could she have done something to cause this destruction—this pain? How much destruction?

She craned her neck, but she couldn't see the agent. Had he catapulted out of the windshield? The glass was broken. But then, he might have shot it out. He had been shooting—trying to stop the other vehicle from running them off the road. According to the paramedics' comments, the other vehicle had been a police car.

The trooper's uniform had looked vaguely familiar to her. Had she seen him before? Was he the one who'd put her in the trunk?

Was there anyone she could trust? Special Agent Reyes had done his best to save her. But where was he now? Pinned beneath the vehicle when it had rolled?

She shuddered as she imagined the worst. And her head throbbed more with dull pain. The pounding wasn't just inside her head, though.

Someone was hammering on the back doors of the ambulance—trying to open them. She struggled against the straps, but they held her fast to the gurney. She couldn't move—she couldn't escape. She could only wait for whoever had run them off the road to finish her off.

Chapter Four

Water seeped through the tuxedo, chilling Dalton's skin. He awoke with a jerk—then grunted as his head slammed against metal. Stars danced behind his eyes as oblivion threatened to reclaim him. But then he heard the hammering and felt the force of it rocking the ambulance.

Fortunately he wasn't beneath the vehicle. Instead of going through the windshield, he had grabbed hold of the dash and had somehow wound up wedged beneath it—between the passenger's seat and the door. Water surged through that door from where the van lay on its side in the ditch. If he hadn't awakened, he may have drowned.

But now, as the doors creaked and finally gave, he still could die because he had no intention of letting anyone hurt the injured woman more than she had already been hurt. He fumbled around on the wet floor, looking for his gun. Finally his fingers grazed metal. He closed his hand around it, but the barrel was stuck—wedged between the seat and the crumpled passenger door.

As he tugged on the Glock, he lifted his head to assess the situation. The bride, strapped to the gurney, was suspended on her side. Her silvery-gray eyes were open and wide with fear. She knew she was trapped. Then she noticed him.

And he saw hope brighten her face, infusing her pallid skin with a hint of color. Of life…

She was okay now.

But he wasn't sure how much hope he offered her—when he couldn't get his damn gun loose. So he turned away from her to focus on those opening doors. And he released his breath in a ragged sigh of relief.

WHEN THOSE AMBULANCE doors jerked open, Dalton had been relieved to see—along with his friends Blaine and Ash—Jared Bell. Now he was worried rather than relieved. While the FBI profiler hadn't said much of anything in the hour since he had arrived at the accident scene, Dalton was pretty sure the man was going to try to snag his case and his witness.

As Dalton rushed into the hospital emergency room, he realized he was more concerned about losing the witness than the case. That concern worried him more. She was easy to find in the small rural hospital; two troopers stood outside the curtain where she was, while the blond FBI agent stood guard next to her bed.

"Is she okay?" he asked Blaine.

Dalton had managed to talk Ash into returning to his wedding, but that hadn't eased much of his guilt over disrupting the reception. Unfortunately, the other agents had heard the trooper's call for an ambulance and thought Dalton was the one needing medical attention. That was why they had all showed up when they had—at the perfect moment.

But none of them had caught the man who had driven the ambulance off the road. He had escaped them just as easily as he had escaped Dalton. And just like Dalton, no one had even gotten a glimpse of him.

In response to Dalton's question, Blaine shook his head. Dread had Dalton's stomach plummeting.

"Is she…?" He turned toward the bed where she was lying, her wedding gown replaced with a hospital gown. The blood washed away from her face, it was devoid of all color now. But her red hair was vibrant against the pillow and sheets. She couldn't be gone.

Wouldn't they have covered her face, her beautiful face, if she were dead?

"God, no, she's not," Blaine hastened to assure him. "But the doctors are concerned about her head injury."

"Why isn't she in surgery, then?" he asked.

He shouldn't have stayed behind at the accident scene with Agent Bell. He should have ridden in the second ambulance, which had arrived to replace the crashed one, with the victim and the injured paramedics. But because he had stayed behind, he had been able to point out things to Bell that the man might not have noticed on his own—like how both the Mercedes and the trooper's car had been hot-wired.

Had Bell's serial killer known how to do that?

But then, Dalton's car thieves had never taken a hostage before.

Whose case was this?

Her heavy lashes fluttered against her cheeks as she lifted her lids and stared at him. "You're back…" Her breath shuddered out with relief.

Relief eased the tightness in his chest. She wasn't dead…

"Where are these doctors?" he asked Blaine. But he didn't look around for the ER physicians; he couldn't pull his gaze from hers.

"She doesn't need surgery," Blaine said.

"But the head wound…" If her head was bandaged,

it must have been beneath her hair, because he couldn't
see any gauze or tape. "It isn't a GSW?"

Blaine replied, "She wasn't shot."

Dalton uttered a sigh of relief—which Bell echoed.
Until now, the profiler had barely paid any attention to
the victim. Of course, as a profiler, he was all about the
perp. Did he intend to link this case—and her—to his
serial killer?

"I have a concussion," she said. "The neuro specialist
said that's probably why I can't remember…"

"You can't remember?" Bell asked. "Anything…?"

She glanced at him but turned back to Dalton, as if
seeking assurance that she could trust the stranger. Earlier he had convinced her that she could trust Blaine.
Hell, Blaine Campbell was well-known for his protec-
tiveness. Dalton wouldn't have trusted her safety to anyone else—not with a man out there determined to kill
her.

Dalton hesitated only a moment before nodding that
she could trust Bell, too. The guy was legendary for his
intelligence and determination. Only one killer had escaped him in all the years he'd been a profiler.

"I don't remember anything," she said. "But him…"
She lifted her hand toward Dalton. "I just remember him
lifting the trunk lid…"

"Nothing else?" Bell asked. "You don't remember
anything that happened before that?"

She closed her eyes as if searching her mind for memories. Or maybe she was just exhausted.

"She's in no condition for an interrogation right now,"
he admonished Bell.

"The doctors said her concussion is serious," Blaine
added. "She lost a lot of blood from the head wound,
too, so she's really physically weak."

Her eyes opened again. "I am not weak."

"She's not," Dalton agreed. Just as he had told her earlier, he repeated, "She's very strong." She had survived two attempts on her life.

"I could handle an interrogation," she said. "I would love to answer your questions—all of your questions—if I had any answers. But I can't tell you anything about how I wound up in that trunk. I can't even tell you my name."

Tears glistened in her eyes, but she blinked furiously, fighting them back. He suspected they were tears of frustration. He couldn't imagine losing all of his memories—to the extent that he didn't even know his name. As he had when she'd been bleeding in the trunk, he reached out and clasped her hand. At that time he had been urging her to hold on to life; now he wanted her to hold on to him.

She clutched at his hand and squeezed. "Since you can't interrogate me, I'm going to interrogate all of you. I need answers. I need to know who I am and what happened to me."

He had been right about her. She was strong—hopefully strong enough to handle the truth, whatever it was.

"Does she have any other injuries?" he asked Blaine.

"I remember what the doctor told me," she informed him. "I just don't remember anything before you opened that trunk."

He didn't want to upset her by asking her how else she might have been injured, but it was important to know what kind of attacker they were dealing with. A sexual predator? Anger coursed through him. He wanted to find this guy. And he wanted to hurt him for hurting *her*.

"What are your other injuries?" Jared Bell asked the

question now, no doubt because he was trying to profile her attacker.

She shivered even though a few blankets covered her hospital gown. He squeezed her hand, offering comfort and reassurance, and she offered him a smile. God, she was beautiful—so beautiful that his breath stuck in his lungs for a moment.

"What you're thinking," she said, "it didn't happen." She shuddered now—in revulsion at the thought and in relief. "I have some bumps, bruises and scrapes—"

"In addition to the head injury and amnesia," Blaine finished for her.

"Amnesia," she bitterly repeated. "I need to know who I am. You're all in the FBI. You must know *something* about me."

"Contrary to public opinion," Blaine said, "we don't have files on everyone. So we don't know your identity. We don't know anything yet."

"We checked the missing person's report in the area," Agent Bell said. "No one's reported a bride missing."

She glanced at Blaine and then Jared Bell before focusing on him again. "None of you have any answers," she said with a ragged sigh of resignation and weariness. "You don't know who I am or why I was in the trunk of that car, either."

"We don't," Dalton admitted.

"So what do I call myself?" she asked. And now her voice sounded weak, thready, as exhaustion threatened to claim her.

"Jane Doe," Blaine suggested.

She wrinkled her nose in distaste. "That makes it sound like I didn't survive. Like I'm a dead body."

Dalton had another suggestion. But he didn't want to upset her. "We'll find out your real name," he said. "And how you wound up in that trunk. I promise you that we will find out." He squeezed her hand again.

While she wasn't weak, she was exhausted, and her eyes closed again as sleep claimed her.

"You shouldn't have made her any promises," Jared Bell admonished him.

"Why not?" Because the profiler intended to steal the case from him?

"It isn't like you," Blaine agreed. "You always swear you're not going to make *anyone* any promises. You're never getting married."

"I'm not marrying anyone," Dalton anxiously corrected him. That was a promise he'd made himself long ago. "I'm just going to find out who she is and how she wound up in that trunk."

"But if nobody reports her missing and she doesn't have DNA on file, there might not be any way to find out who she is," Bell cautioned him. "You can't risk putting her picture out there. You can't risk a news report about her."

"I wouldn't risk it," Dalton assured him. He couldn't risk kooks coming out of the woodwork trying to claim they knew her or cared about her—not in her vulnerable state.

"Why not?" Blaine asked. "Her attacker obviously knows she's still alive, or he wouldn't have tried running the ambulance off the road."

Jared Bell shook his head. "The last thing her attacker needs is any publicity…"

Dalton wasn't worried about her attacker; he was worried about her.

"But it might be the only way," Blaine said, "since the doctors said she might never regain her memory."

Even while his heart sank for her, Dalton shrugged.

"It doesn't matter. *I* will still find out who she is and what happened to her." And he would find out without putting her in even more danger.

SHE MIGHT NEVER regain her memory.

She had only closed her eyes to hold back more tears—not to sleep. So she'd heard what the agent had said.

She had already heard the doctor say it, too, though, so the pronouncement wasn't a shock. But hearing it again made it more real. She might never remember her life before the moment that Special Agent Dalton Reyes had opened the car trunk and rescued her.

Her oldest memory was of him—standing over her looking all handsome in his black tuxedo with his bow tie lying loose around his neck. If not for the trunk and the concussion and the blood, it might not have been such a bad memory. He was such an attractive man. But he wasn't just a man. To her, he had become a hero.

The FBI agents must not have realized that she wasn't sleeping, because they spoke freely over her—as if she wasn't there. Since she didn't remember who she was, it was almost as if she didn't really exist.

She had no name. No history.

"You didn't find anything at the crime scene to reveal her identity?" It must have been the blond man—Agent Campbell—who'd asked, since he had been the one assigned to protect her in the second ambulance. Fortunately, the paramedics from the first ambulance had had only minor injuries from the crash. They'd ridden along with her, too, to the hospital.

"No," Dalton replied. "The glove box was empty, and there was no license plate on the car. I'll have to run the vehicle identification number to find out whose name it was titled in last."

Hers?

She hadn't even seen the vehicle. She had no idea in what kind of trunk she had been found.

"The car was hot-wired, though—like Trooper Little-field's patrol car had been," he continued. "This guy's a pro."

"So you think he's part of that ring of car thieves you've been tracking?" Agent Campbell asked.

"Definitely."

"Have your car thieves taken a hostage before?" the other man asked. Back at the crash site Dalton had introduced him as Agent Bell. She could remember all of their names; it was her own she couldn't recall.

Dalton said nothing in reply to Agent Bell's question before the man asked another. "And would they risk returning to the scene to reclaim that hostage?"

Now Dalton cursed. "I know what you're up to," he said, as if he was accusing the other agent of something nefarious. "You're going to try to make this your case."

She almost opened her eyes then so that she could protest. She wanted Special Agent Reyes on her case—and not just because he'd promised to find out who she was and what had happened.

Maybe it was because her oldest memory was of him—maybe it was because he had saved her life—that she felt so connected to him. Even dependent on him...

She had no sense of herself. Her only sense was of him. But the only thing she actually knew about him was that he was an FBI special agent. She knew nothing of his life. She'd heard him say he was never getting married, but that didn't mean he wasn't involved with someone. That he didn't have kids.

"I hope it's not my case, Reyes," the other man replied with grave brevity. "I don't want to think that he's back—that he's killing again…"

"She's not dead," Dalton said.

"She would have been—if you hadn't stopped him," Agent Bell said. "But you didn't really stop him. He came back and hot-wired the trooper's car. He tried again."

"But he didn't kill her," Dalton said. "It's not him—it's not your serial killer. Or she would be dead. Some of his victims may not have been found, but nobody's ever escaped him. It's not the Bride Butcher."

Bride Butcher…

The words chilled her, but she suppressed a shiver and a shudder of horror and recognition. The name sounded vaguely but frighteningly familiar to her.

But why would the killer be after her? She was no bride. Then she realized there was a slight weight on her left hand, something hard and metallic encircling her ring finger. Was she engaged? Married?

"I hope it's not him," Agent Bell said again, "because if it is, he'll keep trying until he kills her."

So she might not have lost only her memory. She could still lose her life…

BY THE TIME he had made it to the hospital where she'd been taken, the place was crawling with FBI agents and state troopers—just as the crash site had been.

He had just about had those crumpled doors of the ambulance open when those other vehicles had arrived on the scene. He'd slipped back into the woods just as two men dressed in tuxedos, like the dark-haired agent, and another dressed in a suit had rushed to the aid and protection of the crash victims.

He had moved too quickly into the concealment of the dense forest for them to see him. And they had been too preoccupied with rescuing the others to notice him watching them.

The way he was watching them now—at the small hospital near the Lake Michigan shoreline. There were so many of them: agents and state troopers and even some county deputies for added security. So he would have to be careful—because he was damn well not going to get caught.

So he would have to bide his time until the perfect opportunity presented itself. And, eventually, it would. He wasn't going to give up; he wouldn't stop until he had finished this.

Until he had finished *her*…

But now *she* wasn't the only one he wanted dead. He had to kill the FBI special agent, too. He would probably even need to kill him first—since the man had assigned himself the woman's hero.

In order for him to get to her again, the agent would probably have to be eliminated first. But the order didn't particularly matter to him. All that mattered was that he had to make certain that both the woman and her hero died.

Chapter Five

He watched her from the doorway. She was awake now. But she didn't see him. Instead, she was staring down at her hand, studying the diamond on it. Either she was admiring the big square stone or she was trying to remember where the hell it had come from.

Her memory was really gone. He had spoken with the doctors, too, and had confirmed everything that Blaine Campbell had told him yesterday. Now if only Dalton could confirm what Jared Bell had told him.

If she really had been abducted by the Bride Butcher serial killer, then Dalton should turn the case over to the profiler. Jared Bell knew the case best.

But Jared Bell hadn't caught the killer when he'd had the chance before. And he had made no promises that he would catch him now.

Dalton was the one who had made her the promises. Dalton and probably whoever had put that ring on her finger. She had been wearing a bridal gown. Was she married? Or was she only engaged? Who was the man in her life and why hadn't he filed a missing persons report for her?

Dalton had checked, but he had found no report for anyone matching her description. Midtwenties, five foot seven or eight inches tall, red haired, breathtakingly beautiful…

If he was the man who had put the ring on her finger, he wouldn't have just reported her missing; he would have been out looking for her—desperate to find her.

But maybe the man who had put the ring on her finger had also put her in the trunk. Dalton had a name now—for the owner of the vehicle. He also had an address. But to follow up the lead, he would have to leave her to someone else's protection.

Blaine's? Or Agent Bell's? Or Trooper Littlefield's? The guy hadn't left his keys in his patrol car; he hadn't done anything wrong. He deserved a chance to prove himself, but not at any risk to her...

"Do you have bad news for me?" she asked. "Is that why you're reluctant to come into my room?"

A grin tugged at his lips. The woman kept surprising him—with her strength and with her intuitiveness. He hadn't thought she'd even noticed him watching her. However, she apparently didn't miss much. But her memories.

He stepped inside the hospital room and walked closer to her bed. She was sitting up, and thanks to the IV in her arm, she had more color. She looked healthier. Stronger...

"I have no news for you," he said.

She sighed. "Well, that is bad, then."

"How about you?" he asked. "Any memories?"

Had staring at that diamond brought anything rushing back to her? Any feeling of love for whoever had given her the engagement ring?

She shook her head and then flinched at the motion. Concern gripped him. "Still in pain?"

"Not so much thanks to the painkillers they've been giving me," she said. "It's just a dull ache now unless I make any sharp movements."

"You are tough," he mused.

The doctor had said that someone had given her quite a blow—probably with a pipe or a golf club. It had lacerated her skin and fractured her skull. But the fracture had probably actually saved her life since it had relieved the pressure and released the blood of what could have been a dangerous subdural hematoma. That was why there had been so much blood. But transfusions had replaced what she'd lost. According to the doctor, she was doing extremely well.

"I am tough," she said. "So you can tell me about this *no* news. What do you mean?"

Hopefully, she was tough enough to deal with the facts, because he wasn't going to keep anything from her. There was already too much that she didn't know—that she couldn't remember.

So he replied, "Nobody has filed a missing persons report for anyone matching your description."

She flinched again, but she hadn't even moved her head. This pain was emotional. "So no one is missing me."

"I doubt that's the case," he said—because he would have missed her, had he not known where she was, and he barely knew her. "I'm sure there's another explanation."

"Like what?" she challenged him.

And because he believed she was strong, he told her the truth. "Your groom could have been the one who put you in the trunk of that car."

"You think I'm married?" she asked as she glanced down at that ring again.

"I don't know." But part of him hoped she wasn't— the part that had his heart racing over how beautiful she was. Her red hair was so vibrant and her silvery-gray eyes so sharp with intelligence and strength.

"Because this looks like just a solitaire engagement ring," she said. "There's no wedding band soldered to it. So I don't think I'm married."

"She's right," a female voice agreed.

Even if Dalton hadn't recognized the voice, he wouldn't have been too worried about someone slipping past Security and getting to her room. He had a guard stationed near the elevators, so no one would get onto the floor without getting checked out.

The only one who was in danger from this woman was him—for disrupting her wedding the day before. He braced himself, for her understandable and justified anger, before turning toward the doorway.

Their arms wound around each other, the bride stood next to her groom. But unlike Dalton, they had changed out of their wedding clothes. Claire wore a bright blue sundress, while Ash wore jeans and a T-shirt. Of course, more than a day had passed since the ceremony.

Dalton really needed to return the damn tuxedo. And shower…

"Aren't you two supposed to be on your honeymoon?" he asked. He hoped he hadn't disrupted that, too.

"We're on our way to the airport," Ash assured him. From how tightly he held her, he looked as if he couldn't wait to get his bride alone again. "But Claire wanted to stop by and check on you."

"I'm fine," he said.

She clicked her tongue against her teeth, admonishing his dismissiveness. "You were in an accident."

"It was no accident." The man driving the trooper's vehicle had intended to run them off the road.

"That's even worse," she said.

"I'm fine," he said again.

Color rushed to the blonde's pale-skinned face. "Good. Now I feel a little less guilty for threatening your life when I realized you ditched our wedding to chase down a stolen car."

He didn't blame her for being angry with him and could just imagine the words she had probably silently mouthed about him. "I'm sorry, Claire."

She pulled away from her husband, rushed forward and hugged Dalton. "I'm so glad that you did." Then she turned toward the bed and smiled at the patient.

"I'm glad, too," the red-haired woman said, "since he saved my life."

"He does that," Claire said. "Saving lives is kind of his thing." She moved closer to the bed and extended her hand. "I'm Claire Stryker."

Ash chuckled. "She keeps introducing herself to everyone—even her dad."

The redhead took Claire's hand in hers. "I wish I could tell you my name, but…"

"You really don't remember anything?" Claire asked. "No."

"We will find out who you are." Dalton reiterated the promise that, according to Jared Bell, he'd had no business making. "But in the meantime, we need to call you something." Besides *redhead*…

"Special Agent Campbell suggested Jane Doe," she reminded him. "I guess that is what unidentified females are called…" But she hadn't liked it because Jane Doe usually referred to unidentified dead bodies.

But he'd thought she was dead when he had first opened that trunk. He resisted the urge to shudder at the thought of her being dead.

"We could call you Mercedes," he suggested. He had

hesitated to bring it up the day before, but it was better than Jane Doe.

"Mercedes?" she and Claire asked in unison.

"It's the kind of car he found her in," Ash explained. "Of course Reyes would go with the name of a car."

He whistled in appreciation of the vintage Mercedes. "She was a beautiful car…" Before she'd been put in the ditch. And now he knew who owned her. The car. He hoped that there was no guy out there who thought he owned the woman. But she had been put in the trunk like so much baggage…

Claire's blond brows drew together as she considered the choices. "Jane or Mercedes?"

The redhead shrugged as if she didn't care what they called her. "It doesn't matter."

"We need to find out your real name," Claire said.

"We will," Dalton said, but he felt a frisson of unease over how easily he was tossing out these promises. He had never been *that* guy—like Blaine or Ash. He wasn't the marine. He wasn't the hero. He was just the guy who worked hard because his job was his life. It was all he had. It was all he wanted, though.

"I'm really good with computers," Claire said, which was a gross understatement of her world-renowned hacking skills. "Maybe I could do some digging—"

"I already have a team on it," Dalton said. "They're using facial recognition to try to link her to online media pictures. It's being handled, and you two have a plane to catch."

"You sure you don't want our help?" Ash asked. His offer sounded sincere, but Dalton wouldn't blame him if it wasn't.

Selfishly, he would love their help. Claire was a genius and Ash was a legendary agent and former marine.

But there was no way that Dalton would mess up any more of the Strykers' plans. They had been through hell to earn their much-deserved happiness.

"I doubt this has anything to do with terrorism or national security," Dalton said—since that was Ash Stryker's specialty with the Bureau.

"Then maybe Jared Bell is who you need," Ash suggested.

The redhead shook her head again despite the fact that the motion had her wincing in pain. Then she turned toward Claire. "You agreed with me," she said. "You agreed that I'm not married. So if I'm not a bride, I couldn't be a victim of the Bride Butcher."

She had heard them yesterday. He'd thought she was sleeping, but she had heard everything he and Blaine and Jared Bell had said in her room. Now he flinched—with regret. He didn't want to keep anything from her, but there were some things she hadn't had to hear…like anything about the sadistic serial killer.

If that was who had abducted her, it was probably better that she never remembered what had happened to her. She would never recover from the nightmare of confronting such a monster.

PANIC OVERWHELMED HER, stealing away her breath. But she was actually less afraid of having a serial killer after her than she was afraid of losing Agent Reyes. He couldn't pass off her case to someone else.

"The victims of the Bride Butcher aren't married yet," Agent Stryker said. "He abducts the women at their last fitting for their wedding dress."

She shook her head—not in denial of what he claimed but in denial that she could have been at a fitting for a wedding dress. "No…"

"Do you remember something?" Claire Stryker asked. "Something that makes you think you're not really engaged?"

"I can't remember anything…" She stared at the newly married couple. Their love was palpable—like another presence in the hospital room. "But if I was married or engaged, wouldn't I remember…*him*?"

"Maybe you don't want to remember," Dalton suggested. He apparently suspected that was who had hurt her.

Was she such a horrible judge of character that she would have fallen in love with a monster?

The petite blonde stepped closer to the bed and reached for her hand. She twisted the ring on her finger.

"What are you thinking?" she asked. Such intelligence shone in Claire's eyes that she wanted to hear her opinion.

"It looks like this ring has been on your finger for a while," the other woman replied.

Her stomach pitched. And yet the person who'd put that ring on her hand hadn't even filed a missing persons report for her? What kind of man was her fiancé? The monster Dalton Reyes apparently suspected he was?

Agent Stryker glanced at his watch and said, "If we're going to make our flight, we should get going…"

"We should stay," Claire told her husband. "We could help…"

"You could," Dalton agreed. "But you're not. You're going to leave for your honeymoon and have a wonderful time."

Claire hesitated.

Even her husband looked uncertain. "Let's talk in the hall a moment…"

Her stomach sank again as the two men stepped out

of the room. She was certain that Agent Stryker was going to try to talk Dalton into handing her case over to Agent Bell.

"Don't worry," Claire told her. "We only offered to help because we owe him—not because we don't think he's capable of solving the case on his own. Dalton is a very good agent."

She nodded in agreement. "I know. I wouldn't be alive if he wasn't."

"He's not like Ash and Blaine Campbell, though," Claire continued. "They were marines—they grew up knowing what was right and what was wrong."

Anger surged through her, and she opened her mouth to defend him. The special agent obviously knew what was right and wrong.

But before she could speak, Claire continued, "Dalton grew up on the streets—in a gang. He had to figure out for himself what was right and wrong. I think that's even more impressive."

"So do I," she said. But everything about Dalton Reyes impressed her. She couldn't help wondering about herself. What kind of person was she? Was she an honorable person? Did she know right from wrong?

"This must be so hard for you," Claire said, "not having your memories. Not knowing how you grew up— who your family is or your friends…"

She wondered if she had any—since nobody had filed a report about her missing. Dalton and Agent Stryker stepped back into the room, and like the love between the Strykers, there was love between the men—a strong bond of friendship.

Her heart ached with an overwhelming sense of loss. But she hadn't just lost her friends; she had lost herself, as well.

Dalton uttered a long-suffering sigh, even while his dark eyes twinkled with merriment. "I had to give this guy some advice for the honeymoon." He turned toward Claire. "You're welcome."

The new bride laughed. "Like *you* have any experience with honeymoons or will *ever* have any experience…"

Apparently, as well as growing up on the streets, Dalton had grown up determined to remain single. She hadn't been surprised when she'd overheard him telling Blaine Campbell that he wasn't marrying anyone. Ever. She faintly remembered him saying something in the ambulance when the paramedic had mistaken her for his bride. She'd been in and out of consciousness, so she hadn't picked up on his words but on his tone. He had been appalled that someone had mistaken him for a groom.

At the moment she could relate as she glanced down at her hand again. She wanted to take off the ring. She couldn't believe she was engaged. It didn't feel right.

"If you two don't get going, you won't have any honeymoon experience, either," Dalton warned them.

Claire glanced at her. "But I could help…"

"I have help," Dalton said. He wrapped his arm around the young bride and steered her toward the doorway. "I know you two can't stand spending time together, but you're going to have to suck it up for the next fifty or sixty years."

The newlyweds chuckled—confident in their love and their relationship.

She glanced down at her ring again. Why would she be wearing this when she obviously hadn't felt that way about whoever had put the ring on her finger? But then, a love like the Strykers' was rare and special.

"It was nice meeting you," Claire called back to her.

She had met Claire. She wasn't sure if they'd met her—because she wasn't sure who she was, except not Jane or Mercedes. But maybe she would need to start thinking of herself as one of those names since she was unlikely to ever remember her own. She waved at them. "Enjoy your honeymoon."

The Strykers both hugged Dalton before leaving. He stared after them a moment, as if tempted to call them back, before he turned back to her.

"Who is your help?" she asked. While it would have been selfish to keep them from their honeymoon, she would have trusted the Strykers to help her.

"Trooper Littlefield is going to stand guard in your room," he told her, "while I go to Chicago to follow up a lead."

"Littlefield?" she asked.

Was that the trooper whose car had been stolen? Because of that and because something about him or his uniform was vaguely, unsettlingly familiar to her, she wouldn't feel particularly safe with him. But then, she didn't feel particularly safe with anyone but Dalton.

"He's a good officer," Dalton assured her. "He's the one who called me when he noticed the vintage Mercedes. He knew something wasn't right about it."

Her in the trunk—that was what hadn't been right about it. What if he hadn't seen the car? What if Dalton hadn't stopped it?

She would be dead. She was certain of it. She shuddered with the realization that someone out there wanted her dead. What kind of person was she that someone could hate her enough to try to kill her more than once…?

"Are you okay?" Dalton asked, his voice even deeper with concern. "Claire didn't upset you, did she?"

She shook her head. Claire hadn't upset her, but meeting the other woman had. "I just wish…"

"What?" he asked.

"I wish I knew what kind of person I am," she said. "If I'm like her…" Or if she was someone who'd earned another person's hatred? "I just wish I knew who I am…"

"You may not know your name," Dalton said, "but you know who are you are—you're strong and smart and brave."

But she felt like none of those things. She was terrified—terrified of the person determined to kill her, terrified to be away from Dalton Reyes and terrified to find out who she really was.

ALL HE'D HAD to do was bide his time. Eventually the dark-haired agent had left—along with the other federal agents. They weren't bodyguards; they were investigators.

He wasn't worried about what they would find. He'd been careful so that nothing could be traced back to him. Not even her…

But still she had to die.

And it would be easier for him to kill her now that the agent was gone. He'd left behind the bald-headed trooper for her protection.

All he'd had to do was wait him out. With the amount of coffee the man drank, it was inevitable that he would leave her to use the restroom. He was waiting for him there—hiding inside a stall.

He waited until the trooper was preoccupied at the urinal before he stepped out. The trooper didn't have a chance to pull his gun—to catch more than a shadowy movement in the mirrored wall—before he struck him. Hard. Harder than he'd even struck her.

As the trooper dropped to the tile floor, he dropped the bloodied pipe next to him. He was wearing gloves, so it couldn't be traced back to him. He was careful to leave no evidence behind. Anywhere.

He reached for the buttons on the trooper's uniform. Dressed like the trooper, he would have no trouble getting into her room and finishing the job he'd started. He looked quite official in uniform—every bit the lawman he'd always hated. He grinned at his reflection in the mirrored wall.

The woman was going to be dead soon.

Very soon…

Chapter Six

"Are you sure you're all right?" Dalton asked. He glanced over at the passenger's seat to check on her. He expected to find her eyes closed as she rested or passed out from exhaustion. She had been through so much—had lost so much blood.

But the doctor had assured him that it would be all right to take her out of the hospital. And she had insisted that she was strong enough to be released.

Maybe she was right. She wasn't sleeping or passed out. She leaned forward, straining against her seat belt, as she stared through the windshield. She had studied every street and building between the rural area of lower western Michigan and the urban skyline of Chicago as if trying to recognize it or hoping something might jog her memory.

The bridge rattled beneath the tires of the SUV as Dalton drove over the Chicago Skyway into the city. "Anything familiar?"

She groaned.

"I thought this would be too much for you," he said. "You should have stayed at the hospital with Trooper Littlefield protecting you." The local lawman had been offended when Dalton had asked him to protect an empty room. He thought that Dalton didn't trust him anymore.

That hadn't been the case at all, though.

He was pretty certain that the killer was watching her and waiting for another opportunity to get to her. So Dalton had wanted him to think that she was still at the hospital—still protected.

Instead of alone with just him for protection. But Blaine was on standby. Dalton could call him in or several other agents for backup…if he needed it. But nobody had followed him. He had taken a circuitous route and had kept a vigilant watch on the SUV's rearview mirror. So he was certain they had no tail. But her attacker was the least of his concerns at the moment.

"Are you all right?" he asked. Her skin had grown pale again, making her red hair look even brighter and more vibrant. She had exchanged her hospital gown for clothes that Dalton had bought and sneaked into her room. She wore tan pants and a pale yellow blouse. There were other clothes in a small bag in the backseat, too. It had bothered her that she hadn't been able to buy them herself. But along with her identity, her money and credit cards had been lost, too.

With obvious reluctance, she admitted, "My head is starting to hurt again."

"Should I take you to a hospital?" he asked with alarm, even as he mentally clocked the distance to the closest one.

"No, the headache is my fault," she said. "I think I'm trying too hard to remember—to find something familiar."

His tension eased somewhat. Maybe she wasn't medically in danger. But how about emotionally?

"Have you found anything familiar?" he asked.

"It's *Chicago*," she said. "Doesn't everyone know what Chicago looks like—just like they know what New York looks like? It doesn't necessarily mean that they've ever lived there or even been there. Maybe they just saw it on TV so many times or in movies or described in books that it feels familiar."

"So it does feel familiar to you," he deduced.

She uttered a small groan of frustration. "I just don't know…"

"Close your eyes for a few minutes," he suggested. "Relax." He didn't want her hurting herself.

She must have been exhausted, because she took his advice, but her rest didn't last long. When he pulled into the downtown parking garage, she opened her eyes. "We're here?"

"This is the apartment building where the owner of the Mercedes lives," he said.

"Do you think he could have been the one—" her throat moved as she swallowed convulsively, probably choking on nerves or fear "—that put me in the trunk?"

Dalton reached for her, sliding his arm around her shoulders to offer her comfort. She trembled against him and he tightened his embrace. "Of course not," he said. "I wouldn't have brought you along if I thought he could be the one who had hurt you."

She had thought that all this time and had been willing to confront her attacker? He'd known she was strong, but her fearlessness overwhelmed him.

"Then why did you bring me along?" she asked, peering up at him in the dim light of the parking garage. He'd already turned off the SUV.

"Maybe he will recognize you," he said. "Someone stole his car to abduct you. It could have been a theft of convenience—like his car and you were in the same vicinity."

She looked beyond him to peer around the parking garage. "You think I could have been grabbed here?"

Instead of cowering, she opened the passenger's door and stepped out to confront her fear or her elusive memories. Dalton jumped out the driver's door and hurried around to her side of the car. They hadn't been followed. But if the killer had figured out that they might come back here...

He didn't want her far from his side in the dimly lit parking garage. He didn't want to lose her.

CHILLED FROM THE dampness of the parking garage, she shivered. But maybe it wasn't just the dampness that had chilled her blood.

Maybe there were memories there—in the shadows of the steel-and-concrete structure. And maybe she had buried those memories so deeply that she couldn't access them anymore. They were just out of her reach... like Agent Reyes.

He had put his arm around her earlier for comfort and support. But now he stood on the other side of the elevator. Maybe he was frustrated that she couldn't remember—that she couldn't help him solve her case. Before they had stepped onto the elevator, he had called someone—maybe an FBI crime scene tech. He had asked them to come and inspect the garage for blood.

Her blood...

"You have my DNA," she realized. From the trunk of that stolen car. "Can't you find out who I am that way?" Jared Bell had mentioned as much the day before.

"We have your DNA," he admitted. "But it doesn't match any on file. Neither do your fingerprints."

She stared down at her hands. She didn't remember being fingerprinted. But then, there was so much she didn't remember. Like that damn ring on her finger...

Claire Stryker was confident it had been there for a while. Why, then, wasn't she married already?

How long had this engagement been?

And where was her fiancé? Why hadn't he reported her missing? Because he couldn't—because he had been with her when she'd been attacked but had been more critically wounded than she had been?

"Was there any other DNA in that trunk I was in?" she asked.

His mouth curved into a faint grin. "From the way your mind works and the questions you ask, I would almost believe you're in law enforcement, too."

Hope burgeoned. She would rather be on the right side of the law than on the side with people who hurt other people.

"But if you were in law enforcement, your fingerprints would have been on file," he continued and dashed that brief hope.

A bell dinged as the elevator stopped and the doors began to slide open. Panic rushed over her. He had assured her that he wouldn't have brought her along if this could have been the person who'd hurt her. But this person was the link to that car—the car that probably would have been her casket had Agent Reyes not rescued her in time.

He touched her again, his hand squeezing hers as it had so many times before. But this time chills raced over her as her skin tingled in reaction to his touch. His skin was rougher than hers and warm. The man was like that—a little rough around the edges, probably from growing up in a gang as Claire had told her he had, but he was warmhearted.

He cared.

About his cases.

He felt sorry for her. While he felt only pity, she was beginning to feel something more—something completely unfamiliar to her.

"It'll be okay," he assured her. "We'll just see if he recognizes you, if he's seen you around this building before."

As they walked down the hall, she studied the building—the dark wood walls and terrazzo floors. The building was old and dark, but it wasn't run-down. It wasn't even dated. It was fairly ageless.

But the man who opened the door at Agent Reyes's knock wasn't ageless. His body was stooped with arthritis, so that his head barely came to Dalton's chest. His face was heavily lined, his eyes clouded with cataracts.

"Mr. Schultz?" Dalton asked.

The older man nodded. "Who are you? I hope not salesmen. I have no money or time for your pitch." He shuffled back a step as if getting ready to slam shut his door.

Dalton held out his badge. "I'm FBI—Special Agent Reyes," he introduced himself.

"An FBI agent?" the old man asked. He pulled Dalton's badge closer to his face and studied it through narrowed eyes. "Well, I'll be damned." He chuckled. "Tell me what I've done."

"You haven't done anything wrong, Mr. Schultz," Dalton assured the elderly man.

Mr. Schultz chuckled again. "Depending on what kind of day my wife is having, she might tell you differently." He stepped back and gestured for them to step inside his apartment.

She glanced around, hoping to see something familiar. But nothing struck a chord. Like the hallway, his apartment was classic—polished hardwood floors and smooth plaster walls. It looked familiar in that she could have seen it on TV or in a movie or even a magazine.

Magazines and photo albums were piled atop a coffee table. Mr. Schultz gestured them to the floral sofa behind the table. "Take a seat. Would you like some coffee or tea?"

Initially unwelcoming, the elderly man now seemed grateful for company.

"We don't want you to go to any trouble," she told him.

"No trouble at all," he assured her. "I'm the chief cook and bottle washer around here." With that, he waved them down onto the couch before he disappeared through an arched doorway into what must have been the kitchen.

"Does he know?" she asked.

Dalton shook his head. "I don't know. He never reported the car missing."

"Who are you?" a woman asked. She stood in the doorway of what must have been a bedroom off the living room. Her hair was white and neatly combed, her face not quite as heavily lined as her husband's...if she were Mrs. Schultz.

They both stood as she stepped out of the room to join them.

"I'm FBI Special Agent Dalton Reyes," he introduced himself but hesitated when he turned to her.

She hesitated, too. What should she call herself? Jane Doe? Mercedes, as Agent Reyes had suggested with a morbid sense of humor, since that was the kind of car she'd been found in? Mr. Schultz's car.

"You're Sybil," the woman answered for her.

And hope had her heart swelling. "You know who I am?"

The woman laughed. "Of course I do." She reached her arms around her and pulled her into a surprisingly strong embrace despite her fragile build. "You're my daughter…"

Mr. Schultz stepped back into the room, a tray clutched in his gnarled hands. Reyes quickly took the tray from him, but just held it when he realized there was no place to put it on the table.

"I'm sorry," the elderly man said as he tugged the older woman away. "My wife often gets confused."

"So I'm not…Sybil?" she asked.

The old man stared at her with the same pity with which he regarded his wife. "You don't know who you are?"

She shook her head. "I have a concussion that's caused memory loss."

Mr. Schultz offered her a pitying sigh. "And you're so young." He helped his wife into a chair near the couch. "Rose was seventy when she first started having problems remembering…"

She didn't even know how old she was. Possibly late twenties? Maybe thirty? Not much younger than Dalton Reyes, she would bet.

"Does she have Alzheimer's?" Dalton asked quietly as if worried that he might upset Mrs. Schultz. Maybe his edges weren't that rough since he could be sensitive, too.

Mr. Schultz nodded.

"My grandma had it," Dalton said.

"Everyone has someone in their life who's been affected by it," Mr. Schultz said with no self-pity, just resignation. He turned back to her. "But you're too young to be losing your memory. Do the doctors think it will come back?"

She shrugged. "They don't know."

"They don't know nearly enough about the mind." He took the tray from Dalton and found an end table to put it on and then he handed them each a cup of coffee. "And I don't know yet why you're here."

"Did you recently loan your car to someone?" Dalton asked before taking a gulp of the strong black coffee.

She sipped it with a grimace before reaching for the sugar Mr. Schultz handed her.

The older man settled into a chair next to his wife. She'd fallen silent now and withdrawn into her own little world inside what was left of her mind. He patted her hand reassuringly, lovingly, and Mrs. Schultz glanced up at him with confusion and absolutely no recognition.

She didn't even know her husband.

Was her mind the same? Had she passed her apartment and not even recognized it? Had she passed her fiancé and not even recognized him?

"I don't have anyone to loan my car to," Mr. Schultz answered Dalton's question.

"What about Sybil?" she asked. "And her husband or her kids?"

"Sybil died of leukemia in her teens," Mr. Schultz said, "before she even had a serious boyfriend. So no husband. No kids. And she was our only child." Again there was no self-pity in his voice. But there was pain now—pain that seemed fresh even though Sybil must have died many years ago.

"I'm sorry," she said—in unison with Dalton as he expressed his sympathy, as well.

Maybe Mrs. Schultz was better off than her husband. Since she didn't remember her daughter dying, she didn't suffer like Mr. Schultz. The poor man had lost his child, and now he was losing his wife.

"You wouldn't have loaned your car to a neighbor?" Dalton asked. "A friend?"

"No. I have the keys in the kitchen," answered Mr. Schultz, "both sets. I can prove to you that I have the car."

Dalton shook his car. "I have the car—at an FBI garage. It was stolen."

Mr. Schultz shook his head. "No, that's not possible."

"When did you use it last?"

The old man gestured toward his eyes. "Not since my doctor told me I couldn't drive anymore until I get my cataracts removed. So, months…"

The car could have been taken a while ago, and he wouldn't have even noticed.

"And you don't recognize me?" she asked. "You haven't seen me in the building or anywhere?"

He peered through narrowed eyes, studying her face and hair. "I would have remembered a redhead." He shook his head. "No, honey, I'm sorry."

"I know you…" the older woman murmured. "I know you…"

She shivered, uncertain to whom Mrs. Schultz was speaking—her or herself. Would she wind up like that—murmuring to herself—if her memory never returned?

DAMN IT! HE was still furious that he had been duped. He should have known better than to think Agent Reyes would have left the woman to the protection of the inept state trooper. But he hadn't lost much time, because he'd guessed where they were going. Reyes had obviously traced the car back to the owner—in Chicago.

That was *his* city. So it would be even easier for him to take care of them—especially given what he'd learned at the hospital. It hadn't been a total waste of time.

He had managed to eavesdrop on some nurses' conversation. And he'd found out why the only ones coming to see her in the hospital had been law enforcement officers.

She had no idea who she was.

Too bad that she would be dead before she even had a chance to remember…

Chapter Seven

She leaned over the railing, staring at the water below as if she was contemplating jumping into the cold depths. Dalton shouldn't have brought her walking around the city—especially not out here on Navy Pier.

He kept his gaze on her as he stepped away to take a call. His phone had been vibrating in his pocket, but he hadn't dared to take it at the Schultzes' apartment. He'd kept hoping that they would actually recognize her. But with Mrs. Schultz's dementia and Mr. Schultz's cataracts, they probably wouldn't have recognized her even if she had actually been their daughter.

"Agent Reyes," he identified himself to the number who'd kept dialing him. Hopefully, someone else had come up with a lead to the attacker and to her identity since he had come up empty-handed.

"Reyes? This is Agent Bell."

He swallowed a groan. He wanted a lead, but he would have preferred to get one from someone else—because he suspected Bell's would lead him back to the Bride Butcher serial killer. But at this point, he didn't care; he had to have something to follow because Mr. Schultz had given him nothing. "Do you have something for me?"

"Are you all right? You and the woman?" Bell asked, his voice full of concern.

"Yeah, we're fine." He was only speaking for himself, though. She wasn't fine. She had pushed herself too hard in the hopes of finding something familiar, but those hopes had been dashed. By bringing her along to follow a dead-end lead, he had dashed her hopes of learning her identity. "Why wouldn't we be fine?"

"Someone ambushed Trooper Littlefield in the hospital restroom and stole his uniform."

He cursed. "Is he okay?"

"No."

He cursed again—loud enough that he drew her attention from the water to him. He took a deep breath, controlling his anger. He didn't want to upset her any more than she already was.

So he pitched his voice low and asked, "Is he dead?"

"He's in a medically induced coma," Bell replied. "He took a helluva blow to the head. They're not sure he's going to make it."

"I should drive back to Michigan." He had brought the state trooper into this case with that damn bulletin he'd put out for leads to his car theft ring.

"No," Bell replied. "Keep her away from here. Keep her safe."

He was afraid that he had already put her at risk just bringing her here. He clicked off his cell and slid it back into his pocket just as she slowly approached him.

Her legs looked shaky; she looked shaky, as if she was totally exhausted. But before he could ask her, she asked him, "Is everything all right?"

He had promised not to keep anything from her. But he wasn't sure she could handle knowing that Trooper Littlefield might not be as lucky as she'd been. He might lose more than his memory.

"No, it's not," he answered her honestly. "We need

to leave here. All this walking and trying to remember has been too much for you."

She didn't argue with him, so she must have been exhausted—so exhausted that she swayed on her feet. He reached out and slid his arm around her shoulders—for support and protection. He started walking along the pier, toward the parking area. But she stopped and clutched at his arm. Her fingers were cold against his skin, but still her touch heated his blood.

"I don't want to leave," she said.

"Why?" he asked. "Does this area seem familiar?" He'd already asked her, but he didn't know how amnesia worked. Would something just click in her mind and all of her memories would come rushing back?

She shook her head, tumbling her hair around her shoulders. The setting sun shimmered on the shiny tresses, making the red glow like fire. "No. It's just…"

She sounded so lost that sympathy and concern clutched his heart.

"What is it?" he asked.

She turned her face to his, tears glimmering in her pale gray eyes. "I—I don't want to leave here because…"

Maybe it was because she was so strong that her tears affected him so much—as if she'd crawled inside him, and her pain had become his. He tightened his arm around her and pulled her against his chest.

Her breath tickled his throat when she murmured, "I have no place to go."

SHE CRINGED THINKING of how pathetic she must have sounded. Of everything she had been through, it shouldn't have hit her so hard that she had no place to go. She had been released from the hospital, so she couldn't go back there.

Where else could she go?

She didn't know who she was, let alone where she lived.

Dalton hadn't said anything in reply to her pathetic comment. He had just whisked her out to the parking lot and into his SUV. Then he'd driven her here—to another apartment complex near River North.

"Where are we?" she asked as he led her through the parking garage to an elevator. "Do you have another lead?"

She'd hoped that was what his phone call had been about, but he had seemed too upset for it to have been good news.

"No," he said. "But it's too late and you're too exhausted to do any more running around or driving around. You need to rest."

So why hadn't he brought her to a hotel? Or to a holding cell for protective custody?

"Where are we?" she asked again.

But he didn't answer her. He pressed a button for the twentieth floor. They rode the elevator in silence, the only sound the swoosh of air as the car quickly rose. This building was newer than the Schultzes', or at least it had been recently renovated—probably converted from a warehouse or factory into pricey urban lofts. As they stepped off the elevator, she could see that the ceiling was high and exposed even in the hallway—the boards painted black, the walls all exposed brick. He stopped at a door and punched in a code, and then the metal door slid open like a barn door along the wall.

He stepped back and gestured her inside in front of him. "We're home," he said.

Hope flickered in her heart and must have shone on her face because he clarified, "My home."

She stepped into his place and stared in awe at the tall windows looking out over the river. Like the hall, it was all exposed brick and timber and metal ductwork.

"How much do FBI agents make?" she murmured. "Maybe I should become one."

With another punch of the console by the door, it slid closed again. And suddenly she felt very isolated and alone with a man she really barely knew.

Sure, he had saved her life. But what else did she know about him?

He had been in a gang. He'd grown up on the streets. Had he really given up that life? Or was he using it to finance his lifestyle?

He looked around him with a strange mix of pride and sadness in his dark eyes. "I have my grandma to thank for this place."

"She lived here?"

"No, we lived in South Side."

"We?"

He nodded. "She raised me…in a tiny little studio apartment above a convenience store. She worked three jobs and barely spent a dime—saving it all for me to go to college someday. I used that money to buy this condo."

"You didn't go to college?"

"I've got my bachelor's in criminal justice," he confirmed, "but my work as a gang informant and a couple scholarships paid for my tuition. I didn't use any of her savings or life insurance money until I bought this place."

Maybe it was because she knew nothing about her own life that she was so interested in his—or maybe it was just that she was interested in him. "When did she die?"

"Before I graduated high school," he said. "She got

confused…" His usually grinning face contorted with a grimace of pain. "And she got into it with some gang members…"

Now the pain was in his voice. Like the pounding in her head, she could feel it, too. She reached for him, clutching his hand as he had so often clutched hers to offer comfort and support.

His voice cracked with emotion when he continued, "She died…"

She gasped in horror. "They killed her?"

His head jerked in a sharp nod. "A confused old lady. And they showed her no mercy."

"That's when," she said with sudden realization, "that's when you figured out what was right and what was wrong."

"What?"

"It was something your friend Claire said—that you weren't like Agents Campbell and Stryker, who always knew right from wrong," she explained. "She said that you had to figure it out for yourself."

He shook his head. "No, Grandma taught me right from wrong," he said. "I just hadn't paid any attention to her—I hadn't listened to her—until she was gone."

She didn't realize she was crying until she felt the dampness on her face. "I'm so sorry."

He shrugged off her sympathy. "That was a long time ago."

But like Mr. Schultz, he wasn't over the loss or the pain. For Dalton, it was what motivated him to be such a good agent. That motivation had saved her life.

"Don't cry," he said as he lifted his free hand to her face and wiped away her tears. "Don't cry…"

"I'm sorry," she said again. "I shouldn't be crying —"

"Oh, you should," he said. "You have every right to

cry, but for yourself, for everything you've lost. You shouldn't be crying for my loss."

She shrugged. "I don't know what I lost. Maybe I should be happy I don't remember." She glanced down at that ring on her hand—the hand that was holding Dalton's. "Especially if my fiancé is the person who put me in that trunk."

Dalton sighed. "You don't know that."

"Why hasn't he filed a report that I'm missing, then?" she asked.

He spoke slowly, almost reluctantly, when he said, "There could be another reason."

That reluctance had her stomach flipping with dread. "Another reason."

"You already considered it," he reminded her. "That he could have been with you when you were attacked. That was why you asked about other DNA in the trunk."

Maybe it was good that she didn't remember the man—because she couldn't feel the loss that she probably should be feeling.

"You don't think that he just lost his memory, too." What Agent Reyes was saying was so much worse.

"That would be quite a coincidence," he said. "And I don't believe in coincidences."

"Me, neither." She sighed. "At least I don't believe in them now. I don't know what I believed before this."

"I don't think your beliefs would have changed," he said. "You are you—no matter what your name is."

"Sybil," she said.

He drew his dark brows lower over his eyes—confusion etched on his handsome face. "The Schultzes' daughter is dead."

"I don't think they would mind me using her name until you find out what my name is." She wasn't banking on remembering—not anymore. After all, the doctors had said that her memory might never come back. "Because if there are no coincidences, why was I in their car?"

She knew that she really wasn't their daughter. But maybe it had been fate that she would meet them— that she used their daughter's name to keep her memory going since she'd lost her own.

"It must have been stolen by someone who knew they wouldn't notice it missing," he said. "A family member…"

"He said he has no family," she reminded him. Just as she had no family now, either—at least not any family she missed or who missed her.

"Then maybe a neighbor," he suggested. "I have a team already looking into it."

"You will find out who I am," she said. "I believe you."

He sucked in a breath, as if uneasy with her faith in him. Had anyone believed in him since his grandmother?

She doubted he would have brought her back to his condo if he shared it with someone. He had his friends— she'd seen their love for him. But what about a woman— someone important in his life? Even though he didn't want to marry, he could still share his life with someone.

"But in the meantime, I should call you Sybil?" he asked, his mouth curving into a slight grin.

She nodded and then laughed. "The character Sybil had so many personalities, and I feel like I have none."

"Just like your beliefs, you have your personality," he insisted. "The concussion wouldn't have changed that. You are strong and brave and compassionate."

He had more faith in her than she had in herself at the moment. Gratitude and something else, something even more powerful, flooded her, and she rose on tiptoe and pressed her lips to his.

Feeling like an idiot, she froze, even while her face and body heated with embarrassment. But then his arms came around her, pulling her close, and he kissed her back. His mouth moved over hers, teasing her lips apart, and he deepened the kiss. His tongue slid into her mouth with an intimacy that had her skin tingling.

And passion that she was certain was more powerful than she'd ever felt before overwhelmed her. She wanted him with a hunger that consumed her.

Maybe he felt that passion, too, because he lifted her and carried her from the living room. Moments later, her back pressed into something soft as he followed her down onto a bed, his mouth still fused to hers—their bodies tangled together.

WHO WAS AGENT Dalton Reyes?

Maybe he wasn't the honorable federal agent he'd thought he was. Reyes would have been told about the trooper by now. Why wasn't he on his way out of Chicago back to that rural hospital in Michigan?

But maybe it was better that Reyes stayed in the city with the woman. It would be easier for him to take them out here—on his home turf.

It had been easier for him to find them—at the old man's apartment building. Of course, he'd known where they were going. And he had caught up with them before they had even left the old couple.

He would have taken them out in the parking garage—if there hadn't also been FBI crime techs crawling all over the structure. Looking for evidence…

Because of the city, it had been easier for him to follow around the SUV. The agent had skills, but he hadn't lost him. He'd followed him back to River North, but he hadn't been able to get into the parking garage of that condo complex.

Of course, if Reyes had taken her to a Bureau safe house, it wouldn't be easy to get access to her. To them.

He would have to wait until they left. And the moment they did, he would take them both out. Together.

Chapter Eight

Despite the blankets covering her, she shivered. She shouldn't have been cold because, along with the blankets, she wore her clothes, too. So maybe she was cold because she slept alone.

Not that she was actually sleeping. She hadn't been able to sleep since he had left her lying alone and aching on the king-size platform bed to which he had carried her. She had wanted him so much; she couldn't imagine having that desire for anyone else.

And she'd foolishly thought he had shared her desire, that he had wanted her, too. But he had pulled away from her and then, without a word—without so much as a look—he had walked out of the room an hour ago.

"Sybil…"

She shivered again—because the sound of his deep voice had her skin tingling and heating, had her wanting him all over again. Or still…

"You do want me to call you that, right?"

Since when did he care what she wanted? To hold back those petty words from slipping out of her mouth, she bit her bottom lip. So she just nodded.

Sybil was better than Jane or Mercedes. Sybil Schultz was an actual person—someone who had been loved and was still missed. Unlike herself, who, apparently, no one was missing.

"Are you cold?" Dalton asked. "I can get you more blankets."

She didn't want more blankets; she wanted *him*. "You don't have to play host to me," she said. "In fact, you didn't have to bring me back to your home. You could have just dropped me off at a hotel."

"No, I couldn't." He stepped closer and blocked out the light spilling into the bedroom from the hall. "There is someone out there determined to get to you. I won't let that happen."

She shivered again—this time with genuine fear. There was someone out there—someone who had nearly killed her. Someone who had tried killing her again by running an ambulance off the road, by risking other lives than just hers. He wanted her dead that badly that he didn't care about innocent bystanders. He cared only about killing her.

To save face and relieve some of her humiliation, she could have used that as an excuse for kissing Special Agent Reyes, that she'd only done it to get her mind off her situation—about the danger, about the amnesia.

But that would have been a lie. She had kissed Dalton for one reason only—because she'd wanted to. Because she wanted him.

The mattress dipped as he sat down beside her. "That's why I stopped," he murmured, as if he, too, was embarrassed. "It's why I *had* to stop."

With relief, she turned toward him. "You didn't want to stop?"

"God, no," he admitted. "It took all my willpower. But I shouldn't have kissed you. I shouldn't have carried you in here."

Her heart pounded faster with the remembered excitement of being carried in his strong arms—of his kisses. "Why not?"

"Because I can't get distracted," he said. "I have to stay alert. I have to make sure you stay safe."

"So you didn't stop because of this?" She held up her hand. And despite the dim light, the diamond glittered.

He groaned. "No. For one reason or another, your fiancé isn't here." The suspicion was back in his voice. He had pointed out the possibility that her fiancé could be dead, but it didn't sound as if he believed it. "So the only one I'm concerned about is you—about keeping you safe."

She scooted up against the leather headboard so that she sat facing him. "You really take your job seriously."

His dark eyes glittered like her ring had in the dim light. His voice gruff, he murmured, "You're not just a job."

Her heart rate quickened even more, and it was hard to draw a deep breath. "I'm not?"

He uttered a ragged sigh. "You should be. Every other case was just a case…" He shook his head. "But there's something about you—something that's getting to me." He sounded resentful, mad.

Instead of being offended, she smiled.

"I have never lost my head like that before," he said. "I came so close to taking advantage of you. I'm sorry. I am so sorry that I lost control."

"You didn't." She shook her head in disappointment. "You didn't take advantage of me." But she really wished he had.

His handsome face twisted into a grimace of self-disgust. "You were just released from the hospital today. You have a concussion, fracture and amnesia—"

"You're the one who said that wouldn't have changed my beliefs," she reminded him. "Or my personality." It didn't matter what name she was using—her own or someone else's—she had wanted him then.

She continued, "And you didn't lose control." She leaned forward so that her mouth was close to his. "And I'm sorry that you didn't." Because she wanted him yet...

He muttered a curse, and she felt his breath on her face. "You're killing me..."

"Maybe you're the one in danger," she said. And she closed the last fraction of space between them and pressed her lips to his again.

DALTON WAS IN DANGER—more danger than he'd ever been in, even when he had been living on the streets, running with the gang. And secretly informing on all of them.

This woman was more dangerous than any of the bangers he'd known—any of the killers and criminals he had brought to justice. She was more dangerous because she could hurt him more than any of them had been able to hurt him. When he had turned informant, he'd already lost the most important person in his life, so he'd felt he had nothing left to lose.

She was making him think he had something to lose. Like his heart...

And so he had forced himself to pull away from her again. He had forced himself to leave his bed and the tempting woman in it.

Instead of being hurt, the way he had worried he'd previously hurt her, she'd laughed at him. Then she'd added insult to injury, clucked and called him a chicken as he stepped out of the door. He had stopped and nearly turned back.

But she was right.

He was scared. Of her...

Of what she was making him feel.

He hadn't been completely honest with her and not just about Trooper Littlefield. It did bother him that she was wearing another man's ring; it bothered him that there was someone out there—someone she had loved enough to accept his proposal, to wear his ring...

Maybe that was the person who'd hurt her. Or maybe that person had been hurt with her, trying to protect her. If she was his fiancée, Dalton would have willingly given up his life trying to save hers. Maybe the man he wanted to think was a monster was actually a hero.

So he checked again, but he didn't find a missing persons report yet for a young woman even loosely matching Sybil's description: sexy body, flirtatious smile, fiery-red hair.

He checked hospitals and morgues for a man who may have been hurt with her. Of course, bodies had turned up in Chicago and in surrounding areas. He assigned a team to follow up and see if any of those men had a missing fiancée.

Then he made another call—to Jared Bell. "It's Reyes," he identified himself when the man answered. "How's Littlefield doing?"

"No change," Bell replied. "How's the woman doing?"

"Sybil," he automatically corrected him.

Bell's gasp of surprise rattled in the phone. "She remembered her name?"

"No," Dalton replied, with concern that she might never remember. She had tried so hard that she had hurt herself. "She didn't like Jane Doe."

"Or Mercedes?" The profiler must have talked to Ash

and Claire—probably to see if Ash had managed to talk Dalton into turning the case and the witness over to him.

"No."

"She hasn't remembered anything yet?"

"No," he said again. He didn't bother reminding the other agent that the doctor had warned them that she might never remember. Bell knew the odds of her memory returning. It was why he had been so against Dalton making her any promises.

What if he never learned her real identity?

And why did he care less about returning her to her old life than keeping her safe? Maybe he was being selfish—wanting to keep her to himself. But her life was more important than her memory.

Dalton had to find the person so intent on killing her that he would even attack a law enforcement officer assigned to protect her.

"What about you?" he asked Bell. "Did you learn anything at the hospital? Was there any security footage with leads to whoever attacked Trooper Littlefield?"

A gasp drew his attention to the doorway of his darkened bedroom. He'd thought she was sleeping. He had hoped she was sleeping.

"This hospital is too small and rural," Bell replied. "It doesn't have any security cameras."

The killer had obviously known that; he was careful. But not so careful that Dalton wouldn't catch him.

"They've never had anything like this happen here before," Bell continued. "The whole place is in an uproar. There's even media here."

"Local?"

Bell chuckled. "Yeah, the pennysaver reporter." But then the humor left his voice as it became gruff with resentment. "But there are national reporters, too." He cursed—probably for personal reasons. The media had crucified him for not catching the Bride Butcher serial killer.

Dalton echoed his curse—because of the danger national news coverage would put Sybil in. Every kook would come out of the woodwork claiming a relationship with her.

"We'll stay away, then," Dalton said with reluctance and guilt. But he really wanted to see Littlefield; he blamed himself for involving the man and putting him in danger.

"Stay safe," Bell said before clicking off the phone.

Sybil still stood in the shadows of the bedroom doorway. "The trooper was attacked?" she asked, her face starkly white in the dim light. "How badly was he hurt?"

Dalton flinched. He didn't want to tell her. But she stepped forward and gripped his arm.

"How badly?"

"He's in a medically induced coma."

She gasped again—with shock and horror. "He was hit in the head, too?"

He nodded.

"So it was definitely the same person who attacked me?"

They had no evidence of that yet, so he replied, "We don't know that for certain."

"You already told me that you don't believe in coincidences," she reminded him.

He had told her too much about himself—more than he had ever told anyone else.

"You were asking someone about security footage—so he got away again?" Her face had grown even more pale with fear; her voice trembled with it.

That fear broke his heart, so he pulled her into his

arms and embraced her. "It's okay," he assured her. "We're going to catch him."

"You don't know that," she said. "You can't make that promise."

"But—"

She pressed her fingers over his lips. "Bell never caught that serial killer," she reminded him. "Plenty of criminals never get caught."

"But I'm not Bell," he said.

While he respected the other man, he was a different kind of agent. Bell was a profiler; he was all cerebral. Dalton was a street fighter. He had no problem fighting dirty to get things done. And for her, he would fight with everything he had.

So he willingly made her another promise. "I will catch him."

She nodded. But he didn't know if she was agreeing with him or just humoring him. Then she said, "I want to go back."

"Where?" he asked. "Did you remember something?" Because it was only hours ago that she had told him she had no place to go. That was why he had brought her back to his home instead of to some impersonal Bureau safe house.

She sighed. "No. And I am beginning to doubt that I ever will."

He couldn't make her any promises about that. While he intended to find out who she was, he didn't know if she would ever actually remember, herself.

"I want to go back to the hospital," she said.

He cupped her chin and tipped it up to scrutinize her face. Was she in pain and he hadn't noticed?

"Are you hurting?" he asked with alarm. It was good that he'd managed to control his desire for her—no matter how hard it had been. He would have felt horrible if he'd taken advantage of her. "Of course I'll bring you to a hospital."

"Not *a* hospital," she said. "*That* hospital. I want to make sure Trooper Littlefield is all right."

"No." He shook his head. "There are reporters, and the killer could still be hanging around there—waiting for you to come back. You can't."

"I have to," she said. "People are getting hurt because of me. The paramedics, now the trooper."

"They're not getting hurt because of you," he assured her. "They're getting hurt because of the person who's after you."

"Exactly. He's after me, but he doesn't care who he hurts in the process." Her pale gray eyes widened with horror as if she'd had a nightmarish thought. "He's going to hurt you."

Dalton chuckled. "No, he's not."

"You were almost hurt when he ran the ambulance off the road," she reminded him.

He shrugged off her concern. "I was fine," he said. "I didn't even get a scratch."

"Unlike the paramedics."

The driver had a broken arm from getting pinned behind the steering wheel. And the paramedic who'd been in the back with her had cuts and contusions.

"I have to go back," she said. "I have to make sure Trooper Littlefield will be okay." Her beautiful face contorted with a grimace of guilt and regret.

"Why?" he asked. "I've been getting updates about his condition. I'll just keep doing that." And keeping her safe.

She shook her head. "I have to see him." She sighed. "I didn't trust him earlier."

"Why didn't you trust him?" he asked.

"Something about his uniform or how he looked." She shrugged. "I didn't trust him, and now he might not make it. I need to apologize."

"You have nothing to apologize for," he assured her. But he had another question for her. "Why did you trust me?"

"Because you keep saving my life," she said. "You'll keep me safe."

"Yes, I will," he readily agreed. "I will keep you safe *here*."

He wouldn't bring her back. He wouldn't put her in danger because she had a misplaced sense of guilt. "We are not leaving…"

HE JERKED AWAKE as the SUV exited the parking garage. He knew they would leave—eventually. He just hadn't expected them to leave while the moon was still visible in the slowly lightening sky.

It was just light enough that he could see two shadows behind the tinted glass of the SUV windows. They were both inside that vehicle.

But of course Agent Reyes wouldn't have left her alone and unprotected. He had too big a hero complex. Too bad that complex would prove his downfall. His demise.

His hand shook slightly as he reached for the keys and turned them in the ignition. *This is it*.

He turned his vehicle around and followed them in the light morning traffic.

This was his chance to finish this.

To kill them both…

Chapter Nine

Some might have called it his gut instinct. It had kept him alive when so many of his friends and former associates hadn't survived. Ever since his grandmother died, Dalton had figured it was her voice in his head—her as his guardian angel warning him to watch his back. Instead of his back, though, he'd been watching his rear-view mirror.

At a discreet distance, the car had followed them from the city. The luxury all-wheel-drive sedan was a vehicle he would have been following, the way he had followed the Mercedes, if he was still concerned about the car theft ring. It was the least of his problems now.

He glanced to the passenger's seat. Slumped against the leather, Sybil slept now. He didn't want to wake her up; he didn't want to scare her.

But that vehicle had been following them for too long for it to be a coincidence. That wasn't a Bureau vehicle, so it wasn't backup.

That left only one option. Only one person with a reason to follow them…

Sybil's and Littlefield's attacker.

He pressed on the accelerator. The other man had managed to lose him on backcountry roads. But Dalton couldn't be outdriven on pavement.

The closer they came to that hospital in Michigan,

the less pavement there was. Maybe that was why the guy had waited and watched instead of closing the distance sooner. He had been waiting for those back roads again. For his chance to run Dalton off into one of those damn suicide ditches...

Or worse yet, this highway wound close to the Lake Michigan shore, with steep shoulders leading down to the rocky beach below. Unlike the way the ambulance had only crumpled a little in the ditch, the SUV would get crushed if it rolled off here.

Dalton gripped the steering wheel in tight fists. If Sybil hadn't been in the vehicle next to him, he would have spun the SUV around and become the pursuer instead of the pursued. Above all the promises he'd made her, he wanted to keep his promise to catch her would-be killer.

He had called in for backup when he'd first noticed the car following them from the city. Fortunately, she had already been sleeping, and deeply enough this time that he hadn't awakened her.

But he didn't see that backup behind him yet. There were no government vehicles on the road, nor were there any helicopters in the sky. He saw only that luxury sedan bearing down on them. So he couldn't confront the killer with the man's almost victim riding along with him.

He couldn't put her in any more danger than she already was. So he pressed harder on the accelerator.

The car thief had stolen the wrong vehicle if he had intended to catch Dalton's SUV. His engine was far more powerful. But he had to slow for a sharp curve as the tires began to skid across gravel. The pavement had given away as the highway ended and became a two-lane gravel road.

A curse slipped through his lips as he fought the wheel, and the sedan gained on him. The front bumper of the car struck the rear of the SUV, spinning it more—spinning it nearly out of Dalton's control.

SYBIL AWOKE WITH a scream as a jolt sent her flying forward toward the dash. But Dalton's arm was there, catching her before she struck her head. He held her back against the seat.

"Hang on," he warned her.

And she instinctively reached for him. But he was pulling away, putting both hands back on the wheel. He steered the SUV into a circle, gravel and dust kicking up from beneath the tires. And then he was bearing down on a car.

"What's going on?" she asked. She braced her hands on the dash now. How long had she been sleeping? Nothing looked familiar to her anymore.

They weren't in Chicago. Because, for some reason, the city had been familiar to her. This area was familiar only in that she knew she had been here since she'd lost her memory. This was the area in which Dalton had found her in the trunk of that car.

Dalton sped up and knocked the front bumper against the rear bumper of the car. The car fishtailed on the gravel, spinning nearly out of control.

"What are you doing?" And then she knew...

Dread filled her, making her stomach churn—making her nauseated. "It's him?"

"I would love to find out," he murmured. But as the car sped up, he slowed down—letting it get away from them.

"Catch him!" she said.

He shook his head. "I can't risk it. Not with you."

"Why?"

"He's probably armed," Dalton said. "If he shot me

and then something happened to you…" He shuddered as if the horror was what would happen to her.

If he shot me…

He said it as though it didn't matter what happened to him, only what happened to her.

But she cared. She cared too much about Dalton Reyes.

"If I wasn't with you, you wouldn't have cared whether or not he was armed," she said.

"Of course not." He tapped his holster. "I'm armed."

"But it's not the Old West," she said. "You can't just have a shoot-out in the street."

"You need to tell the criminals that," he said. "I've had more than my share of shoot-outs in the street."

Of course he had. He had grown up in a gang and then he had joined law enforcement. If he hadn't been shot yet, he would be shot eventually. Maybe he would survive. Maybe he wouldn't.

That was why she cared too much—because she cared about him more than he cared about himself. And eventually he would leave her—whether or not her memory returned.

"That's why I couldn't go after him," he said. "Because you might get caught in the cross fire." The tires hit asphalt again as he drove down a paved road before turning into a parking lot. "And then I would be bringing you here for you—not for Trooper Littlefield."

As he pulled into a parking space, other vehicles pulled into the lot behind him. The sedan he'd struck wasn't among them. These vehicles were all black, like his SUV. He stepped out just as Agent Campbell came around the front of one of those other SUVs.

"You okay?" the blond-haired agent asked him.

Dalton nodded.

"What about you?" Agent Campbell asked as she stepped out.

She nodded. But she wasn't fine. She had already confronted her own mortality, but now she'd confronted Dalton's. Like the paramedics and Trooper Littlefield, her presence had put him in danger.

But he was used to it. He put himself in danger all the time. And that bothered her most.

"Did you catch him?" Dalton asked.

Agent Campbell shook his head. "Found the car abandoned, though."

"Figured he'd ditch it," Dalton said. "I'm sure you'll find it was stolen."

Agent Bell joined them. He hadn't come from one of the SUVs, though. He'd stepped out of the hospital. "You still think this guy is a car thief?"

"He has stolen at least a few cars that we know of," Dalton pointed out. "So, yeah, he's a car thief."

"He's not just a car thief," Bell insisted.

"Nobody's just *one* thing…" She hadn't realized the words had slipped out of her lips until all the agents turned toward her. "What I mean is that no person is just one thing. A woman is a daughter, a mother, a sister, a lawyer or doctor…" Her face heated with embarrassment over how philosophical she sounded.

"So a car thief could also be a killer," Dalton told Jared Bell.

The profiler shrugged. "Too bad you didn't catch him."

Dalton's hand curled into a fist—as if he was tempted to slug the other man. She and Agent Campbell both stepped closer to him—to hold him back if necessary. "I couldn't risk Sybil's safety."

"Then you shouldn't have brought her back here," Agent Bell told him.

Sybil was tempted to slug the man herself. "I insisted. I want to see Trooper Littlefield."

And she had threatened to take a cab or bus to the hospital if Dalton had refused to drive her. Of course, it had been a bluff and one he could have easily called since she had no money for taxi or bus fare.

"He's in the ICU," Agent Bell warned her. "There has been no improvement. He may not regain consciousness."

Trooper Littlefield may not be able to hear her apology, but she still felt the need to make it. She had doubted him, and he might lose his life because of her.

"I want to see him," she insisted.

Bell shrugged. "We'll have to sneak you in the back, then, because reporters are staked out in the lobby."

She nodded. "Of course, a state trooper being attacked would be big news."

"He's not the only news."

"They've found out about her?" Dalton asked, and his voice was gruff with bitterness and dread.

Bell nodded. "They've been asking questions."

"Bet you love that," Dalton murmured.

The other man shook his head. "Let's sneak her in before someone notices us all in the parking lot."

All the FBI vehicles and agents had drawn attention. A couple cameras clicked, bulbs flashing. She felt as if she was dodging paparazzi as Dalton and Agent Bell rushed her into the back entrance of the hospital.

"This is probably the door he came out," Dalton murmured. "Has it been dusted for fingerprints?"

Bell nodded. "It and the pipe he used to hit Littlefield."

"He left it behind?" Dalton asked as they boarded the elevator.

"There were no prints on it," Bell said. "Or on anything else. He's too careful…like someone else…"

The serial killer who had eluded him.

"No," Dalton said. "He's not that careful or he wouldn't have tried to run me off the road again. I could have had him."

If he had been willing to risk her safety…

"Maybe he just had no idea what a crazy driver you are," Agent Campbell teased him.

Dalton glared at his fellow agent, who, like Ash Stryker, was obviously also his friend, as they stepped off the elevator.

Because the trooper was in the ICU, he could have only one visitor at a time. So she stepped into the room alone—well, relatively alone—since all three agents watched her through the glass wall.

Tubes and machines were connected to the bald-headed lawman. He looked old and small lying in the bed. She couldn't believe how uneasy he'd made her before. He was no threat to her.

She had been the threat to him.

"I'm sorry," she murmured. "I'm sorry you got hurt…" And he hadn't even been protecting her. He had only been pretending to protect her.

What about Dalton—who really was saving her over and over again? What would her attacker do to him?

She knew the answer to her question. She knew that the man would kill Dalton the first chance he got—if only so he could get to her.

HE WAS SO damn mad that rage blinded him. That was probably a good thing since he'd had to rent some flea-bag motel room. But it was the only place that wouldn't have wanted a credit card from him.

His cash was beginning to run low, though. He had to end this soon.

Agent Reyes kept getting in his way. The man drove better than any other lawman he knew. But then, he probably hadn't learned to drive on some driving range. He'd learned on the streets.

He could have caught him…if he hadn't slowed down. The man had probably known the other agents were coming. He'd barely slipped out of the car before those other SUVs had driven up.

They'd searched the area, but they hadn't found him. They wouldn't. He knew how to be invisible. He wouldn't have survived prison if he hadn't learned that. Or maybe he'd just gotten lucky.

He couldn't risk going back. He couldn't risk his freedom.

But he couldn't leave this undone, either. He had to kill the woman. And he wanted to kill the agent.

He knew where they were. So he just had to wait again—until another opportunity presented itself. He wouldn't try to run Agent Reyes off the road again.

His rage dissipating, he could see clearly. The motel room was run-down, the bed lumpy and low to the floor. But in the middle of the mattress lay the gun he'd picked up while he was in the city. Next time he would use that.

Agent Reyes had been able to outrun a car. But he wouldn't be able to outrun a bullet.

Chapter Ten

Dalton hadn't brought her home. Maybe he regretted that he'd brought her to his condo the night before, because he hadn't brought her back.

"So is this one of those safe-house places?" she asked as he closed the cottage door behind them.

It was a small house, but its whitewashed walls and floors made it seem bigger and brighter. Bright furnishings and curtains made it cheerful and welcoming. It reminded her of someplace she'd been before—before she'd lost her memory.

Or maybe it only reminded her of a picture she had seen in a magazine. She couldn't trust her mind—not when so much of it was blank.

"We don't have any safe-house places in this area," he replied. "This is the cottage Ash and Claire rented for their wedding night."

She could see the romance of the cottage—could imagine the dark-haired agent carrying his petite blonde bride over the threshold. Dalton hadn't carried her. He wouldn't even look at her.

He cracked the blinds and peered through them. But he wasn't looking at the view of Lake Michigan. Instead, he was uneasily watching the driveway and the street.

"You have agents out there," she reminded him. "They will watch for him and make sure he doesn't get to us." But he had already gotten to them. He had nearly killed her. She had been lucky to lose just her memory. She could have wound up like Trooper Littlefield, barely alive, or she could have wound up dead.

"I'm not looking just for him," he said. "I'm making sure no reporters followed us, either."

They had ambushed them in the parking lot when they'd left the hospital. More cameras had flashed, and microphones had been shoved in their faces to answer the questions that were hurled at them.

"Who are you?"

"Do you really not know who you are?"

"Were you raped?"

She shuddered at the thought. But that had been one of the first questions she'd asked the doctor who had examined her. She hadn't been violated that way. But she had been violated. She'd been dressed in a wedding dress that she was certain wasn't hers. And she had been shoved into the trunk of a stolen car.

But more than that, her memory had been stolen.

"I don't think any reporters could have followed you," she said.

Nobody could have followed him, given the way he had been driving. If he hadn't told the backup agents where they were staying, she doubted they would have found them, either.

He uttered a ragged sigh and rubbed a hand around the back of his neck. Dark circles rimmed his dark eyes. And she realized how tired he must be.

"You didn't sleep last night," she said.

He shrugged. "You didn't sleep much last night, either."

And not for the reason she'd wanted to be awake—

not because they'd been making love. "No, but I slept in the car."

"For just a few hours."

"It's more than you had," she said. "You should lie down for a while. We're safe here. Nobody could have followed you, and we have other agents watching to make sure nobody hurts us. We're safe here."

"Are you trying to convince me or yourself?" he asked.

"I was scared today," she admitted. "Being that close to him…not knowing who he is…"

Could it be the man to whom she was engaged? Could he be that determined to get rid of her that he didn't care who else he hurt in the process?

She shivered. And Dalton stepped close to her, offering her comfort and protection. She wanted more from him. She would lose him eventually. He wouldn't keep her case forever. He would either solve it or pass it over to Agent Bell. Or he would wind up getting hurt like Trooper Littlefield was hurt. Or worse…

She couldn't think about that. She couldn't lose him before she'd had him—before she'd felt as close to him as she could get to another person.

"We'll figure out who he is," he reiterated his promise. "And we'll stop him. He won't hurt you."

"I'm not worried about him," she admitted. "At least not right now."

He touched the spot between her brows, which had furrowed with anxiousness. "What are you worried about, then? The reporters?"

He was. She had seen his anger and concern. Maybe he'd been irritated because all the reporters' questions had led back to one subject—Jared Bell's serial killer.

"They're wrong," she said. "And so's Agent Bell. I

don't think a serial killer randomly picked me to attack." It felt more personal than that. Or maybe it was just that it felt personal to her. "For one thing I'm not a bride."

"You're engaged," Dalton said.

"Are you reminding me or yourself?" she wondered.

He leaned down, his mouth coming close to hers before he stopped and whispered, "Both of us..."

"I don't care," she said.

"That's because you don't remember him."

"It's because of you," she said. "You're the man I don't want to forget."

"You won't," he said, his breath tickling her lips. "You won't forget me." Then he kissed her. He really kissed her—with passion and desire every bit as fierce as what she felt for him.

He lifted and carried her again to a bed. Like last time, he followed her down onto the mattress. She clutched at him, holding him to her. She didn't want him changing his mind again—didn't want him regaining control.

So she kissed him passionately, sliding her tongue into his mouth. He chuckled even while he panted for breath. And beneath her palm, she felt his heart racing inside his muscular chest. Then she pulled at his shirt, trying to free the buttons.

But he caught her hands.

"Damn you!" she cursed him as he stood up and stepped back from the bed. "Damn!"

But he just chuckled again. Then he removed his holster and put it and the gun inside it onto the table beside the bed. Next, he pulled off his shirt. And then, his pants. And everything else until he stood gloriously, devastatingly naked and aroused in front of her.

Her hands trembled as she reached for her own

clothes, so desperate to remove them that her hands fumbled. But then his hands were there, taking off her shirt and her pants.

His finger flicked over the clasp between the cups of her bra. And the bra came unhooked and fell away from her.

He wasn't laughing anymore. There was no humor in his dark eyes, only desire as he stared at her. Had anyone ever looked at her with such hunger? She doubted it. And she doubted that she had ever felt such hunger herself. She wanted him. So she reached for him, sliding her hands over all his rippling muscles.

And he touched her. Her breath caught in her throat, nearly choking her as sensations overwhelmed her. He caressed her breasts with his hands and then his lips, flicking his tongue over her peaked nipples. She squirmed on the bed as tension wound inside her, begging for release.

"Please..." she found herself begging. "Dalton, please..."

He touched her there, between her legs, where the pressure was becoming unbearable. While his tongue continued to tease her breasts, he traced his fingers over her mound, teasing the most sensitive part of her.

She bit her lip but couldn't hold in the cry as pleasure rushed through her. But it wasn't enough. It barely took off the edge of her mad desire for him.

His hands shook a little as he reached inside his wallet and pulled out a condom. She took it from his shaking fingers. Tearing the packet open with her teeth, she rolled the latex over the hard, pulsating length of him.

He was so big, so hot—so overwhelming. Then he was between her legs, gently pushing and then thrusting inside her. She arched up, taking him deeper— taking him to the core of her.

They moved in perfect rhythm, as if they'd been doing this for years. As if they had always known each other this intimately…

He knew exactly where to touch her to set her off, his fingers moving over her again. And his lips covered hers, his tongue moving inside her mouth the way he moved inside her body.

She clutched at him, her nails digging into his back and then his butt, as she met his thrusts. And sought release. The tension was like a madness inside her, driving her to the edge of reason.

And then she fell over the edge. She screamed his name as pleasure overwhelmed and devastated her. He tensed inside her before thrusting deep and joining her in the madness. He groaned, but he didn't call her name.

He didn't know her name. But he didn't even call her Sybil. Maybe because he knew that wasn't her. She wasn't really anyone anymore.

But now she was his.

No matter that she wore another man's ring, her heart belonged to Dalton Reyes.

CURLED AGAINST HIM, she slept again—her small, pale-skinned hand splayed over his chest. Even in the darkness, the diamond glittered and taunted him. It was big. Whoever had given it to her had money.

While Dalton had a nice condo, he didn't have any extra cash. He wouldn't have been able to afford a ring like that. Of course, he could always sell his place. The thought had him tensing with shock. What the hell was he thinking?

Obviously he wasn't or he wouldn't have made love with an injured witness. No, she wasn't a witness. A witness saw something happen to someone else. She hadn't seen anything—at least not that she could remember. She was the victim.

She had been victimized. And now he had taken advantage of her. She had wanted him, but that was because he was the only person she knew now that her mind had been wiped clean.

He had done some bad things in his life—before he'd finally started listening to his grandmother. But those things had felt wrong.

Making love with her hadn't felt wrong. In fact, he couldn't remember anything ever feeling as right. As perfect.

She was perfect.

And by now her face was probably plastered all over the news. Someone would recognize her and come for her. Of course, he had always known that someone was coming for her. The killer and her fiancé. Were they the same person?

Or was her fiancé another victim?

He had checked in with the agents following up on the male bodies that had been found. So far none of the ones identified had a missing fiancée. But that didn't mean that his body couldn't still be out there. In fact, if this killer was as good as Jared Bell believed, that body might never be found.

But, even though no leads had panned out yet, Dalton wouldn't give up. He had made promises to her. He had vowed to catch the man trying to kill her, and he'd vowed to find out who she was.

Tracking down a killer gave him no pause. He'd been doing that since he was a teenager. But tracking down her identity, giving her back her old life, that gave him pause.

He was reluctant for her memory to return because

then she wouldn't be his anymore. He nearly laughed aloud at that crazy thought. She had never been his.

Maybe he was so sleep deprived that his mind was getting messed up. He wasn't like Blaine and Ash. He wasn't going to fall in love with a witness or suspect or a victim. He wasn't going to rush to the altar so he could live happily-ever-after. Even as a kid he'd never believed in fairy tales.

Her hand moved on his chest, caressing his skin. When he looked at her face, her eyes were open—the silvery gray glittering in the faint light like that diamond. Then her hand moved lower, encircling him.

There was no such thing as happily-ever-after. But he could enjoy the happiness of the moment. He could enjoy the woman while he still had her. He reached for her, tugging her up to straddle him.

She gasped as she came down on him, taking him deep inside her. Then she moaned at the sensation.

She was so hot. So tight. So wet and ready for him. He moved in a frenzy, but she came along with him for the ride. She gripped his shoulders and then his arms.

He pulled her head down for his kiss. He teased her lips with his tongue before moving his mouth lower, to tease her nipples too.

She came apart in his arms, screaming his name, as her body exploded around him. He didn't ease up; he kept thrusting until she came again and again.

Then, finally, when he could bear the tension in his body no longer, he joined her in ecstasy. She collapsed onto his chest, her skin damp against his.

"Oh…" she murmured. "That was…"

"Amazing?"

"Overwhelming."

That was how he felt, too. Overwhelmed with emotions he had never felt before. He closed his arms around her, holding her to him.

After the news reports, people would come for her. But he wasn't sure he would be able to let her go.

Ever.

HER FACE TAUNTED him from the television. No matter what station he flipped to, she was there—looking so brave and beautiful in front of the reporters. And that damn agent stood beside her. A muscle twitching along his clenched jaw, Reyes looked irritated.

He was more than irritated. He was furious. Rage overcame him, blinding him again with its intensity. And he hurled the remote. He wasn't so blind that he missed. It struck the television screen but bounced off onto the threadbare carpet on the floor. The remote broke into little plastic pieces.

But the television, like the woman, was unharmed. She stared at him, her image daring him to finish what he'd started. He would. He always did.

So he lifted the lamp from the table beside the bed and jerked the cord from the wall. Then he hurled that at the television. Both it and the lamp crashed onto the floor. Sparks flew up from the TV as it shorted out and its screen shattered.

She was gone.

And soon both she and Agent Reyes would be gone for good.

Chapter Eleven

"Elizabeth…"

The voice was deep and masculine and familiar. It wound through her, igniting her desire again even though her body ached from making love with him last night. From making love all night.

"Elizabeth…"

While she recognized the voice, she didn't recognize the name.

"Sybil," she murmured sleepily. That was what she'd told him to call her. But even while she'd screamed his name last night, he had never called her anything.

Until now…

She reached out, but her hands only moved over tangled sheets. She was alone in the bed. So she opened her eyes. She was alone in the bedroom, too.

He stood just outside the doorway, as if he didn't trust himself to step back inside the room with her. He'd dressed and armed himself again, his holster lying against the side of his black shirt.

"Why are you calling me that?" she asked. But she knew.

"Because that's your name," he said.

She shook her head. "You don't know that for certain. That must be what someone told you. A reporter?"

"Not a reporter," he cryptically replied. "And I confirmed the identification. I pulled your Illinois driver's license. It's you. Your full name is Elizabeth Ann Schroeder. Nobody calls you Beth or Liz. It's always Elizabeth."

He had talked to someone who knew her better than a reporter would have. She tried hard to think, to summon them, but no memories rushed back. The name was only vaguely familiar to her. She might have once known an Elizabeth.

But was *she* really Elizabeth Schroeder?

And who the hell was Elizabeth? She wanted to ask Dalton a thousand questions, but she was afraid to learn the answers. Maybe it was better she remember on her own—if she ever remembered. But maybe never remembering wasn't a bad thing, either.

"I still prefer Sybil," she said.

"Why?"

"Sybil had people who loved her," she said. "Who still love her." Mrs. Schultz might have forgotten everything and everyone else. But she still remembered her daughter.

"So does Elizabeth," he said.

Her breath caught with alarm. "It was him." She glanced down at the ring someone had put on her hand. "That's who came forward with my identity."

His handsome face grim, Dalton nodded.

"He doesn't love me," she insisted. "Or he would have reported me missing."

She really hoped she wasn't Elizabeth Schroeder because she was afraid the woman was an idiot—that she was engaged to a man who had tried to kill her more than once. Suddenly she had no questions about Elizabeth. She didn't think she was someone she would care to know.

"I'll find out why he didn't," Dalton assured her,

"when I question him. I'll have Blaine Campbell protect you while I'm gone—"

She jumped out of the bed—heedless of the fact that she was naked.

He heeded, his gaze ran over her curves the way his hands and mouth had just hours before. Then he turned away. "I'll see you later."

"No," she protested. "I'm going with you." Wherever he was going. "I want to see him."

"He could be the one who hurt you," Dalton warned her. "Who's still trying to kill you. It could be him."

"That's why I want to see him," she said. "I want to know why. I want to know what kind of person I am that he could hate me that much."

He turned back. And this time he touched her with his fingers, sliding the tips along her cheek. "No one could hate you," he assured her. "No one…"

But he didn't know Elizabeth Schroeder any better than she did. So she had to talk to the person who actually knew Elizabeth—her would-be killer.

Just as he'd had no intention of bringing her to the hospital, Dalton had had no intention of bringing her to the local state police post, either. But she sat in the passenger's seat of the SUV.

She wasn't staring out the window as she had on the way to Chicago. She wasn't sleeping, either, as she had on the way back, even though she'd had as little sleep as he'd had the night before.

He didn't regret making love with her. He was glad that he had. Or he might have lost her without ever fully knowing what he was losing.

God, he was a masochist—because maybe it would

have been easier if he hadn't known how amazing she
was and how amazing they had been together.

But he wouldn't have traded last night for anything—
not even for her memories. Would they come rushing
back when she saw him?

Would she remember the man trying to hurt her?
Maybe it would be enough to put him away for good.
Or would she only remember the love she had for her
fiancé?

Agent Jared Bell met the SUV as he drove into the
parking lot of the small brick building of the police post.
"She really can talk you into anything," the other man
said. "I can't believe you brought her along."

"Maybe she can identify him as her attacker," he explained. "Isn't that why you're here?"

Because he was hoping to finally close his one open
case and apprehend the Bride Butcher.

Jared shook his head. "I already cross-referenced his
name against my files."

"Tom Wilson." It sounded like an alias to him. But
he'd checked him out—just as he had checked her out.

Bell continued, "Tom Wilson never came up before."

But none of the names in those files had led to an
arrest. So maybe it was someone who hadn't come to
his attention yet. Dalton kept that observation to himself, though. He'd already been fighting not to lose this
case to Jared Bell. He didn't want to just hand it to him.

Nor did he want to hand Elizabeth Schroeder over to
her fiancé. He walked around the front of the battered
SUV and reluctantly opened her door. Usually she didn't
wait for him to open it. Usually she would have already
been out and halfway to the building.

She was reluctant, too.

"You don't have to do this," he told her. "It's not like you remember him."

"But I might," she said, "if I see him again."

That was what worried Dalton.

"But if you don't remember him, you can't believe what he tells you," he said. "Because of the news reports, he knows that you've lost your memory, and he might take advantage of that."

Her mouth curved into a slight smile. "Nobody takes advantage of me."

He had. Several times last night.

Her smile widened, and she shook her head, as if she'd read his mind and disagreed with his thoughts. Then she whispered, "Nobody."

He couldn't argue with her in front of Agent Bell. And he didn't want to argue with her about last night. He wanted to argue with her about walking through those glass doors into the reception area of the police post.

But Agent Bell had walked ahead of them and now held open one of those glass doors.

"You don't have to—" he began.

But she pressed her fingers over his lips as she'd done before. "I have to," she said. And then she slid her fingers from his lips, along his jaw.

His skin tingled with desire. He had never wanted any woman the way he wanted her. *Elizabeth*...

It was an old-fashioned name, but it was also a strong name. A classy name. It was her.

He saw the confirmation on the man's face as she walked through that door Bell held open for her. The guy rose from the chair he'd been sitting on the edge of, but he didn't rush forward. He didn't reach for her. He just stood there.

The way she just stood there, studying the man.

Dalton studied him, too. He was tall with a runner's lean build. His hair was blond—blonder even than Blaine Campbell's. He was handsome in that kind of baby-face, smooth-edges kind of way—an all-American-looking guy. Unlike Dalton, who was a mutt of nationalities.

He felt someone watching him, too, and turned toward Jared Bell. Instead of looking at the reunited couple, Jared was staring at him. He had seen Elizabeth touch his face, and he knew they were more than agent and victim. Dalton expected to see disapproval on the no-nonsense profiler's face; he saw only pity. And something he couldn't quite identify.

He couldn't identify the strange emotions between Elizabeth and her fiancé, either. They just continued to stare at each other. Was he waiting for her to remember? Or was he worried that she would?

"You don't recognize me?" Tom Wilson asked, and his voice cracked slightly with emotion.

Just what emotion?

Hurt?

Or relief?

She shook her head. "I'm sorry…"

"Are you all right?" he asked. "The news reports said you'd been near death when an FBI agent found you in the trunk of a car."

How had the damn reporters gotten so many details about what had happened?

"He found me," she said, and she stepped closer to Dalton as if seeking his protection.

She had it. He wouldn't let anything happen to her.

"Dalton saved my life."

The man's eyes widened with surprise—probably that she had used his first name. Jared Bell's head moved in a fractional nod, as if her familiarity confirmed his suspicions about how close they'd become.

Dalton stepped forward and held out his hand. "Agent Reyes," he introduced himself. He didn't want the man using his first name. "We spoke briefly on the phone."

"You're the one who asked me to come here," Tom Wilson said, and he put his hand in Dalton's.

Like his hair and his clothes, the man's skin was smooth and cold. He seemed more like some plastic doll than a real man. But that was just Dalton's opinion, which was admittedly biased.

The man shook his hand, though, in a surprisingly firm grip. "Thank you," he said, "for saving Elizabeth."

Dalton nodded. He hadn't saved her for this man. "Thank you for coming here. We have some questions for you."

Wilson turned toward his fiancée. "Of course, Elizabeth, I will tell you whatever you want to know."

Dalton shook his head now. "No. When I said *we*, I meant the *Bureau*. I have some questions for you." He took his arm now and led him toward a room off the reception area of the state police post. He turned back toward Jared Bell.

The agent nodded. He would make sure that Elizabeth Schroeder stayed safe. And so would Dalton. He closed the door behind the guy and gestured him toward a chair at the table.

Wilson gazed back at the door, as if he could see Elizabeth through it. "Shouldn't she be in here? So I can tell her about her life, about everything she's forgotten…?"

Dalton dropped onto a chair across from him. "I don't want you anywhere near her," he admitted.

"What!" the man exclaimed as he shot back up from his chair.

Dalton waved him back down and continued, "Until I know for certain that you're not the one trying to kill her."

But even if Wilson wasn't the one who had hurt her, Dalton still didn't want him anywhere near her.

"I would never hurt Elizabeth!" the man hotly denied.

Dalton waited, but Tom Wilson didn't add a profession of love to his denial.

He leaned back in the chair so that he wouldn't reach across the table and throttle the man. "Then why didn't you report her missing?"

Wilson looked away, and his face flushed slightly— either with embarrassment or temper. "I didn't *know* she was missing."

"You don't live together?"

He shook his head. "No."

Dalton ignored the relief that flowed through him and focused on his job. But Elizabeth had already become more than a job to him. "You don't talk every day?"

"No," Wilson admitted. "Elizabeth is very busy. And very independent. Sometimes a week would pass before I would see her or talk to her."

"What do you do, Mr. Wilson?"

"I'm a lawyer, like Elizabeth," he replied. "I also work in corporate law—just for a different company."

"So your jobs keep you busy?"

"Elizabeth has more going on in her life than just her job," Wilson said with a trace of resentment.

"Are you saying that Elizabeth is seeing someone else?"

The guy stared at him, and maybe he was more astute than Dalton had thought, because his eyes narrowed in speculation. "I hadn't thought so…"

He wasn't going to answer any of this man's questions, and it was apparent that he had some questions about Dalton and his fiancée. It was up to Elizabeth to answer those questions—if she wanted. Dalton still had questions he needed answered. "Do you have an alibi for the day I found her in the trunk of that car?"

"According to the news reports, that was three days ago?" Tom asked.

Dalton nodded.

"Then I was out of town. My company had flown me to Miami for a conference." He pulled a plane ticket out of his pocket and set it on the table between them. "I just got back this morning."

Was that alibi a little too convenient? Dalton picked up the ticket, but he also picked up his cell phone. And he called a contact at the airlines who verified that Tom Wilson had been on both flights and none in between.

And there hadn't been enough time between the attacks and his flights for him to have driven the distance back and forth. Dalton ignored his pang of disappointment—especially as the other man wore a smug grin.

"Can I talk to my fiancée now?" he asked.

Dalton wished he could refuse, but this couldn't possibly be the man who'd just tried to run them off the road the day before. And it wasn't as if he was going to let the man be alone with her.

He would have Jared Bell or Blaine Campbell sitting with her for her protection. He couldn't do it. He couldn't watch her reunite with her fiancé—not when he had so many feelings for her himself.

THEY WERE AT the damn state police post. He couldn't get them there. And he hadn't dared to try running Agent Reyes off the road again.

It was too risky.

He slammed the motel room door behind him with such force that the windows rattled. He tossed his keys onto the broken plastic and glass already lying on the floor.

Something buzzed and then vibrated. His phone was ringing again. He knew who was calling—who had kept calling since that damn news report.

He didn't have to play the voice-mail messages to know what they said.

She's supposed to be dead.

I paid you well to kill her.

Sure, he'd been paid well, but not enough to risk his freedom again. This was supposed to have been an easy hit. Thanks to Agent Dalton Reyes, it had been anything but.

He could have walked away. He would probably eventually wish that he had. But he had been hired to do a job. It wasn't personal to him, but it was very personal to the person who'd hired him.

To save his own reputation, he had to kill the woman. But he was going to kill the agent, too. Because that had become personal to him.

Chapter Twelve

The man had come out of the conference room alone. She hadn't seen Dalton again. Maybe he was done with her now that her fiancé was found. Obviously he trusted the man. If he hadn't, he would have arrested him. Or he at least wouldn't let him be alone with her.

Agent Bell stepped inside the room where Dalton had questioned her fiancé, and he closed the door. Except for a couple troopers standing behind a glassed wall, she was essentially alone with a stranger.

"How are you doing?" the man asked. "Should you be out of the hospital yet?"

"The doctor released me," she said.

"But you don't remember anything…"

She shrugged. "Amnesia can't kill me." But maybe it could—if she trusted the wrong person. She wanted to go to Dalton—to have his support and protection.

But she couldn't count on him being around her always. He had other cases. She was just one.

"But the concussion…"

She lifted her hair and flashed him the small bandage. "A few stitches." Or so. "And I'm fine. Really."

He nodded. But she couldn't tell if he was relieved or disappointed.

"Are *we* fine?" she asked.

He nodded again. "Yes, of course we are."

But he hadn't ever tried to reach for her—to embrace her—as Dalton had so many times. Despite the man's good looks, she had no desire for him to touch her. She had no desire for him at all.

"Then why didn't you report me missing?" she asked.

Tom Wilson pushed a hand through his hair, tousling the golden strands. It was pretty hair, but it was the kind that was already thinning. It wasn't thick and soft like Dalton's hair.

"Like I just told the agent, we're busy people," he said as if already weary of repeating himself. She wasn't going to get the answers she needed from him. "I was at a conference in Miami."

So he wasn't the one who had tried to kill her.

"And you were busy," he continued. "You're always busy."

She heard the resentment in his voice. "I am?"

He sighed. "I'm sorry, Elizabeth. I know that you're busy. But we have drifted apart since the baby."

She gasped as shock gripped her. "Baby? We have a baby?" She shook her head. "No, no, no, there's no way I would forget having a baby." She couldn't be that horrible a mother.

"Biologically she isn't yours," he said. "You became her guardian after her parents died."

Her heart clenched with intense pain—a pain she remembered feeling. It was the first real emotion she had recalled. "Her parents?"

"Kenneth and Patricia Cunningham," he said. "You roomed with them in college and during law school. They were your best friends."

Shouldn't he have been her best friend? How the hell had they become engaged?

Laughter tinkled inside her head—a woman's laughter. Then a woman's pain-filled cry as she gripped Elizabeth's hand and the hand of a man. A baby's cry echoed the woman's...

Elizabeth's head began to pound as the memories rushed through her mind like a movie in fast-forward. Panic pressing on her lungs, she struggled to breathe.

"Are you okay?" Tom asked. Instead of stepping forward, though, he looked toward the door of the closed conference room—as if he wanted Dalton to step in and take over for him.

She wanted that, too.

But the memories kept coming...of Kenneth and Patricia and little Lizzie. They had named her Elizabeth.

Tears stung her eyes, burning them. And a sob choked her as pain overwhelmed her. It was like losing them all over again. "Lizzie's alone," she said.

Tom shook his head. "She has a nanny. She's fine."

Elizabeth's gut churned with guilt and fear. "No, a nanny isn't fine. I promised Kenneth and Patricia that if anything happened to them I would take care of her like she was my own."

"You remember?" he asked with shock. "Your memory returned?"

"I remember Kenneth and Patricia." Mostly she remembered the pain of losing them. "I remember my promise to them. I need to honor that promise." To honor her friends.

"You have," Tom assured her. "But you have a job, too. I think you were going back to Chicago to handle something for your office."

He thought? Did he have amnesia, too? Or hadn't he cared where she was or what she was doing?

She must not have cared, either, because she couldn't summon any memories of him. All that filled her mind now was images of a curly-haired baby—giggling and then crying as if her heart was broken.

And it had been broken when her parents died—just as Elizabeth's had broken. All they had now was each other.

"You have to bring me to her," she insisted.

Tom glanced toward that door again.

She could have pounded on the door. Or she could have called out for Dalton. But he didn't know where baby Lizzie was. She knew her friends' home was somewhere near here—somewhere in Michigan. She could envision the house that Patricia had decorated like that little honeymoon cottage Elizabeth had stayed in the night before with Dalton. But she couldn't recall the road or the roads she would need to take to drive there.

Tom had been there. They had been together too long for him not to know. And they had been together too long for him to be a danger to her.

As he'd said, he had been in Miami when the man had tried to kill her. The attacker wasn't him. It couldn't have been him.

"You have to take me to her," she demanded. "I have to see her now."

"SHE'S SAFE," JARED BELL assured Dalton as the profiler joined him in the conference room where just moments before Tom Wilson had sat across the table from him. "They're talking in the reception area. He's not going to try anything in the middle of a state police post."

The guy was smart enough not to try to hurt her physically. But emotionally, she was vulnerable. With her memory gone, she could believe whatever the man told her. And he could lie to her about their relationship—claim that they were closer than they had obviously been.

He hadn't even noticed her missing.

Dalton couldn't imagine having a woman like Elizabeth Schroeder and not wanting to see her every day or at least talk to her. Tom Wilson might not be a killer, but he was a fool.

"He's not the perp. He's got an ironclad alibi." Dalton sighed. "I'm not sure it's such a good idea letting them talk, though. If he overwhelms her with information…"

"She's a tough lady," Jared said. He carried a thick file under his arm. That was the kind of agent he was—all cerebral, with his research and paperwork.

Dalton followed his gut and instincts and that voice in his head that sounded so much like his grandmother's. His grandma would have loved Elizabeth Schroeder.

"Yeah, she is," Dalton agreed. "She's tough and maybe a little too brave for her own safety."

"You regret her going back to the hospital yesterday to see Trooper Littlefield."

"I regret nearly getting run off the road," he said, "and I regret the reporters ambushing her."

Jared Bell grimaced at the mention of reporters as he dropped onto the chair across from Dalton. "Yeah, but they probably were a necessary evil. We found out who she is. You kept one of your promises to her."

"I'll keep the other," Dalton said. "I'll find out who's trying to kill her—even if I have to turn the case over to you." Maybe that would be for the best—for Elizabeth—if he stepped back entirely. Then she could regain her old memories and her old life without him being a distraction.

Jared arched a dark brow. "What? Why?"

"I thought you'd be happy," Dalton said. "You've been trying to hijack this case from me the minute I found her in that trunk."

Jared shrugged but didn't deny his intentions. "The bridal gown…it seemed connected."

"There are no coincidences," Dalton agreed. And if her fiancé wasn't a viable suspect, then it was even more likely that Jared's serial killer was involved.

But Jared Bell shrugged. "Maybe not accidentally."

"You think someone was trying to copycat the Bride Butcher?"

The profiler nodded. "He would make a good scapegoat."

"But it could really be him," Dalton pointed out. "It hasn't been that long since he killed last. He could have started killing again."

"But why Elizabeth Schroeder?" Jared asked. "Since you gave me her name, I've checked her out." He passed Dalton that thick file across the conference room table.

"She's engaged," Dalton reminded him. He needed no reminders himself. Even last night he hadn't been able to forget that there was someone else out there, someone with a closer tie to Elizabeth than he had.

"But they haven't set a date for their wedding," Jared said.

"How do you know that?"

"Checked out their social media," Jared said. "They've been asked when the big day is and both say they're in no hurry to get to the altar. That they're way too busy to plan a wedding any time soon."

That fit with what Tom Wilson had told him—about why he hadn't noticed she was even missing yet. He'd been at a conference and she was always busy.

Dalton shrugged. "So…"

"So if there's no date set, she wouldn't have been getting fitted for a wedding dress," Jared pointed out.

"The dress wasn't hers," he agreed. "A bridal shop

had reported it stolen the day before I found her in the trunk." Unfortunately they'd had no cameras and had no idea who'd taken the gown.

"Your guy is quite the professional thief," Jared Bell mused. "Cars. Bridal gowns."

"Yeah, he's a pro." Realization struck him like a blow. "He's a hired killer." So it didn't matter that Tom Wilson had an alibi—that oh-so-perfect and prepared alibi. Dalton cursed. "He could have hired someone to kill his fiancée."

"Seems like kind of an extreme way to break an engagement," Jared said.

So extreme that it probably didn't matter that he was inside a state police post. Dalton jumped up, knocking his chair over, and jerked open the door of the conference room.

But he was too late.

The lobby was empty. They were gone.

HE WASN'T GOING BACK. It was a damn state police post. He'd probably killed that trooper, so it was the last place he should be hanging around. But after listening to all those voice mails left for him, he'd gone back.

He had a job to do. And no matter how damn hard it got, he was going to finish it.

When they stepped out of those glass doors, he grinned. This was perfect.

Well, it would be better if she had been leaving with Agent Reyes. But Reyes would have protected her.

This man wouldn't protect her.

He finally had his perfect opportunity. He waited until they got into the rental vehicle and turned out of the parking lot onto the road. Then he pulled out of the gas station from which he'd been watching them. And he began to follow the car. He didn't wait long—the way he had with Agent Reyes, following them for miles.

He waited only until the rental sedan turned off onto a road that wound around an inland lake. The first hairpin turn he sped forward and struck the rear bumper of the sedan. It swerved off the road, hit the deep ditch and rolled.

It was so easy…

He braked. Then he grabbed his gun from the passenger's seat. This time he would make damn certain that Elizabeth Schroeder was really dead.

Chapter Thirteen

Dalton cursed—mostly himself—for taking his gaze off her, even for a few minutes. He shouldn't have trusted anyone else to protect her.

"She must have remembered him," Jared Bell said from the passenger seat of the SUV. "Or else why would she have left with him?"

"Because he forced her," Dalton suggested. "Maybe at gunpoint."

"He wasn't armed," Jared said. "I searched him before you two got to the post."

Dalton sped up. According to the troopers at the post, Elizabeth and the man had left only seconds before he had rushed out of the conference room.

"He could have coerced her another way," he said. "Or tricked her. But where the hell did he take her?" He slowed as he approached a winding road. It reminded him of the one on which he'd found her.

"Down there," Jared shouted. "I see a car parked off on the shoulder of the road." Then he sighed. "But that's not the rental Wilson was driving."

Dalton saw the car, too. It was another luxury vehicle— a two-seater sports model that would have been much faster than the rental; it would have easily overcome the rental. Dalton jerked the wheel and took the turn nearly on two wheels.

Jared gripped the dash and cursed. "I heard about your driving."

Like his gang days, it was part of his notoriety in the Bureau. Until he had saved Elizabeth with those skills, he hadn't taken much pride in them. Now he hoped he could use them to save her again.

"There's the rental," Jared said.

It lay in the ditch just in front of the parked vehicle. He slammed the SUV into Park and jumped out the driver's door. A shot rang out, followed by the sound of tinkling glass.

He was too late. Too damn late…

He pulled his gun from his holster and hurried around the front of the SUV. Another shot rang out—this one shattering the side window of the SUV.

"Bell?" he yelled, worried that the profiler had been hit.

"I'm okay," Jared yelled back.

Another shot rang out, striking the hood dangerously close to where Dalton stood. The bullet dented and then ricocheted off the metal. He returned fire, shooting at the dark-clothed figure crouched in the ditch beside the turned-over sedan.

Bullets ricocheted off the undercarriage of the car. The man fired back—so many shots that Dalton had to duck low or he would be hit for certain. More shots pinged off the hood and the bumper of the SUV—too close to where he crouched. When he dared to raise his head and look into the ditch again, the man was gone—probably into the woods on the other side of the road.

Dalton hurried down the steep drop-off from the shoulder of the road and approached the car. Heat emanated from the exhaust yet; it hadn't rolled over long ago. And it was still running.

He crouched down, but he couldn't see through the windshield. It had shattered—either from the crash or from the bullet that had bored a hole on the passenger's side. His heart pounded hard and fast against his ribs. He edged around the car to the passenger's side. The window was down and red hair spilled out into the weeds and dirt.

He sucked in a sharp breath—as if someone had slugged him in the gut. "No…" he murmured. "No…"

A few of the tresses moved. Maybe it was just the motion of the wind.

But he called out to her, "Elizabeth? Elizabeth, are you okay?"

Her hair moved, and a hand replaced the red strands—a pale-skinned hand. "Dalton?" Her voice cracked with fear and hope. "Dalton?"

"Yes, I'm here," he said.

"Is he gone?" she asked.

"Yes." He'd gotten away again—which made Dalton feel almost physically ill. But not as ill as he'd been at the thought that he had lost her—really lost her. "Are you okay? Did you get hurt in the crash? Or shot?"

The window eased down more, opening a bigger space. She reached both arms out.

"Are you hurt?" Dalton asked again—before he moved her.

"No," she said. "He missed me. I don't know how… there were so many shots…"

Dalton shuddered. There had been so many shots, but maybe most of those had been at him—since he saw only that one shot through the windshield of the rental sedan. He gently grasped her arms and eased her out the window. Then he lifted her up and held her tightly in his arms.

"Are you okay?" she asked him. "Was he shooting at you, too? Because he turned away and was firing up at the road…"

Agent Bell answered for him as he helped Tom Wilson out the driver's side of the car. "I can't believe Dalton didn't get hit—so many shots came so close."

She shuddered in his arms. "Are you sure you're okay?"

If he had been hit, he might not have noticed it—his adrenaline had been that high because he'd been so worried about her. He almost patted himself down to check for bullet wounds, but her hands were there, trailing over his chest, back and arms. Memories of the night before—of her caressing him—rushed over him. And his heart started pounding madly again.

"I'm okay," he said as he caught her hands and held them in his. At least he would be okay once she stopped touching him. "What about him?" he asked Jared as he held up a shaky Tom Wilson.

"Not a scratch on him," Jared replied with a pointed glance.

He could have set it up—could have had his hired hit man waiting for an opportunity to kill Elizabeth and still make him look innocent.

Anger coursed through Dalton. Through gritted teeth, he murmured, "Yet."

He led Elizabeth around the car, but he took one hand from her to shove Wilson back. "What the hell were you up to?" he demanded to know.

The man blinked and stared up at him as if Dalton had clocked him. "What? What do you mean?"

"I said you could talk to her—not take her out of the police post," he reminded him. "She's in danger—

if you damn well haven't figured that out. She could have been killed."

"I could have been killed, too," Wilson pettishly added. And he was still shaking—maybe with shock, maybe with fear.

Dalton was the person he needed to fear. "Doesn't look like you were really in any danger—the shot was fired at her. The killer was trying to get to her." He stepped forward and shoved the man again. "Is that how you planned it?"

"What?" Wilson asked. "Planned what? Are you…"

"Crazy?" The guy didn't have the guts to utter the word. But Dalton had no such problem. He felt a little crazy—with anger at the moment. "I should have known your alibi was too convenient. You hired this guy to do your dirty work for you, and you tricked her into leaving with you to give him the opportunity."

Wilson shook his head. "It wasn't my idea to leave. She insisted."

Dalton felt again as if he'd been sucker punched. He turned to her. "Really?"

"It was my idea to leave," she admitted.

Why? Had she remembered her fiancé and been too embarrassed to face Dalton again?

"Did either of you see the man who ran you off the road?" Agent Bell asked the question that Dalton should have asked—had he not been so damn angry over nearly losing her.

"I didn't see him," Tom replied. "I must have hit my head when we crashed and blacked out for a minute." He turned toward Elizabeth. "Did you see him?"

She shuddered. "He had a hood pulled over his head, but when he walked up to the car to shoot…" She shuddered again. "I saw his face."

"Did you recognize him?" Tom anxiously asked her.

"I don't recognize *you*," she reminded him. "How would I recognize him?"

"But you remembered Kenneth and Patricia," he said, and that pettiness was in his voice again, along with resentment.

"Who are Kenneth and Patricia?" Dalton asked.

"My friends," she said, and her voice cracked. "My best friends. That's why I had to leave. I have to go to their house."

He understood. They were the only people she actually remembered from her past, so of course she would want to see them immediately. But he needed to see them, too—because they were the only people who could answer all the questions that Jared Bell's thick file couldn't. They were the only people who could tell him all about Elizabeth Schroeder.

"THANK YOU FOR bringing me here," she told Dalton Reyes. He'd insisted on bringing her to the ER first, but the doctor had confirmed what she'd told him. She was fine. Or she would be once she saw Lizzie. Tom Wilson had had to give him the address because she hadn't been able to, but she recognized the house as he drove the battered SUV up the long driveway to the two-story Victorian farmhouse with the wraparound porch.

A Chicago girl like her, Patricia had always dreamed of raising her family in a house in the country with a wraparound porch. Kenneth had given her that dream. He'd had the house built to look old while being modern and safe for his girls.

Dalton shut off the SUV and turned toward her. "You shouldn't have left with Tom Wilson. You should have asked me to drive you."

Her face flamed with embarrassment over how impulsive she had been. "I know," she said. "I know how much danger I'm in." And if her stalker hadn't driven Wilson off the road as quickly as he had, then he would have followed them right to this house that Kenneth Cunningham had thought so safe. "I'm sorry."

He touched her face, his fingertips skimming her cheek, and her skin heated even more—with desire. She had met her forgotten fiancé, but Dalton was still the only man she wanted.

"I am not going to let you out of my sight again," he warned her.

Reassured rather than forewarned, she smiled, but then—remembering how close she'd come to getting killed again—her smile slid away. And she released a shaky sigh.

"Thank you," she said, "for saving my life yet again."

"I understand why you were in such a hurry to get here—to talk to people that you actually remember," he said.

"Oh…" He didn't know that Kenneth and Patricia were gone. She would explain that later. Now that she was here, she didn't want to wait another minute before going inside. "There's someone else that I needed to see here," she said as she shoved open the passenger's door and jumped out.

Despite the fact that she was running to the house, Dalton stayed with her every step—ever vigilant of her safety. She was so glad that he was here. That he would protect her and little Lizzie.

She had barely opened the door when the toddler ran to her, squealing and crying with delight. Elizabeth swung the baby up into her arms and clutched her close. "There's my little girl," she murmured. "There you are…"

"Mommmmmma," the child stammered. "Mommmma…"

"Momma?" Dalton repeated the word—his handsome face draining of color with his utter shock.

He thought the child was hers. But since Kenneth's and Patricia's deaths, baby Lizzie had become hers—because she had promised them she would love her goddaughter like her own.

Her eyes stinging with tears, she nodded. "She's my little baby girl!" She pressed kisses against the little girl's pudgy cheeks.

A man stepped into the foyer. Like the little girl, he had curly dark hair. A pang struck her heart over how much he looked like Kenneth. But, along with Patricia, Kenneth was gone.

She was actually relieved that for a few days she had been able to forget the devastating loss of her best friends. But guilt struck her that she had forgotten Lizzie, too.

"I'm so sorry," she murmured to the little girl.

"Was that you on the news?" the man asked. "Were you the one found in the trunk of a car? What the hell's going on, Elizabeth?"

"Yeah," Dalton Reyes murmured. "What the hell's going on, Elizabeth?"

HE PANTED FOR BREATH, his lungs still burning from his run through the woods. He'd had to do that too many times over the past few days. And for a man whose only exercise had been in a small prison yard for years, the physical exertion was too much.

It didn't help that Agent Reyes was as good a shot

as he was a driver. His arm burned, blood oozing yet from the bullet hole in his shoulder. The bullet had gone straight through, but the wound kept bleeding. His shirt was saturated.

Hopefully, nobody had noticed him bleeding. And if that pain wasn't bad enough, he had another voice mail from his employer. Another diatribe about how badly he'd messed up.

It wasn't his fault. It was all Agent Dalton Reyes's fault.

But the worst part of that message was that the person wanted to meet with him. He took his gun from his jacket pocket and clutched it close to him. He knew he would need it—not just to kill the woman and the agent.

But to kill the person who had hired him…because he had no doubt that person intended to kill him. This person was more ruthless than anyone he had ever met—in or out of prison.

The only thing he knew for certain was that somebody was going to die tonight.

He hoped like hell it wasn't him.

Chapter Fourteen

Dalton had figured there was a fiancé—either dead or alive and trying to kill her. He hadn't figured that she had a baby. How could she have forgotten a baby?

"I'll explain…what I remember," Elizabeth promised, "after I get her down for her nap." She carried the little girl toward a wide oak staircase leading to the second story.

He nearly reached out to stop her. But a gray-haired woman stepped from behind the curly-haired man and hurried after her. "Miss Elizabeth, I was so worried about you. When you didn't call to check on her, I knew I should have called the police—"

And Dalton stopped that woman instead, pulling her up short with a hand on her arm before she could climb the stairs, too. Elizabeth stared down at the woman with the same expression with which she'd looked at her fiancé—as if she didn't remember her.

"Why didn't you call the police?" he asked. "Why didn't you report her missing?"

"Who are you?" the woman asked, her dark eyes narrowing with suspicion.

"FBI Special Agent Reyes," he introduced himself.

The woman gasped. "Is she still in danger?"

He nodded. "The person who attacked her has not been caught. So, yes, she's still in danger."

"Maybe you shouldn't have come here, Elizabeth," the curly-haired man told her.

She didn't even stop—just kept carrying the now-giggling toddler up the stairs.

"She couldn't stay away from the baby," the woman admonished him.

"Not even for little Lizzie's safety?" the man asked.

"Nobody followed us here," Dalton assured him. "I will make sure they stay safe. But I need to know what the hell's going on."

"She really has amnesia?" the man asked.

He nodded. "Yes, but her memory is beginning to return. She remembered her friends—Kenneth and Patricia. She said they live here."

A little cry slipped through the woman's lips, and the man shook his head. "Not anymore. Kenny and Patricia are dead."

Had Elizabeth remembered that yet?

"What happened to them?" he asked, wondering if it was somehow related to what had happened to her. "Were they murdered?"

The woman jerked her head in a quick nod. "Yes, yes…that is what Elizabeth believes."

The man pushed a hand through his curly hair. "It was a tragedy," he said. "Kenny was my brother, and I just can't understand what happened."

"What happened?" Dalton asked again.

"It was a murder-suicide," the man replied. "He killed her and then himself."

The woman began to cry, tears flowing down her face. "Kenneth loved her. He wouldn't have."

"I think that's why he did," the man said. "So that he would never lose her."

"Patricia wouldn't have left him."

"Why don't you go check on Elizabeth and the baby," he suggested, as if annoyed with the woman's interruptions.

She hesitated, either waiting or maybe hoping for Dalton to stop her again, before she climbed the stairs to wherever Elizabeth had gone.

"Marta and Elizabeth don't want to accept it," he said. "But my brother was an insanely jealous man. He was gone a lot for business. And he'd become certain that Patricia was having an affair."

Dalton was assigned to the organized crime division. He didn't understand crimes of passion—or at least he hadn't until he had been tempted to kill Tom Wilson for putting Elizabeth in danger. "You're his brother?"

"Gregory Cunningham," the man finally introduced himself.

"Did he tell you who he thought the other man was?"

Gregory glanced up toward that ornate staircase, as if wondering if Elizabeth was listening. "Tom Wilson."

"Elizabeth's fiancé?"

"The man had an obvious crush on Patricia."

Dalton's brow furrowed. "But he's engaged to Elizabeth…" No man engaged to her had any reason to look at another woman.

Gregory sighed. "And Elizabeth is…smart and driven. But Patricia…"

"Patricia was magic," Elizabeth said as she descended the stairs to join them. "She was beautiful and loving and loyal. It didn't matter who had a crush on her…"

It didn't appear to matter to her that Tom Wilson might have.

"…she would have never cheated on Kenneth," she said. "And he knew that. He wouldn't have hurt her or himself."

Gregory sighed. "Elizabeth, the police investigated. They ruled it a murder-suicide. You have to accept that. You have to accept that they're gone."

She shook her head, and like Marta, tears streamed down her face. She had definitely remembered that her friends were gone, and she was suffering all over again.

"I'll call the investigating officer," Dalton offered, because her tears had his gut tightening with dread and his own heart aching with her pain. "I'll just double check."

The guy sighed. "Thank you, Agent Reyes, and thank you for saving Elizabeth. I don't know how little Lizzie could have handled losing another person in her life."

"She's not going to lose me," Elizabeth insisted. "I'm going to be here for her—just like I promised Patricia and Kenneth that I would be." An earsplitting cry drew away her attention, and she hurried back upstairs to the upset child.

The man sighed again. "That should have proved to her that their deaths were no accident or murder," he said. "They knew they weren't going to be around to raise their little girl, so they made Elizabeth make those promises."

It made sense in that "dying man getting his house in order" way. But how could Patricia have known what Kenneth had planned for them?

"They made Elizabeth her guardian?" He watched the man's face for any sign of resentment or anger.

Gregory Cunningham just nodded. "Elizabeth was their best friend. They named their little girl for her." He chuckled. "They always said Lizzie was more like her than either of them—as if the baby actually was her biological child."

He picked his jacket from one of a row of hooks by

the door. The hooks were actually crystal doorknobs, though. "I am just a doting uncle."

"You don't live here?"

He shook his head. "Not in this house. But I live in the area, and I work in Grand Rapids."

"So I'll be able to find you if I have more questions?"

The man nodded. "Thank you, Agent Reyes, for saving Elizabeth," he said again. "That little girl can't lose anyone else she loves."

Dalton didn't want to lose Elizabeth, either.

ELIZABETH'S ARM HAD grown numb, but she didn't want to move the little girl. She wanted to hold on to her forever. "I'm sorry," she murmured to the sleeping child.

How could she have forgotten her—even for a moment? How could she have forgotten her promise to Lizzie's parents?

"I'm sorry," a deep voice murmured.

She raised her gaze from the curly-haired child to the man standing in the doorway to the nursery. He was so ruggedly handsome—with his dark hair and muscular body. But his handsome face was etched in a slight grimace. Maybe the so-very-pink princess room that Patricia had created for her daughter made him uncomfortable.

Or maybe it was whatever he'd learned about the investigation into Kenneth's and Patricia's deaths.

"I'm sorry," he said again.

And she grimaced and shook her head. "No…"

"I talked to the investigating officer," he said. "He's certain that it was what it looked like…"

Murder-suicide.

"I don't care what it looked like," she said. "It wasn't what happened."

She had been watching Lizzie that weekend a few months ago so that Kenneth and Patricia could sneak away for a romantic getaway. But then she'd gotten the call that their bodies had been found in their little lakeside cabin.

She shuddered even now, remembering it, and the child stirred against her. She didn't want to wake her. Marta said that she'd slept very little while Elizabeth had been gone. She had left her willingly to return to Chicago to handle a work crisis, but then she hadn't returned.

"I'm sorry," she murmured to the baby.

"I asked Jared Bell to review the case, too," he said.

But she heard it in his voice—the belief that Jared would be wasting his time. So why had Dalton asked him to look into it? Just to humor her?

She didn't care what his motivation was, though. At least someone else would look into what had happened. Maybe they would finally discover the truth.

"Thank you," she said.

His head moved in a slight nod. He looked tired, but then, they hadn't slept that much the night before.

Her face heated as she remembered why. She had been insatiable. And she still wanted him.

"Do you want to lay her down in her bed?" Dalton asked.

She had been sitting with baby Lizzie for hours—so long that the sky had grown dark outside the windows. "My arm fell asleep," she admitted.

"You let the nanny leave," he said.

She nodded. "Marta needed a break." Like Elizabeth, the nanny had relived the tragic loss of Kenneth and Patricia. She had worked for the couple since the baby had been born two years ago, and she had loved them like family. "She'll be back in the morning."

"You should get some sleep," he said. "You must be exhausted." He stepped forward so that he stood over the rocking chair in which she sat with the child.

"Because of last night?" she asked.

A spark flashed in his dark eyes. "Because of today," he said. "You've been through a lot." He touched her, accidentally, as he lifted the little girl from her arms.

But her skin heated, and desire flashed through her. He gently cradled the child in his muscular arms and carried her toward her crib as if he'd been carrying a baby for years. He looked more comfortable than she had been—in those early days when she had first been granted guardianship of the little girl based on Kenneth and Patricia's will.

"Have all your memories returned?" he asked.

She shrugged, and her shoulder burned as the numbness left her sleeping arm. "I don't know. I still feel like I'm trying to read a book with a lot of pages missing."

"At least some of it's returning," he said.

She sighed. "The part I didn't want to remember," she admitted as she joined him by the crib. "Maybe I forgot on purpose."

"You had a concussion," he reminded her. "I don't think you had a choice."

Guilt clutched at her as she stared down at the sleeping child. "I feel horrible that I forgot about her." The child blurred as tears filled her eyes. "She deserves better than me as a guardian. She deserves her mother and father."

"Forgetting that they're dead won't bring them back," Dalton said. He slid his arm around her and drew her tightly against him.

Weary and grateful for his support, she leaned heavily on him. "I know."

"Even if Jared finds out that you're right about their deaths, it won't bring them back."

"But it'll clear their names," she said. "It'll take the taint off their love, of their memory for their daughter."

He squeezed her shoulder. "They were right," he said, "to ask you to raise their daughter. You're the perfect person. You're just pretty much perfect."

How could he think that—after getting a glimpse into her real life? She laughed. "You must be exhausted," she teased him. "You're getting delusional."

He chuckled.

And the child stirred at the unfamiliar sound. Kenneth hadn't had a deep voice like Dalton's. Neither did his brother. And she couldn't remember if Tom had ever spent much time around the little girl.

So he wouldn't wake baby Lizzie, she took Dalton's hand and tugged him from the room. Then she closed the door.

"Her baby monitor is wired into intercoms," she explained. "There's one in the kitchen." So she could have brought him downstairs. But it was late and she wasn't hungry…for food. "And in the master bedroom…"

She opened the double doors to the corner room. "I didn't think I would be able to sleep in here," she admitted as she stepped inside the large, airy room with its vaulted ceiling, lightly stained hardwood floors and pale blue walls. "But I had to because of the intercom."

She shook her head in amazement that she had automatically felt so comfortable in this room. She remembered that—she remembered everything about Kenneth and Patricia and baby Lizzie. "And somehow it felt right…"

And for some reason, it felt right that Dalton joined her in that room and closed the doors behind him.

"Like last night," she said, reaching for his hand to pull him farther into the room with her. "Last night felt right."

It was all she managed to say before he pulled her to him again and covered her mouth with his. He was hungry, too; his hunger was in the urgency of his kiss and in his hands as they tugged off her clothes.

She was every bit as anxious, tearing at his buttons and snaps until he was naked with her. But as he had the night before, he put his holster and gun within easy reach of the bed—on one of the end tables. Then he laid her on that feather-soft mattress beneath the wispy canopy. But within seconds he joined her. Then their bodies joined.

She arched up, ready and eager for him, and took him deeply inside her. She clung to him as if he was her anchor in the storm of emotions as her memories returned—along with the danger.

But Dalton brought out more emotions in her, emotions she never remembered feeling before, even though she wore another man's ring. She was falling in love with Special Agent Dalton Reyes. She opened her mouth to tell him, but his lips covered hers before she could utter a word.

Maybe that was for the best. He was unlikely to believe her anyway. He would probably just think that she was grateful that he kept saving her life. And she was grateful.

But she was so much more than grateful. She met each of his thrusts. And she kissed him back with all the passion he aroused in her. She would show him how much she loved him—even though she dare not tell him yet.

She would wait until the killer was caught—as Dalton had promised. And her memory had returned. Then she would tell him—if he was still around. Because once the case was closed, Dalton would have no reason to protect her any longer. If he moved on to the next case, then she would be grateful that she hadn't shared her feelings with him.

Her body tensed, but then he thrust deeper. And ecstasy filled her. He joined her again—with a low groan—as he found his own release.

But he didn't let her go. He wrapped his arms around her and held her tightly against his side—as if he would never let her go. But she worried that he would—as soon as her case was solved.

A DOOR CREAKED, drawing Dalton from his sleep. Elizabeth was curled yet against his side, her cheek on his chest. So it wasn't her moving around the farmhouse. And the little girl was too small to have crawled out of her crib.

Had the nanny returned?

Elizabeth had said that Marta wouldn't come back until morning. The older woman had been upset and had looked exhausted, probably with worry over Elizabeth not checking in. So it probably wasn't Marta moving around downstairs.

He reached for his gun and pulled it from the holster. Elizabeth murmured in protest over his moving away from her. But he had to leave her—to protect her. He shouldn't have been with her at all tonight; he should have been guarding her while she slept—instead of sleeping with her.

Now he hoped he wasn't too late to protect her and the little girl who called her Momma now.

Chapter Fifteen

Elizabeth shivered as her skin chilled. She patted the sheets, but Dalton was gone. Moonlight, shining through the tall windows, illuminated the bedroom enough that she could see his gun was also gone.

Why had he taken the gun? But then he always carried his gun. It didn't mean that he needed it—that he had heard something.

Then she heard something, too. First, creaking, like a door or maybe the stairs. Was it Dalton going down the stairs or someone else coming up?

Marta wouldn't have come back. Elizabeth had implored the older woman to spend time with her daughter and granddaughter and to rest. Marta had promised that she would—and that she wouldn't come back until late the next morning.

So it wasn't Marta.

Was it only Dalton?

She heard a shout—then something else. Something heavy fell over. Something cracked. Something broke.

Dalton was not alone.

He was fighting with someone. Someone had broken into Kenneth and Patricia's home—to kill *her*. Her hands shaking, she grabbed her clothes from the floor and hurriedly dressed. Then she looked around for something she could use as a weapon. Kenneth hadn't believed in firearms, so there were none in the house.

That was what had been so unbelievable about the murder-suicide claim. How could he have shot Patricia and then himself when he hadn't even owned a gun?

Now she wished for one. But it didn't matter whether or not she had a weapon. She had to protect Lizzie. Maybe the best way to do that was by staying away from her. If the killer wanted Elizabeth, he could have her—as long as he left the child alone.

A gunshot rang out, rattling the windows and shaking the floor. A cry slipped through her lips. Had Dalton been shot? Or had he shot the intruder?

She wanted to rush out and check on him. But fear had her frozen to the spot. She couldn't even move when the doorknob began to turn. But then she heard baby Lizzie cry. Maybe the killer was using the baby to draw her out.

It worked. She grabbed a sculpture from the bedside table. The glass dolphin was small yet delicate enough that it had sharp edges. She could use it to stab him—if he got close enough. He wouldn't need to get close to her if he just shot her.

She clutched the sculpture so tightly that the glass cracked inside her palm. Then the doors opened and the man stepped into the room.

In one arm, he clutched the crying child. In his other hand, he clutched a gun.

She screamed. And he stepped closer, and the moonlight washed over his face. His handsome face...

Her breath shuddered out with relief that Dalton was okay.

DALTON WAS FURIOUS. Even more than an hour later, his temper hadn't cooled. How the hell had the guy gotten the jump on him in the dark? He had nearly lost his gun. He had nearly lost his life. And then Elizabeth's would have been lost, too. Maybe even the little girl's.

Lizzie—little Elizabeth.

Her friends had loved her so much that they had named their child after her. And then they'd given her their child. She was so easy to love, though, that he was fighting the feeling himself—as he had fought the man in the dark.

"You should have had backup," Jared Bell said as he surveyed the broken glass and furniture in the formal dining room.

Blaine Campbell had come along, too. Neither of these guys worked cases like this. Jared had ruled out his serial killer as a suspect. And Blaine worked bank robberies.

But then, Dalton didn't work cases like this, either. He worked organized crime. There was nothing organized about the attacks on Elizabeth.

He grimaced over the broken china plates and colored glass. They had even smashed a couple of the oak chairs and toppled over the heavy oak table, they had fought so violently.

As he surveyed the damage, Blaine asked, "Are you okay?"

"No," he said. "I'm pissed. I don't know how the bastard got the jump on me."

"He's a pro," Jared reminded him.

Dalton shrugged. "I'm not so sure. He went for my gun instead of pulling his own."

"What's the point of pulling his if you shot him first?" Blaine pointed out. "That's probably why he went for your weapon."

"We fought over it," Dalton said. That was when the

furniture had gotten broken. "I managed to squeeze the trigger."

"You're lucky you didn't get hit," Jared said.

He had taken the risk—to protect Elizabeth and the child. "I think I hit him…" The guy's breath had whooshed out, as if Dalton had delivered an even harder blow than the ones he'd already hit him with.

His forehead furrowed, Jared looked skeptical. "If he was hurt, how'd he get away?"

"The baby cried—when the shot went off," Dalton said. "We were below her bedroom. I wasn't sure if the bullet hit him or went into the ceiling."

The room bathed in light, he could see no holes in the coffered ceiling.

"So you let him go?" Jared was appalled.

Dalton wanted to hit him. And Blaine must have sensed his intention because he subtly stepped between them and replied for him, "Of course he'd be worried about the child. You'll know when you have a kid of your own."

Jared shuddered. "Not going to happen…"

"That's what I once said, too," Blaine replied. His baby wasn't his own, though. His wife had been pregnant with another man's child when Blaine had saved her from bank robbers. But he loved that baby as if he was his own.

The way Elizabeth loved little Lizzie…

"It's not like I let him go," Dalton defended himself. "The baby crying distracted me for just a second and he wriggled free."

"You didn't chase him?" Jared asked.

"He had to check on the baby," Blaine reminded him.

And Elizabeth. He had wanted to check on Elizabeth

and make sure that someone hadn't gotten to her while the other man served to distract him.

"I didn't know for sure if there was only one guy in the house," he explained. "I had to check on Elizabeth and the baby."

Jared finally nodded in approval. "Of course, there could have been two."

"There are two, at least," Dalton reminded him. "The hired killer and the killer who hired him."

A gasp drew his attention to the dining room doorway—to where Elizabeth stood with the baby. She held a hand over the child's ear, as if the little girl would understand what they were saying. Elizabeth's pale gray eyes widened with fear; she understood—how desperately and deceitfully that someone wanted her dead.

"Reyes?" Jared held up a hand smeared with blood. "You did hit him."

Blaine nodded. "We can track him now."

"We may have to wait till daylight," Dalton pointed out. But dawn wasn't far off. The sky was already growing lighter. And so was Dalton's heart. He may have let the guy get away, but he hadn't been unscathed.

How badly had he been hurt? Enough to seek medical attention? "But in the meantime we can check with the local hospitals and clinics for someone with a GSW."

Blaine nodded. "I'm on it."

"And I'm in the way," Elizabeth murmured as she stepped back out of the dining room.

He should have stayed with the other agents—in the midst of the investigation. But he followed her instead as she climbed the stairs to the oh-so-pink room. He had to make sure that she was really okay.

"You're not in the way," he said.

"Someone obviously thinks so," she said. "Or why would they have hired someone to get rid of me?"

"Now that we know who you are, we can figure out the motive," he explained. "We can find out who's behind these attacks on you."

She flinched. "Maybe I don't want to know."

"We have to know so we can stop him." He touched her face, skimming his fingers across her silky cheek. "And we will stop him." Almost as much as he hated her being in danger, he hated that she was somehow holding herself responsible for that danger—for someone wanting to kill her.

She thought she'd made someone hate her, but he doubted that was possible. She was more likely to make someone love her—even though he had no business falling for her. Not when she wore another man's ring. Not when he'd sworn to himself that he would fall for no one and focus only on his job.

He had to do that now. If Dalton hadn't heard the guy sneaking around downstairs, he might have gotten to her—might have killed them all while they slept. No, Dalton had to stay focused.

THE KILLER NEVER MADE it to a hospital or a clinic. Dalton found him lying on a blood-soaked mattress in a seedy motel room. Like the dining room, half the furniture in the room had been smashed—along with the TV and a lamp that lay shattered on the threadbare carpet.

"Who is he?" he asked the clerk who had called police because he'd noticed a blood trail leading from the parking lot to the door of this room.

The long-haired young man just blinked at him in confusion. "I don't know."

"How did he sign in when he registered at the desk and got his key?"

"John Smith."

Dalton snorted. "I don't suppose you took a copy of his driver's license or his credit card."

The clerk's face reddened. "He paid cash and signed in as John Smith."

Dalton asked the state troopers who were gathering evidence, "Did you find a wallet?"

One of the troopers shook her head. "No, sir. No cell phone—nothing. It looks like he was robbed."

This wasn't a robbery. Maybe he hadn't carried any of those items on him, not wanting his identity to be discovered. Or maybe someone else had gotten rid of those items for him. "How long will it take the coroner to do an autopsy?"

"We use the county coroner," the young trooper replied. "He has a wide area, so he's pretty busy."

Dalton cursed. "I may need to have a federal coroner do the autopsy. I have to know what bullet killed him."

"What caliber?" she asked.

He shook his head. "What bullet—because it could have been mine." But just because the hired killer was dead didn't mean that Elizabeth was out of danger. Dalton had to find out who had hired the man—which might be easier if he knew who the hell he was. "I also need to get his fingerprints and DNA in AFIS and find out who he is."

"Call the FBI lab," Jared Bell said. He had come along with Dalton, while Blaine had stayed with Elizabeth and the child to protect them.

Maybe it was his bruises from the fight in the dining room or maybe it was being away from Elizabeth and Lizzie, but Dalton physically ached. He hated leaving their protection to anyone but himself—no matter how much he trusted and respected Blaine Campbell.

"We need to put a rush on this." The profiler had admitted to Dalton that he didn't think these attacks were related to his open serial-killer case. But he would want to rule out any possibility that it could be related—that this could be the killer he had sought for so long.

"You don't know this is part of your federal investigation," the young trooper dared to challenge him.

Dalton never had time for jurisdictional games. "This person might be the one who attacked Trooper Littlefield," he said. "I figured you would all want to know that as soon as possible, too."

The young trooper jerked her head in a quick nod. "Of course. Of course, I didn't realize…"

The older trooper, searching the room with her, snorted. "What did you think—we're having a crime wave in this area? Of course it's related. The only other crimes we've had in this area before Agent Reyes found the bride in the trunk was that murder-suicide a few months back."

Dalton's blood chilled. He didn't believe in coincidences. Elizabeth just might be right about her friends. He met Jared Bell's gaze, and the other man nodded. He had his suspicions, too. Elizabeth was insistent that her friends' deaths were murder—just murder—and now someone was trying to murder her. To cover up a crime already committed?

Maybe the attempts on Elizabeth's life had less to do with her than with her friends. The little girl couldn't lose her, the way she had already lost her parents.

Dalton couldn't lose her, either. But he was afraid that he would. Eventually. He would keep her alive and find out who was trying to kill her. But he couldn't keep her from remembering her fiancé and returning to him. Unless Tom Wilson was the person who'd hired the hit man.

Chapter Sixteen

Pain radiated throughout Elizabeth's head, blurring her vision. It was as if she had been struck all over again. The throbbing was intense, echoing inside her skull. Was it because of the concussion?

Or was it because her memory was returning? Because along with those memories came pain. It was like losing Kenneth and Patricia all over again.

Or was it because she'd had another sleepless night? Because she was falling in love with a man who wouldn't stay? Since the break-in, she hadn't seen him. Shortly after talking to her, he had left the house with Jared Bell—leaving Blaine Campbell to protect her.

"Are you okay?" Agent Campbell asked as he jostled the little girl on his lean hip. Baby Lizzie giggled now. She'd been crying earlier—tired and cranky from having her sleep disrupted.

Maybe that was why Elizabeth's head was pounding. She had been rocking the little girl in the nursery, but it had only intensified her pain and little Lizzie's crying. So she held the rocking chair still while Agent Campbell held the toddler.

"I'll be okay," she replied. When Dalton returned.

If Dalton returned.

"Thank you," she added. "Not just for protecting me but for helping with the baby."

"I'm happy to help out," he said. "Keeping you safe and helping with this little princess." He'd switched the bouncing to rocking in his arms, and now Lizzie's curly-haired head bobbed as she fell asleep.

"You're a natural," she said.

"My wife and I have a son," he shared with a father's pride.

She remembered Dalton's horror over being mistaken for a groom. He probably felt the same way about fatherhood as he did marriage. He was probably just as averse. But she understood that he was devoted to his job—to avenge the loss of his grandmother and to make her proud.

"He's only eight weeks old," Blaine continued, "so quite a bit smaller than this young lady. But with the way he eats, I'm sure he'll catch up soon."

"They grow up fast," Elizabeth said. She'd been gone less than a week, but the curly-haired toddler seemed so much bigger to her. So much older. She was growing up so fast. How soon before she forgot her parents?

She had already started calling Elizabeth Momma. She had replaced Patricia in her mind. But Elizabeth would make sure that the little girl always knew who her real mother was. She would keep their memories alive for Kenneth and Patricia. But she could only do that if she were still alive.

A door creaked—reminding her of the noises that had awakened her the night before. Then the stairs creaked as someone began to climb them. There was another intruder in the house. Agent Campbell passed her the toddler as he pulled his gun from his holster.

"It's me," a deep voice called out.

The sleepy girl lifted her head from Elizabeth's shoulder. She already recognized Dalton's voice. Her face brightened, and she smiled at him as he stepped inside the nursery.

Elizabeth wanted to smile, too, but she held her breath instead. He had left the house for a reason—to follow a lead. "What was it?" she asked. "Did you find him?"

He pulled his phone from his pocket and turned the screen toward her, displaying the picture of a man's face. His eyes were closed, his face ashen.

She gasped. "He's dead?"

"Yes."

"Are you all right?" she asked. "Was there another struggle?"

He shook his head. "No, the hotel clerk found him dead in his room. I think he might be who I struggled with last night."

But his deep voice held a hint of doubt.

Blaine must have picked up on it, too, because he asked, "You're not certain?"

Dalton shrugged. "I thought he was bigger. Taller. Broader." He sighed. "But it was late. And I was tired."

Which was her fault. She had kept him awake two nights in a row—making love.

"Do you recognize him?" he asked her.

"I wasn't down here when you struggled with him," she reminded him. Embarrassment heated her face. She had been upstairs in her room—frozen with fear— unable to help him or herself.

"I don't mean from last night," he said and clarified his earlier question by adding, "Do you recognize him at all?"

She shrugged now. "I don't know. I remember some things." Like little Lizzie and Kenneth and Patricia and the house. But she didn't remember her own fiancé. "But there's so much I don't remember."

"Could he be the man who shot at you after he ran you and Wilson off the road?"

"I was upside down." Her head pressed against the roof of the car. "And he had his hood pulled tight around his face," she said. "It could be him." She peered closer at the screen. "But I'm not sure."

"It's okay," Agent Campbell said. He offered her assurance, while she felt Dalton's frustration.

Was he upset with her? With her inability to help at all? He wasn't the only one; she was frustrated, too. She wanted her memories back—all of them. She wanted her life back, and the danger gone.

But she knew if that happened, Dalton would be gone, too.

"I got some other news on the way over here," Dalton said. "Trooper Littlefield's out of the coma."

"That's great news!" Agent Campbell exclaimed. "He's a nice guy and a really good trooper."

A memory flashed into Elizabeth's mind—of the uniform and her resentment of it. "He investigated Kenneth's and Patricia's murders," she said as the memory became clearer. "I talked to him before."

While she was relieved that he was all right now, she understood why she had been suspicious and resentful of him even when she hadn't remembered him. "He didn't listen to me, though. He didn't look deeper into their deaths."

Dalton shook his head. "I spoke to the officer in charge of the investigation. It wasn't Trooper Littlefield."

"There were two of them," she conceded. "An older officer and Trooper Littlefield. I talked to both of them. But neither of them listened to me."

"You remember all that?" Agent Campbell asked

skeptically. He looked at her with suspicion now, as if he wondered if she had faked the amnesia.

She sighed. "Yes. I remember—like I remember little Lizzie."

"But you don't remember Tom Wilson," Dalton reminded her.

She shrugged. "I don't know why. Maybe I remember Kenneth and Patricia so clearly because I'm so upset about the injustice. Nobody listened to me then about their deaths and nobody's listening now." Frustration overwhelmed her, and tears stung her eyes and nose. "Their names will never be cleared, their real killer never found."

"I'm listening," Dalton assured her. Over the little girl's head, his dark gaze held hers. "And I'll talk to Littlefield about the investigation."

She snorted in derision. "What investigation? There really wasn't one."

"There will be now," Dalton said. He turned toward his friend. "Can you stay for a while longer?"

Blaine nodded. "Yes, but I want to talk to you before you leave." The other agent stepped outside the room.

Dalton didn't follow him right away. Instead, he stepped closer to her and reached out a hand. He patted little Lizzie's curly head and skimmed a finger along her cheek. "She's asleep. I hope last night wasn't too traumatic for her." But as he said it, he watched Elizabeth's face.

She didn't know if he was referring to the break-in or to her falling in love with him. Did he know how she felt about him? Did it show on her face? Her love? Her longing?

"She's been through a lot," Elizabeth replied.

"I know," he said. And again, she thought he was referring to her and not the child. "Too much."

"Do you know who he is?" she asked. "The man found in the motel?"

"A recently paroled former car thief," Dalton said. "His prints were on file. Ronnie Hoover worked as a parking attendant in the garage where Mr. Schultz kept his car."

"The building looked familiar to me," she said. "I may have an apartment there, too." But she remembered this house better. "That might be how he grabbed me."

"You think he could just be a random stalker?" he asked.

"Clearly, you don't think so," she said as she heard the doubt in his voice.

He shrugged. "You could have picked up a random stalker. But I don't think you've even spent that much time in Chicago since becoming little Elizabeth's guardian."

She shook her head. "No, I don't think so, either—not from what I remember and not from what Marta said. So you don't think this is random?"

"No. But I will figure it out." He made her another promise.

But all the promises he'd made had been about her memory and her attacker, about giving her life back to her—not about sharing it. Once he figured everything out, he would leave. Just as he turned to leave now.

But before he walked out into the hall to join his friend, he leaned down and he brushed a soft kiss across her mouth. Her heart shifted, swelling with the love she felt for him. A love she doubted that he would ever return…

WHY HADN'T TROOPER LITTLEFIELD identified her? When Dalton had found her in the trunk, the trooper had acted as if he'd never seen her before. But Littlefield had seen her; he had argued with her, if Dalton knew Elizabeth at all.

And Dalton knew Elizabeth.

She was strong. And stubborn and determined to prove that her friend hadn't killed his wife and then himself. The lawyer in her—even though her specialty was corporate law—would have had her arguing her case, proving her point.

She would have been memorable. Dalton knew that he would never forget her. And probably never get over her.

He drew in a deep breath as the thought jabbed his ribs with a twinge of pain.

"You okay?" Trooper Littlefield asked him as he opened his eyes and focused on Dalton's face.

Dalton chuckled. "You're the one just coming out of a coma," he said. Actually, he'd worried the man might have slipped back into it when he'd stepped into his hospital room and found him asleep. "Are you okay?"

The trooper lifted a hand to his heavily bandaged head. "Good thing it was already shaved, huh? I don't have to worry about my hair."

"No, you don't," Dalton agreed.

The man's pale face flushed with color. "I'm sorry," he said. "I screwed up, letting the guy get the jump on me again—like when he stole my car."

Dalton had thought it odd that the trooper had left his car down the block. Had that been a mistake or something else? But if the trooper had had some type of arrangement with the paroled car thief, why had he called Dalton to the scene at all?

"It's a good thing you didn't trust me to protect her," the trooper added.

"I trusted you," Dalton said. Then.

"You were right," Littlefield continued, "that he was waiting for another opportunity to get to her."

"He got to you instead," Dalton said. "You're lucky to be alive." And if Littlefield and Ronnie Hoover had been working together, why had the criminal turned on him? Not that that hadn't happened before. According to the old friends Dalton had put away, he had turned on them.

Littlefield shuddered. "The doctors are amazed that I came out of the coma."

"Is your memory intact?" Dalton asked.

"Yes," Littlefield replied. "I'll be able to identify the bastard, too. I saw his face in the mirror right before he hit me."

Dalton held out his phone with the picture displayed.

Littlefield's breath escaped in a shocked gasp. "He's dead?"

Dalton nodded.

"Yeah, that's him," he replied. "What happened to him?"

"I'm still waiting to hear from the Bureau coroner," he replied. He didn't know for certain that his bullet had killed the man.

Littlefield nodded. "That's good that you're not relying on Doc Brouwer. He's stretched too thin, as it is."

"Is he the one who investigated the deaths of Kenneth and Patricia Cunningham?"

Littlefield tensed and cursed. "That's who she is. The amnesia victim—she's related to those people. I remember her now."

"Elizabeth Schroeder," Dalton said. "She's a corporate lawyer from Chicago." And the guardian of a small child and someone's fiancée. As she'd already pointed out, no person was just one thing. But Dalton. He was only an FBI special agent. "We already learned her identity."

"Her memory returned?"

Not all of it. But he nodded. "She definitely remembers her friends."

"She doesn't believe it was a murder-suicide," Littlefield recalled.

"Do you?" Dalton asked.

The trooper hesitated just long enough that Dalton realized he had doubts, too. "Trooper Jackson was the senior investigator. He believed it was a murder-suicide."

"She said that he wouldn't listen to her," Dalton said. "She said that neither would you."

Littlefield sighed. "I think she's right that it didn't happen exactly the way the report reads."

"You don't think so?"

He shook his heavily bandaged head and flinched. "I think that the husband died first."

"You think the wife killed him and then herself?"

Littlefield nodded—but just slightly. "It looked that way. Doc thought he was dead longer. And his blood was under hers on the gun."

"Meaning she died last." Dalton had seen the crime-scene photos. "But the gun was in his hand…" The scene had been staged.

Littlefield groaned. "You think she's right. That the couple was murdered?"

"I think that it's an odd coincidence that Elizabeth is the only one fighting to keep the investigation open, to prove that her friends were murdered, and then she is nearly murdered."

"You think whoever killed them has been trying to kill her?" He pointed toward Dalton's phone. "Do you think it was him?"

Dalton shook his head. "It couldn't be. He was in prison when they were murdered." So if Kenneth and Patricia had been murdered—as he was beginning to believe—then their killer was still out there.

Littlefield grimaced again, but he hadn't moved his head at all. "Maybe I need to rethink my career," he murmured. "I may not be cut out for this job."

Dalton wanted to argue with him, but he was beginning to feel the way Elizabeth felt. Outraged that there had been no justice for her friends yet.

"Get some rest," Dalton suggested. "You'll feel better." He wouldn't feel better until he knew for certain who was trying to kill Elizabeth.

His cell vibrated in his pocket. He didn't click the talk button until he had stepped out of the trooper's room and into the hall. "Reyes here."

"You put a bullet in this guy," Jared Bell said. "But it wasn't what killed him."

"It wasn't?" There had been so much blood.

"That was the knife wound."

"I didn't have a knife in the dining room," Dalton said.

"He was dead before then," Jared added. "You must have shot him when he ran Elizabeth and her fiancé off the road earlier that day. I would bet whoever hired him killed him."

"And then broke into Elizabeth's house to finish the job he had paid Ronnie Hoover to do," Dalton said. "Are you with her?"

"No," Jared replied. "I'm still at the coroner's."

"Blaine had to leave early." That was why he'd called Dalton into the hall—to tell him that he couldn't stay much longer to protect her.

"There are guards all around the place," Jared assured him. "Nobody's getting inside to her."

Dalton wasn't that convinced. The only thing he knew for certain was that he had left Elizabeth and Lizzie alone. And that the person who really wanted her dead was still alive and determined to finish the job.

HER HAND SHAKING, Elizabeth wrapped it around the knob and drew the door open to face her fiancé.

"Thanks for agreeing to see me," Tom Wilson said as he stepped inside and closed the door behind him—shutting out the lawmen who were supposed to protect her.

She wasn't certain she had done the right thing. Maybe she shouldn't have let him past the young FBI agent and the trooper guarding the outside of the house. Maybe she shouldn't have let him inside with her—because, according to Dalton, she was still in danger. The man he had found dead had probably only been doing what he'd been paid to do. What someone else had paid him to do.

Tom Wilson, with his perfect hair, face and clothes, looked like the kind of man who would hire someone else to do his dirty work. But why would he want to hurt her?

To kill her?

Why not just ask for his ring back instead of trying to permanently get rid of her? Unless he had another reason, unless he had done something else—something horrible...

Had he really had a crush on Patricia? She'd been so beautiful with her long blond hair and bright blue eyes. But her inner beauty had been even more captivating. She'd been loving and loyal. She had never looked at any man but Kenneth. She wouldn't have left him for anyone. Tom would have known that he could never have her. And if he couldn't have her, had he not wanted anyone else to?

Tom was looking at her strangely, as if he was worried that she didn't remember him yet. Or maybe he was more worried that she did remember him.

And maybe what he'd done to her…

And to Kenneth and Patricia…

Before she could say anything, he reached for her. His hands closing roughly around her shoulders, he jerked her to him.

Chapter Seventeen

A sense of foreboding and urgency drove Dalton back to Elizabeth's house. He pressed the accelerator to the floor, risking the speed on the dark and unfamiliar roads—because he would risk anything for Elizabeth, to keep her safe.

He had promised to protect her, but he'd left her unprotected. Sure, there were guards outside—a lower-level agent and a local trooper or deputy. That wasn't protection in which Dalton had much confidence. Growing up the way he had, he didn't trust easily. So he only had a few true friends.

And two of those were gone on their honeymoon. Maybe he should have asked them to stay.

The lights of the house twinkled in the distance—at the end of the winding driveway leading up to it. He slammed on his brakes at the squad car that blocked the entrance. He put down the window and flashed his badge at the trooper.

"Special Agent Reyes," the man said as he read Dalton's shield. "You were going to see Littlefield. How is he?"

"Fine," he replied shortly. "Did you let anyone go up to the house tonight?"

The guy tensed—hopefully, just with irritation at

Dalton's curtness. But then he replied, "We let her fiancé through."

"When?" Dalton asked.

"Just a little while ago."

"Move your damn car," he ordered as fear gripped him. He didn't trust Tom Wilson, and it wouldn't take the man long to finish the job he'd hired someone else to do. The car had barely backed up when he squeezed his SUV between it and the fence. Then he pressed hard on the accelerator and raced up to the house.

He slammed it into Park and jumped out while it was still moving. Drawing his gun from his holster, he leaped up the steps to the porch and threw open the front door. Little Lizzie's cries drifted down from upstairs, drawing his concern. Elizabeth would have never let her cry.

Then he heard the struggle—something falling. And he turned toward the front room—where the man held Elizabeth tightly while she pounded her fists on his back and shoulders. She was a fighter.

Rage rushed over him, heating his blood and making his heart race. "Get your damn hands off her!" he shouted. Instead of cocking his gun, he holstered it and reached for the man, jerking him away from her. Then, like Elizabeth, he used his fists. Instead of pounding on his back, though, he pounded on his face—shoving his fist right into Tom Wilson's jaw. Wilson dropped to the floor with a heavy thud.

And Elizabeth dropped to her knees beside him. "Oh, my God, are you all right?" She glanced up at Dalton and glared at him. "Why did you hit him?"

"You were hitting him," he said. "He was hurting you."

She shook her head. "No. He wasn't hurting me." She sighed. "I was hurting him…"

Dalton narrowed his eyes. "What? He was all over you." Then he realized why and wished he'd hit him harder.

Wilson groaned, though, and shifted around on the floor as he regained consciousness.

Elizabeth glanced up again, but higher—toward the ceiling. "Would you go upstairs and check on Lizzie?"

Dalton hesitated. He didn't want to leave her alone to be mauled again by another man—even though that man was her fiancé. "If he tries to touch you..."

He would hit him harder. He didn't care that Wilson was her real fiancé. Dalton felt as though she was his. That feeling of possessiveness overwhelmed and chilled him. He had never felt that way before. But then, Elizabeth Schroeder made him feel a lot of things he had never felt before.

He gave Tom Wilson his most menacing glare before he headed up the stairs to the little girl. He opened the door and stepped inside the pink room. The tiny princess stood in her crib. Her hands gripped the top of the railing as if she was ready to climb out.

He didn't give her long before she figured out how. His granny had always said that there wasn't a crib created that could have held him.

Her chocolate-brown curls were damp and stuck to her face, which was red and flushed from her tears. But the minute she saw him, her tears stopped and her little grimace turned into a smile. And something shifted inside his chest, squeezing his heart. He wasn't just falling for Elizabeth. He was falling for her goddaughter, too.

"Come here, baby," he said as he reached inside the crib for her.

She gripped his arms and clung to him. When he lifted her up, she settled her head beneath his chin and sighed. He rubbed her back. "It's all right, sweetheart. It's all right."

But it wasn't. He didn't like leaving Elizabeth alone with Tom Wilson—even if the man posed no physical threat to her. He posed a threat to Dalton. Wilson was her fiancé. Dalton was just her protector.

And he worried that he wasn't doing a very good job of protecting her by leaving her alone with a man she didn't even remember. He could have been abusive to her. He could have been a danger…

ELIZABETH'S PULSE SETTLED back down to an even pace as the little girl's cries subsided. Dalton had her now. He was taking care of little Lizzie—the way he tried to take care of her.

Tom groaned and sat up. His hand rubbed his jaw, which he moved back and forth as if testing to see if it was broken. Had Dalton broken it? He'd certainly hit him hard enough.

"What the hell's wrong with that agent?" Tom asked, his chest puffing out with righteous indignation.

"What the hell's wrong with you?" Elizabeth asked, and she slapped his already bruised face.

He groaned again and flinched.

"You can't just grab me and try to force yourself on me," she said, and her pulse quickened again with the fear she'd felt as she had tried to fight him off.

"I was trying to get you to remember me," he admitted. "You remember everyone else but me."

Had that really hurt him—as she'd told Dalton she had? Or was it only wounded pride that had brought him here to try to jar her memory?

"I'm your fiancé," he said. "We've been engaged for

two years. We dated three years before that. How could you just forget me?"

"I forgot everything," she reminded him. "My amnesia was complete. I didn't even remember my own name. I didn't remember *myself*." But she hadn't felt any differently then than she did now. Dalton had been right—that her character and her values hadn't changed.

"But you remember all of that now," he said, his voice wavering with a faint whine. "You remember everything and everyone but *me*."

"I remember," she said. But with none of the intense emotion that she had remembered Kenneth and Patricia and baby Lizzie...

"You do?" he asked with skepticism and nerves apparent in his voice.

Did he really want her to remember?

It was too late—if he had changed his mind. His kiss hadn't brought the memories back, but when Dalton had hit him so hard that he'd knocked him out, she had cared. She hadn't wanted him hurt.

"We have known each other a long time," she said.

He smiled then winced and touched his swollen jaw. "Yes, we have."

"We've been engaged for two years," she said, even though she wasn't certain it was actually that long. She couldn't remember exactly when he'd proposed—the night had felt like any other dinner date.

"Yes."

"We don't live together," she said.

He shook his head, and his brow furrowed slightly as if he was growing concerned about her memories.

He had reason to be concerned.

"We haven't set a date for our wedding," she said.

"We've been busy," he said, "especially since Kenneth and Patricia died. You've been dividing your time between Chicago and here—between me and Lizzie."

"Why?" she asked.

His brow furrowed more. "What do you mean?"

"Why haven't we set a date?"

"I just told you—"

"Kenneth and Patricia died a few months ago," she said. "We were engaged over a year before that. Usually the first thing couples do when they get engaged is set a date—because they're anxious to get married." The way Kenneth and Patricia had been. Apparently, Dalton's friends Ash and Claire had also been anxious and ecstatically in love.

"We're not that kind of people," he said. "We don't rush into anything."

"Then why don't we at least live together?" she asked. "Especially now. Why aren't you helping me with little Lizzie?"

He sighed—a churlish sigh of irritation. "*You* are her guardian. Not *me*."

And why was that? Hadn't Kenneth and Patricia approved of him? Hadn't they expected her and Tom to last?

She remembered Patricia broaching the subject, wishing more for her best friend. Elizabeth had defended Tom then—saying how handsome and smart he was, how much she admired him.

And Patricia had sighed with pity.

Now Elizabeth understood why. She had wanted passion and love for her friend, not admiration.

"We weren't even decided on whether or not we wanted children," he said.

But she suspected he was decided. He didn't want

them. While he hadn't told her as much over the past few months, she'd sensed his withdrawal.

"That's why you pulled away," she said. "I thought it was because I was emotional over Kenneth's and Patricia's deaths, and you're not comfortable with emotion."

"I'm not," he admitted. "Neither are you. That's why we're so compatible. That's why we've had such a great relationship, Elizabeth."

She nodded in agreement. "We were comfortable," she agreed. "We talked about work over dinner in exclusive restaurants. We attended plays and art gallery openings."

He smiled. "We loved that life."

"That's not my life anymore," she said.

And she realized that wasn't the life she wanted now. Maybe that had never been the life she'd really wanted—it was only what she'd thought she wanted. It had been her idea of success, the kind of life her parents had lived, still lived. Like Tom, they hadn't offered to help her with little Lizzie. They hadn't comforted and consoled her over the loss of her best friends. If not for Kenneth and Patricia, she might have never known about true love—about true emotion.

"You could sign over custody to her uncle," Tom suggested. And she knew it wasn't the first time he had made that suggestion; he'd just been more subtle about it before.

Anger surged through her, and she wanted to slap him again. Instead, she stared down at her hand, admiring the diamond ring one last time before she pulled it from her finger and handed it back to him.

"What are you doing?" he asked.

"What I should have done months ago," she said. "Giving back your ring."

He wouldn't reach for it. Only shook his head. "Elizabeth, you're not yourself. You shouldn't be making decisions like this."

"I'm more myself than I've been," she said. "And I know now that I never should have accepted your ring. I care about you, but I don't love you like a wife should love her husband."

He gasped as if she'd hurt him. "Elizabeth!"

But she only smiled. "And you don't love me." She actually wondered how much he even really cared. "Not like a husband should love his wife."

"Elizabeth, you've been through so much that I think you should consider this some more before you make any rash decisions," he said.

She laughed. "Nobody's ever accused me of being rash." She had planned out her entire life—her education, her career, even her mate...

Tom Wilson had fit that role—before she'd met Dalton Reyes.

Maybe Tom knew her better than she thought, because he glanced up at the ceiling and nodded. "It's him—isn't it? That FBI agent..."

"What's him?" she asked.

"He's the reason you're giving me back this ring." And finally he reached for it, closing his fingers around the big diamond.

Dalton was definitely part of the reason but not the entire reason. "We're the reason," she insisted. "We're not right for each other."

He shook his head. "We were perfect." But he looked at her now as if she wasn't—as if she was far from perfect.

Because she'd rejected him? Or because she had

fallen for the FBI agent? Could he see that love in her—that love she'd never felt for him?

She would have apologized, but she wasn't sorry—not now. Not with the way he was acting. Her memories back now, she knew that she would have broken up with him earlier. But then she hadn't wanted to hurt him. Now she realized that she couldn't hurt him.

Dalton had, though. Tom kept rubbing his jaw even as he finally got to his feet and headed toward the door. "You're going to get hurt," he warned her.

Fear chilled her, and she asked, "Is that a threat?"

He tensed and stopped his advance toward the front door. "What?"

"Are you threatening me?" Was he the one who'd hired the hit on her?

"I'm warning you," he said. "I think you've fallen for the FBI agent out of gratitude to him for saving your life. But he was only doing his job, Elizabeth. He doesn't love you. And once this case is over, he'll move on to the next one. He'll leave you."

"He will," she agreed. She had already accepted that. But she would enjoy whatever time she had with Dalton—because she loved him. She loved him the way Kenneth and Patricia had loved each other…if only Dalton loved her back.

Tom hesitated at the door. "What we had was good, Elizabeth. We were comfortable. I'll keep the ring. You'll want to wear it again."

She shook her head at his stubbornness and his arrogance. Why had she never noticed it before? She wouldn't be going back to Tom Wilson. Ever. She wanted more out of life than comfortable.

She wanted passion. She wanted love. She wanted Dalton Reyes.

HE WANTED DALTON REYES. Dead.

The FBI agent had a damn hero complex. He had to keep riding in to rescue the damsel in distress. He understood now why Hoover had failed in the job he had hired him to do.

Dalton Reyes was the reason. The FBI agent had shot the ex-con. And he'd shot *him*.

He winced as he wrapped another bandage around his waist. The bullet had gone through his side without hitting anything vital. But he had probably needed surgery or at least stitches to close the wound. Instead, he had taped and bandaged it. And he hoped that nobody noticed it.

It hurt like hell, though. And he had to watch that the wound didn't get infected.

He wanted Elizabeth dead. Yet. Still. But he wanted Dalton Reyes dead even more.

Chapter Eighteen

The first thing he noticed when she stepped inside the nursery was that the ring was gone. Nothing sparkled on her hand—nothing taunted him that she belonged to someone else.

But it didn't matter that the ring was gone. She didn't belong to him, either.

"He left?"

She nodded.

"Did he ask for his ring back?" he asked, although he doubted it.

Tom Wilson hadn't looked like an idiot. But then the man had been so stupid that he hadn't even realized she was missing. Or maybe he had hoped that she was missing.

Forever.

"I gave it back to him," she said.

"Why?" he asked. And he held his breath as he waited for her admission. Was it because of him? Because she had feelings for him, too?

"He suggested that I sign over custody of Lizzie to her uncle."

He tightened his arm around the little girl. "I should have hit him harder."

Her lips curved into a slight smile. "If it makes you feel better, I slapped him—right on his swollen jaw."

It made him feel better. And it made him feel more—love for her. "You yelled at me for hitting him."

"I didn't yell at you," she protested. "I thought it was unnecessary."

His hand that wasn't holding the child fisted. "It was very necessary. He was all over you."

"He was trying to make me remember him."

"Did it work?"

"I remember him," she replied. "I remember that I intended to give that ring back months ago, but I hadn't wanted to hurt him."

"You don't care so much now?" he asked. Hopefully. If she hadn't wanted to hurt him, she must have had feelings for him at some point. Hell, she'd accepted his ring, so she must have loved him once.

"I don't care at all now," she said. And her gaze met his, as if she was trying to tell him something. That she cared about someone else instead.

Or was he only wistfully imagining that?

"That's good," he said. And he returned her stare. But he could only give her a look.

He couldn't give her anything else—not until he'd kept all of the promises he had made to her. To find out who she was. To keep her safe. To find out who was trying to kill her. And now he had promised to find out the truth about her friends' deaths.

He couldn't make any more promises until he'd kept those. And if he couldn't keep those…

"How was Trooper Littlefield?" she asked.

He closed his eyes to break their connection. He couldn't look at her and keep from her the information the trooper had given him. That it might have been Patricia—her best friend since they were kids—who had been the killer…

She wouldn't be able to handle that; she was already devastated from having to relive their loss as if it had just happened all over again.

"Is he going to be okay?" she asked.

"Yes," he assured her. "He will recover from the head injury."

"And he's had no loss of memory?" she asked.

"No." In fact, he had remembered everything very well.

She sighed. "He still doesn't believe me that someone else…" She trailed off, as if not wanting to discuss the baby's parents' deaths in front of little Lizzie.

He laid the sleeping child back down in her crib. Maybe she would stay there tonight—as long as no one else broke into her home. Dalton would make damn sure no one else broke into her home.

He followed Elizabeth out into the hall, but she didn't stop there—she continued to the master bedroom. And she held open the door for him and closed it once he stepped inside with her. His gaze went automatically to the bed, where they had made love the night before. The sheets were still tangled. She hadn't made it.

Her gaze followed his, and her face flushed with embarrassment. "I didn't have time to make the bed. After what happened last night, I didn't want Marta to come back here. Not until we know it's safe."

"There are guards outside," he said. "As long as you don't authorize them to let someone come up to the house, you'll be safe."

"But the man last night…" She shuddered.

Was still out there.

He pulled her into his arms, offering comfort for her fears.

She linked her arms around his neck and clung to him. "I'm overreacting," she said. "He's dead now."

"No, he's not," he corrected her.

She eased away from him and peered up into his face. "But you showed me his picture…"

"That man is dead," he said. "The ex-con is dead. But he was already dead when someone broke into the house. Someone else broke in here last night."

She tensed in his arms. "Someone else broke in."

"We suspected that there was someone else," he reminded her. "Someone that hired the ex-con."

"Someone I know," she murmured. "Someone I trust." She trembled in his arms as her fears returned.

He pulled her closer, enfolding her in his embrace. "That's why you can't let anyone in here," he said. "You were right to tell Marta to stay away."

"Marta would never hurt anyone," she protested. And she tried to pull back, but he held her tightly.

"You can't trust anyone," he said.

"What about you?" she asked. "Can I trust you?"

"I'm the only one you can trust," he said. "I would never hurt you."

Her lips curved into a slight, sad smile. "Don't lie to me."

"Elizabeth…" But before he could say anything else, she rose on tiptoe and pressed her lips to his. He hadn't intended to make love to her tonight. He hadn't wanted to risk being distracted in case someone tried to break in again.

But there were guards blocking the driveway and watching the house. Nobody would get past them without him at least being forewarned. Even if the guards weren't there, he wasn't sure that he would have been able to resist her.

She undressed him—as he had undressed before for her. She removed his holster and gun and put them on the table beside the bed. Then she slowly, teasingly, undid the buttons on his shirt. Her fingertips skimmed over the muscles of his chest, teasing him as her hand traveled down to his belt.

He resisted the urge to take over—to hurry. He understood that she needed to be in control. She was a strong woman whose life was currently beyond her control. So he let her drive him crazy.

She made love to him with her mouth and her body. And finally she collapsed on his chest. Tears trailed from her face onto his neck as she snuggled into him.

He wasn't sure why she was crying. Because of her friends. Because she was in danger. She had so many reasons. So he just stroked her back until her cries subsided and she finally slept. He couldn't sleep, though—not even knowing there were guards outside. He had to stay vigilant.

His phone, which sat next to the holstered gun, vibrated against the table. He grabbed it quickly—dreading that this would be a warning from those guards.

But he didn't recognize the number calling him. "Hello?"

"Agent Reyes?"

Keeping his voice low so he didn't awaken Elizabeth, he asked, "Yes, who is this?"

"I—I got your number from a state trooper," the raspy voice replied. "I—I have some information you need."

"What information is that?"

"I—I think I know where a guy is—a guy that you might have shot…"

He tensed. And Elizabeth murmured. He carefully

rolled her over to the other side of the bed. Then he hurried out into the hall. "Where?"

"I think he's here at Pinebrook Stables," the voice replied in a raspy whisper. "The vet treated him for a wound that looked an awful lot like a gunshot wound."

It was the guy—from last night. "What's the address for the stables?" Dalton asked. "And how badly is he hurt?"

"Bad," the raspy voice replied.

Then it hadn't been Tom Wilson with whom he'd tangled in the dining room the night before. The extent of that man's injuries was the swollen jaw Dalton had just given him. He hadn't had a gunshot wound, or he wouldn't have been able to manhandle Elizabeth the way he had.

"The vet wanted to call an ambulance," the informant continued, "but no matter how much pain the guy is in, he refused. He's gotta be in trouble…"

He would be once Dalton got ahold of him. He couldn't wait to end this, to keep another of his promises to Elizabeth—so that he would be able to make more.

ELIZABETH AWAKENED TO an empty bed again. But the house was quiet. No crashing sounds. No gunshots. But the eerie silence was just as unsettling. She pulled on her robe and stepped into the hall.

A faint cry drifted from the nursery, so she hurried into little Lizzie's room. A shadow stood over her crib. It could have been Dalton. But the child sounded distressed.

So she flipped on the lights and gasped as she realized the dark-haired man wasn't Dalton. He wasn't as muscular or as tall, and his eyes weren't as dark. Agent Jared Bell held the little girl—but he held her awkwardly and as far away from his body as his arms would reach, as if she might detonate if she got too close.

She reached for her daughter and caught her close. "What are you doing here?" she asked.

"Agent Reyes asked me to take over," he said.

Her heart shifted in her chest, pain squeezing it. What had happened? Had she scared him off?

"Why would he ask you to take over the case?" she asked. "He doesn't believe it's that serial killer who's after me."

"No, he doesn't," Agent Bell agreed. "And neither do I anymore. He only asked me to take over protection duty for the rest of the night."

"Protection duty," she said as she soothed the disgruntled child. "Not babysitting. You didn't have to try to pick her up." It was a miracle he hadn't dropped her with the way he'd been holding her.

"That was a mistake," he admitted with a shudder of unease as she changed the child's diaper. "I didn't think it would be that hard—not when Blaine Campbell, and even Reyes, make it look easy."

Dalton was good with little Lizzie. And with Elizabeth, too.

"Some people are probably naturals," she said. "I wasn't one. It took time and practice for me to get used to being around a little one." But, even before her death, Patricia had made certain to train her, as if she knew that someday Elizabeth would be taking over her mothering duties.

"I don't need any practice," Agent Bell said. "It's not like I ever intend to have kids."

"You don't?"

He shook his head. "Working for the Bureau is all-consuming. I don't have time for relationships, let alone a family."

She already knew Dalton felt the same way, but her heart grew heavy with disappointment. "But Agent Campbell has both. And Agent Stryker just got married."

He shrugged. "They're at different points in their careers than Reyes and I are," he said. "They can step back and do more training than fieldwork. We can't."

And she suspected that wasn't just because of where they were in their careers but because of their personalities. They lived for fieldwork. They were fearless. But being fearless tended to get people killed—because they didn't recognize and respect the danger.

"Where did Dalton go?" she asked with a terrifying sense of foreboding that he had put himself in danger again.

"He's following a lead," Agent Bell replied.

She dimly remembered his phone vibrating on the bedside table and then the deep rumble of his voice. "He got a call earlier."

He nodded. "That was the lead."

"He didn't go off alone, did he?" she asked.

"He didn't want any backup," Agent Bell admitted. "He didn't think he needed it."

Her pulse quickened with fear for his life. "He thinks he's invincible."

"From everything I've heard about him and witnessed myself," Agent Bell said, "I kind of think he is, too."

She wasn't convinced—not after everything she'd recently gone through. Even the person hired to kill her had died. Nobody was invincible. "You should have gone with him."

"He wanted me here—to protect you," he said. "That was more important to him."

Her heart warmed with hope that he seemed to care about her—really care about her—as more than just a case. But her fear for him overwhelmed that hope. "Than his own safety?"

Jared Bell shrugged. "I wouldn't worry about him." He obviously wasn't. "He survived the street gang he grew up in and then turned on—"

"Because of his grandmother," she said defensively, in case Agent Bell thought Dalton had betrayed his gang members. They had betrayed him first. "He turned on them because they killed her—the woman who'd raised him."

Jared's caramel-colored eyes widened in surprise and he sucked in a sharp breath. "I didn't know that."

She suspected it was a story that Dalton had told few people. Why had he told her? Why was he letting her so deeply into his life if he didn't intend to stay around once he apprehended whoever was trying to kill her?

But he wouldn't be able to share her life if he lost his while trying to apprehend that killer. He shouldn't have gone off alone.

HE WAITED IN the dark, following the beacon of the SUV's headlamp beams traveling up the circular driveway to the deserted horse ranch. There was only one vehicle coming up that road. And, using the night-vision scope on his rifle, he could spy only one shadow inside the vehicle, behind the steering wheel.

A smile spread across his face. This had been easier than he had even anticipated it could be. He waited until the SUV got a little closer—until that shadow behind the wheel was directly in his scope—then he squeezed the trigger.

Chapter Nineteen

Elizabeth couldn't get back to sleep. Maybe it was because she missed the warmth and comfort of Dalton's strong arms holding her and the reassuring rise and fall of his muscular chest beneath her cheek. Or maybe she couldn't sleep because that terrifying sense of foreboding continued to grip her.

Hours must have passed since he had gotten that call. But he wasn't back. And she worried that he wouldn't be able to come back.

Jared Bell had faith in him. And so did she. But whoever was trying to kill her was determined to finish the job, and like her, he must have realized that Dalton wouldn't let that happen.

While he was alive.

He wouldn't break that promise he'd made her. While he was alive.

But if he were dead…

No. She wouldn't consider that possibility. She would believe—as he and Agent Bell believed—that he was invincible. Nothing could happen to Dalton.

She hadn't even told him she loved him. She should have told him. She had tried showing him tonight—when she'd made love to him with all her heart and soul. She hoped he had understood that hadn't been gratitude. She felt so much more than gratitude for him.

While she wasn't sleeping, she lay alone in the tangled sheets of the bed she'd shared with Dalton such a short time ago. If she stepped outside the door, she would have to talk to Jared—have to listen to his empty assurances. He didn't make promises the way Dalton did.

But while she lay in the dark, she heard that strange sound again—that vibration of the silent ring of a cell phone. And she realized it was coming through the baby monitor. Jared must have gone back into the nursery. For a man so uncomfortable and awkward with children, he was strangely drawn to little Lizzie. But then, the precious girl was as magnetic and magical as her mother had been.

Elizabeth had already lost her best friends. She couldn't lose the love of her life, too.

"Agent Bell." The words came clearly through the monitor as Jared answered his call.

She couldn't hear his caller, though. So she had to wait, with an unbearable pressure on her chest, while Agent Bell listened. His response was a heartfelt curse.

And her heart plummeted.

"How badly is he hurt?" he asked.

"No!" The protest burst from her lips even though she knew the injured man was Dalton. She'd known that he wasn't invincible. She jumped out of bed and hurried down the hall to the nursery.

Jared opened the door and stepped into the hall to join her. But his cell phone was still pressed to his ear as he listened to whoever had called him.

It wasn't Dalton. Because he'd asked how badly *he* was hurt. And she knew *he* was Dalton.

"What happened?" she asked—too anxious to wait until his call was done. "How is he?"

Not dead. He couldn't be dead.

Jared shook his head, and her heart stopped beating for one beat before resuming at a frantic pace, hammering away in her chest.

"No!"

"I'll check back soon," he said into the phone before quickly clicking it off. Then he reached for her.

She hadn't even realized that her legs were shaking so badly that they had nearly buckled beneath her. But she couldn't feel—not even his hands on her shoulders holding her up—since fear paralyzed her.

"Is he dead?" she asked. "Is Dalton dead?"

Jared shook his head again. "No, he's not."

"But he's hurt," she said. "I heard you over the baby monitor. He's hurt."

"He was shot," Jared replied.

She felt a sharp jab to her heart and sucked in a breath of pain. "Oh, no! How bad is it?"

"I don't know yet," he admitted. "He's en route to the hospital right now."

"We need to go," she said. "We need to meet him there." She had to see him—had to see how badly he was wounded. She had to hold his hand, the way he had held hers when she'd been hurt.

But Agent Bell shook his head again. "No, it's too dangerous."

"How?"

"We could be driven off the road or attacked as we leave the house," he pointed out. "We can't leave here."

"You may not care about your fellow agent," she accused him, "but I do." She didn't just care; she loved him. So much. "I want to be there for him."

"I will be there for him," he said. "By keeping you here. Your safety is his priority and my responsibility now. I won't let him down by putting you in danger."

Panic was making it hard for her to draw a deep breath into her lungs. She had to be with Dalton. "You don't know that we'll be in danger if we go to the hospital."

He gestured toward the closed door of the nursery. "It won't be just your life you're risking," he pointed out, "if we put her in the car with us and it gets run off the road."

"You don't know that'll happen," she insisted.

"I'm a profiler," he reminded her. "I'm not Dalton Reyes. I don't drive like he does."

"Then have someone else bring me to the hospital," she suggested. "One of the troopers outside. And you can stay with Lizzie." She cared more about the child than herself; she'd rather have him keeping Lizzie safe.

Panic flashed across his face now, leaving it stark. "No. Absolutely not."

"But—"

"Keeping you safe is my responsibility," he reiterated. "We're staying here."

"What makes you think we're safe here?" she asked. "Don't you think that Dalton was shot to get him out of the way? And now that he's out of the way, that person is going to try to get to me again. It doesn't matter if we're at the hospital or if we're here."

"There are guards outside the house," he said. "And I'm inside with you. You're safe here."

She shivered as that foreboding rushed over her again. And she shook her head. "No. I won't be safe anywhere." Especially not now with Dalton wounded.

How badly was he hurt?

Would he make it back to her?

Ever?

HE WAS GLAD THAT, when he'd cleared out Hoover's motel room, he had saved the uniform the ex-con had taken off

Trooper Littlefield. Without it, he wouldn't have made it past the deputy blocking the end of the driveway. The poor man had had no idea what had hit him…

Just like whoever was guarding Elizabeth would have no idea what had hit him, either. Leaving the squad car blocking the end of the driveway, he headed up toward the house.

The radio he'd taken off the deputy squawked. "This is Agent Bell," the caller announced. "Is everything clear outside?"

He hesitated answering but finally pressed the button. "I've noticed a light shining in the trees at the back of the house. It could be someone walking around with a flashlight. Should I go check it out?"

"Yes," the agent replied. "But be careful. I'm pretty sure the suspect is going to make his move tonight."

He was right. The suspect was making his move right now…onto the front porch. But the beauty was that nobody suspected *him*. He would get away with murder.

Again.

A shadow darkened the glass of the front door. Had Agent Bell heard him step onto the porch? He moved quickly, backing against the side of the house so that he wouldn't be seen.

Yet.

But the front door creaked open.

God, he was making this easy for him.

Agent Bell stepped out, gun drawn.

He waited in those shadows—just waited, his breath held, until the man stepped close enough. Then he struck, lashing out with the butt of the gun he'd taken off the deputy. Just like the deputy, Agent Bell never saw him.

He dropped to the porch with a heavy thud. He was

either unconscious or dead. It didn't matter which. He wouldn't regain consciousness in time to save Elizabeth.

No one could save her now.

The front door creaked again. "Agent Bell?" a female voice called out. "Are you out here?"

The agent didn't even groan. He couldn't hear her.

"Jared?" she called out with obvious apprehension now. "Jared, where are you?"

Maybe she would step out, too, and make it all so easy for him. But instead, she pulled the door shut. The lock clicked as she turned the dead bolt.

Still in the shadows, he grinned. It didn't matter that she'd locked the door. He had a key. He would get to her. She was as good as already dead.

PAIN RADIATED THROUGHOUT Dalton's chest. It wasn't just the bullet. The vest had taken most of the impact of that. And it had only grazed his arm before hitting the vest. His pain was actually panic—the panic that he had left Elizabeth and the little girl in danger.

"Get the doctor in here," he told Blaine Campbell. "I need to get out of here."

"You need stitches in that arm," Blaine said.

Dalton glanced down at the blood-soaked bandage. "It's fine."

"You lost a lot of blood."

He shrugged. "Not like you did."

Blaine had taken a bullet in the neck months before and was lucky to be alive. But then, Blaine Campbell was a lucky man. Dalton had a horrible feeling that his luck was running out.

"This is nothing." He swung his legs over the gurney and stood up, but his legs weren't quite as steady as he'd counted on and he stumbled forward.

Blaine caught one of his arms while another man grabbed his other. "Hey," Trooper Littlefield said. "You need to wait for the doctor."

"I'm fine," he said. "It's Elizabeth I'm worried about."

"Jared Bell is with Elizabeth," Blaine reminded him. Blaine had been with him—crouched down in the backseat. He had insisted on coming along even though Dalton had thought he could handle the situation alone.

He cursed himself. "I knew it was an ambush…" But he'd still walked right into it. "And the only reason someone would want to take me out is to get to Elizabeth."

"From what I understand, a lot of people would like to take you out," Blaine reminded him.

"In Chicago," he agreed. "Not here. I barely know anybody here."

"Somebody could have followed you," Blaine pointed out. He had been followed—on that case that had nearly claimed his life.

It wasn't just pride that had him shaking his head. He was certain. "This isn't about me. It's about Elizabeth."

Trooper Littlefield uttered a regretful and agitated sigh. "Maybe it's about her friends," he said. "The more I think about that crime scene…"

"You think she's right? It was no murder-suicide?" Blaine asked.

Dalton had already determined as much.

"The gun was in Kenneth Cunningham's hand," Littlefield said. "But he died first. He couldn't have killed her after he died."

"Someone staged the scene," Blaine agreed. "Why? And what does that have to do with Elizabeth?"

"Whoever did it wants to shut her up," Dalton said. "She won't stop fighting for justice for her friends and for their daughter."

"She won't stop," Trooper Littlefield agreed. "She was adamant that her friends were so in love that they would have never hurt each other."

Dalton nodded. "She really believes that."

"She's biased," Blaine pointed out.

"She's not the only one," Trooper Littlefield said. "Pretty much everyone that knew the Cunninghams or had ever met them agrees with her."

Pretty much everyone...

The doctor stepped into the room. "What are you doing out of bed?" he asked Dalton.

"I have to leave," he replied. He had to get the hell out of there. Now.

"You have to get stitches," the doctor said—just as Blaine had moments before.

"I have to get back to Elizabeth," he insisted—because he had figured it out.

"Jared is with Elizabeth," Blaine reiterated. "He'll keep her safe. You don't need to worry."

But he was worried. Because someone had tried to take him out for a reason, and he believed that reason was to get to Elizabeth.

He held up a hand—holding the doctor and his suture kit back. "Let me call him."

Blaine cursed as he fumbled his cell phone out of his jeans pocket. "I promised I'd call him back, but I haven't yet."

Dalton held out his hand for Blaine's cell, which the other agent handed over with a sigh. He pushed the redial button. The phone rang once, twice, three times and then four and five before going to voice mail.

"Special Agent Jared Bell. I am currently unavailable, but leave me your name and number, and I will return your call."

"What the hell's going on?" Dalton shouted into the phone, but also at his friends. "If he's waiting for your call, why did it go to voice mail?"

But he knew. And from their faces, so did they. Something had happened to Jared that had, at the least, incapacitated him. And now Elizabeth was alone and unprotected. He headed for the door, and this time nobody tried to stop him. Instead, they hurried along with him.

No matter how fast he drove, he probably wouldn't get to her in time. He had broken one of his promises to Elizabeth. He hadn't protected her.

Chapter Twenty

Fear gripped Elizabeth. Fear for Dalton. How badly was he hurt? Would he survive his gunshot wound?

She also felt fear for Agent Jared Bell. Where had he gone? He had just disappeared. But she knew better than to risk going outside to search for him. She had no gun. No weapon that would defend her and little Lizzie from a gun or a killer.

Somewhere she had a business card for Special Agent Blaine Campbell. She could call him for help. If only she could find his card...

She fumbled around in the drawers of the desk in the office on the first floor. The white-paneled room was next to the dining room—where Dalton had struggled so recently with the intruder.

Where *was* Jared Bell? She had heard no sounds of a struggle. She'd only heard the creak of the front door opening and closing. And footsteps on the porch.

Wood creaked and groaned as someone stepped onto the porch again. Her pulse quickened with fear. But maybe it was just Jared returning. Maybe he'd gone down the driveway to talk to the guards by the road—to warn them that someone could be coming for her.

Not could be. Was.

She knew it. That was why Dalton had been shot. Because of her.

Guilt joined her fear. If only Dalton hadn't been so intent on keeping the promises he'd made to her. If only he hadn't been so good at protecting her…

Then maybe someone wouldn't have been so intent on getting him out of the way. She had to get to the hospital. If that was Jared Bell on the porch, she would convince him to take her to Dalton. She had to tell him she loved him.

More boards creaked as the person crossed the porch. Then the doorbell pealed. And she remembered locking the door. She had locked out the agent. Her breath shuddered out with relief, and she rushed to the door. But when she pulled it open, it wasn't Agent Bell standing on the front porch.

Tom Wilson stood in front of her, his face flushed, his hair mussed. Alcohol emanated from him as if he'd soaked himself in it.

"Eliz…a…beth…" He sounded as if he was trying to sing but was just slurring. Tom Wilson didn't sing—not even in the shower.

"What are you doing here?"

She thought he had left town and returned to Chicago after she'd given him back his ring. But apparently he had gone to a bar instead and had been there ever since. She could never remember him having more than a glass of wine with dinner and champagne on New Year's. When had he started drinking?

He stumbled across the threshold into the foyer. "I have to talk to you, Elizabeth."

She couldn't deal with Tom right now—not when she was so worried about Dalton. And about Agent Bell.

"We have nothing more to say to each other," she insisted. They had been over a long time ago; she shouldn't have been wearing his ring anymore. She actually never should have accepted it.

"That's not true, Elizabeth."

They were done—whether or not his pride could accept it.

"You'll want to hear what I have to tell you," he insisted with an aggression she had never seen in him before. And suddenly his words weren't so slurred.

Had he faked the drunkenness so that she would think him harmless and let him inside the house? But how had he gotten past the guards at the end of the driveway? She was certain that Dalton had given orders that Tom Wilson never be allowed up to the house again.

"How did you get up here?" she asked.

"I walked."

"Nobody stopped you at the street?"

He shook his head. "Nobody was there—just a police car blocked the end of the driveway."

"There was no trooper or agent by the car?" she asked. And if not, where had he gone? Had he disappeared with Agent Bell?

"No." He glanced around the room, as if checking now to see if she was alone. "Isn't *he* here?"

"Who?" But she knew who he was referring to and it wasn't Agent Bell.

"That FBI agent you're in love with," he said. "He's gone already." And a smug smile crossed a face she'd once considered so handsome.

Fear chilled her, lifting goose bumps on her skin. And she asked, "What did you do to him?"

"Me?" he asked, his blue eyes widening in shock. "You think I did something to him?"

"He was shot."

His brow furrowed with confusion. "Have you ever known me to shoot a gun?"

She shook her head. But she wasn't sure that she had ever really known him at all. She already knew Dalton Reyes so much better than she'd ever known the man to whom she'd been engaged for two years.

"I haven't," she said. "But that doesn't mean you don't know how to shoot—that you don't own a gun."

He furrowed his brow, as if trying to figure out what she was saying. But she didn't believe that he was actually drunk anymore.

"We've dated for years," she said. "But we never actually spent that much time together. We never lived together. I don't know what you own. I don't know what you know."

"Are you sure that your memory is back?" he asked. "Because you're not making any sense. But then, you've not been making much sense since Kenneth and Patricia died."

She cocked her head, trying to understand what he meant. "Because I'm determined to keep my promise to them and raise little Lizzie?" she asked. Like Dalton Reyes, she kept the promises she made—or she would as long as she was alive. "I'm not giving her up."

"You would rather give me up instead?" And he was all wounded male pride again. "It's that easy for you to just give me back my ring and walk away from all the years we've known each other."

"We don't know each other at all," she said, "if you expect me to give up my goddaughter."

"It's not just her you're being unreasonable about," he said. "You're being unreasonable about their deaths. Why can't you just accept that it was a murder-suicide?

Why do you have to keep going to authorities—keep pushing them to reopen the investigation?"

She shivered now as fear chilled her. "Why do you care?" she asked.

"Because you're making a fool of yourself."

"Is that the real reason?" she wondered. "Or is there another reason you don't want the investigation into their deaths reopened?"

His flushed face drained of all color. "What the hell reason could I have?"

"Because you were involved," she suggested. "Because you wanted Patricia for yourself."

He laughed. "I didn't even like Patricia."

That surprised her more than anything else. Everyone who had met her had loved Patricia; she had been that special. Elizabeth was certain that she and Dalton would have become fast friends. "Why not?"

"Because she didn't like me," he said. "Because she didn't think I was good enough for her best friend. I didn't want Patricia in my life at all. And I didn't want her in yours."

"Is that why you did it?" she asked. "Is that why you killed them?"

"You're crazy!" he said as color rushed back into his face.

She was crazy to have let him inside the house. And she was crazy with fear.

"Is that why you want to kill me?" she asked. "Because I keep pushing to have that investigation reopened?"

He lurched forward, reaching for her. Before she could turn and run, he caught her. His hands gripping her shoulders, he shook her.

She needed to fight him. But that shaking left her

head reeling with dizziness and nausea. Her memory had returned, but she wasn't completely recovered from the concussion. Summoning her strength, she wriggled and twisted, trying to break free of his hold. And then suddenly his hands slipped away as he dropped to the floor in front of her.

She looked up—expecting to see Agent Bell or even Dalton standing where Tom had stood. But it was Kenneth's brother, Gregory Cunningham, wielding a gun. He must have struck Tom with the butt of it.

"Oh, my God," she said with a shaky breath of relief. "I thought he was going to kill me. Thank you…"

But her gratitude turned to nerves as he stared at her with a strange expression, with no expression on a face that had always reminded her so much of Kenneth's—until now. Now he looked nothing like his brother in appearance or demeanor. And, for some reason, he wore an ill-fitting uniform. A trooper's uniform. From the badge on the pocket, she realized it was Trooper Littlefield's uniform. Gregory turned the barrel of the gun toward her.

"What—what are you doing?" she asked.

A phone vibrated. He reached into his pocket for it, but his grip didn't loosen on the gun. "Agent Campbell keeps calling…"

"That's Agent Bell's phone," she realized. "What did you do to him?"

He shrugged. "I'm not sure if he's dead or just extremely unconscious."

She cursed him.

"Agent Campbell must be calling to report to him about Reyes's condition," he mused. "Now *him*—I'm sure *he's* dead."

She gasped as pain stabbed her heart. "No…"

"I had to get him out of the way," he explained. "He kept messing up my plans for you."

"Why?" she asked. "Why do you want to kill me?"

"I don't *want* to," he assured her. "I've always liked you, Elizabeth. I've always admired your drive and spunk. I even admire your loyalty."

She edged backward—toward that office. If she could get inside and lock the doors…

"Then why have you been trying to kill me?" she asked. He was really the crazy one. Had he always been? Was that why Patricia and Kenneth had left her their daughter instead of him? She had always wondered.

"It's really Kenneth's fault," Gregory said. "I thought my brother would leave me custody of Lizzie."

She gasped again, with another jab of pain. "You killed them."

"That was Kenneth's fault, too," he said. "He cut me off. Stopped giving me money. And without money, I'd lose Miranda."

She flinched because she had advised Kenneth to stop giving his brother money that he'd lost anyway. Gregory had used Kenneth's loans for risky investments—in get-rich-quick schemes to finance his wife's lavish lifestyle. If he didn't keep buying her the expensive clothes and cars she craved, his wife had threatened to leave him.

Elizabeth remembered Patricia's disgust that her sister-in-law cared more about the money than she had about her husband. Patricia had believed in her vows—in sickness and health, in until death do we part…

Tears stung Elizabeth's eyes as she realized that death had parted her friends. No. She had to believe they were still together—that they would always be together. If Gregory killed her, as he had Dalton, would she reunite with him?

But she wasn't about to give up her life without a fight. She slid a little closer to the doors of the den that she had left open. "So you killed them because you thought you would get their money," she continued. "You don't care about Lizzie."

"I'll take care of her," he promised.

She didn't trust his promises the way she had Dalton's. She wouldn't put it past him to get rid of the little girl, too—once he was awarded custody.

"Kenneth and Patricia wanted me to take care of her," she said. She'd assumed it was because they hadn't liked Gregory's mercenary wife. Now she realized that they might have known there was something wrong with him—that his desperation had driven him to madness.

"Kenneth and Patricia always got everything they wanted," he said. "The degrees. The jobs. The house. The kid. Their lives were perfect."

And he had obviously envied them that perfection.

He glanced down at where Tom lay unconscious on the floor, and she edged into the doorway of the den. "I should thank Wilson for showing up like he did," Gregory said. "He's making this easy for me."

"You're going to do to us what you did with Kenneth and Patricia," she said, feeling nausea all over again at his sick plan. "You're going to make it look like a murder-suicide."

"It worked the first time," he said.

She shook her head. "Dalton reopened the investigation."

He shrugged. "Reyes is gone."

"Agent Bell—"

"Gone, too," he said.

She shuddered at his callousness. "Agent Campbell will look into everything, then," she said. The men were too close to not look out for each other—even if some of them were gone.

"And he'll blame Tom Wilson for it all," Gregory assured her. And as he glanced down at the man again, she stepped back and slammed the office doors between them. She twirled the dead bolts even though she doubted they would keep him out very long.

Already he pounded on the doors. And as he pounded, a cry rang out from above as the noise woke little Lizzie.

She crossed the den to the exterior wall and pulled up a window. The opening was big. She could climb out onto the porch and disappear into the darkness of the acreage surrounding the house.

But then the pounding stopped.

"I'll go get her," Gregory shouted through the locked doors.

Elizabeth froze with fear—just inches from saving herself. She couldn't do it. She stepped away from the open window and walked back to the door.

His shaky sigh emanated through the doors before he added, "I probably should have killed her with them— then I would have inherited the money straightaway. I wouldn't have had to go after you. It would have been simpler."

"But you care about her," she reminded him. "She's an innocent child."

"She loved her parents, Elizabeth," he said. "Isn't it kinder to reunite her with them?"

She quickly twisted the dead bolts and pulled open the doors. "No," she said. "Please don't hurt her."

She had promised Kenneth and Patricia that she would take care of Lizzie as if she was her own. She would gladly die for the child.

"You're going to bleed to death," Blaine warned him with a curse.

Blood saturated Dalton's sleeve. But it was only a trickle from the wound now. He didn't care about that, though.

"And you shouldn't be driving," Blaine added, gripping the armrest and the dash as Dalton careened around a curve.

He hadn't trusted anyone else to drive as fast as he could—as he had to in order to get to Elizabeth and the little girl. But no matter how fast he drove, he worried he wouldn't get to them in time.

"Bell won't answer his phone," Trooper Littlefield said from the backseat. He'd taken Campbell's cell and had kept hitting the redial.

"He would answer," Dalton said, "if he could." He had gotten to know the man well over the past few days. He was every bit as focused an agent as Dalton usually was.

Bell was already gone. Elizabeth probably was, too.

The next curve brought the house into view—lights burned in several of the windows. He nearly struck a rental car parked near the police car at the end of the driveway.

"Nobody's here," Blaine said as he took in the empty police car. "I can get out and see if the keys are inside and move it."

But before he could reach for the door handle, Dalton backed up and slammed his SUV into the patrol car—pushing it out of his way. Then he pressed hard on the accelerator and tore up the driveway. As he slammed it into Park and jumped out, he heard the gunshot.

Just as he'd worried, he was too late.

Chapter Twenty-One

A scream of pain tore from Elizabeth's throat. Loss wrenched her heart as Tom's blood spattered her face. He dropped to the floor as he had earlier. But this time she doubted he was just unconscious.

He was dead. While she didn't love him anymore, she once had, so she still cared what happened to him. She cared that he had been killed—because of her. Just like so many others had lost their lives because of her.

Dalton. Her chest hurt, panic and pain pressing so hard on her heart that she couldn't draw a breath. Dalton was already dead. Now Tom.

And she was going to be next.

At least she hoped she was going to be next. Gregory kept glancing up—where the little girl could be heard screaming, too. The terror in her voice broke Elizabeth's heart. She ached to hold her, to soothe her fears and dry all those tears—to take care of her as she had promised Kenneth and Patricia she would.

Gregory Cunningham moved, as if heading toward the stairs. She almost reached out to stop him, but Tom's body lay between them and she nearly fell over him—nearly fell on top of him.

"Please don't hurt Lizzie," she pleaded with the madman—hoping to appeal to his sense of decency, even though she doubted that he had one after all the pain he had already caused.

"She's an innocent child," Elizabeth continued. "She's your niece." But Kenneth had been his brother and that hadn't stopped him from killing him. "She's the only part left of Kenneth and Patricia—the best part." That was what they had always said. "The best part of the best people…"

He turned back to her, and tears glistened in his eyes. Maybe he had a conscience, after all. "I didn't want to do it, you know." But his tears cleared as he justified the horror he'd done. "But Kenny gave me no choice. He stopped giving me money."

That was her fault. She had advised Kenneth that it was time to cut off his brother. Her friends had died because of her. Now Dalton and probably Jared Bell and Tom next.

"Promise me you won't hurt her," she pleaded with him again. "I don't care about *me*. Just please take care of Lizzie. Raise her the way that Kenneth and Patricia wanted her to be raised."

His face—so like his brother's—twisted into a grimace of pain and regret. "Elizabeth…"

"They wanted her to always feel loved," she said, glancing up at the ceiling from which the little girl's cries seemed to emanate. "To be confident and self-assured and fearless."

Like Dalton. He was confident and self-assured and fearless, but he'd wound up dead because of that. Because of her.

Tears streamed from Gregory's eyes. "I'm really sorry about this, Elizabeth."

"Just promise me…" But she knew that even if he gave it, it wouldn't be like the heartfelt promises Dalton Reyes had made her. Gregory's promise would be an empty one. He had already threatened to kill the child. Maybe that had been an empty threat—only meant to draw her out of the office so that he could kill her. "Don't hurt her."

"I won't," Gregory said. "I couldn't harm her before. I won't be able to do it now. I need the money—that's all, Elizabeth."

She could have tried to lie—tried to claim that the money was gone. But Kenneth and Patricia had been fanatical about earning and saving money, and they had already set up a trust fund for their daughter. Unlike his brother, Kenneth's investments had paid off well. There was money; she just hadn't realized that someone would have killed them over it.

And now her.

She bit her lip so she wouldn't plead for her life. It was no use trying to appeal to Gregory Cunningham's sense of decency. If he had one, he wouldn't have already killed so many people. She had already accepted that she was to be the next—and hopefully the last.

So she closed her eyes and waited for the bullet.

DALTON HAD SLIPPED silently into the house—through an open window in the den. Before he'd found the open window, he had found Jared Bell lying on the porch, blood pooled beneath his head.

He had been certain that the man, whom he was just now beginning to consider a friend, was dead. But when he'd reached down for Jared's throat, he had felt a steadily beating pulse. Like Elizabeth, the blow hadn't killed the profiler. But he needed an ambulance.

Blaine had gestured that he would make the call for help. The other agent had kept pace with Dalton on his mad dash to the house. But they had hesitated to burst inside before they assessed the situation. So Dalton had slipped through that open window alone.

Blaine and Littlefield were waiting for his cue. But he couldn't give it and risk one of them startling Gregory Cunningham into killing Elizabeth. He had realized it was him at the hospital when Littlefield had admitted that everyone had shared Elizabeth's opinion of Kenneth and Patricia Cunningham—that they were a loving couple who would have never harmed each other.

The only person who'd offered a different opinion had been the man who'd killed them and tried to make it look like a murder-suicide. Kenneth's own brother.

Now the man intended to kill Elizabeth and not just to keep her from reopening an investigation into the Cunninghams' deaths. Alone in the darkness of the den, Dalton had listened to their conversation through the doors that had been left open like the window.

Through those open doors, he had also seen Tom Wilson lying on the foyer floor. Like Jared Bell, blood had pooled beneath him. The shot he'd heard, as he'd stepped out of his SUV, must have been fired at Wilson.

It was too late to help him. But he could help Elizabeth. Maybe…

He had heard everything Gregory had said—his confession about the murder of his brother and sister-in-law. He had also heard everything Elizabeth had said—had heard her negotiating for the little girl's life. She was willing to give up her own life to keep the child safe. As safe as she would be with a killer for a guardian.

In Elizabeth, Kenneth and Patricia had chosen the right guardian for their daughter. They had chosen someone who loved little Lizzie every bit as much as they had.

Dalton didn't want to lose either one of them. The

child had stopped crying. Either Blaine or Littlefield must have made it up to the nursery without Gregory noticing them. One of them was soothing her fears. At least she was safe now.

It was up to him to secure Elizabeth's safety. But if he shot Gregory Cunningham and the guy squeezed the trigger of his gun...

The barrel was pointed directly at Elizabeth's head. Gregory was doing it again—exactly as he had killed his brother and his sister-in-law. First he'd killed the man and then the woman.

Had Patricia done the same thing Elizabeth had—had she negotiated for her daughter's life and then closed her eyes to accept her gruesome fate?

For Elizabeth, Dalton would fight fate. He would keep his promise to her and make sure that she stayed safe. So he stepped out of the shadows of the den.

Gregory Cunningham caught sight of him. His eyes widened with shock, and his face paled. He must have been pretty certain that he had killed Dalton back at the abandoned horse ranch—so certain that at first he'd probably thought he was seeing a ghost. But now, realizing that Dalton was real and alive, Gregory Cunningham swung the barrel of his gun toward him.

But Dalton was already squeezing the trigger of his gun.

If Gregory fired now, the bullet would hit him. Not Elizabeth. For Elizabeth, Dalton would gladly give up his life.

ELIZABETH FLINCHED AT the sound of the gunshot—so close to her head. She waited for the pain. But it never came. Instead, she felt more drops across her face. Blood...

This time it had to be hers. Didn't it?

But where was the pain? Or was she numb? Paralyzed?

Dead?

"Elizabeth…" Dalton's deep voice called to her.

From the beyond?

Then fingertips skimmed over her face. "Are you okay?" he asked. "Were you hit?"

She opened her eyes to his face—to his dark eyes staring at her with concern. And something else.

She must have died. Or at least she was unconscious and dreaming. Because that emotion couldn't really be in his eyes—although she was certain it was in hers.

"You're alive!" she exclaimed. "You're alive!" She threw her arms around his neck and clung to him. "I thought he shot you!"

"He did," Dalton replied matter-of-factly, as if his gunshot wound was of no consequence.

She pulled back and then she saw the blood, which soaked the sleeve of his dark green shirt. "You're still bleeding!" she exclaimed. The fabric was warm and damp. She jerked her hand away—afraid that she'd hurt him—and her palm was stained red with his blood. "Didn't they treat you at the hospital?"

"I couldn't stay," he said. "Not when I knew you were in danger. And Jared wasn't answering his cell."

She covered her mouth to hold back a cry of alarm and regret. Poor Agent Bell.

"He disappeared," she said. "I don't know what happened to him." But she suspected that it wasn't good.

"I found him on the porch. Blaine called an ambulance for him." But from the concern in his voice, he wasn't sure the ambulance would arrive in time to help his friend.

Sirens whined in the distance as emergency vehicles rushed to the scene. Fortunately, Gregory hadn't noticed those sirens, or he would have shot her before help could have arrived for her.

Before Dalton had arrived.

"You saved me." As he had so many times before. But he needed help now.

Hopefully, the ambulance would be able to get up the driveway. Tom had said that it was blocked.

Tom…

Her breath hitched with regret over all the lives that had been taken—because of greed. If only she hadn't told Kenneth to cut off Gregory.

Then they would all be alive. Her dearest friends would be able to raise their precious daughter. Little Lizzie had stopped crying. How was that possible with all the shooting? She had to be terrified from all the commotion.

Fear gripped her again. Dalton was here—with her. Who was with Lizzie?

Dalton had kept his promise to protect her. But had she failed in her promise to protect the little girl?

"Lizzie isn't crying," she pointed out. "She's been crying since Gregory shot Tom. Why would she stop now? Is there someone else in the house?"

"Yes," Dalton replied. "Blaine Campbell and Trooper Littlefield came with me from the hospital. One of them must be with her now."

She needed to be with her—to make sure that the little girl was really all right. But she couldn't leave Dalton—and not just because he was wounded. She couldn't leave Dalton because she loved him, and she was so grateful that he was alive. She had been so worried about him.

That fear must have been on her face yet, because Dalton assured her, "She's safe now. It's all over."

But just as her fears eased, she heard something else that had her tensing with fear. Someone groaned, and there was a flurry of movement on the floor.

She had thought that Dalton had killed Gregory—that it was his blood that had struck her face when she'd had eyes closed as she'd waited for death. But what if Dalton had only wounded the madman?

What if he was reaching for his gun again?

Dalton reached for his, drawing it from his holster. But would he be able to save her or himself?

Or would Gregory finish what he'd started so many months ago with Kenneth's and Patricia's murders?

Chapter Twenty-Two

"You're a fool," Ash Stryker called Dalton.

He glared at his happy friend. While Stryker and Claire had returned from their honeymoon, it was obviously far from over—if the guy's smiling face was anything to go by.

"Just a few short weeks ago you were begging me to be your best man," Dalton reminded him with just a slight exaggeration. "And now you're calling me a fool?"

"Because you are one," Blaine Campbell said from where he leaned against the brick wall of the living room of Dalton's condo.

They had invited themselves over to his place. He had thought to check up on him and make sure he was completely recovered from the gunshot wound—minimal though it had been. But now he felt as if they were staging some kind of intervention.

"Two against one?" he scoffed at their pitiful attempt to gang up on him. "These are my kind of odds, you know." Hell, he'd always taken on more than two at a time.

"They would have been," Blaine agreed. "If you'd had the guts to go for it."

Now they were talking over his head. "What do you mean?" Nobody had ever accused him of being a coward. A fool—well, that wasn't the first time.

"Elizabeth Schroeder and the little girl," Blaine clarified. "If you'd had the guts to go for the two of them, you could be happy right now."

"Who says I'm not?" he challenged them.

He had a great place in the city with a view of the lake, a fast car. The single lifestyle most married men would envy—most. Not these guys, but most. Maybe…

Ash laughed at him. "I know happy. And you're not it, my friend. You're miserable."

He couldn't argue with him. The new husband radiated happiness like a neon sign—making Dalton want to hurl…something. But they were at his condo, and he liked to keep the place neat, the way his grandmother had taught him.

"You guys don't know what you're talking about," he insisted.

He had seen Elizabeth's face when she'd realized it was her fiancé moving around on the floor—that he wasn't dead. She had been more than relieved; she had been elated. And since the nanny had arrived to care for Lizzie, she had ridden along in the ambulance with him and Jared Bell to the hospital.

"I never had a chance with Elizabeth," he told them.

"If you think that, you really are a damn fool," Blaine said. "That woman's in love with you."

"That woman was grateful," he said. "I found her in the trunk of that car when she was barely clinging to life, when she didn't even know who she was."

But she knew now. She was Tom Wilson's fiancée.

"Her memory didn't affect her feelings," Blaine said.

No. Seeing Tom Wilson nearly die had affected her, though. She loved the man. She wouldn't have been wearing his ring if she hadn't.

He shrugged. "I'm not going to argue this with you guys. The case is over."

Gregory Cunningham was dead. Kenneth and Patricia Cunningham's deaths had been ruled homicides. Just homicides. Their names were cleared because of Elizabeth, because she had been so determined that their memories be untainted for their daughter.

"The case is over," Blaine agreed.

"But you two don't have to be," Ash added.

Of course the happily married men would think that. Who were the fools? They had just been damn lucky that the women for whom they'd fallen had loved them back.

Dalton had never been that lucky. "She's going to marry Tom Wilson." He was certain of that.

"Not if you stop the wedding," Blaine suggested.

Could he? Could he put his heart on the line without knowing if she even returned his feelings?

He'd already been accused of being a fool. What did it matter if he made one of himself? He would rather regret making a scene than never telling her how much he loved her. He should have told her before. He should have told her when they'd made love how much she meant to him. How he had never cared for anyone the way he cared for her.

"I really hate you guys," he muttered, even as he dug his car keys from the pocket of his jeans. They had goaded him into embarrassing himself. "You're enjoying this—enjoying that I'm going to make a fool of myself."

Why would Elizabeth choose him—an FBI agent with a penchant for danger—over the conservative lawyer she had already agreed to marry?

Blaine chuckled. "You've got it bad, Reyes. You're not your usual cocky self."

He wasn't—because he wasn't sure of Elizabeth's

feelings. He was sure of his, though, and he would regret never sharing those feelings with her.

Even if she rejected him...

Ash just laughed and patted his back, urging him, "Go get your bride!"

REGRET PULLED THE fake smile from Elizabeth's face. She shouldn't have stopped by Tom's hospital room. But she had already been at the hospital visiting Agent Jared Bell. So she had stopped in out of courtesy.

Nothing more.

"As soon as I'm released, we should move in together," Tom was saying. He had already reached out for her hand and tugged her down onto the hospital bed next to him.

"What?" she asked. Clearly he must have sustained some brain damage from the gunshot wound to his head.

"You and the little girl can move into my condo in Chicago," he said as if extending a magnanimous offer.

She shook her head.

"It makes the most sense," he said. "It's bigger than your place. And really, you can't stay *here*."

"I can't?"

He chuckled. "Your job is in Chicago. Your life is in Chicago."

The love of her life was in Chicago. He must have been because she hadn't seen him since she had ridden away in the ambulance. She'd expected to see him at the hospital. That night. And maybe today.

That was one of the reasons she had come by to visit Jared Bell. She had been worried about him, too, though. It hadn't been all about Dalton.

"Lizzie's home is here."

"Lizzie is a child," he said. "She'll adjust."

"She only recently lost her parents." She sighed. "And now her uncle…" Gregory Cunningham had always been part of the child's life. The boogeyman. But she might miss him, too. "She's had a lot of adjustments to make."

"Exactly," he said. "She'll be fine. She has you."

"What about you?" she asked, wondering why he had stopped suggesting that she give up the child.

"I understand why you want to keep her."

He made Lizzie sound like a stray to whom she'd gotten attached.

"Why do you?" she asked. Did he have any feelings for the little girl? He had never paid any attention to her.

"To keep you," he said. "I would do anything to make you happy, Elizabeth."

Something cold and hard slid over her finger.

Her skin chilled and she shivered with revulsion. He'd put that damn ring back on her finger. "Tom…"

"Sorry," a deep voice murmured from the doorway. "I didn't mean to interrupt…"

She jerked away from Tom and turned toward the door—just in time to see Dalton's broad back as he walked away.

"Wait!" she called out to him, her heart beating quickly. "Dalton!"

Tom sighed. "I guess I have my answer."

"I didn't realize you'd asked me a question," she said as she tugged off the diamond. "You just assumed."

"You rode in the ambulance with me," he reminded her. "You acted like you cared—like you still have feelings for me."

"We were together a long time," she said. "I have feelings for you. But I don't love you."

"No," he agreed. "I see that now. I see who you love."

She hoped it wasn't too late to make Dalton see that she loved him. Would he care? Did he return her feelings? Her pulse raced.

"I'm sorry." As she passed his ring back to him, he caught her hand and held on to her.

"I feel sorry for you," he said, "because he's going to break your heart. He's not looking to be a husband or a father."

Maybe Tom was right. But that didn't stop Elizabeth. She tugged her hand free of his grasp and hurried into the hall. But Dalton was gone. She should have run faster.

She sucked in a sharp breath along with her disappointment.

"So when's the wedding?" a deep voice asked.

She glanced up and found him standing across the hall, in the doorway of an empty room. She shook her head and lifted her bare hand. "I'm not getting married."

Because Tom was probably right about Dalton. He had made his feelings clear about marriage and fatherhood before. He had no interest in them. The only thing he hadn't made clear to her was his feelings for her.

"Really?" he asked with a dark brow arched in skepticism. He leaned closer and studied her hand. "I swear I saw a ring on there just a second ago."

"Tom got the wrong idea," she said.

Dalton shrugged. "Can't say I blame him. You were awfully worried about him back at the house."

"I thought he was dead," she said. "I was relieved that he wasn't. Enough people had already died because of me."

"Because of Gregory Cunningham," he corrected her. "Not because of you. Nothing was your fault."

Guilt weighed so heavily on her as she admitted, "I told Kenneth to cut off Gregory."

"And you don't think he would have done that without your advice?" he asked. "From everything you told me about the guy, Kenneth Cunningham was smart. He wouldn't have kept giving his brother money."

She released a shaky breath and along with it, a lot of the guilt she'd been feeling. "No, he wouldn't have."

"But giving Wilson the wrong idea, that is your fault," he said. "If you hang out in his hospital room, he's going to think he has a chance."

"I didn't come here to see him," she said.

"Who did you come to see?" Dalton asked.

"Agent Bell," she replied. "I was relieved to see that he's doing well." So well that the profiler was being released later that afternoon—or so he'd told her.

"Jared said you'd been by his room."

She drew in a deep breath, swallowed her pride and admitted, "I was hoping that you would be here visiting him. I was really hoping to run into you."

His dark eyes brightened. "Seriously?"

She glanced uneasily back at Tom's room. This wasn't a conversation she wanted her ex-fiancé to overhear; she wasn't cruel.

"Do you want to come back to the house?" she asked. "And see Lizzie?"

His eyes brightened even more and a smile curved his sensuous mouth. "I would love to see Lizzie."

As they headed down the hospital hall, he took her hand in his—the way he had so many times before. And as they stepped inside the empty elevator, he said, "But I really came here to see you."

Hope fluttered in her heart, lifting it.

ELIZABETH'S FACE FLUSHED with color at her embarrassment over finding the nursery empty. Dalton barely held back a chuckle at her reaction.

"I'm sorry," Elizabeth said as she read the note the nanny had left for her. "I didn't know Marta was taking Lizzie to a playdate with her grandchildren."

"I did," Dalton admitted.

Her eyes widened in surprised. "How?"

"I suggested it when I came here earlier."

"You were here earlier?" she asked, her beautiful eyes widened in surprise. "Why?"

"I played with Lizzie," he said, and his grin slipped out now with the memory of how happy the little girl had been to see him. She'd clung to him. And he'd been so happy to hold her and play with her. "I missed her."

She nodded. "She's such a special little girl."

"Yes, she is," he wholeheartedly agreed. "You're lucky to have her."

She blinked her thick lashes as if fighting back tears. "Yes, I am."

"And she's lucky to have you," he said. "You're very special, too, Elizabeth."

She smiled, but there was a tinge of sadness to it. And she continued to blink furiously, as if she was about to cry.

"What's wrong?" he asked. He hoped she didn't still feel guilty about becoming little Lizzie's guardian.

"I just realized what this is," she said with a quick gesture at his chest.

"What is this?" he asked.

"Goodbye."

When he'd found her in Tom Wilson's room—in what had looked like an intimate moment—he'd thought he might have been too late. But then she had called out to him. And she'd come out of that room without the ring on her finger. Hope warmed his heart—along with all the love and passion he felt for her.

He slid his arms around her and pulled her close. Then he covered her mouth with his. He'd missed the sweet sigh of her breath as she kissed him back. He'd missed her lips and the way she ran her fingers into his hair and clutched him closer. When he could lift his mouth from hers, he asked, "Does that feel like goodbye?"

She shook her head.

He swung her up in his arms and carried her down the hall to that sunshine-filled master bedroom. He undressed her slowly, kissing every inch of silky skin as he exposed it to his sight and his touch.

She moaned and sighed, reacting to his every caress—his every kiss. He made love to her thoroughly and, most of all, lovingly—making sure that she had no doubt about his feelings.

But yet he didn't utter the words that burned in his throat. He wasn't sure how to say something he'd never said before. So, after shouting his release, he collapsed back on the bed, and he fell silent.

She lay on his chest, panting for breath. Once she'd regained it, she pulled away from him. "I'm sorry," she said. "You probably need to go back to the hospital."

He pressed a hand over his madly beating heart. "I'm fine," he said. "I don't need medical attention." He needed her attention, but she wouldn't look at him.

"I meant that you probably have to pick up Agent Bell," she said. "I know he's being released this afternoon."

He nodded. "Yeah, he is," he said, "probably against medical orders."

"Why would he leave, then?"

"A young woman recently disappeared," he said with a shudder as he remembered how Elizabeth had nearly disappeared forever.

If he hadn't stopped that car…

"That's awful," she murmured with a shiver of her own.

He wrapped his arms around her for comfort and warmth and to pull her closer. "Yes," he agreed. "Jared thinks it could be related to his case."

"Do you?"

He shrugged. "I don't know."

He actually thought Jared Bell was a lot like Captain Ahab, and that he was going to kill himself trying to catch the elusive serial killer.

"I guess it's a good thing that I'm not getting married, then," she said.

"Why would you say that?" he asked. He was glad she wasn't marrying Tom Wilson. But did she have no intention of ever getting married?

"I don't have to worry about that serial killer."

"No, you don't," Dalton said, "because you have me to protect you."

"I do?" she asked. And finally she looked at him again, staring up at him with her silvery-gray eyes wide and hopeful.

"This isn't goodbye." He reached for the bedside table where he'd left his holster and gun. But that wasn't all he'd left there. Beneath the holster, he'd hidden a small jewelry case. It wasn't as big a diamond as Tom Wilson had put on her hand.

But she gasped when he opened the case. And tears shimmered in her eyes. "What are you doing?"

"Proposing," he said. "I know I'm not doing a very

good job of it, though. But I've never done this before. I've never even told anyone that I loved them."

"You haven't told me," she said. "But I haven't told you, either."

He tensed in anticipation of humiliation. Had he just made the fool of himself that he'd worried he would?

"But I do," she said. "I love you very much."

And finally the words poured from his lips. "I love you, Elizabeth Schroeder. I love your strength and your courage and your loyalty. I love everything about you."

"Even when I didn't know who I was," she said, "it was like you knew me."

"I do," he said. "I know how amazing you are. And how much I want you to be my wife." He thought fleetingly of that serial killer that was still eluding Jared Bell. "And I promise you that I won't let anything happen to my bride."

"I thought you would never take a bride," she murmured.

"I thought I would never, either," he admitted. "Until I found you in that trunk. Ever since then you were destined to be my bride. Will you marry me?"

"It was destiny," she said, "that you found me. And every promise you've made to me, you've kept. I can't wait to be your bride and your wife."

His hand shook slightly as he slid the ring onto her finger. It fit perfectly—just like the two of them. "I can't wait to be your husband," he said, "and Lizzie's father."

Tears filled her eyes again and spilled over to trail down her beautiful face. He brushed them away with his thumbs. "Don't cry."

"These are happy tears," she assured him. "Kenneth and Patricia would be so happy for us—for all of us."

"We can stay in this house," he said.

"Our jobs are in Chicago," she said. "And wherever we are will be Lizzie's home. Our home."

"We can have two homes," he said. "One in the city and one here. I will do whatever necessary to make you and our little girl happy."

"You already have," she said. "I love you."

She was right. It didn't matter where they lived. It only mattered that they were together—the three of them and the additional children he knew they would have someday.

"I love you," he said. "And I can't wait to marry you."

"I can't wait to marry you."

"I only have one problem," he said with a sudden and sickening realization.

"What problem?" she asked.

"My problem is that I don't know who to ask to be my best man," he replied.

She laughed. "That is a problem."

He laughed, too, as happiness overwhelmed him. He had never realized how much he could love someone—until he'd fallen for her and Lizzie. He didn't really care who his best man was. He only cared that she would become his bride. "Marry me," he said again.

She nodded and eagerly agreed, "As soon as we can get a license."

"There's a cute little church not far from here," he said. "I think you'll love it."

"I love you," she said. "It doesn't matter where we get married or where we live—as long as we're together."

"Forever," he vowed.

They had that same kind of love her friends had had—the forever-and-after, eternal love. Every promise they made each other would be kept.

* * * * *

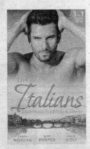

MILLS & BOON®

Want to get more from Mills & Boon?

Here's what's available to you if you join the exclusive **Mills & Boon eBook Club** today:

✦ *Convenience – choose your books each month*
✦ *Exclusive – receive your books a month before anywhere else*
✦ *Flexibility – change your subscription at any time*
✦ *Variety – gain access to eBook-only series*
✦ *Value – subscriptions from just £3.99 a month*

So visit **www.millsandboon.co.uk/esubs** today to be a part of this exclusive eBook Club!

MILLS & BOON®
INTRIGUE
Romantic Suspense

A SEDUCTIVE COMBINATION OF DANGER AND DESIRE

A sneak peek at next month's titles…

In stores from 18th September 2015:

- **Reckonings** – Cynthia Eden *and*
  High Country Hideout – Elle James

- **Navy SEAL Spy** – Carol Ericson *and*
  The Rebel – Adrienne Giordano

- **The Agent's Redemption** – Lisa Childs *and*
  Texas Takedown – Barb Han

Romantic Suspense

- **Second Chance Colton** – Marie Ferrarella
- **The Professional** – Addison Fox

Available at WHSmith, Tesco, Asda, Eason, Amazon and Apple

Just can't wait?
Buy our books online a month before they hit the shops!
visit www.millsandboon.co.uk

These books are also available in eBook format!